Ransome's Crossing

KAYE DACUS

HARVEST HOUSE PUBLISHERS
EUGENE, OREGON

Scripture quotations are taken from the King James Version of the Bible.

The author is represented by MacGregor Literary.

Cover by Left Coast Design, Portland, Oregon

Cover photos © Richard Jenkins; iStockphoto

This is a work of fiction. Names, characters, places, and incidents are products of the author's imagination or are used fictitiously. Any resemblance to actual persons, living or dead, or to events or locales, is entirely coincidental.

RANSOME'S CROSSING

Published by Harvest House Publishers
Eugene, Oregon 97402
www.harvesthousepublishers.com

Library of Congress Cataloging-in-Publication Data
Dacus, Kaye, 1971-
Ransome's crossing / Kaye Dacus.
p. cm.—(The Ransome trilogy ; bk. 2)
ISBN 978-0-7369-2754-3 (pbk.)
1. Ship captains—Fiction. 2. Single women—Fiction. 3. Married people—Fiction. I. Title.
PS3604.A25R355 2010
813'.6—dc22

2009052333

Printed in the United States of America

10 11 12 13 14 15 16 17 18 / DP-SK / 10 9 8 7 6 5 4 3 2 1

For Paul M.,
to whom I owe William Ransome's existence.

The Possible's slow fuse is lit
By the Imagination.

EMILY DICKINSON

HMS *Alexandra*

Commodore William Ransome

First Lieutenant Ned Cochrane

Second Lieutenant Patrick O'Rourke

Third Lieutenant Angus Campbell

Fourth Lieutenant Horatio Eastwick

Fifth Lieutenant Eamon "Jack" Jackson

Sixth Lieutenant Robert Blakeley

Midshipman Josiah Gibson

Midshipman Walter Kennedy

Midshipman Christopher Oldroyd

Steward Archibald Dawling

Boatswain (Bosun) Matthews

Surgeon James Hawthorne

Sailing Master Ingleby

Purser Holt

HMS *Audacious*

Captain Alban Parker

First Lieutenant Montgomery Howe

Second Lieutenant Griffith Crump

Third Lieutenant Lewis Gardiner

Fourth Lieutenant Millington Wallis

Fifth Lieutenant Richard Duncan

Midshipman Thomas Hamilton

Midshipman Cornelius Martin

Midshipman Harry Kent

Midshipman Louis Jamison

Midshipman Charles Lott

Midshipman Isaac McLellan

Master Carpenter Colberson

Boatswain (Bosun) Parr

Sailing Master Bolger

Purser Harley

Captain of Marines Macarthy

Gateacre, England
April 1803

A scream of agony bubbled up in Charlotte's chest, but she stopped it before it could escape.

"The shoulder is reset." The physician poked and prodded more, sending bolts of pain and waves of nausea through her body. But Charlotte managed to hold all at bay—except the two tears that escaped the corners of her eyes and ran down into her hair.

"So long as there is no injury to the spine, the child should recover full use of the arm. But it should be bound for two weeks, and she should be made to rest as much as possible."

"Thank you." Her brother William's voice sounded harsh and gruff. He'd been different since returning from Portsmouth six months ago—he no longer laughed, told stories, or drew pictures of fascinating sea creatures for her.

She kept her undamaged arm over her eyes as the doctor bound her left arm in a sling. Some of the pain was gone, but she couldn't bring herself to look at her oldest brother.

William thanked the doctor again. "That will be all."

She heard the clink of coins and then retreating footsteps. She risked a peek under her arm. William stood beside her bed, arms crossed.

"Tell me exactly how you came to fall off a rotted rope ladder ten feet from the ground." Though soft, his voice carried such a tone of command that Charlotte cringed.

"Philip told me he did not think I could climb it. I told him I could—that I've been climbing it every day to practice for when I join the navy."

William turned his back on her and stalked to the window. After a long pause, he returned to tower over her bedside. "I shall speak with Philip later, but I cannot believe the unladylike manner in which you have behaved. You know better than anyone that girls cannot join the Royal Navy."

Charlotte struggled to sit up. "But, William, I know everything—the flags, the ropes, the bells. I've been practicing climbing the rope ladder to Philip and James's old tree fort so I can be ready to climb the shrouds to the mast tops."

An odd expression flickered across her brother's countenance, and for a moment she hoped he might relent.

"It matters not what you know or what you can do. Females are not allowed to join the navy." He sighed and rubbed his hand over his eyes. "Charlotte, you are almost seven years old. It is past time for you to stop pretending that you are a boy and start acting like a young lady. You will not be climbing shrouds to the top of any mast on any ship. You will stay here in Gateacre, attend to your schooling, and grow up to be a proper lady. Do you understand me?"

He never raised his voice, but her ears pounded as if he'd yelled the words at her. She clamped her teeth down on her bottom lip to keep it from trembling. How could he be such a mean…ogre? She wanted nothing more than to follow in her father's and brothers' footsteps.

"I'm waiting for an answer, Charlotte."

"Yes. I understand."

"Good." He nodded curtly. "Now, you are to rest until dinner." He left her room, shutting the door behind him.

Charlotte stuck her tongue out at the closed door and lay back down. She'd show them—all of them—that if she wanted to join the navy, no one would stop her.

Portsmouth, England
August 17, 1814

Ned Cochrane, first lieutenant, HMS *Alexandra*, stepped out of the jolly boat onto the stone dock and glanced around at the early morning bustle of the dockyard crew. Only nine days remained to fill the crew roster and fit out the ship with the supplies needed for the first leg of a transatlantic voyage. With yesterday lost in celebrating Captain—no, *Commodore* Ransome's wedding—and since the commodore's attention would be necessarily split between distractions on land and his duties to his ship, Ned would shoulder the burden of preparing the ship and crew.

"Sir, look out! Lieutenant Cochrane!"

Ned spun—and fell back just in time to save himself from being swept off the quay by a net full of barrels swinging at the end of a crane. His hat wasn't so fortunate.

The cargo swayed menacingly overhead. Ned scrambled backward, out of harm's way. Once clear, he leapt to his feet. "You, there! Watch what you're about. Secure that crane," he yelled at the negligent dock crew.

"Are you all right, sir?"

The voice—an odd timbre in the chorus of tenor, baritone, and bass tones usually heard in the dockyard—matched the one which had called the warning. He turned.

A young man, not really more than a boy in a worn, ill-fitting midshipman's uniform, stood holding Ned's dripping hat. Sure enough, the lad's right sleeve was wet to the shoulder.

"Nothing injured but my pride." Ned took his hat and studied the midshipman. The boy's tall, round hat concealed most of his dark hair, but…Ned squinted against the bright glare of the sun off the water and surrounding gray stone. "Do I know you, lad?"

The boy touched the brim of the shabby hat. "Charles Lott, sir. We spoke last week. You said there might be a place for me aboard your ship."

"Ah, yes." Ned now recalled meeting the midshipman, who'd answered Ned's questions when the boy had first approached him about a position aboard *Alexandra* last week, even the question Ned had missed the first time he'd stood for his lieutenancy examination. "I'm sorry, but we have filled the positions on *Alexandra*."

Shocked disappointment filled the boy's elfin face.

"However, I have recommended you to the captain of *Audacious*." Ned struggled to keep the smile from his face.

"*Audacious*? Captain Yates, then?"

Ned sighed. He liked Commodore Ransome's friend extraordinarily and had looked forward to the fun to be had on Jamaica station with two such commanders. "Alas, I am afraid to say Captain Yates has resigned his commission. Captain Parker is taking command of *Audacious*." Ned glanced around the quay. "There is his first officer. Come, I shall introduce you."

"Thank you, sir." Midshipman Lott straightened the white collar and cuffs of his too-large coat.

Ned caught his counterpart's attention and met him near the steps to the upper rampart. He made the introduction and stood back as the first lieutenant of *Audacious*, Montgomery Howe, put a series of questions to the lad. Lott answered each quickly and with near textbook precision.

"Well done, Mr. Lott. You are ordered to present yourself day after tomorrow to begin your official duties."

The boy's face paled. "Sir, may I have until next Thursday?"

"The day before we sail?" Howe crossed his arms and glared at Ned and then at Lott.

Ned ground his teeth at the boy's impertinence, which was casting him—Ned—in a bad light. He'd recommended the lad, after all.

"Yes, sir. I am aware it is an inconvenience, but my mother is a widow, and I must see that she is settled—that our business affairs are settled—before I could leave on such a long journey."

"And it will take a sennight?" Ned asked.

"We live in the north part of the country, sir. 'Tis a three days' journey by post, sir." Lott spoke to the cobblestones below his feet.

Aye, well should he be ashamed to make such a request...though many years ago, a newly made captain had let a newly made lieutenant have four days to see to his own widowed mother and sister.

Apparently, from the expression that flickered across Howe's face, he had also received a similar mercy some time earlier in his career. "Very well, then. You are to present yourself to me on deck of *Audacious* no later than seven bells in the morning watch Thursday next. If you are late, your spot will be given to someone else. Understand?"

"Aye, sir!" Lott touched the brim of his hat again. "Thank you, sir."

"Dismissed—oh, and Mr. Lott?"

The boy, a few paces away already, halted and turned, at attention again. "Aye, sir?"

"Make yourself more presentable by next week if you can. You can find plenty of secondhand uniforms available in the shops in much better condition than yours. And get a haircut. I do not allow midshipmen to tuck their hair under their collars."

Lott's hand flew to the back of his neck, eyes wide. "Aye, aye, sir."

"Dismissed."

Ned moved to stand beside Howe as the boy ran down the quay. "Sorry for the inconvenience, Monty, but I have a feeling that boy will do well by you."

"I've never heard a lad recite the answers so perfectly. He's slight. Says he's fifteen? Can't be more than thirteen or fourteen."

"Some boys don't mature as quickly as others. You should remember that quite well." Ned bumped his shoulder against his former berth mate's.

Howe shoved him back. "Just because you gained height and a deeper voice before I did doesn't mean you matured faster, Ned. In fact, you could probably learn manners in decorum and respect from little Charlie Lott."

Ned guffawed and bade his friend farewell. He wasn't certain if he could learn anything from the young midshipman, but he would certainly look out for him and do whatever he could to promote the boy's interest. He had the feeling Charles Lott would make a good officer some day.

Charlotte Ransome dived behind a large shrub and held her breath. Footsteps crunched on the gravel garden path, coming toward her closer and closer.

Had he seen her?

Keep walking. Please, Lord, let him keep walking.

When he reached her shrub, Charlotte squeezed her eyes shut, fearful of blinking. If the gardener had seen and recognized her, he would report her to the Yateses, who would in turn report her to her mother and brother—and all would be lost.

A gust of wind rustled the verdure around her. Her heart thundered against her ribs, and she feared she might be sick.

But the gardener did not stop. Long after his footsteps faded, Charlotte kept to her hiding place. Quiet descended until only the noise of the streets and alleys beyond the garden walls filtered in around the enclosure behind the enormous townhouse.

Peeking around the shrub, she found the path clear once again.

Sneaking into the garden through the servants' entrance in the rear had proven risky but successful. She hadn't been sure she'd avoid being spotted by any of the servants, busy with their early morning duties, but Providence appeared to be with her.

She cautiously made her way across the garden to the back of the house. She peeked through the window of Collin Yates's study and, finding it empty, slipped inside, relieved no one had discovered that she'd left it unlocked when she sneaked out of the house near dawn. She stuck her head out into the hallway, and, hearing no movement, made her way upstairs as quietly as she could. She paused on the landing and looked around the corner, down the hallway on which all of the bedrooms opened. No stirrings, no sounds. Heart pounding wildly and trying to keep her feet from touching the floor, she made her way along the thick carpet to the bedroom at the end of the hall and slipped inside, pushing the door closed with a soft click.

Movement across the room caught her eye. Turning to face the intruder, she found herself looking at a bedraggled boy in an oversized coat and britches, a tall, round hat jammed on his head almost down to his eyes.

She laughed, and the bedraggled midshipman in the mirror did likewise. Yes, her disguise was convincing enough to startle even herself. With a sigh she unbuttoned the coat and pulled it off, dropping it to the floor. When Lieutenant Cochrane had looked at her with recognition in his gray eyes, she was certain her entire plan would crash like a ship against a rocky shore. She sent up a quick prayer of thanks that he hadn't connected her appearance as Charles Lott with her true identity.

Sinking into the chair at the dressing table, she yanked off the hat and pulled her long thick hair out from under the high collar of the uniform coat. She'd tried pinning it flat to her head, but the cumbersome length of it—past her waist when unbound—created too much bulk for even the oversized hat to conceal.

The small porcelain clock on the mantel chimed once. Half-past eight. Panic once again rising, Charlotte peeled out of the uniform—picked up for mere pennies the first time she'd been able to sneak away from her mother's and Mrs. Yates's chaperonage a few days ago—stuffed it in the bottom of her trunk, threw her sleeping gown over her head, and jumped into the bed, still trying to find the sleeves with her hands as the bedroom door swung quietly open.

At the thump of the water pitcher on the commode, Charlotte sat up as if awakened by the sound.

Her maid curtsied. "Good morning, miss. I brought you fresh water for washing."

"Thank you." Charlotte grabbed her dressing gown from the end of the bed and shrugged into it, and then she stepped behind the screen in the corner. The scent of lilacs drifted up from the warm water as she poured it into the porcelain basin in the top of the exquisite dark-wood cabinet.

After running most of the way back from the dockyard, the wet cloth felt good against her skin, especially on her neck and back where her thick braid had been pressed against her by her uniform coat.

With the maid's assistance, she soon stood before the mirror where Midshipman Charles Lott had been reflected less than an hour ago, now looking upon a fashionable young lady. Fear that she wouldn't be able to pull off her plan swirled in her stomach, but she pushed it aside.

"The irons are ready, miss."

Charlotte sat at the dressing table, sipped the coffee which had been delivered while she dressed, and reviewed her plans for the next eight days as the maid twisted and twirled and pinned her hair.

Anticipation, anxiety, and excitement danced within her veins. In just over a week, she would leave Portsmouth on a grand adventure. A grand adventure that would culminate in arriving in Jamaica, being reunited with Henry Winchester, and marrying him.

"Your new rank suits you, Commodore Ransome."

William met Julia's green eyes in the mirror's reflection. Sitting in the middle of the bed in her white sleeping gown, her coppery hair cascading in riotous curls around her shoulders and back, she looked as young as when he'd made the gut-wrenching decision to walk away from her twelve years ago.

Now she was his wife. His knees quaked at the thought.

He returned to the examination of his new uniform coat, delivered from the tailor just this morning. "I am indebted to your father for arranging the promotion. There are many officers more deserving. All will say I received special favor because I am now his son-in-law."

"As you should know by now," Julia said, climbing off the bed and crossing to her dressing table, "my father does nothing unless he thinks it best for the Royal Navy." Drawing her hairbrush through her fountain of hair, she ambled across the colorful carpet toward him. "He secured your promotion before he knew of our engagement, so that did not have any bearing on his decision." She pulled the mass of her hair over her left shoulder and continued pulling the soft bristles of the brush through it. "And when have you ever worried about rumors going around about your being favored by my father?" A mischievous grin quirked the corners of her full lips. "Isn't worrying about rumors and gossip what got us here in the first place?"

The fact she'd forgiven him, that she could now joke about the past, both thrilled and humbled him. He did not deserve her.

She set the brush down and came to stand behind him, looking around him at the reflection. She ran her hand along his sleeve to the braid-laden cuff. His arm tingled in reaction. He did not want to respond to her like this—every time she spoke, moved, breathed, he lost track of everything but her. He had to conquer it; otherwise, her presence aboard ship would be detrimental to his command.

A knock on the door roused both of them. The maid Lady Dalrymple had assigned to Julia entered on Julia's entreaty.

"I will leave you." William inclined his head and made for the door, and then he stopped as soon as he reached it. He turned and smiled at her. "Do not be long."

"I will join you for breakfast shortly."

He stood in the hallway a few moments after the door closed, separating him from Julia for the first time since their wedding yesterday morning. Pleasure and regret battled within him. Marrying Julia Witherington had, in less than twenty-four hours, brought him more joy than he could ever have dreamed or deserved. Yet when he thought of his duty, of his commitment to the Royal Navy, to king and country, he couldn't help but fear he'd made his life more difficult by marrying at such a time.

The east wing of the manor house at Brampton Park, home to Lady Dalrymple, rang with emptiness. While William appreciated the privacy afforded them by the dowager viscountess's invitation to stay in the unused section for their wedding night—with hints she would like them to stay even longer—the grandeur of it made his skin crawl, and he could not wait until he could deposit Julia at her father's house and return to his ship.

After two wrong turns, he managed to find the small breakfast room, unused for nearly a century according to Lady Dalrymple, since the new wing and the much larger dining room had been completed.

The small room, paneled with dark wood, set him somewhat more at ease. By ignoring the narrow, tall windows, he could almost imagine himself aboard a ship in this room.

He paced, waiting for Julia, pondering how he could recover his good sense around her. When she entered the room a little while later—queenly in a purple dress, her hair the only crown she would ever need—he realized the only way he would be able to regain control of his mind would be to limit his contact with her.

Trying not to watch her serve eggs, sausage, and toast onto her plate, nor admire the curve of her neck above the lace set into the neck of her gown, William piled food onto his own plate, held Julia's chair for her, and then took his place at the head of the small table.

"I must return to my ship today."

Julia stirred sugar into her coffee. "Of course. I knew you would need to spend your days preparing *Alexandra* for the voyage."

He cleared his throat of the bite of egg that wished to lodge there. "What I mean is that I must return to *reside* aboard my ship."

Julia's spoon clanked against her cup. Her face paled, and the light which had danced in her eyes all morning vanished.

William's innards clenched. Perhaps he should have eased into the idea instead of blurting it out. He blamed it on her. He could not think clearly in her presence.

"Have…have you received word from your crew that there is trouble?" Her voice quavered.

"No. It is nothing like that." Unable to stop himself, he reached across the corner of the table and took her hand in his. "My duty is to my ship, to my crew. I am needed there. Here, my attentions and loyalty are divided."

For a brief moment, Julia's chin quivered. But she pressed her lips together and drew in a deep breath. "I understand. And I have no desire to draw you away from your duties. I have already created too much inconvenience and upheaval in your life. I do not wish to generate more. However, I have promised Lady Dalrymple we would join her tonight for her dinner and card party as her honored guests. If we were to abdicate from her hospitality today, how would that reflect on her?"

Though well masked, the pain in Julia's expression made William want to retract his words, to promise her he would stay here with her the remainder of the time they had in England. Any other woman would have been offended by his blundering, unreasonable demand. Julia apologized for inconveniencing him.

He raised her hand and kissed the back of it. "Aye. We will stay one more night." Then, giving in to impulse, he leaned over, cupped that quivering chin, and claimed her lips in a searing kiss. "And I will not have you thinking yourself an inconvenience to me."

His action resulted in the desired effect—the spark rekindled in her green eyes. She ran her finger along his jaw. "You lie too well, Commodore Ransome."

"You start off our marriage ill, Mrs. Ransome, if you believe I would ever lie to you." He squeezed her hand and then tucked in to his breakfast.

"Conceal the hard truth, then," she said, cocking her head and sending the spiral curls at her temples dancing, "for the last few days have not been a convenience to you."

"An upheaval, certainly." He feigned a close interest in the piece of sausage speared on his fork. "However, any inconvenience I have suffered has been more than adequately recompensed not just by gaining a wife, but by finally receiving the complete approbation of my admiral."

Julia's gasp preceded a gale of laughter.

A surge of contentment washed away the morning's anxieties. Perhaps being married would not interfere with his duty to the navy as severely as he'd feared.

Chapter Two

Charlotte divested herself of her hat and gloves, absently handing them to the butler. Though she'd spent above an hour here yesterday for William and Julia's wedding breakfast, the lack of scores of well-wishers milling about seemed only to emphasize the vastness of the hall. Overhead, a crystal chandelier sparkled in the sunlight streaming in from the windows high above the front door.

"This way, miss." A woman in an indigo dress with a large ring of keys at her waist bent her knees to Charlotte and motioned her farther into the grand entry hall of Brampton Park.

Paintings of dour-looking men in brown and black velvet coats adorned with gold medallions about their shoulders, and women in various shades of silks and satins, with high powdered wigs, white faces, and enormous skirts, stared at Charlotte as she moved past them. The portraits' eyes followed her as if they knew the secret she carried in her heart, the plan she meant to execute now that she was here.

Nonsense. She raised her chin and infused her gait with confidence. Any risk was worthwhile if it meant she would be reunited with Henry.

The woman in blue opened a set of double doors near the end of the hall. She entered and stepped to one side. "Miss Charlotte Ransome, my lady."

Charlotte stepped forward into the room and dropped into a deep, formal curtsey.

"My dear Miss Ransome." The dowager Viscountess Lady Dalrymple motioned Charlotte into the cavernous sitting room.

Charlotte traversed the distance between them quickly, excitement and trepidation growing with each step. She stopped beside the chair adjacent to the one occupied by her patroness.

She bent her knees in another shallow curtsey. "Lady Dalrymple, once again I would like to extend my gratitude—and that of my mother—for your generous invitation to me."

"Tosh. It is you who are granting me the favor, Charlotte, by bringing youth and vitality back into this house." She looked beyond Charlotte. "Come forward, Melling."

The woman in blue did as commanded.

"Miss Ransome, this is my housekeeper, Mrs. Melling. If you have need of anything, let her know. Melling, please see to assigning a maid to attend to Miss Ransome."

"Yes, my lady."

At Lady Dalrymple's nod, Mrs. Melling curtseyed and left the room.

"Come sit, Charlotte. We must discuss the plans for your ball Saturday night. My dressmaker will be here within the hour to take your measurements." She clasped her hands together in an expression of excitement as if she were no older than Charlotte's seventeen years rather than of an age with Charlotte's own dear mama.

"I am under no delusion that you will want to spend all of your hours with me. And, once your brother and new sister have taken their leave of us tomorrow, I will be installing you in the east wing, where you will be able to come and go as you please."

"Are William and Julia here even yet?" Charlotte had overheard Lady Dalrymple extend an invitation to William and Julia for them to stay here as long as they pleased after the wedding, but she'd assumed William turned it down, given his aversion to grandeur and the appearance of putting on airs.

"They are currently out—something about your brother's ship and Julia's cargo. But they promised to return in time for supper before my card party this evening. I have invited quite a number of young people, so I am certain there shall be dancing." Lady Dalrymple's mismatched brown and blue eyes twinkled. "An opportune way for you to determine with whom you will choose to lead off your ball."

Heat rushed into Charlotte's face as quickly as a certain handsome face filled her mind's eye, but it wasn't the image of Henry Winchester. "Yes, it will be good to have the question of my first partner settled before the night arrives."

"I see your blushes, Miss Ransome. And I can well imagine the honorable Mr. F finds them quite as becoming."

Charlotte flinched and then almost laughed. Yes, Percy Fairfax, second son of the baron, had shown her quite the attentions at his parents' ball a few weeks ago, as well as at the wedding breakfast yesterday. But though she enjoyed his company, it was not his striking tall figure or his curly brown hair she continually dwelled on.

"Mr. Fairfax honors me with his indulgent attentions."

Lady Dalrymple sighed. "If we do not see you married by Michaelmas, I shall be quite astonished."

Charlotte couldn't stop the grin that stole across her face. "Perhaps not so soon, my lady, but hopefully not too long after." They might not make dock in Jamaica before the twenty-ninth of September.

The viscountess's laugh rang through the large room. "Dear, dear, Charlotte. We shall have such fun, you and I." She rang the little silver bell on the table beside her.

Mrs. Melling appeared moments later. "Yes, my lady?"

"Please see Miss Ransome to her temporary quarters so she can refresh herself before the dressmaker arrives."

Both Charlotte and Mrs. Melling curtsied before leaving the room. Charlotte tried not to gape at the antique opulence surrounding her as she followed the housekeeper upstairs and through several long hallways. She counted no fewer than six maids, who all stepped aside and gave a quick dip of the knees to Charlotte before scurrying on about their duties.

Finally, Mrs. Melling stopped and entered a room. Charlotte paused just a few steps in—and wanted to ask Mrs. Melling if she was certain this was *her* bedchamber and not Lady Dalrymple's. Surely not even St. James's Palace boasted rooms so grand.

"This is Martha, your lady's maid."

A girl who couldn't be any older than Charlotte stood near the vanity table. Charlotte inclined her head in response to the maid's curtsey before she remembered her status of honored guest in this house—someone expected to not take notice of people of Martha's station.

Mrs. Melling's lips drew into a disapproving straight line. "My lady receives callers beginning at one o'clock every day. The dressmaker will come to your quarters, so there is no need for you to return to the parlor until she is finished with you." A kindly look entered the housekeeper's dark eyes. "Martha can show you the way. It can take one quite some time to find her way around Brampton." She swept out the door, keys jangling at her side.

Charlotte looked around the room once again. Her eyes lighted on the vanity, where her own ivory-handled brush and mirror sat on a silver tray.

Her heart nearly failed. Frantically, she looked around.

"Is something wrong, miss?" Martha took a step toward her.

"My…valise. Where is it?"

"I unpacked it for you, miss. I was just starting on your trunk. I'll need to send your dresses down to have them sponged and pressed. Terrible wrinkled, they are."

Charlotte's heart raced as if she'd run the three miles here from town. "I'll do that, Martha. I won't need everything out of it." She could not run the risk of Martha's finding the uniform buried at the bottom. *Buried at the bottom*…Henry's letters! Her heart pounded harder. "You unpacked *everything* from my valise?"

"I put all of your underthings in the wardrobe. And your stationery and letters and aught on the desk, miss." The edge of panic in the maid's voice cracked through Charlotte's.

She took a deep breath to try to calm herself. "Thank you, Martha." Though she longed to run to the desk and grab up the ribbon-tied packet of letters she could now see, doing so would only draw undue attention and suspicion.

Julia folded her hands in her lap and observed her father. He seemed to be struggling to digest everything she was telling him about what had happened during his recent absence. "And then Aunt Hedwig—Lady MacDougall—gave me a letter she wanted me to copy in my own hand breaking my engagement to William and announcing my intention to marry Sir Drake. They gave me time to consider my decision. When Lady MacDougall called me into her presence again, I tore up the letter and told them I would not comply. I told them I would not dishonor you or William, or myself, by allowing myself to be party to their lies and schemes."

Sir Edward grunted, but he did not interrupt her.

"They locked me in the bedchamber again. But I knew I had to get away from them to keep them from destroying everything. I picked the lock and had just run out the front door when William and Collin arrived." An involuntary shiver passed over her at the flood of relief—and love—his timely arrival had brought. "The constable and the debt collector arrived shortly thereafter. My cousin tried to run, but they subdued him."

His expression stony, he raised his eyes to meet hers. "It is certain they took your cousin into custody?"

"Yes."

"Clapped in irons, I hope."

"No. But at gunpoint. We did not stay to see what happened next. As you can imagine, we were anxious to return to Portsmouth."

Sir Edward reclined against the back of his chair, fingertips pressed together just under his chin. "If I had not already signed Ransome's promotion orders, I would promote him after his gallantry." He smiled at Julia. "And you are to be commended as well, my dear, for your quick thinking and your defense of the honor of us all."

Pleasured heat filled Julia's cheeks. "Thank you, Papa."

"Your marriage pleases me. I cannot pretend to have been unaware of the events that occurred twelve years ago. Ransome came to me, seeking my counsel on his regard for you. He felt his situation made him unworthy of your affection and unsuitable for you. I told him then, as I could see his potential for future promotion and wealth, that he had my blessing to marry you."

Julia caught the corner of her bottom lip between her teeth to keep from interrupting him with the questions whirling through her head.

"When your mother told me he had not made the offer, I must admit my disappointment. Ever since Michael..." he cleared his throat. "Ever since Michael's death, I filled the gap caused by the pain of that loss with my affection and admiration for William Ransome. And when I saw your open admiration for him during the Peace of Amiens, I dreamed of having the right to call him son."

She dropped her gaze to her twined fingers. She'd always suspected her father had transferred his affection from his real son to William, but to hear confirmation of it dredged up uncomfortable stirrings of resentment toward him she wished she no longer felt.

"When Ransome left," Sir Edward continued, "and I saw how much his abdication pained you, I was distraught. I was faced full force with the truth: William Ransome was not my son and might not ever be. The grief I'd been holding at bay fell upon me like a hurricane. Grief for my lost son, grief for the hard way I treated him to try to make him into my image, and grief from the shame of trying to replace my boy with my dead friend's son instead of facing my pain and loss like a man."

Julia dashed away a tear before it could complete its journey down her cheek. The ring William had placed on her finger yesterday sparkled in the sunlight filtering in through the window behind her father.

The admiral came around the desk and knelt in front of Julia, covering her hands with his. "I know you have struggled with anger toward me over the years."

Julia couldn't raise her eyes to meet her father's. The truth of his words dredged up guilt and shame, built along with the resentment she'd held toward him for too many years.

"And I need you to know that no matter how much I regard and respect William Ransome, he is no replacement for Michael, just as I am not a replacement for William's father. Living with that illusion only made the pain worse when I faced it—for I had dishonored my son's memory by trying to pretend I did not grieve for the loss of my boy."

Julia pulled her hand out from under her father's and wiped at her tears. "Why are you telling me this, Papa?"

"I could not allow you to leave while you thought ill of me and my regard for your husband." He reached into a pocket and produced a handkerchief—one she'd monogrammed for him.

She took it and dried her eyes. "I have spent the last weeks longing for Jamaica. Now that I am about to go, I feel as if it is too soon." She squeezed his hand and searched the depths of his green eyes. "You will come to Tierra Dulce soon?"

The concern written on his face eased into a smile. "Within the twelvemonth, I promise." He patted her cheek and stood, groaning as he did so. "It is a sad day when I have grown too old to kneel before a beautiful woman." He kissed her forehead.

Julia refolded the handkerchief and handed it back to him. "Will you return to London?"

"I must. There are still many cases to be heard. I shall leave early on the morrow."

"And you plan to join us for dinner at Brampton Park?"

"I thought perhaps I might join Admiral Glover at the Spice Island Inn for supper this evening." Sir Edward regained his seat behind the large desk.

Julia laughed. "So, we shall expect you at six o'clock, then?"

"Aye, though I am still uncertain that having dinner in so formal a setting is more preferable to the company of a bore. However, as it will be my last chance to be with you, I shall endure it."

"Lady Dalrymple is not like most other people in society, Papa. It shall be an enjoyable meal, I promise."

They both turned at a knock on the open study door. Creighton inclined his head. "Sorry to interrupt, sir, but the carriage is ready."

Julia turned back to her father, confused. "I did not realize you had plans to go out, Papa."

"I am making inspection of Commodore Ransome's ship. And I thought you might like to accompany me. I shall need to see all areas of the ship. 'Twill likely be your only opportunity to see her from stem to stern."

Julia's mind immediately jumped back to her conversation with William at breakfast. "I do not think that is a wise idea—my accompanying you. I've no wish to be a distraction to William."

Chuckling, her father came around the desk and offered his hand, though she did not need his support to stand. "My dear girl, you are hardly a day married. He *should* be distracted by you." He tucked her hand in the crook of his elbow and escorted her from their favorite room. "As his admiral, I admire his devotion to duty. As your father, I am disturbed that he left the bridal chamber before the three days I gave him to see to his wife."

Julia's face flamed at her father's mention of the bridal chamber and the implication of the duty it held for a new husband and his bride. And, as he continued talking of husbands and wives, reminding herself that her parents had once been bride and bridegroom only made her embarrassment worse.

When she heard the word "grandchildren," though, she burst out in uncontrollable, mortified laughter. "Papa, please, no more talk of a husband's duty to his wife! I did not live to the grand age of nine-and-twenty without understanding something about marriage."

He stopped at the foot of the stairs and turned her to face him, his hands on her shoulders. "I fear I did not do a very good job of showing you what a good husband is like. I should have recalled your mother from Jamaica years ago."

Julia pressed her fingertips to his mouth to stop him speaking further. "But you still would have been at sea and left her here alone where she had no acquaintance in a climate not suited for her delicate health. Though she loathed being separated from you, especially whenever we received word of each naval engagement in which you might have taken part, at least at Tierra Dulce she was surrounded by people who loved her and could care for her, instead of here, in this big house with only servants for company—or worse, her Pembroke relations." She arched her left brow.

"Aye, you are correct, as always." He tweaked her chin. "Come. No more dawdling. I have a task which must be performed. And a new son to remind there are greater duties than to king and country."

"Sir, a boat is coming up."

Along with Commodore Ransome, Ned looked up from the bills of lading the purser had been reviewing for them. William's steward hovered in the doorway between the commodore's dining cabin and the wheelhouse.

"Where away?" William gained his feet.

"Starboard, 'midships."

Ned and the purser rose also.

"Commodore, sir, I believe it is Admiral Witherington...and Mrs. Ransome."

William's face flashed from mildly interested to concerned. "My mother?"

"No, sir, your wife. Miss Witherington, as was."

Ned nearly choked on his laughter at Dawling's comical expression. Though frustrated by the interruption, seeing his commander's brief flicker of uncertainty made William seem more like a mere mortal than usual.

The commodore shrugged into his uniform coat. Ned groaned. Of course. No shirtsleeves if the admiral was coming aboard. He mopped his brow and forced his arms into the woolen sleeves. Readying a ship for sail in August must be God's punishment for a lifetime of sins.

He trailed William out onto the quarterdeck and toward the starboard waist entry.

Lieutenant Eastwick had apparently just given the order for the bosun's chair to be made ready for *Mrs. Ransome*. Scant moments later, everyone on deck snapped to at William's command as Admiral Sir Edward Witherington cleared the accommodation ladder and stepped onto the deck.

The admiral returned William's salute. "As you were."

The swing-style seat at the end of a block-and-tackle rope appeared over the gunwale, and both the admiral and the commodore moved forward to assist Julia Ransome—who hopped off the seat onto the deck before either officer could assist her.

Ned did not bother to hide his smile. Even though her visit meant delaying their work yet again, he couldn't help but admit how very much he admired his friend's wife. She was exactly the kind of woman every officer should be blessed to find.

An image of Charlotte Ransome rose unbidden, but he cleared it straight away. At only seventeen, Charlotte was too young to marry; yet when Ned returned to England in a year—perhaps two, depending on how long the American war lasted—she would most likely be married. And to someone more worthy than Ned. Someone of fortune and property. Someone with ambition and not afraid of advancement. Someone who hadn't killed two men.

After a trying day, made even more so by the admiral and Julia's visit to *Alexandra,* William gladly left the tedium of Lady Dalrymple's card party to join Julia and her father outside as they said their farewells. Though he'd initially believed the admiral's explanation for bringing Julia out to *Alexandra* this morning—that he simply brought her to see the ship—subtlety was not Sir Edward's greatest ally. Julia's father repeatedly hinted and then outright lectured William during their private conference on William's duty to Julia as her husband.

"Ransome."

He stepped forward, planted his feet shoulder-width apart, and clasped his hands behind his back. "Aye, sir?"

"You will remember my words." Admiral Witherington held Julia's right hand in both of his.

"Aye, sir."

Sir Edward narrowed his eyes. "I have my ways of learning whether or not you follow my instructions."

William took in a measured breath. "Aye, sir."

The admiral glanced at Julia and then back at William. He opened his mouth, stopped, and then cleared his throat. "I am entrusting you with what I value most in this world, son. I am depending on you to keep her safe—and to make sure she is happy." He held Julia's hand toward William.

William reached out, took her hand, and tucked it in the crook of his elbow. The hand, along with her chin, trembled. "I shall protect her with my life, sir, and do my best to ensure her happiness."

Julia's grip around the inside of his elbow tightened.

Her father cleared his throat again, but it did not keep the gruffness from his voice. "Elton shall come for you at ten o'clock tomorrow morning to take you home. Creighton has had the staff in a fury today preparing for your arrival."

Julia shook her head. "I've been away only one night. What could..."

When she did not continue her question, William looked down. Her lips had withdrawn into a thin line, and she averted her gaze away from both William and her father.

The admiral, apparently, did not realize his daughter's embarrassment. "They have been preparing your mother's chamber for you. It is larger and should accommodate the two of you better."

Infernal heat climbed the back of William's neck, making him bless the darkness.

Through the open front door echoed the chiming of the great clock in the entryway.

"I should leave. Catching the early stage to London." Sir Edward adjusted his black formal coat. He seemed strangely diminished—and much older—out of uniform. Though perhaps it was a trick of the darkness and the lateness of the hour.

"Goodbye, Papa." Julia's voice came out reedy, strained, thin. "Godspeed on your journey. Write as soon as you arrive."

"I promise." The admiral made no move toward his barouche. After a long moment, Sir Edward—the man famous throughout the Royal Navy for his gruff, irascible demeanor—pulled his daughter into his arms.

William averted his gaze—not out of a desire to avoid watching his commander's emotional outburst, but because the scene made him too keenly aware of his own father's absence. He needed to spend as much time with Mother—and Charlotte—as possible before sailing.

Sir Edward finally broke away from Julia, kissed her forehead, and beat a hasty retreat to his waiting carriage. Julia stood on the top step and waved until the barouche disappeared into the night.

Despite the darkness, William could see the devastation and loss in her expression when she turned around. Her heartache kindled the need to comfort her. He extended his arms, and she flew to him, burying her face in his chest.

She made no sound as she wrapped her arms around his waist and let him support her trembling weight. Fulfilling the second part of his promise to her father had come much sooner than William expected, though he thanked God Julia was not one to weep. He pressed his cheek to her forehead and hoped his embrace communicated his desire to offer her comfort—as he knew not what to say.

Inside, the clock chimed another quarter hour gone.

"I might never see him again." Her voice barely reached his ears.

"We will have none of that." He took her upper arms and moved her back enough to look at her. He then cupped her chin and tilted her head back until their eyes met. "What has you thinking such morbid thoughts?"

"Your father died before you saw him again."

"He died of fever while at sea. The worst thing your father could catch is the attention of the Lord Admiral of the Royal Navy and come down with a promotion to the Admiralty in London." He smiled, hoping to lighten her mood.

"But *we* shall be at sea. I could contract yellow fever and die."

William refused to let her see the cold dread her words caused. "Have you ever fallen ill with yellow fever?"

"Once, when I was a child."

His skin crawled at the idea of the child he had known wracked by such a terrible illness. "But never since then?"

She shook her head.

"Then you are unlikely to die of yellow fever. I have engaged a fine surgeon who also apprenticed with an apothecary. No sickness shall befall you."

"We could be set upon by privateers—or a rogue French ship. I could be killed in the battle." Julia's wide eyes displayed a distant yet frenzied expression William did not like in the least.

Even though his stomach churned at the real—however remote—possibility, he kept his tone light. "I will protect you. No enemy vessel will be able to get within firing range of *Alexandra*."

"I could be captured by pirates—there could be a hurricane—"

He clapped his hand over her mouth. "Enough. You cannot allow yourself to think these things, Julia. I will keep you safe. I will protect you." Originally annoyed by his agreement to neglect his duty once more and sleep off his ship, he now could not imagine leaving her tonight.

Some of the fear in those beloved green eyes abated. "And who will protect you?" she asked against the palm of his hand.

"God will protect us both." Unable to resist, he lowered his hand, leaned down, and kissed her. "Now, my macabre bride, shall we rejoin the card party?"

"I shall ask her when she returns."

"Miss Fairfax, I do not think she will—"

The baron's daughter cut off Charlotte's protest with a light tap of her fan on Charlotte's wrist. "Nonsense. As Miss Witherington, she proved herself very obliging—and talented as well. As Mrs. Ransome, I wager she will be the same. Look, here they come." Penelope Fairfax rose and started toward the entrance of the formal parlor.

The shadowy light cast by a myriad of candles did nothing to hide the paleness of Julia's countenance when she entered the room on William's arm.

"Mrs. Ransome, how fine you look. It is not fair of you." Penelope leaned closer to Charlotte's sister-in-law. "Everyone will no doubt make a mad dash for the warehouses tomorrow morning and buy up all of the dark green fabric to be had in Portsmouth."

Julia's smile tried to convey appreciation for the flattery, but her eyes remained distant and forlorn.

Charlotte's heart went out to her. The idea of saying goodbye to Mama...she shuddered. She moved forward to try to stop her friend from trespassing on Julia's good nature. "Julia, you look fatigued. Perhaps—"

"Of course she does," Penelope interrupted. "We have all been dull company this evening. Mrs. Ransome, might I entreat you to play for us so we can dance? No one plays so well as you."

Charlotte stared at Miss Fairfax. Her demeanor had changed from the commanding, assured young woman of society Charlotte knew to an insecure, uncertain debutante in the space of a wink. But if there was one thing Charlotte had learned about the Honorable Miss Fairfax, it was that Pen always got her way.

Julia's expression took on a resigned air. "Of course, Miss Fairfax. I shall be happy to play for you."

"Oh, thank you." Penelope clapped her hands and hurried off to spread the news.

With slow deliberation, Julia began removing her gloves.

"You do not have to accede to her will, no matter whose daughter she is," William grumbled.

Julia handed him one long, white glove and started on the other. "How can I refuse her? She is the one who warned me of Lady Pembroke and Sir Drake's scheme." She released a short, dry laugh. "The first one, anyway." She glanced at Charlotte. "My aunt and cousin planned to force me to marry him by spreading rumors that Sir Drake and I were engaged. They were certain I would feel honor bound to marry the...man."

Charlotte stood stone still, drinking in every word, grateful to finally be learning some of the secrets held by her family for the past several weeks.

"I can never repay her for the blessing she bestowed on me by not only telling me what she overheard, but also by not telling anyone else, especially her mother."

William received the second glove. "Why especially her mother?"

Charlotte joined Julia in gaping at her brother.

"Lady Fairfax is the person who told everyone you and Sir Drake were to fight a duel. She is a busybody of the highest manner; and I shall never forgive you, Charlotte Ransome, if you ever tell a single soul I said such a thing."

Julia's words came out so fast, it took Charlotte a moment to realize Julia now addressed her. "I promise I would never say a word. Unlike the baroness, I know how to keep confidences." After all, she'd had quite a bit of practice.

"Speaking of the Fairfaxes..." Julia looked past Charlotte and inclined her head.

Charlotte turned just as Percy Fairfax gained her side.

"I hear there is to be dancing. May I claim you as partner for the first, Miss Ransome?" Percy extended his elbow toward her.

Though in looks he was no Ned Cochr—Henry Winchester, Percy Fairfax's attentions flattered Charlotte. "Yes, Mr. Fairfax." She placed her hand atop his forearm.

"Then I had best take myself over to the pianoforte and start playing." A hint of amusement trickled through Julia's words.

"Capital! Come, Miss Ransome. If we are not quick, Pen and St. Vincent will try to usurp us to gain the best position, but as Lady Dalrymple's guest, you should take precedence over her and lead off."

Leaving it to the baron's son to know more about precedence and leading off the dancing, Charlotte followed him to the opposite end of the room, strategically cleared by Lady Dalrymple's staff for just such an eventuality.

Julia struck up a lively country dance on the pianoforte, and Charlotte began the familiar steps. Had it truly been two years already since Henry showed her the steps in Eliza's sitting room? If Mama had heard of it, Charlotte would never have been allowed to see Henry—or visit Eliza—again.

Now here she was, going through the same rounds of patterns with another man, a man whose attentions flattered her vanity. Yet she wondered at the flirtation Percival Fairfax lavished on her. As the son of a nobleman, he could have no serious designs on her. She might not yet be eighteen, but she knew enough of the world to know the heir to a barony—and all the wealth and estates thereto—would never seriously consider marrying the daughter of a common sailor, regardless of Lady Dalrymple's patronage and Charlotte's ten-thousand-pound legacy, settled on her by her sailor brothers.

Mr. Fairfax complimented her dancing. Charlotte gave him a coquettish smile, all the while grateful for the fact of Henry, making her in no danger of having her heart broken by Percy.

When the song ended, Charlotte glanced around for another partner in time to see Penelope and Mr. St. Vincent—the future Viscount St. Vincent—break away from the dancers and step out through the open doors to the porch that ran along the back of the house with grand views of the gardens—or at least grand views during daylight hours.

"St. Vincent and Pen's engagement will be announced tomorrow." Percy's lips almost touched Charlotte's ear; his breath tickled her cheek. "My father is beside himself at the match. Made the expense of my time at Oxford worthwhile, he told me. That is where I met the rascal, you know. He had always been fascinated by the sea and the navy, so I invited him to come for a visit over a school holiday." Percy laughed. "That was almost six months ago. He has only left Portsmouth twice, and he could not stay away long either time."

Charlotte sighed. To have fallen in love with a man of fortune, as Penelope had. To have no barriers of money, rank, or family disapproval to contend with. To have a fiancé who lived right here in England.

Another of Percy's friends bowed to Charlotte, and Percy relinquished her hand with teasing grumbles before leaving her to find himself another partner.

Julia played an allemande next. Charlotte kept her amusement to herself as the names of the sails and rigging of a ship of the line started ringing through her head. As a girl she'd always set things to music to memorize them so she could think about that during the tedious hours of lessons and practice at the small parlor pianoforte William had purchased for Mama with the first prize money he'd ever received, at age fourteen—three years before Charlotte's birth and their father's death. Mama had not touched the instrument since the loss of her husband, but she had insisted that Charlotte learn.

At midnight, when the butler announced supper, Charlotte was grateful for the support of Percy's arm to the dining room. Tonight was good practice for the formal ball next week—at which the dancing would start earlier and end later, and the room would be more crowded.

Of course, she needed to grow accustomed to crowded conditions as well, if she were going to survive living aboard a ship populated by more than seven hundred souls in cramped conditions for two months.

Though not particularly hungry, Charlotte accepted a plate of cold meats, cheeses, bread, and fruit from Percy. Penelope waved at them, and Charlotte stifled the urge to groan with pleasure as soon as she sat, happy to be off her feet. Her new kid slippers pinched her toes and rubbed her heels until they burned.

The noise of conversation—of the dancers and the card players—which had been masked by the piano and the size of the parlor, filled the dining room and reverberated off the portrait-laden walls. What had seemed a small party—when divided amongst whist tables at one end and dancing at the other—now looked to be a hoard. Fifty guests at least gathered around the giant table in the dining room, eating, drinking, and making all manner of noise. A second scan of the room revealed William and Julia with the Yateses and Mama, who leaned close to Julia, listening and occasionally patting her hand.

A pang of guilt coursed through Charlotte. Mama would be so angry when she discovered Charlotte's departure. Even though Charlotte had not yet determined how she would arrange to sneak away to report to *Audacious* next Thursday, she had already resigned herself to the knowledge it would involve lying to Mama. Again. Something she never would have done before she met Henry. Something she would do only for him.

A commotion at the door caught Charlotte's eye. Mrs. Melling, the housekeeper, had what looked like a concerned conversation with the butler. Melling left, and the butler made his way to Lady Dalrymple and leaned down to speak to her.

The dowager viscountess drew everyone's attention a moment later when she stood. She waved the men back into their seats. "Enjoy your supper. I shall return shortly. A family matter to attend to has arisen."

Speculative whispers rose as soon as the doors closed behind their hostess.

"Something to do with her youngest son, I've no doubt," Penelope whispered, though with such effect Percy and St. Vincent heard her remark as well.

"Her youngest son?" Though yesterday Melling and the chambermaid had given Charlotte the names and ages of Lady Dalrymple's children, their husbands or wives, *their* children, and where they each lived, she'd still been so overwhelmed by her surroundings that she hadn't taken much of it in.

"Yes. I do not recall his name, but he went into the navy at a young age." Penelope glanced around, apparently reveling in the attention of not just her three companions, but of everyone else in hearing range. "He rose smartly through the ranks—of course, as the son of Viscount Dalrymple, he would. But then the story took a strange turn. He and the other officers on his ship were accused of mutiny, charged, tried, and convicted. Mama thinks that's what killed the viscount—the previous one, not the current one, obviously—his son's conviction as a mutineer. Sentenced to death along with the other officers, even though he cooperated with the tribunal and gave testimony that proved the guilt of the other men."

Charlotte stared wide eyed at Penelope, hands pressed to her mouth to keep it from falling open. To commit the ultimate treachery at sea—deposing one's captain—and then to turn around and betray his fellow officers...the man must have had a soul as black as obsidian. "Was he executed?"

"Nay. All but two escaped." Percy jumped in, taking advantage of his sister's pause for a drink. "So now, not only is he hunted by the

Royal Navy, he's hunted by the men he betrayed. The miracle is that they managed to keep the entire sordid affair out of the papers, no doubt owing to the family's position and wealth."

Charlotte stole a glance across the table at her brother and Captain Yates. If they knew this story, would they be sitting here? Would William have agreed to holding his wedding breakfast in this house? Allow Charlotte to stay?

Recovering herself, she asked, "How do you know of this? Did not Lady Dalrymple live in Devon before her husband died?"

Percy nodded. "Lived, yes. But they spent many months every year at Brampton Park, so they have always been well known here."

Slowly, the guests returned to the parlor to take up their former activities. Charlotte excused herself from the Fairfaxes and joined her family to say good night to Mama and Collin and Susan.

Walking back down the hall toward the parlor, Julia covered her mouth when a yawn overtook her.

"Do not go back in." Charlotte stopped her sister-in-law with a touch on her arm. "I will play for the rest of the night—for however long everyone wishes to dance. I can see you've no desire for society tonight."

Julia's cheeks turned pink, and William's severe expression eased. Julia took hold of Charlotte's hand and squeezed it. "Bless you. I did not know how I would face another hour or two of playing, but I could not allow you to give up dancing."

"My shoes pinch, and if I dance one more dance, I shall have a blister on my heel." She smiled at their relieved expressions. "Shall I see you both before you leave tomorrow?"

Julia looked to William to answer.

"We shall breakfast at nine, if you wish to join us."

"I will." She was about to return to the parlor, but she could not wait until morning to get her questions answered. "William?"

He turned at the foot of the stairs, his arm around Julia's waist. "Yes?"

"What do you know of Lady Dalrymple's son, the one who joined the navy?"

"Why do you ask?"

She hurried over to him and gave a quick synopsis of the story Penelope and Percy had told at supper.

William's mouth drew into a tight line as she spoke. "Complete nonsense. Geoffrey Seymour, Lady Dalrymple's youngest son, was not a natural sailor or a remarkable one, but he was loyal to the last. Two lieutenants from his ship were convicted of mutiny, and Seymour testified against them—as did the captain and other officers. The two men were convicted and hanged according to the Articles of War."

"You said 'to the last.' So is he dead, then?"

"Not that I have heard. He paid off as soon as the war ended. Where he went after that, I have not heard." And his tone indicated he did not care.

Charlotte cared—not about where Mr. Seymour might have gone, but whether he might have left anything from his life at sea here at Brampton Park. Because any little piece of detritus or perhaps even a forgotten journal or log book would be a wonderful item to help her look like someone who'd served on several ships and traveled many places.

Starting tomorrow, she would take Lady Dalrymple up on her invitation to explore the house and see if anything here could help her build her new identity as Charles Lott.

Chapter Four

Ned jerked awake, skin clammy with sweat, heart hammering. The smoke. The screams. He wiped his face on his shirt hem. Too real.

Lord, how many times must I pray for forgiveness before the nightmares go away? He climbed out of the hammock. Yet one more proof God did not, as William said, listen to his prayers.

The dream had not come so vividly in years. Why now? He stared into the reflection of his own bleary eyes in the small shaving glass.

Ah, yes. Today was Friday and *she* would be here. On the ship, perhaps within mere feet of him. But maybe the visit by Commodore Ransome's mother and sister coming today, a day before the ball in her honor, would be good—would help Ned make peace with his resolve to see Charlotte Ransome as nothing more than his commanding officer's little sister. Not much younger than his own sister, in fact. Someone to be seen, assisted, and, if needed, protected, but not to be looked at with longing in his heart.

Five bells rang on deck, marking half-past six. Ned made himself ready for duty and arrived on deck before six bells, when he officially started his primary duty of supervising the crew for the day. At eight o'clock, with the crew gathered on deck, Ned informed them of the Ransome women's impending visit and the commodore's expectation for the condition of the ship—every area of the ship, including the officers' wardroom and the gun decks and galley.

The crew grumbled amongst themselves. Ned couldn't blame

them—though he did quell the complaining with a sharp look. Making the ship ready for sail was chaotic work. Trying to do that and also clean up the ship to meet with a woman's approval would be nigh impossible.

But for William Ransome, this crew would do almost anything. And Ned would see that they did.

He dismissed them to duty or breakfast—they each knew which, depending on their duty cycle—and then returned to the wardroom to cook his own eggs and toast for breakfast.

The other lieutenants, except O'Rourke, who was on watch, laughed and talked a great deal too much this morning, filling their small common room with a noise Ned usually enjoyed. This morning, however, anxiety stretched his nerves taut, and each peal of laughter after a jest, each voice raised to be heard over another, plucked at him like an archer drawing his bow. He needed solitude and time to organize his thoughts before he let loose arrows of ill temper on his mates. He stuffed the last crust of toast in his mouth, grabbed his hat, and practically ran all the way up on deck.

He glanced around the ship. Men crowded the yardarms, rerigging the sails. Not that the dockyard crew had done it incorrectly, but years of experience on *Alexandra* had taught these seasoned sailors exactly how she needed to be rigged for the best performance.

On deck men hoisted supplies from boats alongside them in the harbor up and over *Alexandra*'s sides and down into the dark chasm of the holds, with the purser, master gunner, and boatswain barking orders over all the noise. Elsewhere, men cleaned the cannons while others scrubbed the deck. Small boys darted in and out, fetching and carrying.

No solitude here.

He climbed up to the poop deck. The younger midshipmen looked around at him—away from the navigation lesson Sailing Master Ingleby was teaching. Toward the stern of the poop, the older mids worked on their calculus with the surgeon, Mr. Hawthorne—a happy discovery for Ned, who had been able to remember enough of the theory behind the arithmetic to pass his examination but was flummoxed when trying to teach it to the mids. And though William seemed more than capable at teaching it, Ned suspected he hated it, as he always assigned Ned that task—until Mr. Hawthorne had observed Ned's fumbling attempts to answer a boy's question. Hawthorne stepped in, answered the question without hesitation, and taught the remainder of the lesson at Ned's invitation. Even Ned had learned something that day.

With a sigh, Ned abandoned his search for solitude and made a tour of the ship, looking over and approving or correcting the work being done where necessary. The morning passed more quickly than he liked, but keeping himself busy held his anxiety over Charlotte Ransome's visit at bay.

When he returned to the quarterdeck a couple of hours later, the boatswain scurried over to him.

"Jolly boat coming up, sir." Matthews knuckled his forehead in salute to Ned. "Commodore Ransome and his party."

As William had insisted the women's visit was not to disrupt the crew's work, Ned did not call the crew on deck to order, but merely made his way over to the starboard waist entry port to properly greet his commander.

William appeared first and returned Ned's and Matthews's salutes by touching the forepoint of his hat. Matthews and his mates were ready with the bosun's chair for the ladies and swung it over the bulwark. Ned stole a glance over the side to see why William had abandoned the women in the boat.

Collin Yates, the former captain of *Audacious*, assisted an older woman onto the seat of the swing. Beside her, a fashionable bonnet hid the face Ned both longed and dreaded to see. Another woman, a little older than Charlotte and with light hair, sat in the center of the boat. She caught Ned looking at her and waved. Oh, yes. How could he forget Mrs. Yates?

Ned stepped forward in case his assistance should be needed with William's mother, but it was not. Soon, all three women and Collin Yates—giving off a melancholic air in his civilian clothes—stood on deck.

To keep from staring at her, to drink in her innocent beauty, Ned avoided looking at Charlotte altogether.

William motioned Ned away from the visitors. "Report."

"All is well and progressing apace, sir." Ned gave William a quick rundown of everything the crew had done since his departure yesterday afternoon.

"Very well." William removed his hat, wiped his brow, and settled the bicorne back over his dark hair. "Thank you for the extra effort you have been putting forth in my absence, Ned. It shall not be forgotten."

"It is my honor, sir." Keeping his commission and a position in these times was worth any manner of imposition. "May I make so bold as to ask, sir, why your wife did not come with you today?"

William gave him a sharp look—as if checking to see if Ned were needling him—but he must have recognized the sincerity of Ned's question. His expression eased. "My—Jul—Mrs. Ransome is fulfilling some social obligations today."

Purser Holt hovered nearby, almost vibrating with his anxiety to speak to the commodore, since he'd been put off yesterday…and the day before. William looked from Holt to the women to Ned.

Ned held in his sigh, steeling himself for the request to come.

"Might I impose on you, Ned, to accompany my guests around the upper decks while I square away Holt?"

"Of course, sir." Ned hoped William's conference with the purser did not last long. The less time he spent in Charlotte's presence, the better—for his own peace of mind.

Mr. Yates offered his arms to his wife and William's mother and set off down the quarterdeck, leaving Ned and Charlotte to bring up the rear. Ned motioned Charlotte to go before him, and he fell in step aft, gripping his hands behind his back.

In the forecastle, the Yateses and William's mother stopped. At first, Ned couldn't understand why—until he recognized the ship off the larboard bow. *Audacious*. Yates's final command.

"How many guns is she?" Charlotte asked, pulling to a stop near them.

"Sixty-four," Ned answered automatically.

"And was she refitted, same as *Alexandra*?" Charlotte looked up at him with raised brows and eyes so blue and clear, Ned couldn't form words.

"Nay." Mr. Yates ran his hand over the bulwark railing. "We did not see nearly as much close action in *Audacious* as your brother did, Miss Ransome. Though I did oversee the repairs to her before..." Yates glanced at his wife.

The silence grew. The knowledge that Captain Yates had resigned his commission on account of his wife's delicate condition had spread through the navy rumor mill like weevils through a biscuit.

Ned cleared his throat. "*Audacious* is a fine ship."

"And will you have command of something like it soon, Lieutenant Cochrane?" Mrs. Ransome asked.

His stomach rolled—in the opposite direction of the harbor beneath *Alexandra*. "No, ma'am. Aside from there being no open ships now that the war with France has ended, I would need to serve as commander of a smaller ship before I could begin to think of promotion to post captain and gaining a ship of the line like *Audacious*." And only if his nightmare came true. He would rather leave the navy—leave the only life he knew, the life he loved—and try to make his living on land than to face taking command of a ship and its crew.

"Shall we continue the tour?" Collin led the two older ladies away. This time Charlotte would not allow Ned to walk behind her, but she paused until he realized her intention to walk beside him. A few paces ahead, Mr. Yates brought the finer points of *Alexandra*'s construction—and masts and rigging—to their attention. Though Charlotte looked everywhere he indicated, she seemed uninterested.

"Are you enjoying your stay at Brampton Park, Miss Ransome?" Ned couldn't help himself. Her bonnet hid her face, but he at least wanted to hear her voice.

"I am, Lieutenant Cochrane. Though I do not see much of Lady Dalrymple. Two nights ago, during her card party, her daughter arrived unexpectedly. I am not certain exactly what happened, but something to do with the husband and an argument over…something." Charlotte's tone indicated she knew more about the situation than she revealed. "She will be entering her confinement any day now, so Lady Dalrymple is constantly at her side."

"You must be lonely."

"I do have much solitude in that big, empty wing of the house by myself, now that William and Julia have returned to her father's house, but I am resourceful. I can always find employment for my time."

As Charlotte launched into a recitation of calls, dress fittings, and excursions to the shops in town, Ned wanted to silence her and tell her to watch her feet and be careful where she stepped to avoid tripping over ropes, which her mother and Mrs. Yates cautiously minced through.

But Charlotte was surefooted as an old seaman, never once putting her foot wrong or needing Ned's ready assistance to step over or around anything.

Before Charlotte exhausted her monologue on how she filled her hours, Commodore Ransome joined them and dismissed Ned to return to his duties. Holt awaited Ned in the wheelhouse, but Ned did not join him right away.

Now that he'd been dismissed from the duty of escorting Charlotte around the ship, Ned wanted to be nowhere other than at her side. However, she spared him no glance, no sign to indicate she thought of him as anything more than a lieutenant on her brother's ship—just one of many.

As well she should.

Julia tried to swallow the bitter tea past the knot in her throat. Lady Fairfax continued relating the latest gossip, apparently noticing nothing awry with her caller's behavior.

Her father had given William permission to sleep ashore for the next week—both of them had informed her so. Wednesday evening, he had agreed to stay with her because she had committed them to attend Lady Dalrymple's card party. She appreciated his willingness to accommodate her—though she wondered what could he possibly be doing at night that would necessitate his sleeping aboard *Alexandra* that he could not accomplish from her father's study.

But then yesterday had only served to confuse her more. After breakfast with her and Charlotte at Brampton Park, he had returned to *Alexandra*, and Julia paid their farewells to Lady Dalrymple. Julia expected she would not see him again that day. But then he arrived for dinner and explained he had not wanted to leave her alone her first night home from Brampton Park. Being in her father's house—even though in a different bedroom and not in the room that had been Julia's for the past year—the very air around them had been laden with tension and awkwardness. For the first time since their wedding, William had not done more than give her a chaste good-night kiss and then lay on his back, staring at the carved wood canopy above them. Yet in the middle of the night, Julia had been awakened from a fretful sleep when William pulled her into his arms—never waking from his own sound slumber.

Why would he not want her when awake, yet want to hold her in his sleep?

Julia needed her mother. The lump of emotion grew, and she set the teacup down before her hands started shaking. She wanted Mama to talk to, to ask questions of, to receive assurances from. She couldn't talk to Susan or Mrs. Ransome—they would not understand. They would believe William had made a poor choice in a wife who complained about him and questioned his intentions to his mother and best friend's wife only a few days after the wedding. But without being able to go to them, she had no one in whom to confide. No one else whom she trusted to keep her concerns and questions confidential.

"Mrs. Ransome, my dear, are you unwell?" Lady Fairfax's concern broke through Julia's emotional turmoil.

"Pardon? Oh, yes. I do apologize, my lady. It would seem my mind is much occupied this afternoon."

"Oh-ho-ho!" Lady Fairfax simpered and smirked. "'Tis always so with the newly married. When Lord F and I were just wed, I could not carry on a serious conversation for months."

The idea of Lady Fairfax having ever possessed the ability to carry on a *serious* conversation forced a smiled through Julia's worries.

"And you have the added distraction of preparing for your removal to the West Indies. Why, the very idea of returning to that pestilential place must have you all in a tizzy when you must have thought yourself finally settled at home."

"But Jamaica is my home, Lady Fairfax. I long to see the plantation again, to spend time with lifelong friends I had to leave behind." To discover if the missing ten thousand pounds from the new steward's ledgers was a mistake or treachery.

Yes. That must be her focus now. Worrying about William's whims of will availed her naught except grief and a headache. She must keep in mind why she married him in the first place: to return to Tierra Dulce and protect her home.

"Well." Lady Fairfax fairly snorted the word. "If that isn't the queerest thing I've ever heard. Home in Jamaica indeed." Her eyes took on a glint. "But of course you are teasing me. No one would prefer that godforsaken place to England."

Julia answered only with a tight smile. She would never be able to convince the baroness Jamaica was her idea of heaven on earth.

"Tell me about your sister."

Julia blinked, trying to hide her confusion, certain the baroness knew about Michael. "I have no sister, only a brother who was lost at sea fifteen years ago."

"Miss Charlotte Ransome, goose." Lady Fairfax tapped Julia's wrist with her fan. "My children are much taken with her. Percy speaks of her constantly."

Ah, yes. *That* sister. The one hiding the letter Julia had accidentally seen in which a man declared his love for Charlotte and asked her to marry him. "Charlotte is a wonderful young woman. Very accomplished. But...I believe Commodore Ransome and his mother think her far too young to entertain any idea of a serious attachment. She is not yet eighteen."

Lady Fairfax laughed. "I know it is no longer the thing amongst this generation to marry young, but in my day, if a woman were not engaged by her eighteenth birthday, she was considered on the shelf. And is it not true that you yourself would have married at Miss Ransome's age if a certain handsome lieutenant would have but asked?"

Julia conceded the point by inclining her head.

"I understand Commodore Ransome has settled a small fortune on his sister. Ten thousand, is it not?"

Julia hated discussing financial matters in public. Mama had taught her it was vulgar and done only by shallow, vain people. But over the past year, she'd learned it was not only accepted, but expected amongst society. "Yes, ma'am. Commodore Ransome and his brothers settled that amount on her."

"I am certain, then, that at her ball tomorrow all the gentlemen will be buzzing around her. It is good you shall be there to help her determine who is of an appropriate social position to pay his addresses to her. No one should be burdened by marrying outside of her station."

And with that, Julia understood Lady Fairfax's position clearly. Her son could be seen to flirt with a young woman with a ten-thousand-pound legacy, but the Fairfaxes would never tolerate his marrying the daughter of a common sailor, no matter her wealth or that of her brothers.

"Yes. I feel my duty in helping Charlotte find a suitable husband as a grave undertaking." And her duty in warning Charlotte about forming any attachment to Percy Fairfax. Not that Julia suspected she had, but young women could be unpredictable, and she did not know Charlotte all that well.

"We would like to play our part." The baroness leaned forward. "Charlotte is such a dear girl, quite a friend to Penelope. We would like to invite her to go with us to the country next week. Pen and Percy always have friends come in for a few weeks—parties and balls every night, practically. It would be a wonderful introduction to a larger society for her, to prepare her for a London Season next year."

While Julia hoped Charlotte would accept the invitation to join the Fairfaxes at their country estate, she knew William and Mrs. Ransome would never agree to exposing Charlotte to the garish, soul-snuffing madness that marked a Season in Town.

"A formal invitation shall be sent, but I hope you might work on her mother tonight."

"If I see her this evening, I will certainly inform her of your intention." To Julia's relief, the mantel clock chimed the quarter hour. "Gracious, I did not realize I had been here so long. I wish I could stay longer..." She let her voice trail off.

"I am certain you have many other visits to make, so I'll not be greedy and keep you to myself. But we will see you again at Lady Dalrymple's ball, if not before."

Julia curtseyed in farewell and finally escaped. In the carriage on the way back to her father's house, she imagined Charlotte interacting with the Fairfaxes' acquaintances. The Fairfax family had been nothing but kind to Charlotte, and the opportunity they offered her to expand her social circle was something that the Ransomes had probably never dreamed of for her. They would be foolish to refuse the invitation. But with the Fairfaxes' penchant for caring about nothing other than gossip and fashion and London, Julia hoped Charlotte's character was strong enough to resist being altered from the innocent, unpretentious girl she now was.

William had told her to think on the prospect of bringing a woman companion on the voyage. What would he say if she suggested Charlotte?

Chapter Five

Ned hated the way the high, stiff collar of his dress uniform chafed his jaw and earlobes. But he wouldn't have missed this night for anything...it might be his last chance to see Miss Charlotte Ransome, and he intended to make the most of it. He had been unable to clear his mind of thoughts of her since her visit to *Alexandra* two days ago. He decided he'd best let his infatuation run its natural course than to try to quell it. Soon enough an ocean would be separating them, making it much easier to forget her.

The jolly boat scraped to a stop at the quay, and Ned and the rest of *Alexandra*'s lieutenants disembarked with much straightening of waistcoats and jackets. As Commodore Ransome had indicated, two carriages waited to convey them to Brampton Park.

In Ned's carriage, Lieutenants O'Rourke and Campbell wondered aloud if certain young ladies of their acquaintance might be in attendance.

"Of course, Ned will be the most honored man there tonight." O'Rourke's brogue broke through Ned's thoughts.

"Whatever are you on about?" Ned asked, adjusting his perfectly fitted gloves.

"You...and Miss Charlotte Ransome. She fancies you, I have no doubt. She'd give you her hand for every dance, were you to ask."

Ned's hope kindled briefly, but he doused it in haste. "Once again, you've allowed your Irish imagination to run wild. She would no sooner look on me as worthy of her affection than the night watchman at the city gate." No matter how much he wished it otherwise.

O'Rourke and Campbell exchanged a look that Ned pointedly ignored.

"Has the commodore said aught else about a traveling companion for Mrs. Ransome?" Campbell asked, turning the tide.

"No. Not to me, at any rate. Why? Do you have someone in mind?"

"Nay. Just wondering if we would be getting a double shot of superstitious nonsense from the crew."

Because she was the daughter of their admiral and a well-respected woman in naval circles, the crew had not raised much of a complaint when Commodore Ransome had announced that his new bride would be sailing with them across the Atlantic.

"What about the wife of one of the warrant officers?" Campbell suggested. "An older woman who isn't going to cause any...disruption to the men below decks."

"How do you suggest the commodore choose which man brings his wife when none of the rest are allowed?" Ned asked.

"Not all of them would want to bring their wives." O'Rourke's brown eyes twinkled. "Eliminate them straight off."

"Hold a lottery for the rest. Whoever's name is drawn becomes Mrs. Commodore's traveling companion." Campbell nodded, the issue apparently settled in his mind.

"And if Mrs. Ransome and the officer's wife don't get on with each other? Then you have two women aboard ship who want to be anywhere *but* in the other's company. And since neither of you has sisters, I will tell you that when my sister and mother row, no one around them is happy or productive." Ned held in his smile at Campbell's crestfallen expression. "Let's allow Mrs. Ransome to choose her own companion if she so desires, shall we?"

O'Rourke and Campbell lapsed into silence, for which Ned was grateful. The carriage rattled on over roads—dirt now they'd left the confines of Portsmouth—rougher than a jolly boat on a stormy sea.

"D'you suppose now the captain's been promoted to commodore that he'll promote you to captain when we make Kingston station, Ned?" Campbell never had been able to tolerate silence for long.

Ned's stomach turned. "I try not to speculate. I am content to consider myself blessed to remain in the service and leave it at that."

"Do you not want your own command?" O'Rourke gazed at Ned as if appraising his worthiness for promotion.

Did he? Horrible screams and the phantom stench of fire whirled around in his head. He closed his eyes and swallowed hard.

"Of course he wants a command, just as we all do. Right, Ned?"

"Right, Angus." Yet he couldn't help but pray God would never bring that circumstance to pass.

The carriage rolled to a stop in front of the enormous manor house. Ned climbed out first—privilege of rank—and adjusted his high-domed, black beaver-pelt hat on his head. Just a few more paces and he would be in the same room as the lovely and intriguing Miss Charlotte Ransome once more.

Leaving his hat in the cloakroom, Ned forced himself into the crush of black evening suits and white gowns pressing toward the ballroom. He'd overheard whispers at the commodore's wedding breakfast that Lady Dalrymple's home was one of the few private homes near Portsmouth to boast a room designated solely for dancing.

If Charlotte Ransome was now swimming in such an ocean of wealth and influence, she would never give it up for his mere puddle of a life. Not that he would be asking her to.

He spotted his commanding officer and detoured that direction to report their arrival and the state of the ship when he'd left her half an hour ago. He stopped a few paces from the commodore and was going to salute, but then he remembered the absence of his hat. He snapped into a more sociable bow instead.

"Mrs. Ransome," Commodore Ransome's voice hitched on the epithet for his wife, "may I present Lieutenant Cochrane?"

Ned bent in another bow to hide his smile. "Mrs. Ransome, it is a great pleasure to see you again."

Her lovely green eyes twinkled with amusement. "Lieutenant Cochrane."

William turned to the uniformed man beside him. "And Admiral Witherington, you will recall, of course, my first lieutenant."

Heat climbed into Ned's cheeks. He hadn't thought about the possibility of William's new father-in-law—and their flag officer—being here. "Admiral Sir Edward."

"Lieutenant. And have you brought your fellows with you?" The admiral's voice came across as gruff, but a hint of humor danced in his eyes—eyes the same color green as his daughter's.

"Aye, sir. *Alexandra* is well represented by her officers."

The admiral nodded and then turned his attention to another vying officer. Ned turned back to William and gave his report, remaining at all times aware of the admiral's presence and occasional attention. Most officers of Ned's experience would have jumped at the chance to be brought to the notice of a high-ranking officer like Admiral Sir Edward Witherington. Ned wished he were anywhere but here.

If he had any other talents or skills, he would have quitted the Royal Navy at the onset of the Peace. But having signed on to his first ship at age ten as a volunteer, he knew no other trade by which to earn his living. And he did enjoy naval life, for the most part. He just wished his career could continue on its current heading: as first officer under the command of William Ransome, the man he trusted above all others, the man for whom he would walk through fire or swim through shark-infested waters.

"Thank you for your report, Ned. Now, go and enjoy yourself."

"I believe Charlotte—and most of the young people—are in the conservatory, Lieutenant." The tilt of Julia Ransome's lips brought renewed heat to Ned's face. He inclined his head to her and took his leave.

Charlotte ducked back into the overcrowded conservatory as Ned

Cochrane parted company with William and Julia. Her traitorous heart gave a leap when she noted he was headed in her direction.

Try as she might, she could not conjure up an image of Henry, her betrothed, while Ned Cochrane, a stranger, was just a few feet away and getting closer.

She'd wanted to save the first set for Ned, to lead off the ball on his arm...but she denied herself that pleasure out of an innate sense of loyalty to her fiancé. And she could not be too cautious in limiting her exposure to him, even if they would be serving on separate ships.

A man stepped out in front of her, halting her progress through the room. "Miss Ransome, I have been looking high and low for you."

She snapped open her fan and fanned her face in what she hoped was a coquettish manner as she returned his bow with a quick curtsey. "Mr. Fairfax. What a pleasure to see you again."

"Mother and I were talking just today about you."

Charlotte's heart quickened. "Oh?"

"Yes. You know we are readying to leave Portsmouth for the country. Mother suggested, and I agreed, that it would be a capital idea to invite you to come for a long stay."

Her throat tightened. When Julia had mentioned to her and Mama that the Fairfaxes would be extending an invitation for Charlotte to go on holiday with them in the country, she had been thrilled at the compliment to herself. But then the logistics of the situation settled in her mind. She could not accept the invitation—the Fairfaxes had already put it about that they intended to leave Portsmouth the very morning Charlotte was to report for duty aboard *Audacious*. Yet how could she decline such an invitation without a reasonable explanation? "I...I shall have to speak with my mother about it."

Mr. Fairfax's brown curls bobbed with his emphatic nod. "Yes, of course you will. We shan't be leaving until Thursday morning, so there is ample time to make all the arrangements."

An idea started to form in Charlotte's mind. Because the Fairfaxes were to leave Portsmouth on Thursday, the same day Charles Lott was to report for duty, Charlotte might be able to use the invitation to her advantage.

"Now, on to other orders of business." Fairfax grabbed the hem of his waistcoat and gave it a tug. "Miss Ransome, I believe I have the honor of your hand for the first set." He extended his arm toward her.

With a grin, Charlotte rested her hand atop his sleeve. "No, Mr. Fairfax, the honor is all mine."

The crowd already gathered in the middle of the ballroom parted before Charlotte and Percy, making her feel, even just for the tiniest moment, what Princess Charlotte Augusta must feel whenever she walked into a room. But unlike the Prince Regent's only child, Charlotte Ransome would, after tonight, return to being just a common sailor's daughter.

She caught a giggle in the back of her throat. Actually, not too much longer after tonight, she'd become just a common midshipman. Her gaze darted about the room from her position of honor to lead off the dance.

So many naval officers here tonight—ah, there by the door to the conservatory. Ned Cochrane carried on a lively conversation with another officer. The other man turned, and Charlotte gasped. Avoiding Ned tonight would be important; avoiding Lieutenant Howe, first officer of *Audacious*, would be vital.

The music started. Percy's bow caught her attention, and Charlotte dropped into a curtsey just in time and then reached out to place her hand in his.

Though distracted by a constant awareness of Ned Cochrane's presence, and the idea he might be watching her, Charlotte acquitted herself quite well in the intricate steps...and in receiving Percy Fairfax's flirtatious remarks.

After the first dance ended and Charlotte once again took her place opposite Mr. Fairfax for the second dance of the set, a flutter amongst the other dancers made her look around again. At the other end of the columns of men and women, William and Julia took their places.

"I see Mrs. William Ransome gets to participate tonight instead of being relegated to providing accompaniment."

"She is an accomplished pianist." Charlotte stepped toward Percy, curtseyed, stepped back again, and then started a circuit around him. "But she is also a lovely dancer. Better than I."

"A woman dancing with her beloved is the most graceful creature in the world."

Charlotte snapped her gaze to Percy. Surely he did not think...but he still looked in William and Julia's direction. She hoped Percy would not be foolish enough to develop feelings for her.

"My mother told me something interesting today concerning your brother and sister." Percy looked down at Charlotte as they wove around the dancers currently standing in lines, awaiting their turn.

"What? Do tell."

But no sooner had she spoken than the figures of the dance separated them—sending them to now stand several feet apart, facing each other, unable to talk as others danced around them.

Charlotte had a weakness for gossip, which made the Fairfaxes perfect companions, as they always knew the latest. They never passed it along in malice, but only in fun to make good conversation.

However, Charlotte had learned long ago that gossip could be hurtful, even when spoken only in fun. Though it pained her, she would tell Mr. Fairfax she did not want to hear it. William's and Julia's lives had almost been ruined by the gossip and rumors spread about them. No matter what Mrs. Fairfax had heard, Charlotte would not be party to its spreading further.

As soon as she rejoined Percy for the end of the number, she asked him about their country home and what one might expect to see and do there. The tactic worked to make him forget what he'd planned to tell her. Charlotte wished it were as easy for her to forget.

The next hour swirled away in a blur of handsome, attentive gentlemen and officers. After a rousing reel with Mr. St. Vincent, Charlotte turned off the dance floor for a respite—and came face-to-face with Ned Cochrane.

His cool gray eyes burned into hers. She dropped her gaze and bent her knees in a quick curtsey.

"Might I have the honor of the next dance, Miss Ransome?"

How could she? What if he then recognized her through her disguise next time they met at the dockyard? But as they would be on different ships, they would likely not see each other at all. "Yes, Lieutenant Cochrane. I would be delighted."

Charlotte's fingertips tingled when they came in contact with Ned's, even though they both wore gloves. A few steps into the allemande, Charlotte had trouble catching her breath. Every time they separated, she felt cold and abandoned. And she could look nowhere but at Ned. His hair was too dark to be blond and too light to be brown. He had a scar in the middle of his forehead that broke up the lines when he raised his brows, the way a rock broke the flow of a stream. And though he was not as tall and lithe as Percy Fairfax, he seemed lighter on his feet, more graceful, no doubt from years of developing a keen sense of balance aboard ships.

The dance ended too soon. Had it not been for Penelope's immediately claiming her and declaring the need for refreshment, Charlotte would have embarrassed herself by asking—begging—Lieutenant Cochrane for another dance...and another...

Penelope pulled her into a corner where a tall vase gave them some measure of privacy. "My dear girl, why did you not tell me?"

"Tell you?" Charlotte glanced around the vase, trying to see if Ned danced with someone else.

"That you are in love."

Charlotte ducked back behind the vase. "How did you find out?"

Penelope laughed. "'Twas quite apparent to me. All it took was one look at your face and I knew. Though I heartily object—you can do so much better, my dear—I must applaud you for falling in love with such a handsome man, for all that he is a sailor."

"A...sailor?" Relief weakened Charlotte's knees. So Penelope did not know about Henry. Imagine. Thinking Charlotte was in love with Ned Cochrane. The very thought of the way his uniform hugged his fit form made her lungs smolder—something that had never happened at the thought of Henry Winchester.

But no. Henry waited for her in Jamaica. She loved Henry...didn't she? "You are mistaken, Miss Fairfax. I am not in love with Lieutenant Cochrane."

"Good. Because when you come to the country with us, there shall be gentlemen aplenty for you to choose from." Penelope hooked her arm through Charlotte's and led her toward the dining room.

In love with Ned Cochrane? Impossible. But her heart called her a liar.

William watched Charlotte and the Fairfax girl until they disappeared into another room. He still was not convinced the Fairfaxes were good companions for his sister, but as Mother and Julia countered all his objections with sound arguments as to the favorability and advantage to Charlotte the connection to the Fairfaxes provided, he kept his concerns to himself.

"Lady Dalrymple, you've returned."

Julia's voice brought William's attention back to the conservatory. The dowager viscountess swept into the room like an admiral into a room full of midshipmen. Julia seemed to be the only woman in the room not flustered by the aristocrat's presence.

"How is your daughter feeling?" Julia asked when Lady Dalrymple stopped beside her.

"She is well. Uncomfortable, but well." The viscountess leaned closer to Julia. "I do not mind telling you, Mrs. Ransome, that I have gone against her wishes and contacted her husband to demand he come here and try to reconcile before the baby comes."

"And if he does not come?"

The brow over Lady Dalrymple's green eye arched. "He will come, even if I have to send my own men to London to fetch him."

William, trying to appear disinterested in the women's talk, allowed the slightest smile to touch his lips. There was something to be said about having the wealth and power a title brought when placed in the hands of someone like Lady Dalrymple, who wielded both well.

"There you are." A shrill voice made Julia startle and Lady Dalrymple close her mismatched eyes. William gritted his teeth at the approach of Lady Fairfax.

"If you will excuse me." Lady Dalrymple inclined her head to William, Julia, and the baroness, and then departed. Fortunate woman.

"I have been wanting to have a word with the two of you all evening. I have heard the most remarkable story and knew I must tell you right away." The portly woman sidled up to Julia, taking up the place Lady Dalrymple had just vacated. The aroma of rotting flowers wafted over William and turned his stomach.

"My lady, I'm certain your story is quite interesting, however—"

"Sir Drake is out of debtor's prison."

It took all William's strength to keep from staggering back from the verbal blow. Julia's hand tightened around his arm, and she leaned heavily into his side.

"How...how is that possible?"

An almost maniacal gleam flickered to life in Lady Fairfax's eyes. "My cousin in London informed me that a certain Lady Henrietta Stokesbury—a woman whose knighted husband died very wealthy, leaving everything to his childless widow—had been a favorite of your cousin's during his time in Town. When she learned of his plight, she paid off his most pressing debts and got him released. The word is that they plan to marry almost immediately."

"I pray my cousin will find...much joy in his new life." Julia's voice came out choked, as if she had a stone lodged in her throat.

"As well you should." Lady Fairfax glanced around, and then she leaned forward as if to reveal a vast conspiracy to Julia. "I have it on good authority that not only is Lady Stokesbury's reputation less than sterling, she is considered to be somewhat of a shrew. My cousin says it is this reason why the lady remains unmarried, though she has been on the hunt for a titled gentleman for many years."

Against him, Julia's body began to tremble. William removed her hand from the crook of his elbow and placed his arm around her waist to lend her additional support—physically and emotionally.

"Thank you for informing us, Lady Fairfax."

The baroness gave a little squeak at William's statement, as if heretofore unaware of his presence.

"If you will excuse us, I believe I promised my wife the next dance." Though dancing was the last thing on his mind, he had to get her away from the baroness to somewhere quiet and private. He took Julia by the hand and led her across the ballroom, through the front hall, and up the stairs to the small sitting room in which they'd had tea the first afternoon after their wedding.

He used the candle he'd snatched from the sconce in the hall to light the tapers in the two candelabra on the mantel and brighten the room a little. Turning his back to the dark chasm of the fireplace, he clasped his hands behind his back and waited. Julia paced the other side of the room, one arm wrapped around her waist, one hand clamped over her mouth. The elaborate gold embroidery at the neck, high waist, and hem of her blue-gray gown sparkled in the flickering candlelight. The gold ribbon peeking through her hair made him want to remove it to release the mahogany curls so that they could tumble freely around her shoulders and back.

Closing his eyes, he schooled his thoughts. He would never be able to return to the ship tonight if he allowed himself to continue in that vein.

"All that time." Julia's voice came as if from a distance, drawing him back to the present.

He opened his eyes and looked about the room for her, finally seeing her before the windows at the opposite end. "All that time?"

She spun, her skirt flaring slightly, and threw her arms wide. "All that time he pursued me whilst knowing there was a woman in London who would be willing to pay his debts *and* marry him. He—and his mother and Aunt Hedwig—tried to ruin me. He tried to ruin my father in order to force me to marry him." Her nose crinkled as if at a distasteful smell. "Why could he have not married this Lady Stokesbury and left me alone to live my life in peace? Why did he have to spoil everything?"

William clamped his teeth on the inside of his bottom lip to keep from reacting. Spoiled everything? While marrying Julia had not been his idea—not since he made the decision to walk away from her twelve years ago—he could not see how their marrying spoiled anything, with the exception of his own peace of mind.

"All I wanted was to go back to Jamaica, to manage Tierra Dulce. But they tried to take it away from me. For what? To pay his gambling debts?" Julia's pitch rose, and she started pacing again. It took almost all of William's strength to keep from mirroring her.

Julia stopped directly across the room from William and turned to face him. "They locked me in a room and were going to force me to write you a letter breaking off our engagement." Her expression underwent a radical change—from fury to something akin to astonishment. "But if they had only known..."

He raised one brow in question. "Known what?"

She walked slowly toward him. "That threatening to take you away from me was the best way to ensure I would never capitulate to their demands." She stopped directly before him, the hem of her dress brushing the toes of his shoes. "Because I would never have given you up. I have loved you, William Ransome, since I was ten years old, and I was not going to part ways with you again."

The granite hardness that had settled in his chest melted away. He reached out and touched the ringlet that caressed her cheek, and then he bent to kiss her, cupping her jaw with his palm. Her arms encircled his waist, and he pulled her into an embrace, almost frightened at how much contentment he drew from her nearness.

"So are you sorry your relations' actions led you to propose marriage to me?" With his cheek pressed to Julia's forehead, William did not hide his smile.

She let out a long sigh, the tension palpably ebbing from her body. "Nay. I am not sorry that the mistake made a dozen years ago was finally put right."

He squeezed her tighter until she let out a yelping laugh, and then he released his hold so he could look into the green eyes that had haunted him since he was fifteen. "I cannot make up for the years we lost, but I promise I will do my utmost to make what years we have the happiest you have known." He kissed her again to seal the vow.

After the several long moments it took for Julia's eyes to focus on him again, she released another deep sigh. "We should return."

"Aye, we should." But he made no move to release her or leave the privacy of the sitting room.

"Susan and Collin will wonder where we are. Your mother, as well."

"Aye, they will." He ran his finger from her temple down the side of her face and along her jaw to her stubbornly pointed chin.

"Charlotte might need watching after."

"Aye, she might." However, William rested in the knowledge that his mother, Collin, and Susan would all look after Charlotte—and he could depend on Ned Cochrane to protect her from the puppies and macaronis who filled the ballroom if need be.

"Lady Dalrymple might be offended if we were to leave so early." Julia's eyes grew increasingly hazy.

"Nay. Lady Dalrymple would understand."

Julia stared up at him for a long while. William leaned forward, ready to kiss her again.

"Do you think Sir Drake's betrothed will pay the mortgage on Marchwood to stave off the foreclosure proceedings you've begun?"

Now it was William's turn to sigh. Instead of kissing her, he dropped his head to press his forehead to hers. "I am leaving that in the very capable hands of Collin and his solicitor." He straightened, disentangled himself from Julia's arms, and began snuffing the candles he'd lit. "As the son of an earl, Collin knows so much more about estates and mortgages than I ever will. And with the preparations to sail in less than a week, I do not have time for it."

Julia looked offended. "You should have let me know. I am well versed in financial matters such as these."

He rested his hands on her shoulders, which had tensed again. "I know. But this is a legal entanglement that will continue long after we have departed these shores. And Collin needed employment to keep his mind occupied now that he is no longer an officer in His Majesty's Royal Navy."

The indignation left Julia's expression. "I had not thought of that. Yes, it is good for Collin to have something to occupy his time."

William opened the door and ushered his wife through.

"What do you think Collin will do now that he has left the navy?" She waited for him in the hallway and slipped her hand under his elbow when he joined her.

"Collin Yates will do what earls' sons do best—become a gentleman of society and give dinners and balls and purchase a country estate, where he and Susan will give dinners and balls and raise their children."

"You need not sound so appalled at the idea of a country estate, dear husband. Do not forget that you are now heir to one of the largest sugar plantations in the Caribbean. Does not that make you a gentleman of society and property?"

Heir to Sir Edward's sugar plantation. William had not thought through the ramifications of that aspect of being married to Julia. His son, if he and Julia were blessed with a son, would be the first generation of Ransomes born with the expectation of an inheritance other than life consigned to the sea.

"Our sons will go to sea when they are old enough. I do not want them raised like overprivileged popinjays."

Julia stopped; William nearly lost his balance on the step below. The single candle he carried did not give much light, but enough to define Julia's frown. "Our sons?"

"If we have sons."

"But to go to sea…all the dangers that could befall them there… my brother…"

"Yes, there are dangers. Even the risk of death. But there are also lessons to be learned about duty, loyalty, and honor that cannot be taught in a schoolroom or even on a plantation. My forebears have been sailors as far back as we have family records. I want my sons to follow in my family's tradition."

Julia's frown increased.

"We do not need to decide the question tonight." He smiled at her. "But in a year or so, when you give me my first son, we shall have this conversation again."

Her lips twisted up at the corners, and her brows raised. "Your *first* son? How many do you intend me to give you?"

"Oh, a full compliment of lieutenants for a seventy-four, at least."

"Six?"

"Aye. And then perhaps a daughter. After all, Collin and Susan's son will have need of a wife."

"If their child is a son."

William knew his friend well. After twelve years of marriage and disappointment after disappointment, Collin claimed that he cared not whether the child Susan now carried was a son or daughter. But all Collin could talk about were the things he wanted to do with his son when he arrived. "Collin will have a son."

Julia shook her head and started down the stairs again, pulling William with her. He had no desire to return to the gathering below, but he did so to please Julia. His wife. His beloved. The mother of the sons of whom, until now, he'd never allowed himself to dream.

She paused once more before leaving the stillness of the unused wing of the house. "What think you of Charlotte's accompanying us to Jamaica as my companion?"

Charlotte—a lovely, unmarried seventeen-year-old—aboard a ship crewed by seven hundred sailors and marines for two months? He pressed his lips together while he conjured up an appropriate response. "I shall speak with my mother if you like, but I believe it would be better for my sister to remain in England. You yourself commented on the advantageous opportunity presented to her by the Fairfaxes' invitation."

Julia nodded. "Yes, you are correct. I am being selfish, wanting her with me so I can get to know her better." With a sigh she said, "We had best return before someone comes looking for us."

William could not resist the advantageous opportunity now presented to him by the privacy of their surroundings. He bent and kissed her once more, appalled at the memory of the men's unguarded reactions—the stares, the murmuring, the neglect of their duties whenever she was in sight—to Charlotte's brief visit to *Alexandra* yesterday and at the same time pleased by Julia's desire to know his sister better.

Upon reentering the ballroom, William looked around for Charlotte. When he did not see his sister amongst the dancers, his concern rose. If Fairfax, or one of the other men who'd swarmed around her all evening, had invited her for a stroll in the garden...He glanced down at Julia beside him and almost smiled. He knew all too well the kinds of conversations that took place in gardens during balls.

Ned Cochrane appeared out of a knot of officers gathered near the card room. Julia excused herself and crossed the room to join her mother-in-law, Collin, and Susan.

"Have you seen my sister recently?" William asked his first officer without preamble.

"No, sir. Not since Miss Fairfax took her away after our dance. She said something about refreshments, sir."

The knot in William's chest eased. He was correct to have trusted Ned to keep an eye on Charlotte in his absence.

"Sir, as it is near midnight, the boys and I were preparing to take our leave."

William snapped his gaze to the large clock in the corner. "I had no idea the hour had grown so late." He shifted his gaze to Julia and sighed. He could not leave now, and the harbor lay at least half an hour's carriage ride from Brampton Park. "The ship is yours for one more night, Lieutenant."

Ned's gaze also slid to Julia, and he grinned when he looked back at William. "Aye, aye, sir."

William gave him a look that would have sent any other officer scurrying. Ned's smile only widened. The officer knuckled his forehead—the salute given by the common seamen—and then flourished a bow and made his exit. The other five lieutenants inclined their heads toward William before taking their leave.

Julia's laughter drew him across the room to join her, just in time to hear the end of Collin's anecdote. He envied his friend's ability to tell tales of life aboard a ship of war in a way that they were at once humorous and yet did not lose any of the gravity of the truth.

William's arm tingled when Julia slipped her hand around his elbow. Rather than pleasure, however, all he could feel was annoyance. Once again, he'd let his emotional attachment to her get the better of him. He should be on his ship. He should be sleeping in a canvas hammock this night rather than in the large, plush bed with Julia. Where did duty to one's wife begin and duty to the Royal Navy end? Admiral Witherington had not been able to adequately explain.

Sir Drake Pembroke. Julia had been correct. If her cousin had not sailed in and fired his broadside, trying to force Julia into marriage, their lives would not have been capsized. Julia could have gone about her life, and William could have gone about his—no interruptions, no interference, no distractions.

Except…he glanced down at the white-gloved hand tucked into the crook of his arm.

There was nothing for it. He owed Julia's meddling cousin and aunts a debt of gratitude he'd never be able to pay. At twenty-two, he'd run from what he'd been certain God had told him to do. Twelve years later, divine intervention had come in a strange form; but though William hated feeling torn between duties as a husband and as a naval officer, he could not deny that marrying Julia had brought him more joy than he'd dreamed possible.

Silently, he repeated the vow he'd made to her, to make what years they had together the happiest she'd known—and he added a vow to God: to thank Him every day for bringing Julia back into his life.

Mama, it is only for a month." Charlotte flapped the letter from Lady Fairfax in the air. "And they have offered to provide transportation back to Gateacre for me at the end of the visit. I know you are anxious to return home. This way you could still leave as planned the day William sets sail, but I would be able to spend more time in society."

Mama had to say yes. For when the invitation arrived this morning confirming the Fairfaxes planned to depart Portsmouth the day before the convoy weighed anchor—the day Charles Lott was to report for duty—Charlotte knew her plan would work.

If only Mama said yes.

"Julia believes it would be beneficial to you, and as William has raised no objections, how can I say no?" Mama smiled softly, and then tears clouded her eyes.

Charlotte rushed to her and dropped to her knees beside the chair. "What's wrong?"

"I knew the day would come when all of my children would be gone from home, but I had hoped to have you with me a few years yet."

Charlotte swallowed hard. Tears burning her own eyes—tears of guilt over what she was about to do. "Mama, I am not going off to live with the Fairfaxes forever." Nay, she was instead stealing away on a ship to sail to the other side of the ocean.

"Yes." Mama dabbed her eyes with a handkerchief. "It is only a month. I want you to go. It might prove to be your greatest opportunity to meet and fall in love with a gentleman who can give you the kind of life none of the young men in Gateacre, or even in Liverpool, can."

Charlotte swallowed back a bitter taste. Henry Winchester did not fit her mother's ideal of a husband for her only daughter. Mama had made *that* abundantly clear when Henry had first come to Gateacre to visit his cousins.

But Charlotte loved him. And Mama had always told her to marry only for love.

The middle of Charlotte's back tingled, and the memory of Ned Cochrane's warm hand there as he led her through their dance rushed in with such force that she trembled.

"I can see you already fancy a certain gentleman." Mama's pale brow creased. "Mr. Fairfax is a fine young man, Charlotte, but..."

Charlotte worked to clear the memory of the sweetest moments she'd experienced last night from her mind and patted her mother's clasped hands. "Do not fear. I have not set my sights on the eldest son of a baron. I am well aware of my standing in the eyes of the Fairfax family—that of a follower, someone to look up to and admire them. A personage of no consequence, whose acquaintance does not adversely affect them and may serve them well, given the fact I managed to catch the patronage of Lady Dalrymple."

Relief eased Mama's frown lines. "Do not forget while you are with the Fairfaxes that there are people who place more emphasis on someone's character than her rank—and we love you for who you are. Find a young man who feels the same."

Charlotte wanted to cry out that she had fallen in love with such a man, but Mama did not approve of him. The contradiction served to firm Charlotte's resolve.

A bang and loud footfalls in the entry hall startled both of them. Charlotte got to her feet and turned. A man she'd never seen before charged into the sitting room.

"Where is she?" The man—who looked a good decade older than William—stopped but a few paces from Charlotte, his cheeks mottled red and his dark eyes narrowed. He had not removed his hat, and to that affront—in addition to his rude entrance—Charlotte took umbrage on Lady Dalrymple's behalf. After all, this was Lady Dalrymple's home.

"Don't just stand there like a simpleton, girl." The man reached as if to grab Charlotte by the shoulders. She stepped back, and his hands grabbed empty air. He blinked at her as if seeing her for the first time.

Charlotte instilled all the command presence she'd been practicing for when she became a midshipman into her stance. "Sir, you will first apologize for the very rude manner of your entrance and your speech in front of my mother."

"I..." He looked about the room. "I am in the manor house at Brampton Park, am I not?" The anger had left his voice to be replaced by confusion.

Charlotte released a shaky breath. "You are, sir. If you will calm yourself and let me know your business here, I will try to assist you with whatever—or whomever—you seek."

He frowned at her for a long moment. "And who, pray tell, are you?"

Perhaps a show of decorum from her would remind the man of his manners—if he had any. She bent her knees in a curtsey. "I am Miss Ransome, a guest of Lady Dalrymple's." She moved so she no longer stood between Mama and the stranger. "And this is my mother, Mrs. Ransome."

Mama, who'd risen as soon as the man had reached toward Charlotte, also curtseyed.

After staring at the two of them for another long moment, he sighed and jerked his tall hat off his head, revealing hair the muddy brown color of the streambed in the field behind their house in Gateacre. He inclined his head. "Lord Rotheram."

"Oh, I see. Lady Dalrymple has been expecting you all morning." Charlotte crossed the room to ring the bell for Mrs. Melling.

The housekeeper, apparently having been alerted by the commotion, appeared a scant heartbeat later. "Yes, miss?" Her lips drew into a tight line when she looked beyond Charlotte and saw her ladyship's son-in-law. She also made the proper curtsey toward the marquess. "My Lord Rotheram. I shall take you up to see Lady Dalrymple."

As soon as the two departed, Mama collapsed into her chair, hand pressed to her heart.

"Mama? Are you ill?"

"Do not frighten me like that again, please." Mama fanned herself with her handkerchief.

"Frighten you?" Charlotte reviewed the confrontation. She had done nothing horrible, had she?

"Lord Rotheram looked angry enough to strike you. You should not have provoked him by using such a rebuking tone."

Charlotte let out a small laugh. "Oh, Mama! I could see by the quality of his clothing—and his boots—that he was a gentleman. And a gentleman would never strike a woman."

Mama stood and grabbed Charlotte's hands. "Do not believe that. Do not ever suppose that wealth and title mean a man is a true gentleman at heart. Some of the most ruthless, violent men are those parading around in expensive clothing, carrying titles of nobility. Position and privilege of birth do not make one a gentleman. It is his character, which cannot be seen so easily on the outside."

Charlotte made sure to keep her expression earnest, as she always did whenever Mama imparted an Important Lesson like this. Charlotte knew, probably better than Mama, some men's tendency toward ungentlemanlike behavior. She'd listened far too often to her brothers' conversations when they were home and thought her and Mama asleep and exchanged stories of things they had seen and heard at sea. And then there were the novels her friend Eliza had managed to sneak past the mistresses at school. Charlotte recalled with fondness the many afternoons spent giggling over tales that would have made even the cantankerous old headmistress swoon when they were supposed to be concentrating on their needlework or dancing.

Best bring the conversation back around to safer mooring. "So I may go?"

Mama frowned. "Go?"

"With the Fairfaxes." Charlotte waved Penelope's letter in front of her.

"Yes, you may go." Mama rubbed her forehead. "We shall have much to do. You will need at least one new gown. Your lilac day dress is too faded and frayed to be worn in such a place as the Fairfaxes' country house."

Though the cost for a new day dress would not be injurious to their personal finances, the idea of her mother spending money on a dress she might not ever see her daughter wear sent a pang through Charlotte's heart. "Lady Dalrymple has been more than generous in filling out my wardrobe, Mama. I have everything I need."

Tunics, trousers, uniform coats, the stout, round midshipman's hat...yes, in the few times she had managed to sneak out and go into town, she had aquired all the wardrobe pieces she needed. Including the muslin to wrap around her chest—which did not need much wrapping to give her the physical appearance of an adolescent boy.

The door opened, and Charlotte and her mother stood to dip into deep curtseys when Lady Dalrymple entered the sitting room.

"Oh, tosh. I have told you that is not necessary." She extended her hand to Mama. "I do apologize, Mrs. Ransome, for not being available to receive you when you arrived."

Mama pressed Lady Dalrymple's hand between hers. "No apology is necessary, my lady. The pending arrival of a grandchild is a blessing."

"Yes." The viscountess's smile clouded. "Her husband is with her now, so I do not feel any guilt upon leaving her. Are you ready to go?"

"Yes, my lady," Charlotte and her mother answered in unison.

In the hall, maids assisted each of them with their spencers, gloves, and bonnets. Charlotte thanked Martha and exchanged a furtive smile with her maid, drawing the expected remonstrative narrowing of Melling's eyes.

A day making calls with Lady Dalrymple was not the most beneficial use of Charlotte's time. In her exploration of the house this morning, she found the bedroom that must have been used by Mr.

Geoffrey. But before she could do more than look in and see what appeared to be an officer's sea chest, Mama had arrived, drawing Charlotte from her quest.

On the calls, Charlotte followed Mama's example and remained quiet except when directly addressed by one or another of the society matrons Lady Dalrymple felt it important for Charlotte to meet—those with unmarried sons of an appropriate age whom Lady Dalrymple considered to be of the proper social status. Not a baron's son or a Royal Navy officer or a poor plantation steward amongst the lot.

Charlotte spent most of the afternoon reviewing her preparations and plans to keep from falling asleep. Lady Dalrymple extolled Charlotte's virtues—and her handsome legacy—well enough without any assistance from Charlotte. Though the social niceties observed in these interactions made them seem civilized, was this really any different than the slave auctions Henry had written about in the first letter he'd sent her from Jamaica?

Charlotte thanked God that Julia's father had freed the slaves at Tierra Dulce so Henry hadn't had to compromise his values and work for a slave owner.

Their last visit was the one Charlotte had looked forward to all day. Lady Dalrymple's carriage rolled to a stop before the impressive façade of Collin and Susan Yates's townhouse. Having lived with the Yateses for the first few weeks in Portsmouth, Charlotte warmly greeted the wizened butler who opened the door, drawing a shocked expression from the younger man behind him.

"Pay him no heed, Miss Ransome." Fawkes took Lady Dalrymple's gloves and hat, and then he turned to take Mama's. "My new apprentice will soon learn how things go here." Fawkes winked at Charlotte.

She laughed and started to lead the viscountess upstairs.

"A letter arrived for you today, mum."

Charlotte looked over her shoulder just in time to see Fawkes hand Mama a folded packet of paper. She paused, Lady Dalrymple with her. "What is it, Mama?"

"Why, it's from Philip." Mama broke the wax seal and scanned the contents. "He will be arriving in Liverpool at the end of the week."

Mama's face fell. "I would need to leave day after tomorrow to arrive in Gateacre in time to make the house ready for his homecoming. He cannot arrive back after so long to find no one there to greet him."

"Then we shall do whatever must be done to get you home in time to greet your son." Lady Dalrymple gave a quick nod as if to indicate the matter settled in her mind.

Indecision nearly tore Charlotte's heart in pieces. She wanted to see Philip. Closest to her in age—with only seven years between them—she'd spent more of her childhood with him and missed him most of all. Yet if she returned north with Mama, she would miss the ship to Jamaica and possibly her only chance at happiness.

In the sitting room, Susan and Julia rose to greet them. Susan glowed with her usual good humor, but Julia looked nearly as low as Charlotte now felt.

"Will William be joining us for dinner?" Mama asked, sitting beside Julia on the gold-and-white striped settee.

"No, ma'am. He is returned to his ship. We shall not see much of him before we sail."

Ah, so that explained the state of Julia's spirits. Charlotte could sympathize—except that an ocean separated her from Henry, not merely a fifteen-minute carriage ride to the harbor.

"Oh, I see." Mama clearly held back tears.

Charlotte explained to the others the contents of Philip's letter, still crushed in Mama's hand, along with the need for Mama to leave two days early.

"I will send Collin to fetch William tomorrow and tell him he must come for dinner so we can all bid you farewell and you can have time to say your goodbyes." Susan nodded very much like Lady Dalrymple just had. "And tomorrow Julia and I will help you and Charlotte pack."

Charlotte's heart nearly burst out of her chest. She opened her mouth to protest, but no words would form.

"Nay. Charlotte's plans will not change."

She stared at Mama. "They shan't?"

Mama gave her a gentle smile. "No. You shall go to the country with the Fairfaxes for the month as planned. Philip's ship was decommissioned, so he has been turned out until another ship comes available. He expects to be in Gateacre for some time. So you will see him after your holiday with the Fairfaxes."

Charlotte could have cried from relief over the way obstacles kept being cleared from her path, from the knowledge Mama would not be left alone by her elopement, and from her disappointment that she would not get to see Philip.

The churning sea of emotions hindered her from eating much at dinner, and she clung to Mama when Lady Dalrymple's carriage was summoned.

"Good heavens, child, you act as if we will never see one another again." Mama laughed, but her voice came out thick.

Charlotte blinked back the moisture pooling in her eyes. "I have never been without you. I had not realized…I had not thought our parting would be so…" Charlotte could not find the words to articulate the overwhelming panic now surging through her.

"You must not be afraid, Charlotte." Mama gently extricated herself from Charlotte's embrace and cupped Charlotte's face in her hands. "It does not matter how much distance separates us, whether land or sea. You will never be far from my thoughts, and you will always be in my heart and prayers."

At the words she'd heard Mama speak to William, James, and Philip every time they left home for the sea, Charlotte dissolved into tears and flung herself back into her mother's arms, on the verge of confessing everything, on the verge of insisting she wanted to go home with Mama forever.

But how could she abandon her plan now, when it appeared divine Providence was helping her out by clearing her way?

"Go, Charlotte. You must not keep Lady Dalrymple waiting." Mama shooed her down the stairs. At the bottom, Charlotte turned to say her farewell and caught sight of Mama dabbing her eyes with a handkerchief.

"Good night, Mama."

"Sweet dreams, daughter."

Early the next morning, Lady Dalrymple's driver delivered Charlotte to the Yateses' house—just as they were sitting down to breakfast. Charlotte joined them, but once again she found herself with no appetite.

Julia arrived not too long after Charlotte. The day was spent in packing Mama's trunk; and, after much sitting on its lid by Charlotte and Julia while Mama and Susan tried to lock it, amid gales of laughter, Susan insisted on giving Mama one of her own valises to ease the burden on the trunk.

Late in the afternoon, after a long visit from Admiral Hinds's wife, Susan's new butler entered the sitting room to inform Charlotte that the carriage had returned for her.

"And they brought this for you, madam." He bowed and held a silver salver toward Mama. Startled, Mama lifted a letter from the tray. The butler bowed again and departed.

"From Lady Dalrymple." Mama unfolded it and her eyes flicked back and forth over the page. "She has arranged for one of her carriages to pick me up at half-past seven tomorrow morning to take me home." She let the letter fall to her lap. "I do not know how I will ever repay her."

"I have some money set by, Mama," Charlotte said, though she knew she would need every bit of it on her journey.

Mama's mouth quirked up on one side. "It is not monetary recompense of which I speak, my dear. Lady Dalrymple would never accept it. Her kindness and generosity toward me, toward William and Julia, and especially toward you, can never be adequately repaid."

Relieved she would not have to part with any of her money, Charlotte made her farewells and hurried downstairs. She had less than an hour before the shop closed.

The Dalrymple footman bowed and opened the carriage door for her. "Driver, please take me to Madame Rousseau's Millinery in the High Street."

"Yes, Miss Ransome." From his high seat, the driver inclined his head. Charlotte climbed up into the carriage, grateful Lady Dalrymple's men had brought the closed coach instead of the open-top barouche. As soon as she sat down and the footman closed the door behind her, she yanked off her bonnet and gloves and started pulling all the pins from her hair. She hated to ruin all the hard work Martha had put into creating the cascade of curls, but Madame Rousseau would need to see its full length.

She removed the last pin just as the coach rolled to a stop before the shop. She put her bonnet back on and tied the ribbons loosely under her chin before accepting the footman's assistance to dismount to the street. His brows raised slightly at her loose hair, but he quickly hid his reaction. Charlotte smiled and almost forgot to wait for him to open the shop's door for her. The inability to do anything for herself in the presence of the Dalrymple servants was becoming an annoyance.

An assistant waited on a customer at the front of the shop, but Charlotte knew what she needed. She moved toward the back of the room, toward where she had seen the sign that brought her here today.

Hair Bought.

"Welcome to Madame Rousseau's Millinery. How may I be of service to you today?" A tall, large woman came through the curtains that separated the shop from the workroom behind.

Charlotte removed her bonnet. "I understand that you buy hair. I wonder if you might tell me how much mine is worth."

Madame Rousseau—at least Charlotte assumed this woman was the shop's owner, though she did not sound French, as her name indicated—took Charlotte by the shoulders and turned her. She combed her fingers through Charlotte's hair. "Takes a curl well." She gathered it all together at the nape of Charlotte's neck. "Good, thick texture." She then pulled a comb from the pocket of her apron and ran it through the length of Charlotte's hair. "I could get a clean eighteen inches."

From the corner of her eye, Charlotte noticed the woman pull something else from her pocket—something that flashed, reflecting the late afternoon sunlight beyond the shop's front windows. She spun around just in time to keep Madame Rousseau from cutting off a chunk of her hair.

Her heart thudded. To make her plan work, she would have to lose her hair. But not now. Not yet. "I do not want it cut today. I just need to know how much you might pay for it if I do decide to cut it off."

The woman's mouth twisted into disappointment. "Ten shillings."

Charlotte looked around at the display of hairpieces already in the shop. The least expensive sold for two guineas. Her hair could make three of those. "One guinea."

Rather than anger, Madame Rousseau's eyes glimmered with humor. "Eighteen shillings. One per inch of hair."

Charlotte stood her ground. "I believe you said my hair is thick. One guinea."

The woman's mouth curved into a smile. "If you need employment, young miss, you are to come to me and no one else."

Charlotte returned the smile. "Thank you, but I already have a position."

"When can I expect to receive this guinea's worth of hair?"

"I...my brother, Charles Lott, will bring it by on Thursday morning before he goes to his ship. May I have your offer in writing so that he can bring it with him when he comes?"

A few minutes later, Charlotte departed with the note promising one guinea for her hair and the promise that her "younger brother" could stop by early, before the shop opened, to deliver it.

The motion of the coach lulled her into a stupor on the long drive back to Brampton Park. She played with her hair, curling a thick lock around her finger or pulling it straight and watching it bounce back into a fat curl again. Her breath caught in her throat.

When Mama had seen the young women in Gateacre begin to bob their hair like the women in the fashion plates from London, Mama had quoted something from either the Scriptures or the prayer book about a woman's hair being her crowning glory and that those girls should be ashamed for cutting theirs short.

To become a midshipman, Charlotte needed to look like a boy, which meant short hair. She combed her fingers through the length of hers. Did she love Henry Winchester enough to endure the shame of short hair?

Chapter Eight

Floorboards creaked. Charlotte paused. No one else should be in this wing of the house, but she looked over her shoulder to make sure no one had heard her. Certain of her solitude, she continued down the hall to the fifth door on the left.

The latch clicked loudly when she turned the knob, but this time, she did not pause until she was on the other side of the door. Glancing around the room, she made a plan for the most methodical way to search it. One item looked out of place amidst the fancy furniture: a rough, small trunk. A sea chest. It would most likely yield treasures beyond what she imagined, but she would save it for last. The rest of the room could be searched much more quickly.

She started with the wardrobe. Not much there: a coat, a few old waistcoats, some mismatched stockings in a drawer, two neckcloths in another. She moved on to the desk: some blank stationery and a dry ink bottle. None of the other furniture in the room yielded anything of interest.

Finally, she knelt before the sea chest. Black script lettering on the lid confirmed it had indeed belonged to *Lt. Geoffrey Seymour*. She rubbed her palms together, unclasped the latch, and then lifted the lid. A musty, dank smell wafted out—the decayed smell of the sea and a ship of war.

Reverently, she lifted out the folded lieutenant's jacket, followed by a flattened bicorne. She punched it back into shape and had it halfway to her head before she thought of what it might do to the curls

Martha managed to coax her hair into this morning. She set it aside with the jacket.

Charts and books made up most of the remainder of the contents. And a wooden box. She pulled it out and slid the top open. Like sails released from their rigging, all manner of folded pages unfurled themselves and beckoned her to pull them out. Most were from Lady Dalrymple. A few were from the former viscount. And no matter how her curiosity ate at her, Charlotte refused to read the letters. She flattened the pages and slid the box's top closed.

Underneath the stationery box lay the real treasure. Charlotte pulled out three leather-bound volumes. She untied the thong wrapped around the top book and opened it. Faded script filled the pages warped by long exposure to damp environs. Geoffrey Seymour's journals. Not every officer kept personal diaries in addition to their logbooks, but a perusal of the pages revealed Mr. Geoffrey's detailed records of his voyages. He hadn't written more than the date, ship's heading, and his assigned duties for many of the entries, but others went on for pages—when and where they'd docked, incidents and disciplinary actions he'd witnessed, storms, and, best of all, battles.

Layering everything else back into the chest, she closed it; and, with the thick journals hugged to her chest, she hurried back to her room, ready to curl up on the chaise lounge and spend the rest of the morning reading about Mr. Geoffrey's life at sea.

Her stomach gurgled. Perhaps breakfast first. She tucked the journals into the bottom drawer of her wardrobe, under Henry's letters, and then skipped down to the bright, sunny breakfast room in the main part of the house.

She drew up short in the doorway. Lord Rotheram sat at the table with a decanter of spirits in front of him. She'd heard of men who were well into their cups by breakfast, but she'd never expected to see it, especially in a marquess.

Remembering her station, she made a quick curtsey, though he paid no heed. Perhaps she should return to her room and give up the idea of breakfast. But the hunger gnawing at her stomach wouldn't allow her to move farther away from the sideboard laden with all manner of good things to eat.

Her penchant for timidity around men she did not know would not serve her well in the near future. With a plate piled with eggs, sausages, and toast, she took a chair at the far end of the table from Lord Rotheram.

She ate much faster than usual, ready to get back to her room and Mr. Geoffrey's journals. She didn't slow or stop until Lord Rotheram finally moved. He downed his drink and then poured another, leaned back in his chair, and pinned his narrowed eyes on Charlotte.

The bite she'd just swallowed stuck in her throat.

"Tell me, Miss Ransome, why it is that a wife must be a nuisance and do the most idiotic things, like run away from her safe, secure home in London when she is in no condition to travel." The alcohol slurred his words, and his rising anger added a harsh edge to his tone.

"I am sure I do not know, my lord." Charlotte laid her fork on the rim of her plate. On second thought, she picked it back up again.

Lord Rotheram drained the glass in one swallow and stood. Charlotte was mildly surprised he was so steady on his feet. He paced the length of the room, passing behind her twice, mumbling to himself. She caught only words and snippets of phrases, but enough to understand he was angry at his wife's impulsive flight from London to Portsmouth and Lady Dalrymple's insisting he come to be with Lady Rotheram during her confinement.

Then he stopped behind Charlotte. Dread trickled down her spine, which went stiff as a ship's mast.

"You look like someone who would understand a man's need, not a cold, spiteful harpy."

Charlotte's pulse throbbed. Mama had warned her about men who took to too much drink.

She nearly jumped out of her own skin when he touched the curl that lay against the side of her neck.

"You do look like a tasty morsel."

She shot out of the chair, gasping in pain when he did not immediately release her hair. "My lord, please remember yourself."

Instead of becoming contrite and apologizing, the marquess laughed. "But I am acting precisely like myself. Or did not my lady complain to you about me? She has done so to half of London society."

Charlotte backed away from the drunken man with ill intent in his gaze—until her back pressed against the sideboard.

"Did she not complain to you of how her husband has humiliated her by carrying on a dalliance with one of her closest friends?" Lord Rotheram took a few menacing steps toward Charlotte. "Did she not tell you how she had me followed, how she tried to humiliate me into changing my ways?"

"Nay, my lord. Please. I do not want to hear—"

He came within reach of her, but his hands remained at his sides. "You would not be such a shrew, would you, Miss Ransome? You would understand that a man's needs must be fulfilled, and if his wife refuses to meet them, then he must seek to fulfill them elsewhere. Even if it means debauching young women with seductive eyes." His arm snaked around Charlotte's waist before she could move away. She tried to resist but was no match for his strength. She opened her mouth to cry out just as his lips crushed down on hers.

She slapped and punched at his arms, but he only increased the pressure of his hold on her. She tried twisting her head away, but he grabbed a fistful of her hair and subdued her by pulling it until she yelped.

Anger overcame her fear, and everything her brothers had ever taught her about men came crashing in. She tightened her fist around the fork but stayed her hand. Instead, she shifted her balance and, once sure of her footing, brought her knee up as hard as she could and connected right where Philip said a man was most vulnerable.

Lord Rotheram yowled and doubled over, releasing her—a string of curses flowing from his lips like bilge. When he dropped to the floor, Charlotte stepped around him, ready to put as much distance between them as possible. But she only made it two steps before Lord Rotheram grabbed her ankle and pulled her foot out from under her.

She cried out and tried to catch herself but hit the wood floor with her chin. Pain shot through her mouth, and she tasted blood where she'd bitten her tongue.

"If you think you can get away with that—I am Lord Rotheram. You are no one. I could have you arrested for assaulting me."

Charlotte grabbed for purchase as Rotheram pulled her toward him, but nothing solid lay within her reach. He flipped her over and straddled her.

Charlotte punched him as hard as she could. Blood spurted from his nose. He howled with outrage and backhanded her. White spots exploded in her vision. His hand clasped around her throat and squeezed.

A fleeting image of another time when she lay prone, unable to breathe, looking up into a man's face, flooded her mind. Only that time, Ned had saved her life. Why couldn't he be here now to do the same? Darkness obscured her peripheral vision. Metal bit into her palm.

Metal. The fork. Unable to see enough to aim her blow, Charlotte swung her arm and prayed God would guide her weapon—not to kill, but to cause him to release her and leave her alone.

Consciousness began to slip away. The comfort of darkness beckoned.

Lord, please let me live.

Julia lay the package of new stationery in the bottom of her lap desk and checked the wax seal around the cork in the new bottle of ink. She couldn't imagine she would need more than that in the next two months—especially as she would be able to post her correspondence only once, when they docked at Madeira to resupply. But she wanted to be certain she had enough on hand, since the days would be long and filled with tedium.

She flinched at a brisk knock on the door and looked up.

Creighton inclined his head. "Sorry to disturb you, ma'am. A carriage has arrived from Brampton Park along with a message requesting your presence urgently."

"Brampton Park?" Julia's mind whirled. She rushed to her wardrobe for gloves and a bonnet—and remembered only when she looked into the empty space that everything had been moved to the room she had shared with William.

She retrieved the necessary items from the other room and followed Creighton downstairs. The footman in Lady Dalrymple's green livery bowed. Julia jammed the bonnet over her unruly hair—no time to put it up now—and worked at tying the ribbon under her chin as she turned to face Creighton.

"Send word to Mrs. Yates that something has come up and I'll be unable to accompany her on calls this afternoon, but with reassurances I will be there in plenty of time for Mrs. Ransome's farewell dinner."

"Aye, aye, ma'am."

"Send Elton to Brampton Park to fetch Miss Charlotte and me at three o'clock, if I have not already returned by then."

"Yes, ma'am."

She tugged her gloves on and then turned to slide her arms into the sleeves of the spencer Creighton held. "Thank you, Creighton." She gave him a half smile. "Are you absolutely certain I cannot convince you to come with us to Jamaica?"

"What would the admiral do without me?" Amusement tugged at the butler's studied dour expression.

Julia allowed her smile to linger until the Dalrymple footman closed the coach door behind her. She could not think what emergency required her presence with *urgency*, but she refused to imagine that something bad had happened to Charlotte...though she did wish the coachman would drive a little faster.

Fifteen minutes later the coach rolled to a stop before the imposing manor house. Alighting from the coach, Julia managed to constrain her pace to a quick walk up the curving steps that led to the main entrance.

The housekeeper met Julia inside the front door. As quickly as she could, Julia divested herself of jacket, gloves, and bonnet and followed a tight-lipped Mrs. Melling upstairs and down a silent corridor. If Julia had been summoned because Lady Dalrymple's daughter had gone into labor, it was one of the quietest birthings Julia had ever witnessed.

Mrs. Melling stopped and opened a door. Instead of entering, she moved aside and motioned for Julia to go in. Wary of what she would find, Julia stepped into the room.

At first she thought she'd entered Lady Dalrymple's apartment, so lavishly was the bedchamber appointed. But the dowager viscountess stood at the end of the enormous, curtained bed, while a man leaned over a prone figure obscured by the hangings and coverlet.

Julia cleared her throat.

Lady Dalrymple spun around. "Oh, dear, dear Julia. I was not certain for whom I should send." She extended her hand toward Julia.

"What has happened?" Julia joined her at the foot of the bed.

"I should have listened to my daughter. I should have believed her. But she was always given to the melodramatic and exaggeration. Now, poor Charlotte..."

Panic flooded Julia's chest. "Charlotte?" She skirted the bed to the opposite side from the man, climbed up on it and crawled across to Charlotte's side.

A red welt marred Charlotte's right cheek. But that mark was nothing compared with the ugly bruises around her throat, as if...

Julia looked at the man, and then at Lady Dalrymple. "What happened?"

"Lord Rotheram, as my daughter has been trying to tell me since she arrived on my doorstep, is no gentleman. He is a philanderer of the worst sort, and apparently he has become so depraved that if a woman does not give herself willingly to him, he takes her by force."

Julia's head throbbed with the force of the anger pounding in her heart. She'd heard of men in Jamaica who treated their slaves in such a manner. She had even allowed Jerusha to give refuge at Tierra Dulce to a woman who'd escaped a master who'd done such a vile thing to her. But Charlotte?

She covered her eyes with one hand. "Did he…?"

"No. Charlotte managed to fight him off before she fainted. Stabbed him in the side of the neck with a fork."

Julia dropped her hand and gaped at the viscountess. "Stabbed—with a *fork*?"

"She had been eating breakfast." A slight smile started playing around Lady Dalrymple's mouth, and her eyes filled with fondness as she gazed upon Charlotte's prone form.

"Lord Rotheram…is he…he is not…how badly did she injure him?"

"The marquess bled a fair amount," said the man beside the bed, "but he will recover."

"Mrs. Ransome, this is my personal physician, Mr. McKeith."

Julia nodded at the doctor. "How is Charlotte?"

"A bit knocked around. She will be sore and will sport a bruised throat for some weeks, but she will survive with no lasting physical effects." He pulled out a vial of smelling salts and flicked it under Charlotte's nose a few times.

Charlotte jerked, started, opened her eyes, and would have flown from the bed had not Julia stopped her. It took several moments' soothing for Julia to calm her sister-in-law enough to convince her of her safety.

"Lord Rotheram?" Charlotte's voice came out as a croak.

"My men bundled him into his carriage and watched as it drove away to take him back to London," Lady Dalrymple said, coming over to stand behind the physician.

Julia stroked Charlotte's hand, silently grateful Rotheram would shortly be too far away for William to chase down and challenge to a duel.

Charlotte turned to Julia. "Do not tell William or Mama."

Julia considered the request. What had happened had happened to Charlotte, and nothing William or their mother could say or do would change it.

Julia nodded. "I promise, I will not say anything. But how will you explain the bruises?"

Charlotte reached up and touched her throat, wincing at even the light pressure of her fingertips. "Lady Dalrymple's dressmaker brought me some beautiful lace collars. Between those and a little powder, we should be able to conceal them." She looked at the doctor. "May I assume the injuries are not life threatening?"

"It will take the bruises some time to heal, but you will make a full recovery." Mr. McKeith patted Charlotte's hand. "I have done all I can. Tea will soothe your throat. Rest is the best medicine for you." He packed several vials into a bag and then stepped away from the bed and flourished a bow. "Mrs. Ransome. Miss Ransome."

Julia inclined her head. Lady Dalrymple left the room with the doctor. As soon as they were alone, Julia helped Charlotte sit upright in the bed, piling pillows behind her, and then she asked Charlotte for her version of the event. Julia kept her disgust and outrage over Lord Rotheram's behavior to herself, though she did climb off the bed and set to straightening the coverlet when Charlotte got to the most harrowing part of the tale.

"And I must have fainted, for I do not know what happened from then until I awoke here."

Julia started to tell Charlotte that the impromptu weapon she had wielded had found purchase, but the young woman had been through enough turmoil for one morning.

"Julia?"

"Yes, Charlotte?" She stopped fussing with the bedding.

"I am monstrous hot." Charlotte kicked off the neatly arranged coverlet, revealing herself to be fully clothed still. "Since the doctor said I am well, I see no need to malinger."

"I agree." Lady Dalrymple swept back into the room. "I know it is far too early, but I have ordered a full tea service to be sent to Sophy's room. She has been quite anxious to meet you, Julia."

"I would be delighted to make Lady Rotheram's acquaintance." Julia turned to offer Charlotte assistance from the bed, but her sister-in-law had already sprung from its confines.

In an apartment more grandly appointed than Charlotte's, a woman who resembled Lady Dalrymple so greatly their relation was undeniable greeted then. Julia's sympathy went out to her. She had never seen a woman so heavy with child.

Sophy—who insisted on Christian names, as she could not bear to hear herself called Lady Rotheram—fussed over Charlotte, apologizing every few minutes for her husband's dastardly behavior.

The mother and daughter kept Julia and Charlotte entertained with stories from their lives—from both of their presentations at Court to Sophy's coming out to humorous anecdotes of family life, carefully avoiding anything unpleasant.

Sophy then questioned Julia about Jamaica and life on a sugar plantation, which seemed to enthrall Charlotte as much as the two ladies. Julia dismissed renewed disappointment at William's decision to stay Julia from asking Charlotte to travel with them to Jamaica.

The tea and food disappeared, but the conversation continued—as did Sophy's fussing over Charlotte, and Lady Dalrymple's fussing over both of them—until Mrs. Melling interrupted.

"Mrs. Ransome's driver has arrived." She held up a small valise in one hand. "He brought this for you, Mrs. Ransome. And a gown hangs in Miss Ransome's dressing room for you."

"A gown?" Julia looked down at her lap—and heat instantly flooded her cheeks at the sight of the ancient yellow work dress. How had she not had the presence of mind to change into a suitable gown before leaving the house? What must Lady Dalrymple and her daughter think?

Bless Creighton, for she knew he was behind the action. She should write her father and demand he raise the butler's pay immediately.

After farewells to Sophy and Lady Dalrymple, Julia took the valise from Mrs. Melling and followed Charlotte back to her suite. She quickly changed into the ivory silk underdress and indigo velvet overtunic she had worn to the Fairfaxes' ball—the night she had asked William to marry her. Had Creighton remembered the significance of the last time she'd worn this gown and asked Nancy to send it? Or had he left the choice to the maid, who knew Julia had not worn this gown to an event recently? Whichever was the case, wearing the same gown in which she had made the most courageous—and most momentous—decision of her life infused her with a sense of peace over seeing William tonight for the first time since their awkward farewell kiss before he returned to *Alexandra*.

But would it give her the strength to keep Charlotte's secret?

Chapter Nine

Charlotte's hand hovered over the sparkling silver utensil. The sharp tines seemed to taunt her with the knowledge of what she had done. For all that she had told Julia she did not remember anything after Lord Rotheram wrapped his hands around her throat, every time she closed her eyes, every time she was still or it grew quiet around her, she relived the moment when she felt the fork connect with Lord Rotheram's flesh. She still did not know where she had poked him, but her stomach turned at the thought of picking up the fork on the table before her and piercing the quail breast on her plate. However, if she did not eat, Mama would want to know why.

She fingered the lace collar to ensure it remained in place, covering the marks that would mock her for weeks to come. She still could not believe her good fortune that the redness in her cheek was mostly gone, making its puffiness unnoticeable—until she touched it and was reminded of its tenderness.

She plunged back into the conversation with Mama and Susan about fashion. William and Collin discussed William's ship and preparations, to which Charlotte listened with half an ear. She also noticed Julia did not join either conversation but appeared to be listening to both. She hoped Julia was not angry with her for asking her not to say anything about the incident to Mama and William. She was grateful Lady Dalrymple had sent for Julia and not one of the other two. Yet she had known Julia for so short a time, and Julia was married to William—meaning her loyalty should be first to her husband, not his wayward sister. Deep down, though, Charlotte was certain that Julia would honor her commitment of confidentiality.

The hour grew later. The food grew colder. The conversations grew harder. And Charlotte's conscience grew heavier. On the morrow, Mama would leave for Gateacre, believing Charlotte would be joining her there in less than six weeks, possibly with a beau or even a marriage proposal. Instead, Charlotte would be nearing the Caribbean and the one man her mother would least approve of.

"That lace is lovely, Charlotte. You must let me examine it tonight to see how it is made." At Mama's words, Charlotte's hand once again flew to her throat. Though the cosmetics on her skin provided some camouflage, they did not completely hide the finger-shaped bruises.

"Susan, was not there a piece of the lace from your mother's dress left when my wedding dress was finished?"

Afraid what her expression might reveal, Charlotte avoided looking at Julia. She would try to find some way to pay back the debt of gratitude she owed her new sister.

"There was the piece we used for your veil." Susan nodded. "Are you interested in learning to make lace, Mrs. Ransome?"

Mama's blue eyes glinted Charlotte's direction. "I have thought for a while now that being able to net such beautiful patterns would be a wonderful skill to have—when one has a young daughter who, one day, might want more lace trim on a dress than I could purchase."

A wedding dress. Something to wear to church in which she would proudly declare her undying love for Henry Winchester. She had not thought about that. And one of the new dresses from Lady Dalrymple would be perfect. But she could not take it with her. Who would believe her as a midshipman if she had a pale lavender silk gown in her sea chest?

❧

"I do believe it is time for the ladies to retire."

William stood at Susan's words, as did everyone else, and fought to keep the words crowding his mind from spilling out of his mouth.

"I see no reason why William and I should not join you." Collin tossed his napkin on the table and rounded it to offer his arm to his wife.

William stopped clenching his teeth and assisted his mother with her chair. But now he was torn again. Should he escort Mother or Julia? Would one be offended if he chose the other?

Julia solved the problem for him when she slipped her arm through Charlotte's and turned to follow Collin and Susan from the room. William extended his arm to his mother, but instead of taking it, she watched the others over her shoulder until they were gone from the room. She then looked up at William, her brows knit over her gray-blue eyes.

"It pains me to see strain already between you and Julia. I know getting your ship ready is no mean feat, but do not allow your duty to the Royal Navy to overwhelm your feelings for your wife." She reached into the folds of her skirt and withdrew something from a hidden pocket. "Your father was one of the most loyal sailors to ever defend king and country, yet he never let that duty come between us."

She held out a yellowed, folded piece of parchment toward him. "I have held on to this letter for many years. I received it the day I realized I was carrying Charlotte. I now realize I should have let you read it many years ago."

William took the letter and gently unfolded it. The paper was so old and worn, it felt more like silk than parchment in his fingers. A chill washed over him when he recognized his father's distinctive handwriting.

Gibraltar
18 November 1796

My darling Maria,

As I write this, it has been fifty-one days since I left you standing on the quay in Liverpool as we put to sea. I carry the memory of your beautiful face, your generous nature, and your loving heart with me wherever I go. I will never be able to say often enough how much I love you and the boys. You are my life, my reason for continuing on in so brutal an occupation that keeps us cruelly separated for so long.

We will round the Cape soon and should arrive in the East Indies before year's end. I pray God I and my shipmates will survive the voyage and whatever faces us when we arrive at our new station in these foreign waters. As I have prayed, God has burdened my heart to write this letter that the boys may know their father and his love for them if I do not return to say so myself.

Fighting to catch his breath without giving in to the emotion coiled tightly around his chest, William flipped the page over and began reading what looked like another letter.

For my dearest William, James, and Philip—

You are the joy and treasure of my life. Each of you is unique and special in my eyes and in God's eyes. When you read this, I may not be present on earth to be able to tell you these things. You may be ship captains or perhaps still working your way up through the ranks. Know I am proud no matter what life you have chosen.

However, it does not matter what rank you achieve if you do not have someone to share your life with. Find love, my sons. Do not let your profession come between you and the woman you love. Let her know the depth of your love for her as often as you can.

You may not understand as you read this, but please believe me when I say that your heart is big enough to love your wife, your children, and the Royal Navy. It may seem to tear you apart at times, but if you shut yourself off from love, you will never have a complete life. There is strength and joy to be found in love. Find it and cherish it, all your life.

With all my heart,
Father

William cleared his throat and held on to the letter until certain he could hand it back without his hand trembling. Mother kissed the letter before returning it to her pocket, and then she reached up and touched William's cheek. "Love takes courage. But you are your father's son. I know you have it within you to do your duty and love your wife."

The back of William's neck prickled under his high collar. Between his mother and Julia's father, he'd had his fill of being told how he should be feeling and acting toward Julia. Though his father's letter expressed love for Mother, William could remember the bouts of melancholy she suffered whenever Father left for sea or a letter arrived. And from what Julia related, her mother spent most of her life in Jamaica pining for Admiral Witherington. William did not want to do that to Julia. They had a mutual affection right now and enjoyed each other's company when they were together. But if he could keep her at arm's length, if he could keep her from falling further in love with him, his conscience would be clear, knowing he did not leave her in a state like his mother's or her mother's. He needed to protect her from such a fate, from such a life of pain.

He escorted his mother up to the drawing room in silence. If he spoke, he feared he might express some of his annoyance, and he did not want anything to ruin their last evening together.

Though everyone tried to put on happy faces and speak in cheery tones, a doleful air hovered in the room. When the mantel clock struck ten, William's gaze flew to Julia. She let out a soft sigh and nodded.

He stood and adjusted his uniform coat with a swift tug at the waist. He cleared his throat twice before he could speak. "The hour grows late. I must see Julia home and then return to *Alexandra*." He leaned over and kissed his mother on the cheek. "I will pray for your safe journey."

"And I, yours. Write as often as you are able."

"I will. And Julia will be an excellent correspondent, I am certain."

"Yes." Julia appeared at William's side. "I will write often as well."

William stepped back to give Mother room to stand. She hugged Julia and said much to her, though in a low whisper William could not make out.

Mother turned to him next and clasped his hands in hers. "I am so proud of you and all you have accomplished in your life. And I know the Lord has many more wonderful blessings in store for you."

He gently returned the pressure of his mother's grip. "Tell Philip I wish I could have seen him, and that if a command is not forthcoming, he is more than welcome to come for a long visit in Jamaica."

"You should be careful, William, with your hospitality. Philip might just take you up on that."

They all turned at a rustle at the door. The butler's apprentice stood framed there. "Beg pardon. The Lady Dalrymple's carriage for Miss Ransome."

Charlotte let out a little squeak, leapt up from the settee, and flung herself into Mother's arms. William stood back and watched in consternation. Never before—not even when she'd fallen from the old rope ladder when she was six and dislocated her shoulder—had he witnessed such a display of emotion from his sister.

Julia slipped her hand under his elbow. He released his fists—clasped behind his back—and brought his arm around front. With her free hand, Julia reached over and squeezed his forearm. It struck him that she was trying to comfort him.

But he did not need comfort. He had done this so many times, said farewell to his mother and sister, that he had grown beyond becoming emotional at partings. Though he did usually throw himself—and therefore his crew—into such a frenzy of work the several days after a parting that he suspected they cursed his name below decks.

Julia's attempt to comfort him *dis*comforted him. If he still reacted to parting with Mother after so many years, what would it be like the first time he had to leave Julia behind?

He stole a glance at his wife. If leaving her at Tierra Dulce when he put back out to sea were half as wrenching as when he'd walked away from her twelve years ago, his crew might mutiny within hours of weighing anchor. And he would not blame them.

Chapter Ten

It was only hair.

Charlotte swiped at the tears streaming down her cheeks and took up the shears again. The curtain of silky brown hair hugged her shoulders and flowed down her back. Her crowning glory, as Mama would say.

"It will grow back," she whispered to her own image in the accusing mirror. She pulled a thick lock forward, wrapped her fist around it close to her scalp, held her breath and…

Shrrrrrp.

Laying the section of hair on the dressing table before her, she released her breath. Slowly, she raised her eyes to the mirror. The short ends remaining looked vulgar and unseemly. She glanced down at the other item on the dressing table.

Henry's letter.

Resolution stopped her tears and steadied her hand. To keep from having much of a mess, she quickly plaited her remaining hair into two long braids—and just as quickly hacked them off. She tied the cut ends with twine. Madame Rousseau owed her a guinea.

Not quite sure what she was doing, and more by feel than sight, she trimmed the back and bottom until she could barely pull it a finger's width from her scalp. She left the top long enough to part at one side and comb both sides down almost to her ears.

Her head felt strangely light, her neck bare and exposed. But when she looked into the mirror, Charles Lott stared back at her, wide-eyed with uncertainty.

She still had time to back out, to go to the country with the Fairfaxes and then go home to Gateacre to see Philip and let Mama take care of her as she'd always done. With Lady Rotheram's baby having come yestereve, just before Charlotte took her leave of Brampton Park, Lady Dalrymple's attention had been understandably distracted when Charlotte had bade her benefactress farewell. Distracted enough to not notice that Charlotte's large trunk was not in the carriage, only a much smaller chest.

The boy at the Yateses' home had taken the sea chest up the back stairs to Charlotte's room, so they did not know she hadn't had her trunk sent straight on to the Fairfaxes'. Staying her last night in Portsmouth at Collin and Susan's home in town had been Charlotte's idea—along with hiding her trunk, filled with the beautiful gowns Lady Dalrymple had commissioned for her, in one of the rooms in the closed, unused portion of the east wing of Brampton Park.

But now, could she go through with it?

She closed her eyes and searched deep within the recesses of her mind for an image of Henry. He was tall—about as tall as William, perhaps taller than Ned Cochrane. She shook her head, trying to erase the vivid memory of Ned in his uniform as he'd danced with her just a few nights ago. Henry. Henry had blond hair and mysterious hazel eyes. Yes. Mysterious and fathomless—not gray and searching like Ned's.

Frustrated with her inability to keep Ned from her thoughts, Charlotte set about the task of cleaning up the signs of her haircutting. She dusted herself off first and then the chair, which she then picked up and set aside. Thank goodness she'd remembered that Mama had always put an old sheet down on the floor before cutting Philip's hair when they were young. She picked up the corners of the spare sheet she'd found in the trunk at the foot of the bed and carried it to a window and shook it out—thankful for no wind.

The mantel clock chimed five times. Her heart jumped. She'd calculated she needed to leave no later than half-past five to walk to

Madame Rousseau's to collect her guinea and still be at the dockyard in plenty of time to report in to Lieutenant Howe aboard *Audacious* by seven thirty. She'd made her farewell to the Yateses last night. They believed she would be walking early to High Street and meeting with Penelope Fairfax there, so they would not be surprised when no carriage came to collect her.

Once she arrived at the dockyard, she would need to arrange to have the note delivered to the Fairfaxes—

The note! At the desk, she scrabbled for a piece of stationery and then sat for a long moment, trying to determine how to word it to raise no suspicion. With their intended departure at eight o'clock, they would have no time to corroborate her story with Lady Dalrymple, but she needed to be certain they would not—in concern for Charlotte—send a note to Brampton Park for her.

Finally, she dipped her quill into the inkwell.

Dear Miss Fairfax,

It is with deepest regret, yet also a sense of joy, that I must inform you I will be unable to travel with you today to your country home. Lady Dalrymple's daughter gave birth yesterday evening, and I discover I am much needed in Portsmouth, at least for a few days. I am assured that transportation will be no issue when the time comes that I can depart. As soon as I know when, I will send word ahead to inform you of my arrival.

I apologize for any inconvenience this may cause. Until we meet again, I am most sincerely…

Your friend,
Ch. Ransome

She tapped the end of the quill against her chin as she read and reread the note. By disclosing the news of the arrival of Lady Rotheram's baby, Charlotte hoped that Penelope's—and her mother's—attention would be so focused on receiving knowledge of it before anyone else in Portsmouth that they would not think twice about Charlotte's absence. The rest of the note…well, she'd been as honest as possible and bought herself a few days before the Fairfaxes would start wondering why they had not heard from her. By then the convoy would be at sea. She would post a letter to Mama explaining everything when they put in at Madeira to resupply.

She hoped everyone would forgive her for making them worry about her for a few weeks.

The clock showed she'd managed to fritter away fifteen minutes. She grabbed Henry's letter off the vanity and tucked it into the back of Mr. Geoffrey's journal, which she returned to the sea chest. With one spare uniform, two sets of everyday tunics and trousers, and the smaller sundry items she'd need, the chest was barely half full. But since she had to carry it herself down to the dockyard—three miles—the less weight it contained, the better.

She pulled off the chemise she'd slept in and stuffed it, along with the dress and other articles she'd worn here, into the very back of one of the deep drawers in the wardrobe. She watched herself in the mirror as she donned the midshipman's uniform she'd purchased at a secondhand shop, as Lieutenant Howe had ordered. It looked almost new. The trousers were slightly too short, but she'd been around the dockyard enough to know that trouser length was arbitrary.

The black neckcloth, while concealing her bruises, gave her a little trouble; but once she put on the white waistcoat with its high collar, it hid her ineptness with the neckwear.

Stockings and shoes, and then the coat. Once she had it on and buttoned, she marveled at how it hid her figure completely. Though the rest of the clothes did a good job of masking the slight curve of her hips and the smallness of her waist, the coat did what no other garment could—made her broad at the shoulders and straight everywhere else.

The clock struck the half hour.

Excitement, trepidation, and nausea struck her like successive tidal waves. She took a few deep breaths. Though her heart would not settle down, her stomach did. She tucked the heel of bread and chunk of cheese she'd swiped from the kitchen an hour ago into her pocket, snuffed the candles, clapped the tall, round hat on her head, and hoisted the sea chest.

If Susan and Collin were not awakened by the creaking of the floorboards, surely the sound of Charlotte's pounding heart would be loud enough to wake the dead. But she made it to the service stairs with no incident. At this hour, only the cook would be stirring, and as she lived in quarters beside the kitchen, she never used this staircase. Still, Charlotte paused often to listen for footfalls or other telltale signs she was not alone.

None came. As she had so many times before, she sneaked out the back of the house into the garden. In less than twenty feet, she would be in the alley.

Ned sauntered around to the area where Howe oversaw the delivery of supplies for *Audacious*. "Any sign of Lott yet?"

Howe grunted. "Not yet. I will be very put out, Cochrane, if after waiting all this while I have to secure another midshipman when I could have had one a week ago."

Ned pressed his lips together. He was usually a good judge of character, and Charles Lott had struck him as someone he could take a risk on. Actually, Charles Lott had struck him as something entirely different than any other midshipman Ned had ever met, but he couldn't quite put his finger on what it was. There was something so familiar about the lad, yet Ned knew he'd never met the boy outside of the few times he'd seen him here at the dockyard.

Matthews signaled him from their entrenchment on the quay, so he left Howe, trying to not feel betrayed by the young midshipman.

He turned at the sound of pounding feet. Down the quay ran a slight figure in a midshipman's uniform. Lott. The boy stopped a few paces from Ned and dropped his sea chest onto the stones beneath their feet.

Ned grinned and pulled out his pocket watch. "Five minutes to spare. Well done, Lott."

Panting, Lott bent down and braced his hands on his knees. "Would have been here earlier…had to find a messenger…send a note. Let them know…" He waved his hand and took a few gulping breaths, and then he straightened and touched the brim of his hat. "Midshipman Charles Lott reporting for duty."

Ned cocked one eyebrow. "Don't report to me." He used his thumb to point over his shoulder. "Your commanding officer is over there. But I'd suggest you wipe the bread crumbs off your jacket before you see him. He's a stickler for those things."

Lott turned even redder than he already was, looked down, and frantically brushed away the remains of his breakfast.

"Better hop to, Mr. Lott. You only have about a minute and a half to report in before Lieutenant Howe gives away your spot."

"Aye, aye, sir." Lott whisked away a few more stray crumbs, and then he bent down and picked up his sea chest with a grunt. "Thank you, Lieutenant Cochrane."

Ned inclined his head to the junior officer, and then he made his way down the dock to rejoin his own crew, unable to shake the feeling that he knew Charles Lott from somewhere.

Julia glanced around the room one more time. Memories of the evenings she'd spent in this study with her father over the past year flooded her mind, causing swift tears to sting her eyes, but she refused to give in to them. William had been so stoic two nights ago when they bade farewell to his mother, she'd almost been embarrassed remembering her own outburst upon parting with Papa.

Once she returned to Jamaica, there were so many events, so many people she would miss. Papa. Susan and Collin—and the birth of their child. Lady Dalrymple, who had become a friend in past weeks. The Naval Family Aid society. Admiral and Mrs. Hinds.

Even Admiral Glover and his incessant and repetitive anecdotes of his life at sea.

She closed her eyes and held her breath for a moment until the urge to sob dissipated. Instead of focusing on what she was leaving behind, she needed to think about what she had to look forward to: Jamaica, Tierra Dulce, Jerusha and Jeremiah and the rest of the families who worked and lived at the plantation, the hot days and warm nights, the crystal clear water in her cove…

"The carriage is ready." Creighton's soft voice drew her out of her reverie.

She turned toward him and imagined that her own face mirrored the stricken expression he wore. "The admiral has promised to come to Jamaica next year. Make sure he brings you with him, Creighton."

He smiled at her, a rare sight from the former sailor who took his position as butler so seriously. "Not only would I revel at the idea of being at sea again, but it would bring me great pleasure to visit you in your other home, ma'am."

Julia gulped for air. "I suppose this is farewell, then." She crossed to the doorway and took his hand and pressed it between hers. "Thank you for everything you've done for me, Creighton. My father and I—and Commodore Ransome—will never be able to repay you for your dedication and quick thinking that saved me from an ignominious fate."

"I am proud—" His voice cracked. He cleared his throat before continuing, "I am proud to have been able to serve you and Commodore Ransome, ma'am. And I wish you much joy in the future."

She squeezed his hand, released it, and then exited past him into the hallway. The few remaining pieces of her baggage had been taken to the dockyard earlier this morning. As far as she could tell, all evidence that she had resided in this house for the twelvemonth past was gone.

She preceded Creighton down the stairs—and stopped short when she reached the landing that overlooked the entry hall. Lining the walls in the wide hall was every single member of the staff—from the stable boys to the cook, with every maid and man in between. Though she'd been responsible for paying their salaries since Papa had gone to London, seeing them all collected in one room astonished her.

Creighton gave a slight bow and continued on down the stairs and took his place beside the housekeeper. Nancy, Julia's lady's maid, held a handkerchief over her face with both hands and wept softly into it.

"Thank you, all of you, for making my time here comfortable and enjoyable. Each of you is vital to the running of this house, and without you, we would be lost. I wish each of you happiness and health, and I pray we will one day all meet again."

Cook joined Nancy in tears—though the heavyset woman's flowed freely down her cheeks accompanied by loud snuffling.

A sense of serenity—which could only be God-given—settled over Julia. She made her way down the steps and went to Nancy, who held Julia's gloves and hat.

Julia waved aside the maid's attempt to hand her the items and pulled Nancy into an embrace. Though she wouldn't have thought it possible, Nancy wept even harder. Julia murmured words of comfort, and slowly Nancy calmed enough so that she only sniffled a few times as she pinned Julia's hat and helped her with the gloves.

Creighton escorted her out to the carriage. Instead of a footman, Elton stood beside the barouche, ready to hand her up. His expression was just as stricken as Creighton's had been earlier—until Creighton stepped forward as if to assist Julia into the carriage.

To keep them from coming to blows, Julia turned and once again pressed Creighton's hand in hers. "Farewell, Creighton. I do hope to meet you again someday."

He bowed, his throat working madly when he came upright again, as if swallowing repeatedly. "Godspeed, ma'am."

She pulled her hands away and turned to accept Elton's for assistance to ascend the steps into the barouche.

Most of the household staff assembled on the front steps. Julia raised her hand to wave her farewell as the carriage pulled away from the house.

Leaving Tierra Dulce had not been this difficult. But when she left the only home she'd known since age ten a year ago, she'd known she would be returning, that she would see all of her friends and loved ones in Jamaica again. Once she left England, she would probably never see any of these friends and acquaintances again—because she planned to never return to England.

The now-familiar sights, sounds, and smells of Portsmouth rolled past her, bringing to mind the first time she'd seen them—coming off of an eight-week voyage that had passed in a grief-blurred haze, so soon after her mother's death.

Mama. What would life at Tierra Dulce be like without her? Considering how Mama's melancholia had affected them all over the past few years, with a touch of shame Julia suspected life might be a little happier and more joy filled now. And with William there…

But he would not be there—not all the time. Though he would be in command of a group of ships sailing from the Royal Navy's Jamaica station, he would still be at sea most of the time.

The bustle of the dockyard brought Julia back to the present. Before she could think of and try to make plans for her future with William in her home in Jamaica, she needed to get through the next two months with him in his home on *Alexandra*.

Jolly boat coming up, Commodore." The midshipman of the watch stopped beside William and touched the brim of his hat. "Lieutenant Cochrane and—"

"Very good. Pass word for the purser." William did not glance away from the cargo currently being lowered through the yawning opening in the deck. Complaints from the sailors about the prices Holt was asking for certain items already had reached William's ears. They'd gone through this on their last voyage, and William was none too happy to have to revisit the conversation. The purser continued trying to explain his reasoning after the midshipman left them.

"Permission to come aboard, Commodore?"

William spun around at the sound of Julia's voice. The sunset-orange of her dress set off the russet tones in her hair—at least of the curls peeking out below the straw-brimmed bonnet she wore.

He dismissed Holt, composed himself, clasped his hands behind his back, and regarded her as he might a midshipman asking for a position aboard *Alexandra*. "Have you any qualifications for service aboard a ship of His Majesty's Royal Navy?"

Julia mimicked his stance, but rocked up onto her toes even as her eyes began to twinkle. "I know all the ships and their ratings, can name all of the sails and rigging, and have even been known to climb to the foremast top to identify French warships." She rocked to her heels and back to her toes again. "Oh, and my father is a rear admiral of the Blue, and my husband is a commodore under his flag."

William paused, as if considering her words—all the while simply admiring the figure she presented, standing here on the deck of his ship. "I suppose, for reasons of patronage if nothing else, I must allow you to come aboard, then."

The dimples appeared in her cheeks even as she curtsied. "My most humble thanks, Commodore Ransome."

"Welcome to your new—albeit temporary—home, Mrs. Ransome." The inescapable knowledge that every man on the quarterdeck watched them added starch to William's spine and made him wipe all expression from his face. "Come, I will show you to your—our quarters." He motioned Julia to walk beside him.

The young midshipman in the wheelhouse with Master Ingleby gaped open mouthed at Julia as they passed through—until Ingleby elbowed the lad, and he fumbled to remove his hat.

The marine standing guard at the door reached to open it, his eyes never leaving Julia. William sighed. Bringing Julia on board today instead of tomorrow morning before they weighed anchor might have been better for more than matters of time management. The crew would all have a chance to see her and, William hoped, that would put the staring to an end.

Beyond the dining cabin, William stepped into the day cabin, suddenly nervous and self-conscious. What kind of home was this to offer someone accustomed to the grandeur of her father's house in Portsmouth—or the plantation, which he pictured as something akin to Brampton Park.

"That's my—" Julia gasped and crossed to the writing desk in the far corner, taking advantage of the light from the stern windows. "My desk and chair. How did you…?" She turned, her hand gripping the back of the carved banana-wood chair. "These were my mother's. But I did not think we would have room for them. I was fully prepared to leave them behind."

"But, as you see, there was no reason to leave such a prized possession behind." He kept his self-satisfied smile to himself, proud that he'd been able to do something to both surprise and please her.

"How did you know?"

"How does anyone know anything in your father's home?"

"Creighton." Though a smile coaxed the dimples back into Julia's cheeks, her eyes glittered as if filling with tears.

"Aye, Creighton. It is easy to see his bad habits of being a busybody steward have remained with him as a butler."

As hoped, Julia laughed and her eyes cleared. "Yes, he does know more than he should upon occasion, but we owe him so great a debt, I could forgive him almost anything." She returned to where he stood beside his own desk and then looked past him, toward the sleeping quarters.

William cleared the returning nervousness from his throat. "Dawling stowed your dunnage, that which you indicated you would need, in there." He fixed his eyes on the ship fifty yards off *Alexandra*'s stern.

"William?" The vulnerability in Julia's voice tugged at his heart.

He drew his eyes away from the windows and met her gaze. He unclenched his fists from behind his back and rested his hands on her shoulders. Tension ebbed up through his hands.

"I am sorry to be such a disruption. I promise I will do my best to keep to the cabin so my presence does not interfere with the crew."

His left hand trailed up the side of her neck to touch the curls her bonnet held captive beside her cheek. "The men will perform their duties to the best of their abilities, no matter where you happen to be on the ship. And I shall remind them of that shortly. Though I would ask that you limit your movements to our cabins and the poop deck. A ship—"

"Is no place for a woman." She grinned up at him, leaning her cheek into his hand. "I well remember your saying that."

William frowned. "When did I say that?" He had said it many times, but he would never have said it in front of her.

"You said it to Collin shortly after you saved me from being swept overboard during that storm when Mama sent me to fetch the doctor."

He blinked. "You have remembered that for twenty years?"

A red glow climbed Julia's face. "I remember almost everything I saw you do or heard you say on that first crossing to Jamaica." She settled her hands on his waist and leaned closer. "I told you—I fell in love with you then."

He chuckled, calling upon his own somewhat vague memories of that voyage. The image of Julia dressed as her brother was the only clear picture coming to mind. "I never would have guessed you fancied you fell in love with me on first sight."

"Oh, no. Do not flatter yourself, sir. It was not on *first* sight. I do believe I hated you the first two times I saw you—both times I climbed to the mast top."

"Hated me?" He found the pin securing Julia's bonnet and pulled it out. Julia reached up and untied the ribbons under her chin, and William pulled the thing off her head and tossed it onto his desk.

"Yes, because you knew my secret—and you knew I was caught and punished for sneaking out dressed as a boy. But you showed me the dolphins. And later you saved my life. And I think that's when I fell in love with you. Had I not been confined to quarters, you would have known. For I would have followed you all over the ship otherwise."

William had never felt vain—until now. He had written off his curiosity about Julia after that crossing, ascribing it to the fact that Sir Edward had become a surrogate parent in the years following Father's death. He could now admit to himself, however, he'd harbored the idea—from age fifteen—that he would eventually marry Julia Witherington.

"I always knew you were a woman of impeccable taste and discernment."

She gasped, but he leaned down to kiss her before she could say anything else. Being on a ship with her again, reminiscing about the past, was making him feel like that much more reckless and carefree midshipman again.

But the sound of a throat clearing snapped him out of it. He pulled away from Julia, set her aside, and turned to fix Dawling with a remonstrative glare.

"Beggin' pardon, Com'dore. Purser Holt's compliments and could the Com'dore please meet him below, sir." The burly sailor shifted from foot to foot, his gaze firmly affixed to the floor.

"Let Holt know I will attend him presently."

"Aye, aye, sir."

"And Dawling?"

"Yes, Com'dore?"

"I know it is customary for you as my steward to be allowed to come and go as you please from these cabins. But so long as Mrs. Ransome is aboard, please knock before entering."

Julia felt sorry for Dawling, who scurried away as soon as William dismissed him. When William turned back to her, he'd once again retreated behind the mask of command. She'd best accustom herself to it, for she had a feeling it was the side of him she would see the most from now on.

"Do not let me keep you from your duties, William. I have disrupted your schedule enough already."

He gave a terse nod, turned on his heel, and left.

Julia stood in the middle of the day cabin for a moment, gathering her thoughts. For the first time on a transatlantic crossing, she would not have her own private quarters, cordoned off with makeshift canvas walls in the main cabin itself. She closed her eyes, released the back of William's desk chair, and widened her stance slightly, letting her knees absorb the gentle motion of the harbor. Staying to their quarters would be no sacrifice the first few days—she'd never succumbed to the slight nausea she always had the first day or so out at sea, but it took her a while to find her sea legs. And she did not want to embarrass William, nor endanger herself or others, by lurching about the deck like an alleyway drunkard. Finding the rhythm of the sea was much like dancing to an unfamiliar tune: If one practiced long enough, one became proficient.

She opened her eyes and, with a determined breath, entered the sleeping cabin.

Though it took up more than half of the tiny space, the box bed, with its rustically embroidered hangings, looked smaller than it had the first time she'd seen it, on the inspection tour with Papa. By naval standards, it might be deemed a bed for two, but by Julia's standards, it would take some getting used to.

On the opposite side of the small room, over the menacing bulk of the cannon, hung William's plain canvas hammock. A strange, unfamiliar sensation trickled down into the pit of her stomach. While she did not want to be a distraction to William, she had hoped that in private he would be willing to let his guard down and just be William—her husband—rather than Commodore Ransome.

Lord, please help me be what he wants me to be...

A knock reverberated through the removable bulkheads separating the sleeping quarters from the day and dining cabins. Julia stepped back into what would be, for the next two months, her sitting room and opened the door.

Dawling knuckled his forehead. "Com'dore's compliments, mum. He sent me to see if there's aught I can do for you, mum."

Julia looked around the pristine cabin, her bonnet on William's desk the only thing out of place. "That wardrobe—is it full, or might there be some room to hang a few of my dresses?"

Dawling's eyes lit up and he scurried over to the tall cabinet—tall enough it looked securely wedged between the hull and the beam of the floor joist overhead. He opened the doors and turned with a flourish so out of character with his appearance, Julia almost laughed.

William's dress uniform and a spare coat were all that the wardrobe contained.

"He had this brought on special for you, missus."

Julia's cheeks warmed. One more piece of evidence of William's consideration of her comforts. "Would you please bring my trunk and valise out here so that I can unpack them?"

Dawling saluted again and, with a comical grin and rolling gait, slipped into the sleeping cabin, returning a moment later with the large trunk—and the valise atop it—as if it weighed nothing.

Julia hung her bonnet on one of the hooks on the side of the wardrobe to get it out of the way. She opened the valise first, shaking out the plain cotton and muslin day dresses. In the dampness inherent on a ship, the wrinkles would eventually ease up.

"I've a flatiron, mum, and would be happy to take care of anything for you."

The image of the big sailor with the scarred face and rough hands leaning over a table, ironing one of her dresses, brought a laugh bubbling up. She tried to mask it with a cough. "Thank you, Mr. Dawling, but I shall have plenty of hours that need filling. You already have enough work to do without my adding to it."

"Mr. Fawkes says 'twill be good for me to learn how to serve a lady as well as the com'dore. Says if I leave the Royal Navy, it'll help me to be able to get a position on land if I can show a lady I can be more than just a valet."

"Did you enjoy the time you spent at the Yateses' home?" Julia asked, as Dawling seemed in no hurry to leave.

"Oh, aye, mum. I'd always thought of service on land as something pitiable. But once I saw what a butler and a valet do and what kind of life they have when they get a good house and master, I started to think that I might consider making it a life if I ever find myself without a ship again."

Julia continued unpacking as Dawling enumerated many of the duties he had learned from Collin and Susan's butler, Fawkes. After setting the last stack of folded petticoats from the valise into one of the drawers, she turned and found that Dawling had opened the trunk for her.

"Thank you, Mr. Dawling."

"Please, mum, just Dawling. 'Mister' don't suit my rank."

She ducked her head and bent over the trunk so he would not see her smile. Though he did not have the skills or polish of the stewards who had served her father, including Creighton, Dawling would make the voyage more interesting.

Not much of what she had packed in the trunk would be needed during the voyage. Julia removed several personal items she thought she might want, as well as two of the many formal gowns her aunt had insisted she have made. If William invited any of his officers to join them for dinner, she wanted to show her respect—for William and for the crew—by dressing her best.

After rummaging through what remained, she finally stood, hands pressed to the small of her back. "That is all I need. Is it possible for this to be stowed with the rest of my baggage?" She glanced back into the sleeping cabin. "Oh, and the bandboxes as well. I will keep two bonnets, but the rest could be stowed if there is storage room for them."

"Oh, aye, mum. I can find room for them." He motioned toward the valise by her feet. "If you'll give me that, mum, I'll put it in here until it's needed again."

"Good thinking, Mr…Dawling." She handed him the empty tapestry bag and then went in to find her plain straw bonnet and send the rest to be stowed away until Jamaica.

A quick rap sounded on the door. Dawling latched the trunk lid and went to answer it.

One of the midshipmen—one Julia had not yet met—came in and swept his hat off his head, revealing a sheaf of sandy hair. "Commodore Ransome's compliments, ma'am, and will Mrs. Commodore please join him on the quarterdeck."

Her heart tripped over itself. "Please let Commodore Ransome know I will join him presently, Mr…?"

"Oldroyd, ma'am."

"Thank you, Mr. Oldroyd."

"Ma'am." He nodded and backed out through the door.

Julia took the bonnet from the hook and tied the ribbons under her chin as she hurried through the dining cabin. The blast of sunlight brought her up short. She blinked until acclimated to the light and then scanned the deck for William. He stood just beyond the wheelhouse, hands clasped behind his back.

He said nothing when she joined him but motioned her to follow him up onto the poop deck. When he took up a position at the railing overlooking the quarterdeck, Julia stood beside him, her eyes taking in the vast expanse of ship laid out before her—a veritable floating city populated with nearly eight hundred souls. And William was responsible for the lives of all of them. She wanted to reach over and squeeze his hand to let him know she understood the enormity of his task, but she stopped herself before her arm left her side.

"Signal all hands, Mr. Cochrane."

Julia looked over her shoulder. The young first officer grinned at her in his affable way and then stepped to the rail of the poop. "Bosun," he called in a booming voice that surprised Julia, "signal all hands on deck."

From below the boatswain made a shrill signal with his brass whistle, which was soon almost drowned out by the multitude of feet pounding the decks and companion stairs as the men rushed from the far reaches of the ship to gather on the deck.

Once all had gathered and quieted, William leaned forward a bit. "Crew of His Majesty's Ship *Alexandra*"—a cheer went up from the men—"tomorrow morning, we weigh anchor." Another cheer. "As you all know, my wife will be joining us for the crossing to Jamaica. It is the wish of Mrs. Ransome as well as myself that her presence on board does not disrupt the efficient operation of this ship. Therefore, whenever you see Mrs. Ransome on deck, you may pay her the respect of salute or doff, but then you are to go about your duties as usual. Is that understood?"

"Aye, aye, sir" rang out from hundreds of voices.

"Mr. Gibson." William did not turn his head when he spoke the name.

One of the midshipmen Julia had met—he had been one who delivered William's notes to her before their wedding—came forward. "Aye, sir?"

"Has noon been called?"

"Not yet, sir, but 'tis almost marked."

"As you were."

The mid touched the brim of his hat and returned to his sextant. A few seconds later, "Noon, sir. I mark noon."

"Very good, Mr. Gibson. Master Ingleby, ring noon."

Below, the ship's master hammered four couplets of chimes on the big brass bell.

"Mr. Cochrane, dismiss the men to dinner."

"Aye, aye, sir." Cochrane once again stepped forward to relay the orders.

Just as quickly as they had come on deck, the crew dispersed. Julia released the breath she hadn't realized she held and followed William back down to the quarterdeck and then into their quarters.

She bumped into his back when he stopped just a step into the dining cabin.

"Dawling!"

Not wanting to get involved in something between William and his steward, Julia skirted around him and entered the day cabin. The trunk and bandboxes were gone, so she had a pretty good idea of where the seaman had disappeared to.

"Aye, Com'dore?" Dawling's brusque voice carried through the ajar door between the cabins.

"Dinner?" The weight and inflection of William's voice made no other words necessary. Julia cringed. Dawling had neglected to prepare their midday meal because she had kept him from his duties.

As soon as Dawling left to rectify the situation, William entered the main cabin, shrugged out of his coat, and hung it on the back of his desk chair.

"William, it is my fault Dawling did not have time to prepare luncheon. He came in and offered to help me with the trunk, and...I am sorry. It will not happen again."

William sighed and closed his eyes. "I appreciate your trying to take the blame, but you do him a disservice by so doing. As my steward, he well knows what his duties are—and one of those duties is to see that he does not get distracted by anyone else aboard this ship."

A crash, followed by loud swearing, reached them, even through the closed cabin doors.

William grabbed his coat and punched his arms into the sleeves at nearly a run. Julia followed closely behind. She navigated the companion stairs much more slowly than his leap down them. For a moment, she could not see in the darkness of the main gun deck, but when her eyes adjusted, she drew in a gasp.

Covered in food, a rotund seaman sprawled on his back like a harpooned whale. Midshipman Kennedy scooped food off the man and back into a bucket.

"What happened, Mr. Kennedy?" William barked.

The teen jumped to his feet and saluted. "Cap'n, sir. Cook fell, sir."

William swallowed, annoyance fairly oozing from him. "Yes. I can see that. *How* did Cook fall?"

Matthews arrived, lamp in hand. Around Cook and covered with the victuals now scattered across the floor, Julia could make out the shapes of half a dozen somewhat crushed bandboxes. Her stomach turned. *Her* bandboxes. She opened her mouth to apologize again, but closed it when William turned a questioning gaze on Matthews.

"Beggin' pardon, sir, but Dawling was looking for a couple o' boys to get this dunnage moved afore you called for him."

"See to it, then. Mr. Kennedy, get some of the boys up here to clean this up and then return to your station." He turned on his heel and finally looked at Julia.

In that moment she saw it—in his eyes, in his stance. His ship was no place for a woman. Not even his wife.

Chapter Twelve

Vast hauling!"

Charlotte's hands cramped around the rope as she and the other midshipman stopped pulling. Her arms trembled. Sweat drenched every inch of her body. She had never experienced pain so excruciating in her life.

And she had been aboard *Audacious* for only half an hour.

Until thirty minutes ago, everything had been going well. On the quay, Lieutenant Howe had quizzed her extensively—she once again gave silent thanks to Geoffrey Seymour and his journals for supplying her with answers to Howe's inquiries about Charles Lott's previous experience. She had chosen Geoffrey's first years—those unlucky years in which every ship to which he was assigned ended up at anchor in some harbor for months on end—so that if she did not do well with her gun crew during the first few drills, Howe would excuse her inexperience, not question it.

She had been the first midshipman to mark noon—though she regretted it when it drew some scathing looks from a few of the older mids. But during their quick midday meal, there was no time to discover who would be friend or foe amongst the midshipmen. They had hardly sat down when they were once again ordered back on deck to help with bringing cargo aboard.

"On my mark…two…six…heave."

Charlotte mustered every reserve she possessed and threw her weight against the line.

The quartermaster and purser scurried about, checking cargo, while Charlotte and the rest of the junior officers hauled the barrels of water aboard—some of the most precious cargo they would carry.

The sun beat down relentlessly. Twice more they had to haul dozens of barrels that seemed filled with lead rather than water.

Charlotte nearly collapsed onto the deck in relief when the purser announced that was the end of the hauling. But rather than respite, "Beat to quarters!" followed by a drummer's quick tattoo rent the air.

Around her the other mids hurried away. *Beat to quarters* meant for the gun crews to take up their battle stations for battle, for drill, or for inspection.

Charlotte alone stood still in the midst of the bustle.

"Why are you just standing there?" A tall boy with golden-brown hair grabbed Charlotte's arm and dragged her in his wake.

"I do not know where I am supposed to go." She thought the other midshipman's name was Hamilton, but between the pain each movement brought and the confusion surrounding them, she could not be certain.

"You're at the guns beside mine. I've been covering your stations 'til now."

Being stationed beside Hamilton proved to be Charlotte's best luck to date. He did everything with efficiency and ease, and by mimicking him, she issued her final command—"Run 'er out!"—to both of her gun crews before at least half a dozen others.

Her heart leapt into her throat when Captain Alban Parker came down the companion stairs to inspect the lower gun deck.

Charlotte tried to ignore the fact that Captain Parker cut a fine figure in his uniform. In the dim glow of light from the candle-filled lanterns, he looked a good few years younger than William and Collin. He walked past most of the cannon and gun crews with barely a glance.

Until he reached Hamilton. He made quite a show of inspecting Hamilton's station and finding fault with the angle of the fuses, the condition of the cannons, the comportment of the men on the crews.

None of which Charlotte could see were any worse—and actually looked better to her—than anyone else's.

"If you ever expect to be recommended for lieutenant, Mr. Hamilton, you must do better than this."

Charlotte's skin tingled with dread when Captain Parker turned his attention on her.

"And you are the new mid, just reported. Tell me, Mr. Lott…are you going to live up to the expectation you've created by making us wait a week for you to decide to grace us with your presence?"

She swallowed the panic rising in her throat. "Aye, sir. I mean, I will try to, sir." Embarrassment flamed in her cheeks at the high-pitched squeak in her voice.

Captain Parker laughed. "We shall see. We shall also see if we cannot get you talking like a man before we reach the West Indies."

He turned and looked around the deck, where everyone still stood at the ready. "Kent!"

"Aye, Cap'n?" A reed-thin midshipman stepped forward, across from Charlotte. His white-blond hair seemed to glow in the lamplight.

"My quarters at one bell in the first dogwatch for supper."

A smug smile broke over Kent's sharp face. "Aye, aye, sir."

"Lieutenant Howe, dismiss the crew."

At the shouted order from Howe, Charlotte—and the rest of the gun captains—yelled "Dismissed!"

"Come, Lott. No rest for the wicked."

Charlotte followed Hamilton back up into the blinding sunlight on the quarterdeck. "What do we do now?"

Hamilton motioned larboard. "More cargo to haul."

She leaned her head back and groaned.

"Take heart. By this time tomorrow, we will be out at sea. Or at least clearing Spithead." Hamilton threw his arms out and swelled his chest with a deep breath. "The open sea again at last."

Somehow, she had to survive until then. By the time eight bells sounded the beginning of the first dogwatch and Charlotte sat down to her supper of stringy, fatty mutton and soggy peas, she could barely raise the food to her mouth. Her entire body ached. And having slept only a few hours last night made it difficult to keep her eyes open.

"You there!"

She wished everyone would quiet down, even for just a moment. Her head swam from hours of ceaseless noise and voices.

"You—new boy!"

Something hard slammed into Charlotte's shoulder—a fist. She yelped in surprise and pain.

"Do not ignore me when I call you." Kent towered over her, a sneer marring what could have been a striking—if not handsome—face.

Standing did not gain Charlotte any advantage, as Kent still stood more than eight inches taller. "Since you did not address me by name, how was I to know you were speaking to me?"

The cockpit grew silent. Charlotte sensed she had overstepped a line, breached some sort of protocol she was unfamiliar with.

Kent leaned closer. Charlotte clenched her fists at her sides and stood her ground.

"I am senior officer of this mess." A tittering of dissenting voices behind Kent drew his attention from Charlotte momentarily. "I have served Captain Parker longer than any other mid here, and that means I'm in charge of the cockpit and everything that happens down here."

More grumbling—which sounded like it came from a few boys seated across the table from her with Hamilton. But Charlotte did not turn to look, afraid to take her eyes off Kent.

"I need a clean shirt to wear to supper with the captain. Give me your spare, new boy."

Charlotte stared at Kent, incredulous. "Wear your own shirt."

Kent grabbed her jaw and shoved her back. Charlotte braced her hands on the edge of the table to keep from falling backward into her food. She gulped for air, trying to keep panic at bay. This could not happen to her again.

She desperately wanted to fight back; but since Kent seemed to enjoy the captain's favor, she could not risk being disciplined for fighting.

"And I believe I'll borrow your neckcloth as well."

Charlotte swallowed a cry of pain when Kent's fingers pressed against her throat. But then his hold on her jaw eased. She took the calculated risk of pushing him away. She straightened her uniform and worked her jaw back and forth.

"What—what happened to your throat?" the boy beside Kent asked.

Her hand flew to her neck, now exposed. "A marquess wanted… something from me. And when I would not give it to him, he tried to take it by force."

"And did he get what he wanted, after giving you those bruises?" the boy on Kent's other side asked.

"No, he did not." She looked directly at Kent. "He got my fork in the side of his neck." She felt around behind her on the table and wrapped her fingers around her utensil.

The movement of her arm when she brought it down to her side caught Kent's eye. He looked down at her fist—now wrapped around a fork—and took a step back.

His eyes narrowed. "You wouldn't dare."

Charlotte raised her brows in what she hoped was a good imitation of the haughty expression she'd seen him wear. "I plunged a fork into the neck of a *marquess*. What makes you think I would be afraid to defend myself by whatever means necessary from you?"

Kent's chest heaved, and his already-thin lips practically vanished. "We're not finished, Lott, you and I. But I don't have time to teach you manners right now. Jamison!" He kept his narrowed eyes on Charlotte. "Give me your spare white shirt." With one last sneer, Kent finally walked away to harass a clean shirt out of Midshipman Jamison.

Once Kent left the cockpit, the rest of the mess returned to their chatter and eating. Charlotte tried to finish her meal, but the greasy meat caught in her throat.

"Lott, I don't know if that was brave or idiotic." Hamilton leaned his elbows on the table across from Charlotte. "But if you'll accept some friendly advice, try to get along with Kent. He has Parker's ear and favor."

"Is he truly the senior officer of the mess?" She shoved her plate away, feeling a touch ill.

"No." The tall, homely, dark-haired boy she had seen Hamilton with most of the day shook his head. "Ham and I are both eighteen with six years' service, one year senior to Kent on both counts. But as he said, Kent has the captain's favor."

"And he has a mean streak," Hamilton added. "You should have a care. When he promises retribution, he always takes it."

"But when he does these things, cannot you speak to the first lieutenant?" Charlotte's stomach churned a bit more.

"Martin, tell Lott what happened when you went to Howe."

The dark-haired boy—Martin—nodded. "I made the mistake of trying to exert my seniority over Kent the second day he was here. You see, Ham and I—and a little more than half the mids here—all served on *Audacious* under Captain Yates. Ham and I shared command of the mess—he over one watch, I over the other. But when Parker arrived with half a crew from his previous ship, they took over. Kent and his mates came into the cockpit and told the rest of us how everything would be run. I asked him his experience and informed him Hamilton and I have seniority over him. We ended up in fisticuffs...I say 'we,' but Kent came through with nary a bruise on him, though I am confident I landed several blows. I, however, sported a blackened eye and split lip. Lieutenant Howe tried to advocate for me with Captain Parker, but the captain said he did not believe that Kent could have been fighting with me since he bore no marks."

While Charlotte could understand the captain's reluctance to believe that Kent, who was a few inches shorter and many pounds lighter than Martin, would have won a fight between the two of them, it did not make her think any more kindly of the handsome captain to hear of his bias against Collin's former crew. "What happened?"

Martin rubbed his left wrist. "I was seized to the rigging for a watch, then assigned thirty-six hours' continuous watch." He cast his gaze at Hamilton. "When Captain Parker heard Hamilton arguing with Kent over the command of Hamilton's own gun crews, he mastheaded Ham—six hours up on the mainmast top alone."

Even now, Kent could be telling Captain Parker the things Charlotte had said and done. The idea of being tied up in the rigging or being forced to climb up to the masthead and stay there for hours on end, while preferable to whipping, frightened her.

She shook off the fear and straightened her shoulders. She had survived the dandies and bucks who had fawned over her at the ball—some making no pretense about being more interested in her legacy than in her person; she could put up with Kent.

She had no choice.

After supper with William's lieutenants, Julia set about organizing her few personal items—replacing her stationery and writing supplies in her desk, finding a place for her sewing basket where it would be convenient for use but out of William's way.

Each time the bell sounded, her stomach gave a jolt. William had not spoken directly to her since Cook's accident below deck. She wavered between the resolution to apologize to her husband the moment he entered the cabin and the determination to not speak of it until or unless he did.

Setting out her belongings did not take long. She sat down at the desk. Perhaps she should keep a record of her daily activities and observances. She withdrew several sheets of paper and her writing implements and then stared at the blank page for a long while. What would she write of today? *I arrived aboard safely. I mortified William by kissing him in front of his steward. I then kept the steward from his duties and landed him in trouble. And as if that were not enough, by asking the steward to move my trunk and bandboxes into the hold, I infuriated William by causing an accident and the waste of precious foodstuffs.*

She put the blank paper, quill, and inkstand away. She hoped and prayed the voyage would not be all worthy of forgetting, but so far nothing had happened worth remembering. She turned sideways in the chair and surveyed the cabin. William's cabin. The quarters that had been her husband's home for the past few years.

Draping her arm across the back of the chair, she rested her chin on her wrist. Just as on her father's ships, she would never truly belong here; she would be a guest for however long it took to get from one side of the Atlantic to the other. And so far, she had made herself into a most unwelcomed guest.

With a deep sigh, she returned to the sleeping quarters and opened the small crate wedged in beside William's sea chest. The contents must have shifted in transport, because the book she sought was no longer on the top. She found it after a brief search and carried it and a candle to the sofa tucked snugly in the corner beside her desk. She lit the candle in the wall sconce and settled in to read until William returned.

At ten o'clock, halfway through the first watch, Julia roused from a doze at a knock on the door. She considered just pulling her skirt down to cover her feet instead of moving from her reclining position, but she had embarrassed William enough for one day. She sat up and set her book on the desk. "Come in."

Dawling entered and knuckled his forehead. "Evening, mum. Come to see to the com'dore."

"He has not returned yet, Dawling. I am certain he will call for you when he is ready."

"Yes, mum. Is there aught I can do for you?"

"No, thank you." She kept her smile until the door closed behind Dawling. If Dawling had come in expecting William to be here at this time, she could think of only one explanation for his absence. He was avoiding her.

She doused her reading light and crossed to the wardrobe to retrieve a sleeping gown. If William did not want to speak to her, she would make matters easier for him by going to bed and feigning sleep when he finally did make his way back here.

As soon as she entered the sleeping cabin to change, the door to the day cabin opened. Voices—William's and Dawling's—reached her.

"Where is Mrs. Ransome?" William asked.

"Don't rightly know, sir. She were here just moments ago."

"I am here." Julia stepped out into the main room, trying to affect a serene expression until she could gauge William's mood. In the dim light provided by the few candles still lit, his expression was inscrutable.

"Good. That will be all, Dawling."

"Sir?"

William's brows raised.

Dawling knuckled his forehead and backed out the door. "Aye, aye, sir."

William's stance almost immediately changed, like a marionette whose strings went suddenly slack. He unbuttoned his coat and draped it over the back of his desk chair. The neckcloth was the next divestment, followed quickly by his waistcoat.

"Shall I hang those in the wardrobe for you?"

"Dawling will see to everything in the morning." William tugged at his blouse, pulling it free from his trousers. The voluminous shirt floated away from his body but could not hide his fitness and strength.

She longed for him to hold her, as he had not done since before returning to *Alexandra* several days ago. How could just a few days of marriage have changed her so completely from a person who found all the strength she needed within herself to a woman who longed for the shelter of her husband's arms?

"Julia?"

She closed the gap between them. "Yes?"

He reached up and touched her cheek, his thumb wiping away a streak of wetness. "Why the tears?"

Blinking rapidly to clear the tears she had not noticed herself, she wiped her other cheek dry. "I am sorry I disappointed and embarrassed you today."

"I made something of a disaster of your first day aboard. It is I who should be apologizing to you." He let his hand trail down her shoulder, her arm, to her hand—which he raised to his lips. "Please forgive me for not making you feel more welcome."

"Gladly, though I feel there is nothing to forgive. You must work, William. You cannot allow—"

He pressed the fingertips of his free hand to her lips. "Madam"—his voice was low and gruff—"lest you forget, I am a commodore in His Majesty's Royal Navy. I believe I should be the judge of what I can and cannot allow to happen aboard my ship." He slipped his hand around behind her neck and drew her in close for a kiss.

As William's had moments before, Julia's body finally released the tension she'd carried all day. Long and sweet, William's kiss held restoration and peace and a promise tomorrow would be a better day.

He broke the kiss at the sound of raised voices out on deck.

"Do you need to go see about it?"

"If it is urgent, someone will come get me." He released her to snuff the candles, throwing the cabin into almost complete darkness, and then tucked her into his side with his arm wrapped around her. "Tomorrow begins very early. It is time to get some sleep."

Julia wrapped her arms around his waist, making it necessary for him to turn sideways to enter the sleeping cabin, where a few candles yet burned. As soon as she saw the hammock hanging at the far end, she released her embrace.

"Dawling." William grumbled the name with a tone of exasperation. He pulled his arm from her shoulders, stepped over to the hammock, and started untying the ropes holding it up. "He was supposed to have taken this down before you arrived."

"Oh. Then you..." Julia broke off, shyness stopping the rest of her statement.

"Plan to share the fancy box bed I purchased for my wife?" He smiled at her. "'Tis too late to petition for an annulment now, Mrs. Ransome."

"We will stand for no cheekiness from you, Commodore Ransome. And since I travel with no lady's maid, it is your task to see to my buttons." She turned her back to him. The skin between her shoulders tingled at the touch of his fingers. He finished the task with a kiss on the side of her neck.

By the time she pulled her sleeping gown on, William sat on his sea chest, in his breeches and blouse, barefoot, his arms crossed.

"Are you waiting for something?" She reached up and began to hunt amongst the pile of curls at her crown for the pins digging into her scalp.

"I do believe it takes you nearly twice as long to prepare for bed with no maid."

The relief that came with removing the hairpins nearly made Julia giddy. "I shall get faster as I accustom myself to it. Besides"—a large lock of hair fell forward, and she pushed it back, dropping a few pins with the motion—"after today, my hair shall not see a coiffure like this until we reach Jamaica."

William came up off the chest. "Wonderful." He lifted both hands and ran his fingers through her hair, finding two stray pins in the process. "You know I prefer your hair down."

Julia raised her face to meet him for a kiss. His lips found hers, and—

Pounding on the cabin door drew groans from both of them. Though she knew she should probably stay put, Julia pulled on her dressing gown and followed William into the main cabin.

She stopped short, with a gasp. "Collin! What is it? Is Susan—?"

"Susan is well." But Collin still looked grave in the light of the lamp Dawling had brought in.

William dismissed his steward and invited Collin to sit. Collin refused and stood with his feet braced shoulder-width apart, hands clasped behind his back.

Julia sank onto the edge of a nearby armchair.

"I was not sure if I should come—if I should tell you what happened." Collin kept his gaze affixed on the stern windows.

"You are here, which means you decided to tell me." William mirrored Collin's stance.

"Aye." Collin sucked in a deep breath. "Two men came by the house this evening looking for Charlotte."

"For Charlotte?" Julia jumped to her feet to stand beside William, dread increasing.

"Aye, for Charlotte. One of them was a solicitor from London who said he works for Lord Rotheram, and that the marquess has sworn out a charge against Charlotte for assaulting him and causing him, as he said it, 'grievous injury.'"

Julia pressed one hand over her mouth and wrapped the other arm around her waist. "That awful, horrible man."

Both Collin and William turned to stare at her. "What know you of this?" William demanded.

She prayed Charlotte would forgive her for breaking her promise of confidentiality. "The day of your mother's farewell dinner, I was summoned to Brampton Park. Charlotte had been attacked and very nearly strangled to death by Lord Rotheram—Lady Dalrymple's son-in-law. Apparently, when Charlotte did not give in to his seduction, he decided to—take what he wanted. They had been at breakfast, and when the man started to strangle her, Charlotte defended herself with the only weapon she had available—a fork. Lady Dalrymple sent him back to London."

Stony coldness made William look a different man than the one who had been kissing her moments before. "And you kept this from me?"

"Charlotte begged me to keep her confidence, William. It was her story to tell, not mine."

He gave her one last look, as if to say they were not finished speaking of it, and then returned his attention to Collin. "I shall send word to Admiral Glover immediately that we must delay weighing anchor tomorrow—"

"Nay, William. You will do no such thing. I did not tell the solicitor and constable where Charlotte had gone, only that she was no longer living with us. I imagine they will eventually learn that your family home is in Gateacre. But do not worry"—he cut off William's interruption—"I sent word to your brother Philip as soon as I was certain I could get the messenger out without being seen. I will wait a few days and then go to the Fairfaxes' country home myself to retrieve Charlotte, once I have had time to confer with my solicitor. I will see her safely home to her mother and will do whatever is necessary to clear her name and protect her reputation."

Julia began pacing as William and Collin discussed the details of how Collin would handle the situation. Only when exhaustion made her unsteady on her feet did she quit the main cabin and snuff the candles in the sleeping cabin so she could retire. But even as tired as she felt, once she climbed into the box bed and found a comfortable position on the feather tick inside, sleep eluded her.

Nearly an hour later, the sound of the main door alerted her to William's impending appearance. He carried the lamp in with him but put it out almost immediately. He did not, however, climb into the bed.

"William?"

"Aye." He sounded tired, resigned.

"I made a promise to Charlotte. I could not tell you without breaking my word."

"Yes, I understood that when you mentioned it before." He sighed, and she could sense him moving toward the bed. Indeed, the bed's slight swaying with the rhythm of the harbor below stopped with a bump against something solid. "Now it is my turn to extract a promise from you."

"Yes, William."

"Never keep anything that important from me again."

The letter from Charlotte's secret fiancé fluttered before her mind's eye. "I promise, William. I will not keep anything like that from you again."

Chapter Thirteen

Excitement drove Ned from his hammock well before the appointed hour. Food held no interest for him—though he forced himself to eat something. The rest of the lieutenants were not stirring when he left the wardroom. He took the stairs three at a time in his hurry to arrive on the quarterdeck. The crew on the morning watch had just started washing and holystoning the decks, polishing the brightwork, and flemishing any loose lines—activities Ned rarely witnessed, as on a typical day he was not required to be on deck for two more hours.

But this was no typical day. Today, the open sea beckoned and *Alexandra* would answer.

The indigo sky became gray on the eastern horizon. When three bells marked five thirty in the morning, all of the other lieutenants joined him on deck. At six o'clock, the time chosen by William as the most advantageous for wind and tide, Commodore Ransome appeared, accompanied by his wife.

Ned saluted Mrs. Ransome, who graced him with a beautiful, if somewhat tired-looking, smile. At a nod from William, she ascended the steps to the poop deck, from whence she would have a good overview of the activity of weighing anchor and getting under sail.

"Gibson," William called to the senior midshipman.

"Aye, Commodore?" The young man stepped forward.

"Signal the convoy it is time to weigh anchor."

A wide smile split the junior officer's face—and Ned knew his own expression matched the joy in Gibson's demeanor. The lad took the steps to the poop in two bounding leaps, and his shoes pounded the deck in rapid succession as he made his way aft to hoist the appropriate signal flags.

"Matthews." William acknowledged the boatswain's forehead-knuckle with a nod. "Signal all hands."

"Aye, aye, sir." The older, experienced seaman appeared just as excited as young Gibson. Ned rocked up onto his toes as the shrill signal sounded from Matthews's brass whistle—followed by eerie echoing whistles from the twelve cargo ships and *Audacious*.

Hundreds of sailors, marines, and midshipmen scurried around on the decks and up the masts. Energy vibrated through Ned's body; he tapped his hand against the side of his leg.

"Lieutenant Cochrane."

The moment had come. Ned tried to hide his smile as he stepped forward. "Stand by at the capstan."

His order was echoed by midshipmen and warrant officers in charge of the crews at the capstans both above and below deck.

"Heave away." As soon as the first syllable left Ned's lips, the order echoed from the crew captains. As the thick anchor line went tight, *Alexandra* began to move slowly toward its only connection to solid ground.

At a signal from Matthews, Ned turned to William. "Anchor's hove short, sir."

William nodded, his face serious as ever. "Very good. Mr. Cochrane, get us underway to weather the point and then set course."

"Aye, aye, sir." Having completed his calculations in the half hour of solitude he'd had above deck, Ned needed no time to check the wind or decide the bearing. "Loose the heads'ls. Hands aloft to loose the tops'ls."

Men already aloft on the masts scurried out along the yardarms to free the sails from the ropes binding them to the yards. Pristine white canvas billowed out in brilliant contrast against the grayish-pink sky.

Once the sails were loosed, Ned turned to the sailing master. "Master Ingleby, weather the point and then set course south-by-west-quarter-west."

"Weather the point then sou'-by-west-quarter west, aye, sir." Ingleby and his mate took hold of the large double wheel and turned it to steer *Alexandra* south and slightly east. The ever-present harbor breeze caught them from aft, filling the sails and pushing her forward to round the easternmost point of the Isle of Wight and enter the Channel, whence Ingleby would set the southwesterly course.

Now that the hardest work had been accomplished, many men took their attention off their action stations and turned back toward the dockyard for one last look at loved ones who had come down before dawn to bid them a final farewell—though from here in Spithead, without a telescope, none of them had a hope of being able to distinguish individual figures through the distance and gloom of the dawning day.

For the first time on leaving England, a pang of regret struck Ned. He wished...but, no. He cut his gaze toward William, who alone still seemed focused solely on *Alexandra*. Even if Charlotte Ransome were on the quay, she would have been there for her brother, not for Ned.

He needed to put the unattainable young woman out of his thoughts. A distracted officer was a bad officer. And though he had no desire for further promotion, he still wanted to be the best lieutenant he could be. Then perhaps one day he might be worthy of a young woman of half Charlotte Ransome's charms and beauty.

Charlotte still marveled at the sheer strength it had taken to raise *Audacious*'s anchor. The rope—thicker than her leg by half—had groaned as sixty sailors put all their weight against the bars. And another few dozen men had worked the capstan on the deck above, to give them extra leverage.

The motion of the ship beneath her sent strange—wonderful and frightening—sensations up through the soles of her feet that reverberated through her body. She was on a ship under sail—on a man o' war not as a guest for a few hours' tour, but as a member of its crew. She'd dreamed of joining the navy as a small child, leading her to study all of the books her brothers had left behind and procuring more with the small allowance they'd provided for her, but she had always believed it to be nothing more than a dream. After all, as William had told her when she was six years old, women could not join the Royal Navy.

Her only regret was that she wished she could have been above deck when the sails were loosed. What a glorious sight that must have been.

The rolling movement of the floor below her increased. When Julia had talked about finding what she called her sea legs, she had mentioned that keeping her knees bent a little bit helped considerably to account for the unusual motion of the ship. She'd also mentioned feeling nauseated the first few days at sea.

Charlotte hoped she would not be ill. She would never live it down—Kent had a way of finding each boy's weakness and exploiting it.

"Hamilton, Jamison, Martin, Lott, McLellan!" Third Lieutenant Gardiner's voice expanded into the lower gun deck.

"Aye, sir?" they all called back.

"Inform your crews of their watch orders and then dismiss them to breakfast."

"Aye, aye, sir." Charlotte called upon years of singing lessons to try to deepen her voice to match the timbre of the boys in their late teens answering with her. Twelve men—the two gun crews under her charge—gathered nearby, wiping sweat from their faces and necks with kerchiefs. When Charlotte pulled her watch bill from her pocket, the seamen's expressions turned from expectant to suspicious.

Trying to keep her hands from shaking and her voice deep, she let them know they'd be part of the starboard watch, meaning that until the afternoon watch began at noon, they were amongst the idlers.

"With the crew split in two, that means you are on watch and watch," she informed them, though their rolled eyes and cleared throats at this news presented evidence they had no need of being told they would alternate watches with the other half of the crew. "Dismissed."

The sailors grumbled as they cleared the deck.

"Lott, if I didn't know better, I'd think you'd never served in a ship before." Hamilton cuffed Charlotte's shoulder. "Never let the men see you don't know what your orders are. They must trust you implicitly, and part of that is trusting that you are confident in your knowledge of the orders you give them."

"Right."

"So tell me, Mr. Lott…" Hamilton drew himself up to an attention stance. "What are your orders?"

Charlotte came to attention also. "I am to report to Master Carpenter Colberson to begin my lessons in seamanship, sir."

"Very good, Midshipman Lott. McLellan!" Hamilton looked over Charlotte's left shoulder.

A young boy scurried up beside Charlotte. "Aye, sir?"

A twinkle sparkled in Hamilton's blue eyes. "What are your orders?"

McLellan, a lad no older than thirteen, drove his hand into his pocket after his watch bill. "I…I am…" He scrutinized the piece of paper. "I am to report to the master carpenter for seamanship lessons."

Hamilton gave Charlotte a *what did I tell you* glance. "Mr. McLellan, learn your orders before you come on deck. The lieutenants will not be as understanding and kind as I."

"Yes, sir, Ham—I mean Midshipman Hamilton."

A dimple appeared in Hamilton's right cheek. Though he was a year older than Charlotte, that he could not keep his expression stern in reaction to McLellan's eager tone made Charlotte feel much more advanced in years than the senior midshipman.

"You had both best be off then."

Midshipman McLellan—Isaac, he introduced himself—chattered the entire way down to the orlop, the lowest deck of the ship.

"You're late," Colberson said gruffly, by way of greeting. Three other midshipmen stood near the man charged with keeping the ship in good repair.

"Sorry, we got turned around." Charlotte squinted at the others in the dim interior, glad she didn't see any of Kent's mates amongst the other boys. Hopefully the midshipmen who'd come aboard *Audacious* with Captain Parker were on a different rotation for taking daily lessons from each of the masters on the ship. Most midshipmen, including her brothers in their day, complained about having to make the rounds for seamanship lessons on each new ship they served, but Charlotte was glad of it.

Or she was until Colberson set them to breaking down barrels. They could not just smash them. The wood had to be saved, stacked neatly, and stored.

"How can there be this many empty barrels already? We are less than an hour from weighing anchor." Charlotte used her teeth to try to remove a splinter from the palm of her hand.

The carpenter's mate nearest her snorted. "This ain't anything. It takes lots more barrels than this every day to keep the crew watered properlike."

In addition to splinters, Charlotte's hands smarted and stung where blisters had started forming yesterday from heaving the ropes to bring all these barrels aboard.

After what felt like all day, Charlotte and the other midshipmen were dismissed from their carpentry duties. Though what she wanted to do when she returned to the cockpit was lie down for a while, instead she retrieved her sextant, log book, and slate and trudged up to the quarterdeck for the navigation lesson, followed by marking noon.

She squinted against the midmorning sun, leaning her head as far back as she could without losing her balance to take in the spectacular sight of the sails carrying the wind, taking them away from England. The last of the cargo ships preceded them a hundred yards off their larboard bow. Off the stern to starboard, the Isle of Wight was only a hazy lump.

"Will you be joining us, Mr. Lott?"

Lieutenant Howe's stern look drove all excitement from Charlotte, leaving only a residue of fear—fear of discovery, fear of the unknown, fear of what she would find in Jamaica and what she would encounter along the way.

She sat on the empty stool between Martin and another boy who'd served under Collin Yates. At the other end of the semicircle, Kent narrowed his eyes at her. Though it had been the only available seat, her sitting with the mids from Collin's crew served to indicate with whom she'd chosen to align herself.

Sailing Master Bolger gave them their bearing and speed, and Charlotte and the rest of the older midshipmen set about calculating their current position—not that they had much to calculate, as they had not yet traveled far.

Charlotte reveled in the mathematics required to calculate their position. She carefully wrote out each step of her figuring along with the final position, confident in her answer. She hoped that if she proved her adeptness at this task, she might be assigned to help the senior midshipman of her watch with keeping the log board and their dead reckoning on the charts.

A shadow passed over, and she looked up—and almost gasped. Captain Parker walked along behind the row of stools, pausing occasionally to glance over someone's shoulder and shake his head. He paused behind Kent the longest. Kent wore an expression of agonizing concentration—and he did a lot of wiping out and refiguring as he worked. Parker's face grew grimmer, and he turned and made his way back up the line.

"Lott."

She stood, grabbing her slate before it slid to the deck. "Aye, Captain?"

"You do not appear to be working."

"Aye, sir…I mean, no sir. I am finished."

Parker's pale brows shot upward. "Finished?" He extended his hand. "Show me your calculations."

She handed the slate over to him. The numbers fairly danced on the dark gray surface.

The longer he scrutinized her work, the more Charlotte's doubt expanded. Her palms grew damp, and her knees, aching from the effort to absorb the movement of the ship, began to tremble beneath her.

Finally, he handed the small shingle back to her. "You've a neat hand and a good understanding of arithmetic, Lott, but your attitude is bordering on arrogance. See that you check it. That is a quality that can bar you from advancement."

Tears stung the corners of Charlotte's eyes at the reproof, but she fought against them. "Aye, aye, Captain."

"Mr. Howe, see to it that these men know how to calculate the ship's position properly." With those words, Captain Parker turned on his heel and retreated to the starboard side of the quarterdeck.

"Aye, aye, Captain." Howe launched into the lesson on calculus.

Charlotte dropped back onto her stool, fighting the urge to run down to the cockpit, fling herself into her hammock, and weep. Of course, her hammock was not down there but stuffed into the netting lining the sides of the ship along with everyone else's.

However, listening to Howe's lesson soothed her, and soon she found herself lost in his explanation of the advanced arithmetic. He finished the lesson in plenty of time for them to prepare to measure the sun at its zenith and mark noon.

"Lott."

She stopped and received pitying looks from Martin, Hamilton, and a few others.

"Aye, Lieutenant?"

"Your slate." Howe extended his hand toward her very much the same way Parker had.

She handed it over. He chewed his bottom lip as he examined her numbers. If Charlotte had met him socially, she might have considered him a handsome man—his hair and eyes both somewhere between golden and brown, his build pleasantly average. But nothing compared to Ned—to Henry Winchester.

"Who taught you?" Howe returned the slate to her.

"I learned it mostly on my own, sir. I studied every book I could lay my hands to, including mathematics."

Howe inclined his head. "I am duly impressed. And while I do not consider it arrogant of you to say so, you might want to keep that information to yourself." He cast his gaze to the opposite side of the ship where Parker conversed with Second Lieutenant Crump. "Dismissed."

"Aye, aye, sir." Charlotte kept her smile to herself, relieved to know Howe was on her side. She set up her sextant as far away from Kent as she could get and set about measuring the sun's position in the sky, determined she would not be the first to mark noon today.

Granted, she might have to if no one else got it—

"Noon, sir. I mark noon." Hamilton turned toward Parker, cheeks bright red—as Charlotte was coming to realize they usually were whenever Hamilton faced the captain.

Parker's eyes narrowed. "Master Bolger, mark it on the log board and sound noon."

Bolger wiped everything from the slate log board and started the new day's entry with the ship's position, the wind speed, and their heading, while one of his mates rang out four couplets of chimes on the brass bell.

"Mr. Parr, pipe crew to dinner."

The boatswain knuckled his forehead and blew the appropriate signal on his whistle.

An hour later Charlotte returned to the cockpit with the rest of the mids. The smell of so many perspiring bodies in wool uniforms in such a close space nearly made her sick, but she managed to maintain control of her stomach. In fact, it was the first time she had felt at all nauseated. Perhaps coming from a long line of seamen meant she was built of sterner stuff than those who fell prey to seasickness.

She endured quite a bit of jostling before a mug and plate were thrust into her hands. She sat on what was becoming known as the Yates End of the table, but when she looked down at the gray muck on her plate, she was uncertain she would be able to eat. She grabbed her mug instead and took a gulp.

Her stomach heaved, and she retched, turning just in time so that the liquid hit the floor instead of the table. "That is *vile*." Coughing, she wiped her mouth on her sleeve, wishing she had water to rinse the foul taste from her mouth.

Everyone around her laughed. "You act as if you've never had grog, Lott." Hamilton pounded her back until her coughs subsided.

Grog. Rum mixed with water and a bit of lime juice to ward off scurvy. She should have remembered that everyone aboard was allotted a certain amount, half served at dinner, half at supper.

Another mid picked up her mug and sniffed it. "I don't think grog is all that's in here, lads." He set the mug down on the table and leaned forward, dropping his voice. "Smells like turpentine."

Hamilton looked down at the other end of the table where several of Kent's mates leaned together, whispering conspiratorially.

"They're behind this." He started to rise, but Charlotte stayed him by grabbing his arm.

"Nay, do not create trouble on my behalf. No real damage has been done." And real damage would be caused for Hamilton's career if he were to get into a fight with the midshipmen favored by the captain. She stood to take the mug to the slop bucket to empty.

"What have we here?" Kent pushed through a group of boys standing near the end of the table and blocked Charlotte's path.

She sighed. "Let me pass."

He snatched the mug from her hands. "I'll be taking your grog ration today, Lott."

She reached for the mug and opened her mouth to tell him not to drink it—but then she thought better of it and let her hands drop to her sides. She stepped back quickly.

Kent spewed the vile concoction in an arc that sprayed it onto several bystanders. "What is this? You've tried to poison me!"

Charlotte's sense of revenge froze into fear. "I did not. If you had not been greedy and tried to steal what was not rightfully yours, you would have seen I was about to throw it away because it somehow got tainted with turpentine."

Kent's mates who'd been whispering jumped to their feet, wide eyes focused on the mug in Kent's hand. The remaining dozen midshipmen grew deathly silent, all attention now on Charlotte and Kent.

"Turpentine? You tried to poison me with *turpentine*?"

"Turpentine is not poisonous. It is used all the time as a remedy for stomach complaints. It just does not taste very good." Charlotte crossed her arms.

"Aha! You see?" Kent turned to make sure everyone was listening. "She put turpentine in the grog and then made sure I would drink it."

"I did no such thing."

"We shall see about that." Kent grabbed the collar of her coat and dragged her from the cockpit. "We shall see what Captain Parker has to say about a midshipman who tries to poison his superiors."

Chapter Fourteen

William had to admit that the time Dawling worked with the Yateses' staff had not been ill spent. Though still simple, his food was much better prepared. William tucked into his dinner—but paused when he realized Julia had not yet lifted her fork.

"Is the food not to your liking?"

"It looks wonderful. I am...I have no appetite." She gave him a wan smile. "I never do, the first day or two." She glanced over at Dawling, standing behind William. "If I could have a cup of tea and perhaps a piece of bread, that might help settle my stomach."

"Ri' away, missus." Dawling swept her plate from the table and disappeared, returning moments later with the bread and a steaming teapot.

As soon as Julia started picking at the crust of the slab of bread before her, William returned to his own food. It should not surprise him Dawling had taken to having a pot of tea ready at all times. No doubt something he had learned from Collin's cook. Indeed, he appreciated his steward's efforts to make Julia feel comfortable and welcome.

It meant he did not have to do it himself.

Weighing anchor and setting sail this morning had gone well. With Julia standing behind and above him on the poop deck, she had been out of his line of sight. He wished he could put her so easily from his thoughts.

He signaled Dawling to remove his empty plate but hesitated before leaving the table. Julia's pallor and the tightness around her eyes tugged at him. "Would you like to take a stroll on deck? Perhaps some fresh air will be good for you."

"If it is not an imposition, I would enjoy that."

Every time she suggested her presence was a burden or a distraction was like a cutlass to William's gut. What did he have to do to help her understand he had reconciled himself to her presence aboard his ship?

The three lieutenants already returned to deck from their dinner vacated the starboard side of the quarterdeck when William appeared with Julia on his arm. He made a quick scan of the activity on deck. Mostly quiet, as the majority of the crew were still below at their midday meal.

He turned and started back toward the stern. Lieutenants O'Rourke, Campbell, and Eastwick hastily turned away—as if the log board, with only two entries on it, was the most fascinating object they had ever seen.

"Is that your commodore's flag?"

Julia's question startled him. He followed her gaze upward. "Aye. That is my pennant." While the rank of commodore gained him the right to wear the same uniform as a rear admiral—with all the gold braid about the collar, lapel, and cuffs he could bear—the swallow-tailed flag flying high above *Alexandra*'s deck bearing the Cross of St. George was the true insignia of his new rank.

"I am so proud of you." Julia squeezed his arm. "I know I have said it before, but it bears repeating." She swayed, dropped her gaze, and covered her eyes with her free hand.

William paused, prepared to direct her to the side and hold her to keep her from falling overboard. "Are you ill?"

"I should not have leaned my head back for so long. It made me dizzy."

He wanted to put his arms around her, to offer her the promise of shelter and care. But he could not do so with an increasing number of crew milling about. The bell chimed thrice, and the balance of the watch came up onto the deck.

One of the sailing master's mates scurried over, stopping a respectful distance from them. "Master Ingleby and Lieutenant Cochrane's compliments, Com'dore, and they wish to inform you we are now at the coordinates designated for formation."

"Very good. Let them know I will join them presently."

The sailor saluted again and hastened off with William's message.

"Thank you for the airing, William. I shall retire and see if lying down will be a curative for me." Julia dropped her hand from his arm and bent her knees in a perfunctory curtsey.

William bowed before he realized how out of place the social gestures were on a warship—and between husband and wife. He took her hand and started toward the wheelhouse with her. "Send for Mr. Hawthorne if you need him."

"I do not believe that will be necessary."

"He would be glad of the duty of seeing to you. This shall be an otherwise dull voyage for him and his mates." William tried to keep his focus on his wife, but Cochrane and Ingleby's intensity of conversation over the chart made him impatient to join them.

"If I do not feel better after a rest, I will send for Hawthorne."

Both Ned and Ingleby swept their hats off when William and Julia stepped into the shade of the wheelhouse.

"Mrs. Ransome, you are looking lovely today."

"Enough of that, Lieutenant Cochrane." Julia laughed, but the sound came out just as pale as her countenance. She turned to face William, closed her eyes a moment, and then looked at him again. "I shall leave you to your work."

The marine guard at the door to the dining cabin opened it for her.

"Show me the dead reckoning on the chart." William leaned over the small table where Ingleby's chart lay spread open.

Neither Ned nor Ingleby complied with the order. William straightened. Both men had their backs to him, staring at the door where Julia had just disappeared.

He cleared his throat. "As you were, men," he barked.

Ned snapped to first. "Apologies, sir. Is Mrs. Ransome unwell, sir?"

"A touch of seasickness. It shall pass. As we shall pass our formation point if we continue to dither."

"Aye, aye, sir." Cochrane quickly showed him their position on the chart, well within a box William himself had marked on it.

"How far behind is the *Golders Green*?"

"About a hundred yards. We have gained distance on her over the past few hours. She doesn't draught as well as *Alexandra*." Pride laced Ned's voice.

"If there is a hundred yards between each ship, that means our line is more than half a mile long. No. We must close the distances between ships. With twelve cargo ships between us and *Audacious*, that makes the ships in the middle of the line too vulnerable."

"Vulnerable to what, sir?" Ingleby asked. "We are at peace with France and Spain. And their privateers would not dare risk the treaty and attack an English convoy."

William rubbed the bridge of his nose. "I am not so certain. And there are still self-styled pirates throughout these waters, waiting for easy prey. We must be vigilant and keep the line as tight as we can." He glanced over at the master's mate hovering nearby. "Pass word for Lieutenant Jackson and Midshipman Gibson."

The two young men must have been waiting nearby, for the mate returned with them less than a minute later.

"Mr. Jackson, Mr. Gibson, it is time to call the convoy into formation." William wrote out his instructions and handed the slip of paper to the fifth lieutenant. "Signal the other ships to close ranks. No more than twenty yards between ships." Two abreast—six pairs—would be better, but harder to coordinate and control. "Have the ships signal their progress and position up the line, and report to me regularly."

"Aye, aye, sir." Jackson and Gibson chorused before hurrying off to climb up to the poop to start hoisting flags to send William's instructions to the rest of the convoy.

"Mr. Cochrane, have the crew reef tops'ls so *Golders Green* can close with us."

"Aye, aye, sir." Cochrane stepped out from under the overhang of the poop deck above to relay William's orders to the crew, which immediately sprang into action to shorten the uppermost sails.

"Carry on, Master Ingleby."

"Aye, aye, Com'dore."

William glanced at the door to the cabin but returned to the captain's walk along the starboard side of the quarterdeck. Though confident his orders would be carried out to the letter without his presence on deck, he could not bring himself to retreat to his cabin as he would have in the past. Not with Julia there. Not with the crew knowing Julia was there. In the past he would have gone to his cabin at such a time to write in his log book or journal or to deal with other paperwork. But if the crew were to see him retreating to his cabin now, it might appear as if he were shirking his duties.

He stopped amidships and turned to look out over the water, squinting against the glare of the reflected sunlight. He set his feet shoulder-width apart and clasped his hands behind his back, breathing deeply of the briny air.

Nothing like the chop of the waves under him and the open ocean spread out in its diamond grandeur before him.

Lord God, thank You for bestowing upon us the blessing of good wind and fine weather. Speed our journey, and if it be Your will, keep us safe from those who would do us harm, from disease and storm—

"Com'dore, sir?"

"Yes, Dawling?" William did not bother turning around.

"'Tis Mrs. Ransome, sir. She asked me to fetch Doc Hawthorne."

"And did she ask you to send for me as well?"

"For you…no, sir. I…I reckoned you ought to know, sir."

William clenched his teeth and then forced himself to relax. "I suggested Mrs. Ransome send for Hawthorne if she continued to feel unwell. Please do as she bids and fetch the doctor."

"Aye, aye, sir."

William fixed his gaze on the horizon. *Lord, help me find the fortitude necessary to set aside my belief that a ship is no place for a woman. Not even a wife.*

Lieutenant Howe would not make eye contact with Charlotte. She mimicked his stiff stance as they waited in the captain's dining cabin and tried to wipe every trace of anger from her expression.

From the corner of her eye, she could still see Kent's smirk, which made hiding her anger all the harder. She counted the number of chairs around the table. Eight. Two fewer than William's set aboard *Alexandra*. It stood to reason—*Audacious* was a smaller ship, carrying fewer cannons, fewer crew, and fewer officers. And right now, she wished she were counted among *Alexandra*'s larger crew, even with the constant fear of discovery she would live with there. William would never countenance his crew behaving in this manner.

The door between the dining cabin and the day cabin opened and Captain Parker entered, straightening his coat as if he had just donned it. He sat at the head of the table and folded his hands atop it.

Charlotte was again struck by how young the captain appeared. Perhaps that was why his crew was so disorderly. He had not William's experience in handling the crew of a ship this large.

"Speak, Lieutenant."

"Sir. Mr. Kent came to me with a very serious accusation against Mr. Lott. He has accused Mr. Lott of trying to poison him."

Parker's expression did not change. Charlotte's heart pounded an alarm. The captain seemed unsurprised by this statement—unlike Howe's shock at hearing Kent utter the charge against her—which meant Parker had somehow learned of it beforehand.

"Kent, state your case."

"Captain Parker, sir, I returned to the cockpit for dinner. Lott here handed me a mug of grog, and when I drank from it, I could tell it was laced with something meant to fell me."

Charlotte chewed the inside of her bottom lip as Kent spun a tale worthy of the most tortured of souls. Howe's mouth grew tighter, his eyes grimmer, as Kent's fable unfolded. Parker appeared mildly amused.

"Lott."

Charlotte flinched. "Aye, Captain."

"Why did you try to poison Mr. Kent?"

"I did not, sir." She took a breath to continue, but a line from one of William's old letters strayed through her mind. *I would say no more, as it is best to stay one's tongue and speak no unnecessary words before a superior officer, especially when said officer is relatively unknown.* She clamped her lips closed on the story wishing to spill forth.

Parker's pale brows twitched. "Oh? Then, pray tell, what did you do?"

No unnecessary words. "Sir, when I sat down to dinner with the plate and mug that had been handed me, I tasted the grog and realized it had been tainted with turpentine. I was on my way to dispose of it in the slop bucket when Mr. Kent"—*stole* was too incendiary a word to use—"took the mug from my hand and drank before I could warn him."

"Turpentine?"

Howe motioned toward the mug, sitting on the table before him. "It is here, sir, if you wish to test it yourself. I agree with Mr. Lott's determination that someone has indeed added turpentine to the cup, based on odor and taste."

"I am curious as to how you recognized it as turpentine, Lott." Parker made no move toward the grog.

"When I was small, I had a stomach ailment which our apothecary treated with turpentine, sir. I recognized the smell and taste of it almost immediately." No sense in bringing one of the Yates-crew midshipmen into the story.

"Did you put the turpentine into the grog intending to make Mr. Kent ill?"

"No, sir, I did not."

"Where did you get the turpentine, Mr. Lott?"

"As I said, sir, the cup was handed to me with the turpentine already in it." Frustration warred with amusement. This was the same method Philip had always used to try to get information out of her when they were children: circular questions hoping to snare her if she were lying.

Charlotte, Howe, and Kent all jumped at a knock on the door.

"Enter," Parker called.

A man Charlotte had never seen, in civilian clothing, entered.

"Mr. Carberry, do come in." Parker motioned the man to join Charlotte, Howe, and Kent. "Tell me, Carberry, have you prescribed turpentine or had any come up missing from your stores since coming aboard?"

"Yes—aye, sir." The young doctor twisted his watch chain around his bony forefinger. "One of the midshipmen came to me with a stomach ailment and said he'd had turpentine before and it had helped."

"Is that midshipman here now?" Parker looked pointedly at Charlotte.

She stood firm with the confidence of being innocent.

Carberry turned to scrutinize Charlotte and Kent. "No, sir. But he said his name was Lott, sir, if that helps at all."

"He said his name was Lott, but you do not see him standing before you?" Parker's veneer of calm began to crack. He pressed his palms on the table and stood, leaning over it.

"As I said, sir, I do not recognize either of these young men."

"Thank you, doctor. That is all." Parker straightened and waved his hand in dismissal.

The doctor inclined his head and backed out the door, as if leaving a royal chamber.

Parker ran his hands through his light hair. "As there is no clear indication of wrongdoing on Lott's part, I cannot justify whipping or any such severe punishment. But I also cannot have the midshipmen making mischief and setting a bad example for the rest of the crew." Parker's fierce gaze fell on Kent as well as Charlotte. She fought against smiling. "To set an example for the rest of the midshipmen, you are both on continuous watch for the next twenty-four hours."

The dismayed expression that slackened Kent's jaw made the punishment worth whatever toll the loss of sleep and unceasing work would have on Charlotte; for Kent now understood that he did not have the liberty to do or say whatever he wished with no fear of rebuke from the captain.

Parker's expression hardened. "If either of you are found shirking your duties or asleep, I will revise my judgment and you will be subject to corporal punishment. Lott, Howe, you are dismissed. Kent, a word."

"Aye, aye, sir." Charlotte should not have sounded so chipper for someone who had just been meted out punishment for a crime she had not committed. However, the idea that Kent was being punished along with her raised her spirits.

Howe followed her out onto the deck. "Lott, a moment."

"Aye, sir?" She jammed her hat on her head, wishing for one of her wide-brimmed bonnets to block the glaring afternoon sun.

"I heard about your encounter with Kent yesterday. You…you did not put the turpentine in the mug and give it him as retribution, did you?"

"No, sir, I did not."

"You believe the turpentine was intended for you?"

"Aye, sir."

"Do you know who might have done so?" Howe fiddled with the adjustment of his bicorne, crossing his eyes to center the forepoint over his forehead.

Charlotte and the other midshipmen's speculation that Kent's mates had spiked her grog were unfounded and based merely on suspicion born from animosity. "No, sir. I would not hazard a guess as I have no evidence to support any accusation."

Howe drew the corners of his mouth down in a disappointed expression. "Very well. What is your duty this watch?"

"I was idle, sir."

"Report to—" Howe broke off when Hamilton rushed up to them.

"Lieutenant Howe, sir. Message from lead ship. Close ranks and form line. No more than twenty yards between ships, sir."

Howe nodded. "Very good. I'll inform the captain. You"—Howe included Charlotte with his nod—"return to the forecastle and continue to report on movements and orders."

"Aye, aye, sir."

"What happened?" Hamilton asked as soon as they were out of earshot of Howe.

She gave him a condensed version of the story.

"You are being punished for something you did not do?" He growled low in his throat. "Kent will pay."

"Yes, he will, because he is being punished as well. And I believe the captain kept him to rebuke him privately for overstepping his authority." She paused and stopped Hamilton by grabbing his sleeve. "You cannot take revenge on him, Mr. Hamilton. The captain was very angry at what he sees as mischief amongst the midshipmen. If there are any more incidents, I believe the punishments will be much harsher. He has been alerted to Kent's conduct now. Let Kent be the one who brings reproach down on his own head."

Hamilton stared at her a moment. "How can you be so calm about this?"

Charlotte shrugged. "Because nothing will come of my being upset over it." And because she had to do what was necessary to keep from drawing undue attention to herself. "Come on. I cannot be seen shirking my duties. I have no desire to be whipped."

Ned relaxed back in his chair, sated from the simple yet tasty food prepared by Commodore Ransome's steward. He was happy at the second invitation to join his commander and Mrs. Ransome for supper, but he had to wonder at the reasoning behind it. Though William had almost always had the officers in to dine a couple of times each week before, now that Mrs. Ransome was aboard, Ned had expected the invitations to become less—not more—frequent.

Mrs. Ransome sat at the foot of the table, enthralled by a story about one of their many engagements with a French warship in the Mediterranean as spun by O'Rourke. She looked much heartier than earlier this afternoon. Apparently, Dr. Hawthorne, who sat to her left, had been able to find a restorative that worked for her.

"How many times have you made the crossing, Mrs. Commodore?" Midshipman Kennedy asked. Both Kennedy and Gibson, the two most senior midshipmen, were infatuated with the commodore's wife, having had the duty of carrying messages between William and Julia for several days before their wedding. Gibson had worn much the same dewy-eyed expression yesterday as Kennedy wore tonight.

"This is my third sailing from England to Jamaica. I made it the first time when I was not quite ten years old. It was on that voyage that I met Midshipman William Ransome. My mother and I returned to England during the Peace of Amiens, twelve years ago. When renewed hostilities with France seemed imminent, my father sent us back to Jamaica." She let out a sigh. "And I was happy to go. Jamaica had become my home, you see. And...well, suffice it to say events conspired during my stay in England that made me long for home."

When Mrs. Ransome stole a glance down the table at the commodore, Ned thought he understood it. And he was certain he was not the only one at the table who had heard the rumor that William and Julia had been intended for each other but that William had walked away.

"And why did you return to England this time?" Kennedy persisted.

"My father believed the war to be coming to an end, so he came to Jamaica to retrieve my mother, to bring her back to England for good. But she died just before he made port. I had intended to go with them to help my mother get settled in before I returned to Jamaica to continue running the sugar plantation. I had planned to stay only a few months, but once I was in Portsmouth, I found I could not leave my father so readily, so I stayed on." She looked down the table again, this time with a twinkle in her eyes and dimples in her cheeks. "I believe the timing worked out rather well, do not you, Commodore Ransome?"

William wore the same bored, emotionless expression as always. "Aye, Mrs. Ransome. I would say the timing seemed providential."

If Ned knew no more about Julia Ransome than the fact that she did not let her husband's seeming disinterest in everything bother her, he would mark her down as the perfect wife for the commodore. But having heard much more about her over the years through the Royal Navy's rumor mill, he envied William for the blessing of a wife who knew and understood naval life in a way the majority of women would not. Ned's own mother and sister did not begin to understand the power the sea had over him, drawing him to the shore just to hear the waves rushing against the sand.

During this last visit, to the farm owned by his sister Becky's new husband, she and Mother could not understand his disinterest in the way the crops lay in the fields or the husbandry of the animals. Nor could they fathom the bound-up, closed-in feeling he tried to express after several days there. Surrounded by fields and trees and low hills, they were happier than they had ever been in their small, rented rooms in Plymouth. And Ned was happy for them. But he'd been happier for himself the moment he'd stepped on the ship that transported him from Plymouth to Portsmouth. Hanging his hammock in their wardroom, though it afforded him no privacy whatsoever, had been more refreshing to him than the early morning strolls through the fields Becky and Mother had taken to.

"What of you, Lieutenant Cochrane?"

Mrs. Ransome's voice broke through his musings. "Ma'am?"

"Have you ever been to the Caribbean?"

"No, ma'am. I have never been south of the Mediterranean or west of Ireland."

"Oh, but you have been south of the Mediterranean," O'Rourke contradicted. "You told me you once made landfall in Tripoli. That is most definitely south of the Mediterranean."

Aye, a mistake that would haunt Ned for the rest of his life. "'Twas nearly ten years ago, and not something I think of often." Except when the memories of the dying men's screams invaded his sleep.

William gazed at him over his steepled fingers. Ned looked away rather than face the knowledge in his commander's eyes. William knew the facts of the tragedy and Ned's involvement, but only to the point of Ned's being cleared of any implication of wrongdoing by his captain at the time. He did not know that Ned had not been so lenient with himself.

"Ah, Tripoli. Then you must be well versed in dealing with pirates, Mr. Cochrane." A hint of a smile danced around Julia's lips.

"Pirates—no. Our encounter was with a French ship, not pirates." His shoulders and neck tensed as memories started breaking loose of his tight blockade of them. "Wh–what do you look forward to the most about returning to Jamaica, Mrs. Ransome?"

Her eyes took on a dreamy quality, and Ned tried to focus on that instead of the turmoil building in the back of his mind.

"My reunion with friends. I have been away so long, I fear they will have learned they can do quite nicely on their own without me."

Ned kept his gaze trained on Julia as she talked about the people she'd left behind in Jamaica, but his focus wandered to a newly made lieutenant in command of a small, captured prize vessel. He'd thought to make a name for himself and capture a more heavily armed French frigate by pretending to be part of the detachment of American ships docked in the harbor off Tripoli just after the Americans had taken the city by force from the Barbary pirates.

They had been kind enough to let Ned lead a party ashore to resupply with fresh water—and it had been they who'd told him of the French frigate sighted just outside the bay. The timing had seemed providential, to use William's description.

But it had been naive and arrogant and should have cost Ned his commission—except that one of his men who managed to make it back from the ill-fated boarding attempt found a packet of dispatches the frigate had been transporting. The intelligence gleaned from those letters, along with the tale of the harrowing escape told by what remained of the crew, earned Ned a commendation rather than the condemnation he'd deserved for the two sailors he sacrificed in the engagement—watching them be run through on the deck of the French ship even as he ordered his helmsman to tack and flee.

No. He would not—could not relive that again. He had told William the truth of the matter years ago; and although he appreciated the trust and level of responsibility William lavished on him, he could take comfort in the idea that William would make the hard decisions, especially when it came to sending men to certain death.

Ned would resign before being faced with that responsibility again.

Charlotte covered her yawn with the back of her hand. The darkest hours of the night still stretched before her. The reflection of moon and stars off the undulating water beyond the beakhead lulled her into a stupor. Even after dancing until dawn at the ball Lady Dalrymple held for her, Charlotte had not been this exhausted. Of course, last week she had been able to sleep the morning away after staying up all night. On *Audacious*, she would have one four-hour watch to sleep before returning to duty

"Mr. Kent, careful what you're doing there!" Lieutenant Gardiner's voice sliced through the thick night air.

Charlotte smiled. She had found Kent nodding off once already. He'd dared her to tell Wallis, the fourth lieutenant, who had been on watch at the time. Charlotte had merely shrugged and gone about her business. If Kent could not stay awake before midnight, he would surely fall asleep sometime during the early morning hours.

She turned at the sound of footfalls on the deck behind her, straightened, and saluted the third lieutenant.

"Mr. Lott, I assume since I have not heard from you that our position relative to the *Buzzard* is good?"

"Aye, Lieutenant Gardiner. Though it is hard to tell in the dark, I believe we have not gained on it significantly."

Gardiner nodded. "Very good." He looked her up and down. "You seem to be faring better than your mate Kent. How long have you been on duty now?"

"Since just after one thirty this afternoon, sir. About twelve hours."

"On my first ship, the captain believed in meting out punishment that was swift and rather brutal. I do not know which is worse: the beating when it is happening or a long, drawn-out continuous watch. At least the beating is soon over with. But," he sighed and rubbed his backside, "the effects do linger several days."

He turned and leaned against the bulwark. "It is unfortunate that you should be punished for something you did not do."

Charlotte blinked a few times, unsure she'd heard him correctly. "Sir?"

"It is my understanding that Kent fabricated the charges against you as revenge for your standing up to him in an altercation your first day aboard. Is that not so?"

Though less that forty-eight hours had passed since she first stepped foot on *Audacious*, no one could accuse her of being a slow learner. "It was a misunderstanding, sir. A simple misunderstanding."

Gardiner tapped the side of his nose with his forefinger and then pointed at her. "A wise answer, Mr. Lott. Now, as I know Mr. Kent has already found occasion to nod off during his time on deck, it is only fair that you should have a few moments' relief to refresh yourself. You have ten minutes, Mr. Lott. Make the most of them." He handed her his lantern.

"Thank you, sir," Charlotte called, already dashing toward the forward companion stairs.

The cockpit reverberated with the snores of her fellow midshipmen as she cautiously made her way through the common area. At her stall—made only semiprivate by two canvas curtains along the sides—she dug out a washrag from her sea chest and dipped it into the nearby bucket of seawater provided for washing.

She continued on through the cockpit to the roundhouse, just under the masthead in the bow of the ship. Fortunately, the privy was vacant. She looped the piece of rope hanging from the door around the peg in the wall to keep any of the boys from walking in on her.

With the ocean visible through the open grating below her feet, Charlotte shucked her uniform and unwrapped the muslin banding from her chest for the first time since she'd left Collin and Susan's house. After making proper use of the facility and bathing as much of the sweat and grime from her body as she could, she rewrapped her chest and dressed.

Uncertain of how much time had passed, she hastily returned her washrag to her area, took a drink of water from the dipper in the barrel, and, returning only to grab the lantern off the table, hurried back up on deck.

"Efficient, Mr. Lott. You returned with a few minutes to spare." Gardiner took the lantern from her. "Continue as midshipman of the forecastle. Report if there is any signal from the leading ship or if any change in position becomes necessary."

"Aye, aye, sir." It took her eyes a few minutes to readjust to the darkness after Gardiner retreated to the stern quarter of the ship with the lantern. She stood, hands clasped behind her back, making certain she did not allow herself to become drowsy by looking at one point too long. She studied the sky, picking out as many constellations as she could name. She challenged herself to try to make out as many details of the supply ship ahead of them as she could. She reviewed the names of the sails and riggings in her head.

Each half hour, the bell sounded, counting down the time remaining of her punishment. Four o'clock came with the sound of eight bells, which meant a brief flurry of activity as the crew on middle watch left the deck and the morning watch took over. Cook lit the fires in the large stove two decks below—Charlotte could smell the smoke from the chimney just behind her.

The boatswain greeted her as he toured the decks to see what his mates and the crew assigned to him would need to do today. "All's well, Mr. Lott?"

"All is well, Mr. Parr." Her voice sounded nearly as deep and gravelly as his.

An hour later, at two bells, the boatswain set the crew to holystoning and washing the deck. In the gray, predawn light, Charlotte watched as the men rubbed large pumice stones the size of Bibles across the deck to clean it while others came behind them with water to rinse it. It looked like onerous work, and she was thankful she did not have to do it. But it was the most interesting thing that had happened on deck since lights-out at eight o'clock last night.

As the morning dragged on, the time between bells seemed to stretch from the standard half hour to an hour…two…three. Charlotte stayed on duty in the forecastle, carrying messages from one officer to another on opposite ends of the ship just to keep herself awake. A high-pitched ringing settled into her ears, and her mouth felt as though she'd been licking knitting wool.

A yawn crested, but she clamped her lips shut to stifle it.

"Storm building to the northeast." Wallis, the fourth lieutenant, raised his telescope to look behind the ship to starboard. "Wind's picking up as well. We may be in for a rough day."

Charlotte squinted her gritty, burning eyes, trying to focus her mind on the activity at *Buzzard*'s stern a score of yards ahead. Several small flags of different colors and patterns fluttered in the wind.

With leaden arms, she raised her own small scope. "Message from lead ship."

Wallis—and Martin, who'd come on duty a few hours ago as midshipman of the forecastle—whipped around. All three translated the message at the same time.

"Lott, my compliments to the captain." Wallis then turned to Martin. "Respond 'message received.'"

Charlotte collapsed her telescope and tucked it into her coat pocket. She mustered all her energy reserves and hastened to the aft end of the ship. Last time she'd carried a message to one of the officers, Captain Parker had been on the quarterdeck—but not now. She wove her way through sailors and officers and into the shade of the wheelhouse.

The marine guard knocked on the door to the big cabin for her. The captain's steward opened it. "Cap'n's occupied. Can't see anyone at the present."

"This is urgent—orders from lead ship." She repeated the message over and over in her mind so she would not forget it, even though she'd written it in her log book. She did not want to have to pull that out and have the captain doubt her competency.

The steward quirked a brow as if he did not believe her, but after a moment he stepped aside to admit her entrance.

Charlotte hurried in—but drew up short at the sight of Kent and Lieutenant Crump standing at the table as if about to pull out the chairs they stood behind and feast…on her.

"Ah, Mr. Lott." Parker slouched in his chair in much the same manner as she'd seen several of the young dandies in Portsmouth do.

"Captain Parker, sir, Lieutenant Wallis's compliments—"

"Tell me, Lott, was it not just yesterday when both you and Mr.

Kent agreed to serving out your punishment on twenty-four hours' continuous watch?"

"Aye, sir." She itched to tell him the message before it got lost in her muzzy head.

"And did I or did I not warn both of you that if you were caught sleeping on watch, you would be beaten?" Parker scraped at a spot on the table with his thumbnail as if bored by this conversation.

"Aye, sir, you did." The ringing in Charlotte's ears intensified, now throbbing along with her pounding heart. Even though she had done nothing wrong, she could not trust Kent, especially since he knew she had caught *him* asleep on duty.

Captain Parker released a long sigh. "Lieutenant Crump and Mr. Kent have just reported to me that over the past hour, they witnessed you sleeping in the forecastle, protected by another midshipman."

Bile rose in the back of Charlotte's throat. She never suspected Kent would stoop so low—or that he would be able to convince the second lieutenant to go along with him. She fisted her hands at her sides, digging her blunt nails into her rough palms.

Parker looked up when Charlotte made no response. "Well? How do you respond to this accusation?"

"Sir, my only response can be the truth. I have not been sleeping on duty. If they believe they saw me sleeping within the last hour, they are mistaken. I believe you yourself have seen me moving about the ship, passing messages regarding our position relative to the ship off our bow to the officers and sailing master." She longed for a cup of tea to soothe both her throat and her nerves—and then a long sleep in a soft, not-moving bed. Anger and exhaustion were the only things keeping at bay regret over her decision to make this voyage.

The corners of Parker's mouth tightened. "Show me your log book, Lott."

Charlotte pulled it out and walked to the head of the table to hand it to him. "Sir, the reason I came to your cabin—"

He quelled her with a sharp look. He opened the small journal and flipped the pages until he found the final few entries. "You have three entries for the past hour, including—" He looked up. "How long ago did this order from lead ship come in?"

How long had she been standing here enduring false accusations? "About five minutes ago, sir. That is why I came to see you. Commodore Ransome orders us to alter course to compensate for the increased northwesterly wind and the approaching storm."

Parker stood and handed the log book back to Charlotte. "My compliments to Lieutenant Howe, and have him ready the crew to alter course."

"Aye, aye, sir." She escaped the cabin without a glance at her adversaries.

The first lieutenant gave her an expectant glance when she stepped out into the sunlight on the quarterdeck.

"Sir, Captain Parker's compliments, and ready the crew to alter course." She opened her log book to give him the heading that had come in William's message, as the numbers and compass directions had become inexorably scrambled in her head.

As soon as he handed the small book back to her, Charlotte scrambled off to her station in the forecastle, climbing halfway up the shroud to supervise the crew responsible for the fore topsail as Howe gave the "all hands" order followed immediately by the boatswain's whistle. She had to listen carefully amongst all of the orders being relayed from one end of the ship to the other for any regarding her sail.

Finally, it came. "Reef tops'l," she yelled, putting all of her strength into her voice to make it carry to the men above her on the yard. She tightened her hold on the ropes and eyed the burgeoning sail carefully as the men shortened the sail to the next reefband, but the sailors were well trained and the sail rigged correctly, putting the canvas in no danger of damage.

Half an hour passed, along with several additional changes and alterations in the positioning and reefing of the sails. Charlotte's muscles burned from her tight grip on the rope shroud, and her feet cramped in her hobnail shoes from the pressure of the ropes against her arches.

"Aloft there, lay off!"

She almost cried with relief. Before passing along the order, she started her descent from the shroud, more concerned about getting back down to the flat surface of the deck than the increased tossing of the ship. The wind had a chill bite to it, a welcome relief from the sun's heat.

Leaping from the shroud to the deck only increased the pain in her feet. She needed to take off her shoes and rub away the knots—but before she could find a place to sit and do so, young Isaac McLellan rushed up onto the forecastle.

"Captain wants to see you in his cabin, Charlie, and you too, Mr. Martin. Oh, and you as well, Lieutenant Wallis, sir."

Charlotte exchanged a glance with Martin. The senior midshipman shrugged. She had not had a chance to tell him what had happened when she reported the course correction to Parker.

Rushing to the other end of the ship helped ease the cramping in Charlotte's feet, yet she could not quell the fear that she hurried along to her own demise. She'd read that when sailors were flogged, they had to remove their shirts. For a midshipman, the boatswain's rattan was applied to the backside of the wrongdoer; so she was not certain if the recipient of the punishment remained fully clothed. If the captain had decided to believe Kent and Lieutenant Crump instead of her and she was about to be whipped, she might be only minutes away from being revealed for a trespasser.

Her fear increased when she entered the cabin to find all of the lieutenants, warrant officers, and senior midshipmen—including Kent—standing in a tight crowd around the captain's dining table.

She prayed William would be understanding when Captain Parker turned her over once her masquerade was revealed.

The division between the officers of *Audacious* could not be clearer. On the aftside of the athwartships table stood Lieutenants Crump and Wallis along with Kent and his mates; on the foreside, Lieutenants Howe, Gardiner, and Duncan, with Hamilton, Martin, and two other senior midshipmen formerly of Collin's crew. Among the last to arrive, Charlotte necessarily stood with the latter group—though she would have stood with them anyway, if given a choice.

The sailing master came in, and the captain's steward left the cabin, closing the door behind him. Charlotte set her feet wider apart as the rolling motion of the ship increased, along with the wind outside. She had not known until now that Lieutenant Wallis was part of Parker's crew and not Collin's. He had always been genial with her.

"It has come to my attention that we have a problem aboard this ship." Parker swept his gaze across the assemblage.

Charlotte stared at the second button of his waistcoat to keep from seeing the accusation she knew would be in his eyes when he looked at her.

"There seems to be a misconception that I favor the officers and sailors who were with me before we came to *Audacious*. Let me assure you, this is not the case." Parker clasped his hands behind his back and began pacing at his end of the table. "It does not matter if you served on *Audacious* under Captain Yates or if you came with me from *Lark* or if you never served either captain. We will be respecters of rank and order on this ship."

Charlotte heard and felt the shuffling and fidgeting of the men surrounding her, but she did not dare look at any of them.

"Mr. Hamilton."

Beside her, Ham flinched. "Aye, Captain?"

"I understand you are the senior midshipman, yet you have abdicated your position of captain of the cockpit to someone with a year's less experience?"

"I—"

The question put Ham in an untenable position. If he said yes, not only would he be lying, but he would also be destroying any chance of a good report and recommendation from Parker at the end of this posting. If he said no, he would be accusing Kent of usurping his power. Charlotte wished she could reach out and squeeze his hand to let him know she understood his dilemma.

"Sir," Hamilton started again, "you mentioned the division you have noticed amongst the officers. This is true of the midshipmen as well. There has been a bit of a struggle establishing the order of seniority in the cockpit as we have felt as if there was a division between the two groups. I have been leading one; Mr. Kent has been leading the other."

And terrorizing anyone who gets in his way. Charlotte clenched her teeth to keep a smirk from betraying her thoughts. Her fate had not yet been pronounced, and she did not want to draw any attention to herself.

"This will end as of now." Parker stopped pacing. "Mr. Martin."

As Hamilton had, Martin flinched when the captain spoke his name. "Aye, sir?" the eighteen-year-old's voice cracked.

"You are next in line of seniority behind Mr. Hamilton?"

"Aye, sir."

"Very well. Henceforth, the midshipmen will be split into three watches rather than two. Mr. Hamilton, Mr. Martin, and Mr. Kent will be captains of the watches. With eighteen midshipmen aboard, that means each of you will have five mids assigned to your watch. At least two of them must be from the other ship's crew. Lieutenant Howe and Lieutenant Crump will oversee the choosing of the watches.

The crew will remain on watch and watch. That way, with the mids in three watches and the crew in two, the midshipmen will not always be on duty at the same time as the men in their gun crews, reducing opportunities for favoritism or collusion in troublemaking." He paused and looked around the group again. "Mr. Lott."

Charlotte's heart nearly burst out of her chest. The ringing in her ears increased, and her knees almost buckled. "Aye, Captain?"

"I cannot help but wonder what it is you've done that has drawn such animosity toward you from Mr. Kent. It is vital that all the members of a ship's crew, especially her officers, learn to work well together. Therefore, you will be assigned to Mr. Kent's watch."

Being flogged 'round the fleet, exposed as a girl, and then sent to William in disgrace would be preferable to being at Kent's mercy. The announcement of her true identity was on the tip of her tongue when Parker spoke again.

"Lieutenant Howe, Mr. Kent's watch will be under your command. Hamilton, you will report to Lieutenant Crump; and Martin, you will report to Lieutenant Gardiner."

More shuffling and fidgeting.

"If any accusations are leveled against a midshipman of the *Lark* crew by someone of the *Audacious* crew, or the converse, and they are deemed to be frivolous, petty, embellished, or false, punishment will be swift and severe for the accuser. And you will observe the chain of command and take any problems to the lieutenant of your watch."

Charlotte's head swam. This was not how she'd imagined her third day as a midshipman going. On Kent's watch? As if life at sea weren't miserable enough.

"Those are my orders, and I expect them to be followed rigorously. Do you understand?"

"Aye, sir," everyone chorused together.

"Dismissed—except for Mr. Lott, Mr. Kent, and Lieutenants Howe, Crump, Gardiner, and Wallis. Lieutenant Duncan, you have command until you are relieved."

"Aye, sir." The young fifth lieutenant saluted, and his expression revealed his relief at being dismissed before he turned and escaped the cabin.

Charlotte swallowed hard to keep her stomach from releasing its contents. Hamilton bumped her shoulder on his way past, and she took it as a sign of his sympathy and support.

As soon as the door closed behind Lieutenant Duncan, Howe moved to stand at the foot of the table, leaving Charlotte standing with Gardiner across from Kent, Crump, and Wallis.

"Lieutenant Crump, before we were interrupted by Mr. Lott's arrival with the orders from the commodore, I believe you and Mr. Kent were telling me of how you witnessed Mr. Lott asleep on duty."

Kent and Crump exchanged shifty glances. Neither spoke, but both paled significantly.

"Mr. Gardiner, I believe you had the middle watch last night, did you not?"

"Aye, Captain." Gardiner seemed uncomfortable but not concerned.

"Did you witness either Mr. Lott or Mr. Kent asleep on duty?"

Gardiner flicked his gaze across the table and then back at the captain. "Sir, I—I discovered Mr. Kent about to fall asleep on two occasions—dozing off, as it were—but never fully asleep."

"And Mr. Lott?"

"Always alert from what I could tell. I relieved him of duty just after three bells. He went belowdecks to refresh himself and returned in less than the allotted ten minutes."

"Thank you, Mr. Gardiner. You are dismissed."

Gardiner inclined his head and left the cabin. Charlotte had never felt so alone as she did now.

"Mr. Wallis, you were on duty in the forecastle during the forenoon watch, correct?"

"Aye, Captain." Wallis, tall and slender, with an abundance of curly, dark hair, could not be much older than Hamilton and Martin.

"Did you have occasion to witness Mr. Lott sleeping in the forecastle, being watched over by another midshipman to keep him from being caught?"

Wallis's mouth hinted at a smile, but it vanished as quickly as it appeared. "No, sir. Mr. Lott was never still long enough to have fallen asleep. He was running messages between the forecastle and the quarterdeck. He was also the one who noticed the ship ahead signaling us with the commodore's orders."

"Thank you, Mr. Wallis. You are dismissed."

Charlotte kept her eyes affixed on a point over Parker's left shoulder as Wallis hastened out of the cabin.

Parker pulled out his chair and slumped into it, head propped in his hand. "Lieutenant Crump, how came you to the belief that Mr. Lott was sleeping on duty this morning?"

Crump—a small man with a pinched face, large nose, and bulging eyes that reminded Charlotte of Lady Fairfax's prized pug dog—cleared his throat. "Well, I…I…" His mouth opened and closed several times before he collected his thoughts. "Sir, what happened is that Mr. Kent came to me to tell me he had observed Mr. Lott asleep in the forecastle. As I know it is a serious offense to be asleep on duty, I deemed it proper to inform you, sir, of the offense."

"But you did not take the step of going to the forecastle to see this sleeping midshipman for yourself?" Parker sounded and looked more and more exasperated with each passing moment. William would never have shown his frustration the way Parker did. No wonder Parker was having so much trouble with his officers.

"N-no, sir, I did not. Haste…I thought haste was in order. And I had no reason to doubt Mr. Kent's veracity. We have served together four years, sir, as you will recall."

Parker's eyes narrowed. "Aye, I do recall. And it is for that reason I am giving you and Mr. Kent a chance to rethink what you may have seen—or not seen—on deck this morning." He watched them for a long moment. "Mr. Kent, what say you? Did you see Mr. Lott asleep on deck during the forenoon watch?"

Kent's face was as pale as his silver-blond hair. "Sir, I believe… I mean, that is…I fear I might have been mistaken in what I saw. I thought I saw something that looked like a person in a prone position on the deck. However, it may have merely been a shadow on a pile of rope I saw, sir."

Parker rubbed his jaw. "I wondered if that might not be what you had seen. However, I cannot let it pass that you brought a false accusation against one of your mates before me. Mr. Kent, you will serve an additional twelve hours' continuous watch at the end of your original twenty-four hours. And you will report to Mr. Crump and the lieutenant of the watch at the sounding of each hour of each watch. Understood?"

"Aye, sir." Kent and Crump looked none-too-happy about the punishment. Charlotte's outlook began to improve.

"All of you are dismissed. Lott, you remain on continuous watch until three bells of the afternoon watch."

"Aye, aye, sir." Charlotte could not leave the captain's cabin fast enough.

When she stepped out into the wheelhouse, Hamilton gave her a questioning look. She gave him a slight smile as she hurried past, wanting to put some distance between herself and Kent. With an added twelve hours of continuous watch, he was bound to be furious. And she held no illusions that he would learn from his mistakes and leave her alone. No, he would find more ways to make her life aboard *Audacious* miserable. From now on, she could never let her guard down.

The idea of being under Kent's command frightened her, but she had a means of escape if it got too bad. She could always reveal her identity, be sent to William's ship, and travel in relative comfort on *Alexandra* as a guest—or, rather, the condemned awaiting execution. Right now, though, the thought of facing William and owning up to her subterfuge and lies filled her with more dread than that of being the recipient of Kent's maliciousness.

She had a means of escape if she needed it. But she hoped she would not.

William snapped the spyglass closed and tossed it to the midshipman hovering nearby. He'd been anxious to keep his ship and crew from being decommissioned, but he had not realized how frustrating commanding a fleet of merchant ships could be. They took orders in their own time and could not keep their ships on the heading he commanded. Even with the course correction an hour ago, the convoy ships were once again stretched too far apart.

The wind blew harder, and *Alexandra* responded by digging into the waves and surging forward. Not so the merchant ship behind her.

He ground his back teeth together. Until this storm blew itself out, he'd have to slow *Alexandra* down to allow the other ships to come in closer. Though he did not expect to meet with any hostile ships, predators were always a risk, especially to a supply convoy as tempting a target as this one made. He crossed the poop deck to tell Cochrane to signal all hands to reef the sails again, but when he looked down on the quarterdeck, the sight he saw shredded the last ounce of his reserve.

On the starboard side of the quarterdeck—*his* part of the deck—stood Cochrane and Julia. Though she'd bound her hair in a single, long plait, loose wisps blew around her face. She pushed them back even as she looked up at Ned and laughed at whatever he was saying. She spoke a few words, and then Ned touched the forepoint of his hat and walked away.

William barely touched the steps on the way down to the quarterdeck. The crew parted before him and backed away. He paid them no mind. He would not have breaches in discipline on his ship.

A tiny voice in the back of his head told him he was overreacting, but he doused it and clamped his hand around Julia's elbow.

"William..." Her expression of delight quickly changed to concern. "Is something wrong?"

"I would see you in my cabin." He propelled her along beside him, pausing once they reached the wheelhouse. "Mr. Cochrane, reef topsails."

He did not stay to observe Cochrane's acknowledgment, and the dining cabin door slammed on Cochrane's shouted commands.

As soon as they reached the day cabin, he released his wife's arm—and experienced a twinge of guilt when she rubbed it. Here, in the relative silence and privacy of their quarters, his initial reaction to seeing her with Ned seemed unwarranted.

"You should not be on deck in this heavy weather."

She turned stormy green eyes on him. He waited for her to release the full measure of the temper he knew she possessed. Her whole body tensed. But instead of lashing out at him, instead of rebuking him for his highhanded treatment of her, she closed her eyes and took a few deep, ragged breaths.

The muscles in his shoulders and neck ached for some kind of release. "Have you nothing to say to me?"

She opened her eyes with what appeared to be great effort. "I am sorry if my need for fresh air came at an inopportune time, William. I assure you, I will gauge the wind more carefully before venturing out again."

He dropped into his desk chair and covered his face with his hands. "Stop. Please."

Julia wrapped her arms around her middle. "Stop what?"

"Stop apologizing. Stop agreeing with everything I say to you." Flinging his arms wide, he stood. "Stop being the imitation of a submissive wife and be...be..." Frustration saturated his brain so fully he could not think straight.

"Be what?"

"Be...*you*. Be Julia Witherington. Be the woman who defied her relatives and escaped from their captivity. Be the woman who manages her father's sugar plantation. Be the woman who convinced him to release his slaves. Be the woman who dressed in her brother's clothes and climbed the shrouds to the foremast top just to see a French ship."

"I cannot. That is not the kind of wife you need. My father taught me long ago that a ship's captain must be seen to have a disciplined, well-behaved family if he expects the men under his command to respect him. If I keep my thoughts to myself and do not disagree with you, it is only out of respect for your position and a desire to see you successful in your command."

William thrust his fingers through his hair and turned to stare out the stern windows at the choppy sea behind them. At least now he understood why she behaved this way. "But here, in our cabin, I need you to speak your mind. I need you to be frank and forthright. I have enough problems and frustrations to contend with as commander of this vessel. I need you to react when I ignominiously drag you from the quarterdeck in front of all my officers."

When she did not reply, he looked around at her.

She moved closer. "I cannot believe you embarrassed me that way before all of your officers, William." Her chin quivered with the effort to keep a smile from her lips.

"You were distracting Lieutenant Cochrane from his work."

"Nay, husband. He came to me to suggest I should not be on deck in such heavy weather. I was about to take his advice and return to the cabin when you so unceremoniously came to retrieve me." She took another step closer.

He settled his hands on her shoulders. "That is the woman I married. I began to wonder if I had accidentally left her behind in Portsmouth and picked up a stowaway in her place."

"Most men would be pleased with a wife who agreed with everything they said."

"Then it is well I am not like most men." He gave her shoulders a squeeze before releasing her and turning to again stare out the windows.

Julia sat on the bench built into the stern wall of the cabin below the windows. "I can see you've need to vent your spleen about something other than seeing me on deck."

William sat down beside her and spilled his worries about the convoy, his concern that the storm could give a predator the chance to steal the supplies, and his frustration over having to slow *Alexandra* to compensate for the more poorly rigged and handled supply ships.

Julia had no advice or insights to offer he had not already thought of, but the simple act of speaking everything aloud to her brought him relief unlike anything he had ever experienced in his career.

Perhaps having a woman aboard was not as bad as he'd originally feared.

Chapter Seventeen

As soon as he saw Commodore Ransome emerge from the wheel house, Ned left the quarterdeck and headed to the forecastle. He was not certain if his own interaction with Mrs. Ransome had played into the commodore's reaction earlier, but he did not want to exacerbate the situation further.

William's treatment of his wife surprised Ned. He'd never seen the commodore betray such emotion in front of the crew before. He smiled. Indeed, being married was changing William Ransome.

Kennedy, midshipman of the forecastle, touched the brim of his hat when he saw Ned. "Sir."

Ned returned the salute, turned, and braced himself against the wave breaching the starboard bow, spraying everyone in the forward part of the ship. "Wind's freshening."

"Aye, sir." Kennedy glanced over his right shoulder. "Storm'll be on us soon."

Ned's stomach lurched along with the bow of the ship. With a wind this strong leading it, this would be no typical rainstorm—quickly begun and quickly ended. He turned again to keep from taking another wave in the face.

"Take all due precautions, Mr. Kennedy."

"Aye, aye, sir."

Ned hurried aft. William wasn't on the quarterdeck, so Ned climbed up to the poop where, as he expected, William stood at the stern bulwark studying the storm through his telescope.

"Mr. Cochrane, call all hands to strike topgallant masts and yards. Mr. Gibson, signal fleet to do the same."

"Aye, aye, Commodore," both answered. Ned leapt down the steps to the quarterdeck and called for the boatswain. Matthews immediately appeared at his elbow. Most of the lieutenants, senior midshipmen, and warrant officers were already on deck, anticipating the orders to come.

"All hands to strike topgallant masts and yards!" Ned's voice, followed by Matthews's and the boatswain's mates' whistles created a flurry of activity—like a swarm of rats escaping a sinking ship—as sailors boiled up onto the deck through the companionways. *Alexandra* plunged and reared over the increasing waves, and Ned thanked God he no longer had to climb up in the shrouds like the midshipmen supervising the sailors, who put their lives in jeopardy to lower the topmost parts of the masts and sails.

Less than fifteen minutes later, the sails, yardarms, and highest sections of each of the three perpendicular masts had been removed, taken below to the gun deck, and lashed together to keep them from damage and the crew from harm.

After the crew belayed the main braces and shortened sails again, William gave the order for the hands aloft to lay off—just as a sheet of cold rain washed over the quarterdeck. The seamen on the deck struggled against the driving rain, the bucking of the ship, and the wind-driven waves pummeling them to cover the hatches with tarpaulins and secure them with battens.

"Dismiss all nonessential crew." The wind and pounding rain and waves nearly drowned out William's yelled command. Ned passed the order along. In less than twenty minutes, *Alexandra* had gone from fully rigged and racing along to short sheeted, battened, and storm ready.

Once only a skeleton crew remained on deck, Ned joined William under the awning of the poop in the wheelhouse.

William acknowledged him with a grim expression. "I suppose it is a blessing that the merchant ships have been unable to close ranks as quickly as I had hoped. At least there is no danger of damage from collision."

"Aye, sir. But if they have not been able to navigate efficiently enough to complete the maneuvers you commanded, is there danger they might allow themselves to be blown off course in this squall?" Ned removed his hat and shook the excess water from it.

"A scenario we shall handle when and if the time comes. For now, all we can do is pray this weather blows over quickly."

Charlotte wrapped her arms through the ropes and held on with whatever strength she had left. She'd just finished stringing up her hammock for a much-needed nap when the all-hands signal came. When she'd reported to Kent, he took great delight in assigning her to supervise the crew dismantling and lowering the foremast topgallant and yards. That meant climbing far enough up the shrouds to have a clear view of the sail and its rigging.

One side of the sail bunched funny. "'Vast hauling there. Clear the tackle!" Even with her oilskin coat on, the chill rain permeated every fiber of her uniform. She'd left her hat below in the cockpit rather than lose it to the wind, and she blinked against the water running into her eyes. She risked drowning every time she opened her mouth to scream orders at the crew.

As soon as the tackle that had become twisted in the rigging was cleared, she ordered the continuation of the operation. Her brothers had spoken of having to go aloft during storms, but they had never mentioned the terror that came from looking down to see nothing but sea below as the ship heaved over until it seemed that the yardarms would touch the water—pushing her body into the grid of ropes—and then fell backward until she felt as if she were about to be ripped from the ropes and plunge to her death in the churning waves below.

If she had stayed in England, at this very moment she might well be dressed in one of the beautiful, expensive gowns Lady Dalrymple had commissioned for her, sipping tea and flirting with a wealthy, handsome acquaintance of Percy and Penelope Fairfax. Though that scenario had been a deciding factor in leading her to this decision, that interminable boredom now seemed preferable to the position she found herself in.

Hot tears joined the cold rain on her face. How could she have been so foolish? She did not want to die like this.

The yards, sails, and topgallants were lowered to the deck below and the order to lay off given. Charlotte repeated it to the crew for whom she was responsible. But even as she watched them scurry across the remaining yards and down the mast to the relative safety of the deck below, she could not bring herself to release the ropes. Each time she thought she could start her descent, the ship pitched and rolled, leaning farther and farther to the sides, assuring her that if she unwrapped her arms and released the ropes with even one hand, she would surely plummet to her death.

She could not move, but she could not stay here. She pulled her right arm out from the grid and clutched a rope beside her. Most of the men had made it to the deck. She could justify her presence in the shroud no longer. And if Kent realized how much this frightened her...

Whimpering, she pulled her right foot off its ratline and bent her left knee. She found the next line down with the toe of her shoe and transferred her weight. She did the same on the other side. Down and down and down until she got to where she had to flip around to the underneath side of the shroud so she was over the deck instead of dangling over the side of the ship. Finally, she was close enough. Waiting until the ship was halfway through its side-to-side roll, she released the ropes and dropped to the deck.

She didn't time it quite right, and the deck fell out from under her. She slammed into the bulwark between two cannons. Pain shot through her hip and side. But she was alive. And no longer aloft. She hauled herself upright by grabbing the frame of the cannon on her left. She looked up at where she'd been just minutes before and shuddered.

"Secure those booms. Get that hatch covered." The youngest of the lieutenants, Duncan, stood amidships trying to direct the chaos of men around him. "Lott. Are your men down from the tops?"

"Aye, sir." Charlotte tried to control her shivering, but now out of danger, her body shook uncontrollably.

"Get below. There's nothing more you can do up here."

"Aye, aye, sir." She tried to hurry toward the companionway, but every step shot pain through her hip. Lovely. Another bruise to add to her growing collection. Darkness enveloped her when she reached the bottom of the stairs. With the hatches covered, almost no light came through, but she could still see the vague forms of the sailors taking refuge from the storm. All of the lights had been doused, and most would stay unlit as long as the storm raged. They could not risk fire. That also meant no hot meals. Not that she would miss those in the least.

Someone came toward her with a lantern, its glow a warm beacon in the damp darkness.

"Lott!"

She cringed at the sound of Kent's voice.

"Why are you belowdecks? You're on my watch, and I didn't dismiss you."

"No, Lieutenant Duncan did." He could not fault her for taking an order from someone superior to him. Although, this was Kent…

"You will address me—"

The ship careened to starboard, throwing everyone off balance. From above a crash, followed by a scream, carried down the stairs. Charlotte looked at Kent, whose eyes widened before he ran up the stairs. Indecision anchored her feet, but only for a moment. She ran up the stairs, gaining the deck just seconds after Kent.

Far above the deck, a sailor dangled upside down from the mainmast topgallant yardarm, his ankle tangled in a rope. The man closest to him on the yard struggled to try to reach him—his own life in jeopardy with the severe motion of the ship.

Charlotte held her breath. A length of rope was fed by the line of men up the mast and along the yard—but it was moving so slowly. The sailor continued to flail and scream. There—the rope was almost to the man at the end. He started lowering it for his mate to catch hold of.

But rather than let the rope come to him, the dangling man tried to flip himself upright to grab the lifeline—and the rope around his ankle gave way.

Charlotte's scream was lost amongst the yells and gasps of the men on deck. She squeezed her eyes shut and covered her mouth with both hands. But she should have covered her ears to keep from hearing the thud when the man hit the deck.

For what seemed an eternity, only the sound of the storm pounded Charlotte's ears. Then Parker's voice rang out clear and calm. "Take that man to the surgeon. Get the topgallant stricken and get those men off the yards. Clear the deck of nonessential personnel."

Nauseated, Charlotte spun on her heel and ran back down the stairs. She didn't stop running until she reached the roundhouse—where she emptied her stomach in the necessary.

That could have been her. She could have plummeted to the deck from her precarious position on the shroud.

She sank onto the open grid-work floor, sobbing. She shouldn't be here. She should be back home, in Gateacre, with Mama and Philip. Safe.

Closing her eyes, she tried to conjure an image of Henry—but all she saw was the man falling from the yard. Did she truly love Henry this much? To risk her life to go to him, when he did not even know she was doing so? What if, when she arrived in Jamaica, she discovered she was no longer in love with him? What if the time apart had changed them?

What if she died at sea and no one ever discovered who she was so they could let Mama know?

Julia stood beside the door of the dining cabin and watched the activity beyond through the narrow window. Most of the crew had been sent below. William, Lieutenant Cochrane, and Lieutenant O'Rourke huddled in the wheelhouse with the sailing master. The efficiency of William's crew in striking the topgallants had been impressive.

"Your tea is ready in the big cabin, ma'am." Dawling motioned over his shoulder when Julia turned. "'Twill be the last until this storm blows itself out."

"Yes, thank you, Dawling." She'd hoped William might come in and dry off for a little while, but he seemed determined that if any of his crew must be out in the weather, he would remain there with them—even if in the partial shelter provided by the wheelhouse.

She glanced up at the skylight as she skirted around the dining table. Rain lashed against it as if trying to break the small panes of glass.

"Don't you worry none, missus. Ol' *Alexandra*, she's been through worse than this before. And the com'dore will see us safely through."

She grabbed hold of the door frame to keep her balance before continuing into the day cabin. "I have every confidence in *Alexandra* and her commander to keep us safe."

Rather than the more comfortable sofa near her desk on the starboard wall, Julia made her way to the window seat. One thing her many voyages had taught her was that staying in the center of the ship during a storm like this made her much less seasick.

Dawling was about to pour the tea, but Julia waved him off. "I will do that, thank you, Dawling."

He took a step back. "Anything else I can do for you, ma'am?"

"No, that is all."

Knuckling his forehead, Dawling turned to leave the cabin, but he turned again when he got to the door. "Ma'am, it mayn't be my place, but I just wanted to say that if the com'dore is worried about you walking about on deck unescorted, all you need to do when you feel like a breath is call ol' Dawling, and I'd be pleased as punch to provide you with an escort."

Slightly taken aback at the offer, Julia was not certain exactly how to respond. She settled for simply thanking him. He grinned and left the cabin.

How had he known she and William had discussed that very thing earlier in the day—that William was uncomfortable with Julia going about on deck without an escort? She stood and stepped over to William's desk to pour her tea. Though it had sounded odd coming from rough, burly Dawling, it was the type of thing Creighton might have said to her in a similar situation.

The tea did nothing to settle the renewed nausea, even though she could taste the ginger Hawthorne had given her for it. But past experience told her the seasickness would pass once she became accustomed to the new rhythm of the ship—so long as the storm did not worsen.

Twenty years ago, a storm like this had hit them on her first crossing. Her mother had been prostrate with seasickness that time. She had sent Julia for the doctor, but as soon as Julia left the safety of the cabin, the strong wind had knocked her over. If it hadn't been for William, who saved her by falling on top of her when she rolled into his legs, who knew what might have happened? Moments later, Michael had almost died as well—struck in the head with a giant iron hook, escaping with a wicked scar across his brow and forehead.

The cabin door opened, and Julia looked up, half expecting to see her father enter with an unconscious Michael in his arms.

"Julia?" William paused just inside the door. "Are you all right?"

She shook her head to clear it. "I was remembering the first voyage—thinking of Michael."

"Your brother?" William divested himself of his oilskin, handed it and his hat to Dawling, and then closed the door to the dining cabin, shutting Dawling out.

"It was a storm just like this when he was injured." She shuddered. "There was blood everywhere." She closed her eyes a moment and then opened them as a happier memory took hold. "Michael was so proud of that scar. Made him look like a real sailor, he said."

William eased himself onto the bench beside her. "My brother James fell out of a tree when he was ten years old. Ended up with a scar across his nose and down his cheek. He was thrilled. Thought it would make everyone believe he was already battle scarred by the time he was old enough to sign on to a ship." He reached for her half-empty teacup.

"Let me refill that for you." Julia started to rise, but William stayed her with a hand on her arm.

"Nay, do not trouble yourself." He drained it. "What is in this? Pepper?"

She smiled at his pained expression. "Ginger. Dr. Hawthorne recommended it for my nausea."

He set the cup on the desk and resumed his seat beside her.

"All is well with the fleet?" Julia turned to face her husband. She enjoyed studying his profile: his distinct nose and chin, the lines that fanned out from the corner of his eye.

"*Audacious* lost a sailor while striking topgallants. Fell from the yard and broke his neck." William rubbed the bridge of his nose.

Julia could not stop the grim scene from playing out in her mind. She'd seen men fall from the rigging twice before. It was a part of life at sea, something that could happen to anyone who climbed the shrouds or masts or went out along the yardarms. As an adult, she understood her parents' fury when they learned she had climbed to the foremast top several times. One wrong step, one improperly placed hand, and her life could have ended.

William reached for her hand, lifted it to his lips, and kissed the back of it. "I must return to duty. I am requiring the officers to be on deck only two hours at a time, and I volunteered for the first watch."

She squeezed his hand. "Be safe."

He nodded and exited the cabin.

Be safe. Something no one in the Royal Navy could guarantee. If she worried about William's safety this much now, after less than a fortnight of marriage, what would she be like in a month? In a year?

For the first time in her life, Julia finally understood—and forgave—her mother. No wonder she had wasted away to almost nothing, worrying about Papa not just at sea, but at war.

Julia buried her face in her hands. She had gone and done what she'd sworn she would never do. She had become just like her mother.

Chapter Eighteen

Charlotte was tired of being wet. After spending four hours each watch in and out of the rain above deck, all the pieces of her uniform had been soaked through multiple times over the past two days. And because the six to eight hours between watches were not long enough for even the muslin blouse to dry out in the dank darkness of the cockpit, she had no choice but to continue wearing damp clothes.

At least she was not alone in this misery. Everyone, even the officers, shared in it.

"I'll have your grog ration today, Lott." Kent swiped the mug off the table in front of her once again. She did not have the energy to pretend to protest. If he thought it bothered her, he would continue to take it, giving her the excuse she needed to not drink the vile stuff—almost as vile without the turpentine as with.

Kent laughed and carried the mug to the other end of the table. Parker might have succeeded in mixing his midshipmen with Collin's on the three new watches, but the segregation remained in the cockpit during meals and idle hours.

"You can have half of mine, Charlie." Isaac offered his cup.

Charlotte waved it away. "No, thank you." She gave the boy the best smile she could muster. "I really don't like it anyway."

She shoved her plate away.

Hamilton pushed it back in front of her. "Eat. That's an order. You're already skin and bones. Even if you aren't on my watch anymore, we can't risk you becoming faint because the food doesn't meet with your overscrupulous tastes. I don't know how you've lasted three years, Lott, if you've always turned up your nose at the perfectly acceptable food good King George provides for us."

Charlotte picked up her fork and pulled off a few strings of the grayish meat. She had never cared for mutton, especially plain boiled mutton like this. But Hamilton had a point. She needed to keep up her strength.

"Listen. Quiet, everyone!" Martin rose, holding out his hands, head cocked. A slow smile showed his excessively crooked teeth. "It stopped raining."

Charlotte strained her ears, but she did not notice a difference in the sound of the ship. Isaac took it upon himself to verify Martin's proclamation.

He reappeared moments after disappearing up the companionway. "He's right. It stopped raining. I could see clear sky to the northwest."

Charlotte joined in the cheers, drinking her water along with the toasts. If the heat returned with the sun, perhaps by tomorrow evening she would once again be wearing dry clothes.

After dinner many of the idlers, including Charlotte, went up on deck to view the clearing sky and try to guess how soon the bank of clouds still hanging over them would be gone. When the afternoon watch began, she took her place in the forecastle with much more energy than she'd had just an hour before.

Audacious had fallen far enough behind *Buzzard* that Charlotte needed her telescope to see it clearly. About halfway through the watch, something caught her attention and she raised the glass to her eye.

"Signal from lead ship." She watched as the colorful, patterned flags were raised. "Mr. McLellan, my respects to Lieutenant Howe. Lead ship signals we are to make all sail and close to within fifty yards of the ship ahead."

"Aye, aye, Charlie—Mr. Lott." Isaac grinned and ran aft. Charlotte shook her head and wrote the message in her log book.

A few minutes later, the boatswain's whistle shrilled the all-hands signal. Charlotte headed for the shroud—but stopped a few feet from it, stomach churning. She needed to climb halfway up to monitor the crew on her station on the foremast. The memory of the sailor who'd fallen during the storm flashed before her.

She had to do it. She had to climb up there. She grabbed the ratlines and willed her arms to tighten, to pull her body up. After three false starts, she swung her legs up and hung from the inside of the shroud, face to the sky. One…two…three steps up, and she managed to flip around to the outside of the grid of ropes. Her heart surged when she looked at the deck several feet below.

Don't look down. She raised her chin and kept her eyes on the sails and yards above her. Somehow she managed to climb up to the spot from which she could see the men hoisting and rerigging the topgallants. Every time one of the sailors moved along the footropes hanging below the yards, her breath caught in fear he was about to plunge to his death.

But the longer she stayed up on the shroud, the easier it became. She relayed orders from the officers and soon the sails unfurled and billowed as they caught the wind. Finally, the order came to lay off, and she climbed down as fast as she could, not wanting to stay aloft any longer than necessary.

Within minutes of the crew coming down from the masts, the rolling tattoo of the drummer beat to quarters for evening inspection. Charlotte ran down to the gun deck to command her two gun crews at their battle stations.

Captain Parker seemed slow in his inspection tonight. Charlotte eyed the twelve men under her command critically, trying to see anything with which the captain might take exception. Seeing nothing, she turned to stand at attention just in time.

The captain strolled down the line of cannon and men, pausing occasionally to silently observe a gun crew more closely. Finally, he came to a stop halfway between Hamilton and Charlotte. His frown dug lines around his mouth.

"Lott—your log book." Parker extended his hand toward her without a glance in her direction.

She pulled the small leather journal from her coat pocket and handed it to him, confident he could find no fault with it. Her penmanship was better than anyone else aboard—at least so Howe told her—and she scrupulously wrote down every message, every position, every course change, just as all midshipmen were required.

Parker handed it back to her without a word. "Lieutenant, release the men to supper." But even as Howe shouted the dismissal order, Parker remained standing near Charlotte. She turned and dismissed her crews.

"Lott, a moment." Parker looked at her now.

Heat flooded her face and her heart hammered. What did he want? Had he learned her identity? Had Kent gone to him with some falsehood about her again?

After the deck around them cleared, Parker clasped his hands behind his back. "You seem to be a fair hand with numbers and arithmetic, Lott."

Numbers? "Y-yes…aye, sir."

"I have decided to ask Lieutenant Howe to make some assignment changes in your watch. From now on, Mr. Kent is to be the midshipman of the forecastle, and you will be on the quarterdeck, primarily responsible to the sailing master for keeping the log board and assisting with reckoning our position."

"But Mr. Kent is senior to me, sir."

Parker's brows raised. "I am aware of the seniority of the midshipmen on my ship, Mr. Lott. However, it is a captain's prerogative to observe the strengths and weaknesses of the men and boys under his command and make changes in assignments when necessary. Mr. Kent is still senior of the watch, but the ship will be better served by having you on the quarterdeck. Report to Mr. Howe there on your next watch."

"Aye, aye, sir."

She remained rooted to the spot until long after Parker disappeared up the companionway; then, as soon as she knew she was alone, she bounced on her toes and clapped her hands. She'd be on the quarterdeck—working with the ship's sailing master, doing something more than just staring at the back end of the ship ahead of them waiting to see if they were going to signal another message from William.

She started toward the cockpit at a half run, eager to tell Hamilton and Martin and the others about the honor...but then she came to an abrupt halt. Kent would be furious. The senior midshipman of the watch served on the quarterdeck by virtue of his being the senior midshipman of the watch.

Trepidation weighed her feet, and she trudged the rest of the way back to the midshipmen's berth. Loud voices and laughter emanated from the cockpit—Kent's being the loudest. He sounded happy—perhaps Captain Parker or Lieutenant Howe had not informed him of the change yet.

She'd hardly entered the room when Kent's voice rang out over everyone else's. "And so I told Cap'n Parker that I did not want to be the sailing master's clerk, that I wanted an assignment that took a true man to do. So he agreed to make Lott do the sailing master's bidding and allowed me to choose which place I wanted during the watch. Of course I chose the forecastle."

Martin let out a snort. "More like he wanted a posting where he didn't have to do so much work." After glaring at Kent a moment longer, Martin turned to Charlotte. "Congratulations, Charlie. The captain must be very impressed with you to have given you the quarterdeck."

Charlotte's teeth rattled in her head from the back-pounding congratulations she received from Martin, Hamilton, and a few others. "I only hope I can live up to his expectations."

"I wouldn't be at all surprised to see you promoted to lieutenant before Kent." Hamilton kept his voice low. "You seem to have a knack for making the superior officers like you—even when they originally set out not to."

As the boys went back to what they'd been doing when she arrived, Charlotte allowed herself a rueful smile. Two weeks ago she had purposely set out to make the men surrounding her pay attention—flirting and dancing with them while rebuffing their puppyish attempts to make her like them in return. Here, she had wanted nothing more than to stay unnoticed, to blend into the sea of faces and do whatever was necessary to ensure herself safe passage to Jamaica—and once there, to disappear without anyone from *Audacious* being any the wiser as to her true identity.

Now, looking around at Hamilton, Martin, Isaac, and the others, she realized she might have a hard time saying goodbye.

Julia tucked her book by as four bells signaled ten o'clock. William was usually back in the cabin by now. Though she risked his ire by leaving the cabin unaccompanied, she exited through the wheelhouse. The sailor at the wheel and midshipman of the watch both knuckled their foreheads.

"Good evening, missus." The fourth lieutenant touched the forepoint of his hat.

"Good evening, Lieutenant Eastwick. Is Commodore Ransome about on deck?"

"He's aft, on the poop, ma'am."

"Thank you."

Eastwick looked as if he wished to say more but stepped aside. "Ma'am."

She climbed the steep ladder steps to *Alexandra*'s highest deck—the roof of their cabin. One solitary figure stood at the stern, silhouetted by the moon and stars, his back to her. Halfway across the deck, she stopped. Was she making the situation worse? Not knowing his current temperament, she could not be certain if her presence would be welcomed or if she would make him angry by her willful disobedience.

She turned to leave, trying to be as silent as possible. The water and the wind gave her some measure of cover—until she gasped when her toes smashed into the raised dining-cabin skylight. She hopped on her left foot, pain shooting through the two small toes of her right one.

"I used to do that all the time." William's deep voice was soft as his hands settled on her waist to steady her. "Except I was more likely to break glass than toes in these shoes."

"I..." Embarrassment clogged her throat.

"Here, try to put some weight on it."

She did. Though it hurt, she wasn't about to let on that it did. "I think the pain is beginning to subside." She noticed the sextant and journal he'd set down on the deck. "I had no wish to disturb you."

"Come, let us get you to the cabin where you can sit."

"No. I believe I am well." She gritted her teeth and put weight on the throbbing foot.

"Then I shall be glad of your company, if you would join me in a stroll."

Though each step felt worse than the step before, Julia took William's arm, grateful for the support he offered—and his acceptance of her presence here when they both knew she had broken her promise to not come on deck unless accompanied by him.

"I have just finished calculating the distance between *Alexandra* and *Audacious*. The convoy is still far too spread out for my liking. And after this weather, we are likely to have thick fog by morning."

Julia looked out into the silvery blackness. "How have you taken measurements when the next ship is but a shadow in the dark?"

William stopped at the aft railing. "See the yellow light there?" He pointed slightly to the left.

"Yes, I can just...oh, is that a signal light?"

"Aye. Each ship in the line has one. It is how we communicate after sundown."

"Is it very dangerous to have the convoy spread too far?" The wind blew loose curls into her face.

William reached up and gently brushed the hair back. "I am not overly concerned. We shall see where we stand in the morning, and

I will make adjustments then as needed." His palm cupped her jaw, and he caressed her cheek with his thumb.

Julia's knees nearly buckled. She held onto the balustrade with every ounce of strength.

His eyes, deep blue as the night sky above, roved her face and then rested on her mouth—followed by the soft touch of his lips.

She released her grip on the railing and rested her hand on his shoulder, raising up on her toes—

Her gasp of pain ended the kiss. William looped his arm around her waist for support and then pressed his forehead to hers. "Foot feeling better, is it?"

Even though her breathing hitched with each throb in her toes, Julia had to smile. "Tell me, would you admit to the pain caused by tripping on the skylight? Or any sailor aboard—would he confess or just suffer to save himself humiliation?"

He raised his head, his expression serious. "You are not a sailor, Julia, and I would be very displeased should you start acting like one."

Offense rose in her throat, but before she could speak, William pressed the tips of his fingers to her lips.

"You are the strongest woman I have ever known. I well remember you climbing the shrouds and doing everything else your brother did—usually better. But that was twenty years ago when you were a child, the captain's *daughter*." He brushed more unruly curls back from her face. "Now you are my *wife*, the lady of my household, and it makes me unhappy that you are in pain and trying to hide it from me. I wish for us to always have honesty between us, even if it causes either of us embarrassment. Agreed?"

Lost in the sapphire depths of his eyes, Julia couldn't help feeling like a besotted schoolgirl. "Aye, aye, Commodore."

William shook his head and kissed her again. "Do you think you can walk, or shall I carry you?"

"You'll carry me only if you clear the entire quarterdeck and dismiss the marine standing guard at the cabin door."

William indulged her stubbornness—for the moment. As soon as she gave any indication she would be unable to continue, he was ready to sweep her into his arms and carry her to her bed.

In spite of his doubts, Julia managed to make it all the way back to their quarters, where she collapsed on the small sofa in the corner of the main cabin.

William knelt and untied the pink ribbons at her ankle. She drew in a sharp breath through her clenched teeth as he slipped the shoe off her foot. Even through the silk stocking he could see that the side of her foot was beginning to swell and bruise.

"You stay right where you are—and remove your stocking. I'm going for Hawthorne." He stood and reached the door in two strides.

"No—William, please. Let me…at least let's have a look at it privately first." She uncovered her foot.

He brought a lamp from the desk to get a better view. The pool of light shone on her swollen, black-and-blue skin. He looked up at her, cocking his left brow in question.

"Oh, all right. Get the doctor." She lay back with a huff. "But when he says it's nothing—"

William closed the door on her complaint. Most of the crew were turned in for the night, so he met no one on the main deck as he made his way through the sea of hammocks. Their loud snores made it unnecessary to try to muffle his footsteps.

As he expected, a light still gleamed in Hawthorne's quarters. He knocked.

The young doctor looked shocked to see the ship's commander at his door at such a late hour. "Commodore Ransome, sir, is something wrong?"

"Yes. Mrs. Ransome is injured and in need of your services."

The doctor shrugged into his civilian coat and gathered up some medical supplies into a large black bag. As soon as he doused his lamp, William spun on his heel.

"How did she acquire the injury, sir?" Hawthorne panted, climbing the stairs behind William.

"She..." What had she said about humiliation? "She hit her foot against something in the dark."

The main cabin was brighter than William recalled, and Julia sipped a cup of tea, a damp cloth covering her bare foot.

Dawling lowered the glass chimney over the lamp on the wall behind Julia and then knuckled his forehead. "Com'dore. Doc."

"That will be all, Dawling." Had Julia's protestations of not wanting anyone to know been to make William somehow more sympathetic toward her plight? He paced the width of the room while Hawthorne examined Julia's foot. A couple of times, William paused at her sharp intakes of breath.

"The two smallest toes are dislocated. I need to reset them and then bind your foot until they've straightened. Commodore—"

William joined them.

"Mrs. Ransome may need you, as this will be quite painful."

He sat beside her. She sat up, and he put his arm around her. As soon as Hawthorne began manipulating the toes, Julia grabbed William's left hand with both of hers and buried her face in his shoulder with a groan.

A few minutes later, William pulled his hand from hers to assist the doctor by holding a small board to the bottom of Julia's foot while the doctor swathed it in bandages.

Julia seemed to regain her composure quickly, though a sheen of perspiration shone on her forehead.

Hawthorne knotted the bandage and trimmed the excess. "Now, you must stay off your foot for several days, Mrs. Ransome. Else, we'll be right back here putting those toes in place again."

"Thank you, Dr. Hawthorne."

He inclined his head. "Ma'am. Sir."

William waited a few moments to ensure that Hawthorne was out of earshot. "Julia—"

"William," Julia said, her voice low. "I really do believe you should speak with Dawling. I think he listens at the door. No sooner had you left than he came in and started propping a pillow behind me and telling me I needed tea and a cold compress."

William sank into the desk chair and untied his neckcloth. The truth of her statement made him feel guilty for doubting her. "Yes. I have been meaning to speak to him. He seems to have gotten worse about it since our time in Portsmouth."

"You know I'm fond of him," Julia quieted her voice even further. "And I do not believe he does it with any ill intent—on the contrary, I think he does it to try to improve his service. But it worries me to think that our private conversations may be…not private."

"I will speak with him first thing in the morning."

"Thank you. Of course, he did tell me he's seen a crutch down in the hold—"

William glanced at her, noticing for the first time her pallor, emphasizing the dark circles beneath her eyes. She sat up, swinging her legs over the edge of the sofa.

He was immediately at her side and lifted her into his arms, smiling at her surprised, "Oh!"

"Hawthorne said you are to stay off your feet. No crutch. At least not until he gives his approval."

"And what am I to do all day? Lie abed?"

"How are you getting to that bed?"

She finally stopped frowning at him. "I do thank you for this." She reached her hands behind her to steady her descent as he settled her into the box bed. "But you cannot stay with me all day. I will need to dress and move about the cabin to…take care of necessities. A crutch would be a great help."

He opened his mouth to argue further but was interrupted by a knock at the door. "We are not finished with this conversation."

"I tingle with anticipation." Her green eyes sparkled with humor.

He went out through the main room and opened the door. "Hawthorne?"

"I thought your wife might need this, sir." The doctor thrust a long stick at William. "She will need to use extreme caution, though, until she is accustomed to it."

It took William a moment to realize the stick was a crutch. He thanked the doctor and sent him on his way.

Julia had somehow managed to get her dress off before William returned.

Her lips trembled with what looked like an effort to restrain her smile when he propped the crutch in the corner. He crossed to his sea chest and withdrew a large canvas bundle. He started to hang his old hammock from the iron rings in the ceiling beams.

"William, I…meant no disrespect."

The fear in her voice surprised him. He turned and tried to reassure her with a smile. "Disrespect? No. Stubborn you may be. Strong willed, certainly. But never disrespectful."

"Then why…?" She motioned at the hammock.

He laid the ropes and canvas aside and moved to lean over her, his hands on the feather tick on either side of her. "Because I've no wish to hurt you while we sleep."

"You won't." She held her foot out. "He has so swathed it in bandages that no harm will come to it."

He dropped his head and sighed. He had no desire to give up sleeping beside her, but it was nice to hear she wanted him with her. "Fine. But the first time you so much as twitch…"

She kissed the top of his head. "Good. Now, it is late. You need your rest."

When he finally doused the last lamp and climbed into bed, Julia was nearly asleep, on her side facing away from him. He pulled her close, careful to be aware of the position of her foot.

"Good night, husband." She twined her fingers in his where his hand rested at her waist.

"Sleep well, wife."

Chapter Nineteen

Fog's as thick as turtle soup." Bolger, *Audacious*'s sailing master, continued to grumble and mutter under his breath.

Charlotte stifled a yawn. The thick fog cast an eerie silence around the ship in the predawn gloom. She rubbed her eyes when the writing on the log board blurred before them. Martin's handwriting was nearly as crooked as his teeth, but she could make out the ship's position as recorded at each hour of the watches that came before hers. But the final entry for this hour…

She looked up at the tall young man. He held the chalk in his hand, but instead of writing, he stood frozen, frowning, head slightly cocked, a distant expression in his brown eyes.

"What is it?" she whispered.

He shushed her and wandered out onto the quarterdeck, seemingly led by his left ear. Charlotte glanced at the sailing master.

"I've learned to trust that lad. He can hear things no one else can." With a jerk of his chin, he motioned Charlotte to follow Martin.

She followed him all the way to the forecastle.

Kent jumped up from his seated position. "What's the meaning of—"

"Quiet!" Martin snapped. Charlotte was impressed—it was the first time she'd seen Martin stand up to Kent.

She moved to stand beside Martin and squinted, as if that would help her see better through the fog. A flash of lightning a fair distance off the larboard bow caught her attention. But the boom that followed a moment later wasn't thunder.

"Get down!" Martin grabbed her arm and pulled her toward the deck. She spun and caught sight of Kent staring at them in annoyance. She grabbed his arm and pulled him down with them.

The cannonball hit the bulwark not two feet from where Kent had stood seconds before.

Martin jumped to his feet and started running back toward the quarterdeck. "Beat to quarters, beat to quarters!"

Charlotte leapt up and tried to follow, but her feet twisted with Kent's. She fell, pushed herself back up, and chased Martin, weaving between the sailors pouring onto the deck. She stumbled at another impact, chest tightening with terror.

The war was over. Who could possibly be attacking them?

Captain Parker came out of his cabin, stuffing his arms into his coat sleeves. "Report!"

Martin gave a breathless recounting of the past few minutes.

"Clear for action. Run out the guns!"

Charlotte did not wait to hear the remainder of Parker's commands but spun and ran down the companion stairs.

Her two gun crews were already at work readying the cannons.

"Who is it, Mr. Lott?"

"Be it the Frenchies starting the war again?"

"We don't know," she snapped. "Prepare to run out the guns." She glanced at Hamilton. The pallor of his skin was the only betrayal of his unease. Gulping a few deep breaths and hoping for the ship to somehow get through this safely—and for William to come to their rescue—she managed to achieve a small measure of control over her fear.

"Don't fire until you can see their hull!" Lieutenant Gardiner paced behind them.

The ship shuddered with another impact. Bile rose in the back of Charlotte's throat. She had read so many accounts of battles that she'd thought she'd be prepared for it if anything like this happened. But reading about it could not compare to experiencing it.

"Prepare to fire!"

Charlotte repeated the order to her crews. At least they knew what they were doing. Through the gun portals she could make out the shadow of the enemy ship.

"Fire when you bear!"

She closed her eyes, summoning her strength. Beside her, Hamilton gave the command. Before she could think, she opened her mouth and cried, "Fire!"

The whole ship rocked in recoil when the starboard battery fired at almost the same moment.

"Reload!"

Acrid smoke filled the gun deck. She coughed hard enough to bring tears to her eyes and struggled to catch her breath. She wanted to be a child again, to have dreamed all of this, to wake up, climb into her mother's lap, and be comforted.

But she had made this choice. She must live with it now.

"Gun ready, sir!"

"Gun ready, sir!"

"Run 'er out!" she called to her crews. She bent down to sight the other ship through the portal. The enemy's battery fired at that moment.

She jumped back just as a cannonball shattered the side of the portal. Pain worse than she'd ever felt slammed against the side of her head.

Pounding feet overhead awakened William. Outside, dawn lay gray and pink on the horizon. He listened a moment longer before untangling himself from Julia, leaping out of bed, and hastening to dress.

Julia propped up on one elbow, eyes bleary, hair tousled. "What is it?"

"I'm not certain. But I intend—" Loud banging on the door cut him off and set his heart to racing. *God, please. Not hostilities with Julia aboard.*

He punched his arms into his uniform jacket and ran his fingers through his hair as he rushed to the door.

Cochrane, white faced, stood on the other side. "Message come up the line, sir—*Buzzard* is under attack. *Audacious* is engaging the enemy."

"Beat to quarters and clear for action. Boxhaul the ship. Send word to the convoy they are to remain on course." The drumming and pounding of feet matched the hammering of his heart. For the first time since he'd been made commander of a vessel, he paused before leaving his quarters and joining the fracas on deck.

Julia stood in the doorway between the sleeping cabin and the main cabin, balanced on her uninjured foot, straightening the dress she'd pulled on in haste, eyes wide with fear.

In that moment he resented her—resented loving her, resented her presence. Never before had he experienced fear in the face of an enemy attack.

He crossed the cabin, grabbed her by the shoulders, and kissed her with the force of anguish his fear created. "Stay in the main cabin—but away from the windows." His men were already shoving their trunks aside in the sleeping cabin to get to the cannon in there.

Julia caressed his cheeks. "Do not worry about me, William. Go. See to your ship."

Cochrane had already relayed William's orders and the deck swarmed with crew. *Alexandra* shuddered as the crew threw the canvas aback, catching the wind with the fronts of the sails to halt their forward progress.

"Heave to. Hard to larboard." William climbed to the poop where he had a better vantage as the ship swung around. A lingering fog limited visibility but not the distant echoes of cannon fire. William braced himself against the bulwark as *Alexandra* heeled, leaning far over as she came about.

"Cleared for action, sir, and guns run out." Ned stopped next to him, breathing heavily.

If Captain Parker had made more of an effort to exploit his position at the rear and bring the line tighter together, this might not have happened.

The rising sun burned away the fog. They passed two ships; and through his scope, William could see the next four in line.

Silence descended. Even with all canvas spread and catching a fair wind on the starboard tack, *Alexandra* seemed to crawl through the water.

Ahead—smoke. William tried to will *Alexandra* to gain speed. He scanned the water for any signs of an enemy vessel.

"Enemy ship sighted, Commodore!" came a cry from the quarterdeck.

"Where away?"

"Seven points off the starboard bow."

William swung his telescope that direction. Two vessels came into view—the larger looked like one of the cargo ships. The smaller... "Thirty-two gun French frigate. Make chase, Lieutenant Cochrane."

"Aye, aye, sir." Ned's heart raced, though he tried to keep the excitement from his voice. He leapt down the steps to the quarterdeck and relayed William's orders. *Alexandra* almost immediately changed to the more easterly course on a pursuit path.

The smoke billowing from *Audacious* appeared to be waning, meaning the ship was in no danger of burning, so Ned put it out of his mind, focusing solely on their enemy. But after several minutes they had drawn no closer to the French scavenger and the captured cargo ship. *Alexandra* was under full sail, yet the smaller ships had the advantage of at least half an hour's lead. At this point, they could chase them all the way back to France and never close the gap.

He turned and looked up at William, who stood at the fore of the poop. "Sir, we are not closing." The words seemed unnecessary, given the grim expression on the commodore's face.

"Lay off pursuit. We shall return and render assistance to *Audacious*."

Ned saluted. "Aye, aye, sir." As soon as Ned gave the orders to turn the ship and return to *Audacious*, the men made their disappointment clear. But they obeyed and brought *Alexandra* around.

He examined *Audacious* through his glass. The privateer's cannons had ripped holes in the bulwarks and around the gun portals, but the masts appeared to be intact. So long as she was not hulled below the waterline, it looked as though most of the damage could be repaired under sail.

If he had been in command of *Audacious*, he would not have allowed an enemy vessel to get the better of his ship, fog or no fog. Of course, he would never find himself in such a position, as he would never accept a command.

As they drew nearer, Ned could see the chaos that still prevailed on deck.

William joined him on the quarterdeck. "Matthews, haul in the ship's boats. Mr. Cochrane, choose a crew to take with us to *Audacious*—including the doctor and the carpenter and his mates."

"Aye, aye, sir." Ned ran through the crew and chose several he knew could help the *Audacious* crew put their ship to rights. Minutes later he climbed out of the jolly boat and up the accommodation ladder onto the other ship's deck.

The frenzy on deck was worse than it had looked through his glass. Ned stood slack jawed for a moment. A thirty-two gun ship had created this much carnage? He moved closer to the mainmast and saw that it was pocked with holes. The frigate had used grapeshot in some of their cannon, and the small pellets had done what they were meant to do: take down as many sailors as they could, throwing the rest into panic.

"Where is Captain Parker?" William called over the screams of the injured.

A young lieutenant saluted him. "Captain Parker's dead, sir. Along with the first and second lieutenants."

Ned's stomach lurched. Howe had been a friend—someone he had looked forward to being on station with in Jamaica.

"Who is in command, then?"

The young lieutenant looked as if he were about to be sick. "I am sir. Third Lieutenant Gardiner, sir."

"How long have you held your commission, Mr. Gardiner?"

"Two years and five months, sir."

William nodded, his mouth set in a thin line. "Show me your captain."

Ned followed them to the starboard side of the quarterdeck. Three bodies lay on the deck, covered with ragged pieces of canvas from the shredded sails now being lowered and replaced. William pulled the material down to look at each man's face and then straightened.

"Mr. Cochrane, a word." William headed for the captain's cabin, the only place they could be assured of privacy. He closed the door as soon as Ned entered. "Sharpshooter killed them. Best way to render a ship ineffectual, killing the senior officers." William clasped his hands behind his back. "Gardiner is too young and inexperienced to command this ship."

Fear wrapped around Ned's heart. The screams of the injured outside the cabin mixed with the phantom screams in Ned's memory.

"I am making you acting captain of *Audacious*."

No. Sweat trickled down Ned's back. He could not take command. He could not risk having more men die because of his poor decisions. "Sir...I cannot leave *Alexandra*."

"You do not have a choice, Mr. Cochrane. *Audacious* and her crew need you. And I have every confidence in you."

He'd always sworn he would resign his commission before accepting a command. But here, now, in the middle of the ocean with a ship in need of an experienced officer...William was right. He had no choice.

"Thank you, sir. I shall do my best."

"I expect nothing less."

Charlotte's throat was raw—from yelling commands to the gun crew and the pervasive, acrid smoke filling the gun deck. She spat, trying to get rid of the taste of blood from her split lip. Her left eye and cheek throbbed. Leaning her torso out the gun port, blasted to twice its size, beyond *Alexandra* she caught sight of the hostile ship and the captured cargo ship slipping away over the horizon.

"Who d'ye think they be, Mr. Lott?" one of the gun crew asked, joining her at the portal.

"I can't be certain," Charlotte rasped. "Pirates or privateers, most likely."

"They tuck tail and run like Frogs, sure enough."

"Charlie! Did you see me?" Isaac darted through the sailors now trying to clear the debris—and casualties—from the deck. She was relieved to see that the young boy had survived his first combat. "Did you see? I broadsided her for certain."

"Well done, Isaac. Now, before the master gunner or the first lieutenant comes down for inspection, you need to get your gun and crew set to rights."

Isaac waved and ran off. Charlotte followed her own advice and got her crew to work clearing their stations and cleaning the cannons.

As soon as the guns were cleaned and the deck cleared, Charlotte dismissed her crew and went toward the cockpit to change into her clean uniform.

She was almost there when she heard the whistle for all hands to assemble on deck. Her heart hammered. What if William recognized her?

Dread weighing each step, she made her way up to the quarterdeck, pulling the brim of her hat low on her forehead. She squeezed into the crowd of midshipmen, standing directly behind Martin, before glancing around.

William stood above the wheelhouse on the poop deck, hands behind his back, the forepoint of his hat hiding his eyes in shadow. Ned stood beside him, looking more handsome than Charlotte remembered. On William's other side, stood Lieutenant Gardiner, his waistcoat and shirtsleeves soaked with blood. Charlotte's stomach churned, bile rising in the back of her throat.

Where were the other officers? Captain Parker? She shivered in spite of the morning's heat.

"Officers of His Majesty's Ship *Audacious*," William's voice rang out over the deck. "I regret to inform you that Captain Parker and Lieutenants Howe and Crump were killed in the effort to protect the convoy ship. Many others of your number have also been wounded, some grievously, such as your doctor. I am promoting Lieutenant Cochrane to acting captain of *Audacious*. Your own lieutenants will also be promoted, and between them, they will choose two midshipmen to promote to acting lieutenant."

The young men around Charlotte murmured, each hoping he would be so distinguished. Charlotte chewed her bottom lip. In the nine days since leaving Portsmouth, she'd had quite a bit of interaction with Captain Parker. She could only hope that Ned would be so consumed by matters of command that she would have no interaction with him.

She released a rueful snort as a thought occurred to her. Thanks to the chunk of oak hull that had smacked her face, she wouldn't have to try so hard to hide her identity, at least for a little while.

Ned's heart thudded in his ears. The bodies of the dead officers lay in a line behind him. Blood still stained the deck and the men assembled there. He'd seen battle before, had witnessed friends maimed or killed, but never before had he been tasked with taking command in the aftermath.

"We've been delayed too long." William lifted his hat to mop the sweat from his forehead. "Nearly six hours gone already." He shook his head and stuffed his handkerchief into his pocket. "Did you retrieve everything from *Alexandra* that you needed?"

"Aye, sir. Captain Parker's..." Ned swallowed hard. "*My* steward is preparing the big cabin for me."

A large sailor approached, knit cap in hands. "Beggin' pardon, Captain Cochrane."

Ned jolted at hearing himself called *captain* for the first time. "Yes?"

"Colberson, sir, master carpenter." He knuckled his forehead.

"Yes, Mr. Colberson. What do you have to report?"

"All the damage below the waterline is repaired as best we can, sir. All other repairs can be completed under sail, sir."

"Good." Ned squeezed his hands into fists to keep himself from looking to William for commands. "Return to your duties. Continue using all necessary hands until the repairs are complete."

The carpenter saluted again. "Aye, aye, sir."

"Dismissed." After the subordinate returned to his work, Ned turned to William. "What are my orders?"

"I've given them to you." William laid his hand on Ned's shoulder—the one absent an epaulet signifying confirmation of his true promotion to post captain. "You are now acting captain of this ship. I suggest a conference with the three remaining lieutenants and all the warrant officers as soon as possible. The sailing master can be invaluable to you in deciding which mids to promote to acting lieutenant." His blue eyes bored into Ned's. "You are ready for this, Ned. It is a daunting task to help a crew heal after a tragedy, but I have faith you will rise to the occasion."

"Thank you, sir." He moved with William toward the waist entry.

"We shall signal once we regain the head of the line. If the captains followed my orders, and it appears they have, we should be back on course and at full sail within the next hour." William glanced around the deck one last time. "Let them have a day to grieve and adjust to your command, but do not let them get the better of you."

"Aye, aye, sir."

"And Ned?" William lowered himself onto the accommodation ladder on the side of the ship.

"Sir?"

"Our prayers are with you."

"Thank you, sir."

Chapter Twenty

Ned fought the urge to pace. He could not understand how William managed to stay so calm, so still, so unemotional when he stood before a room full of men looking to him for guidance and direction.

"Commodore Ransome suggested I solicit recommendations from you as to the midshipmen who are ready for promotion." He flexed his fingers, resisting his nervous habit of tapping them against his legs. "I assume it will be between the three midshipmen of the watches?"

The remaining lieutenants exchanged a glance. "Sir, I believe we would all agree upon two names of mids who are ready." Gardiner glanced at Wallis and Duncan again, and they nodded. "Hamilton and Martin. Not only are they the two senior mids, and both have passed their examination for lieutenant, but neither has yet been recommended to a ship for promotion."

Understandable, as the Royal Navy had been of a mind to decommission ships and cut down on the number of officers, not make new ones.

"Master Bolger, what is your opinion?"

The sailing master seemed surprised to have his opinion solicited. "I agree, sir. None better 'an Hamilton and Martin. 'Twas Martin who first alerted us to the enemy ship and gave the order to beat to quarters."

"I shall see that he receives the proper commendation." A dull ache started just behind Ned's eyes. But a headache was nothing compared to the gashes and bruises sported by almost every man in the room with him. "I understand your crew is on watch and watch."

"Aye, sir," Gardiner answered.

Ned pulled out the head chair and sat. "I would like to put them into three watches instead." The sooner he got this ship and her crew working more like *Alexandra*'s, the happier he would be. "Mr. Gardiner, you will work with the warrant officers to create a new watch schedule."

"Aye, aye, sir." Gardiner looked anything but confident. Ned understood. The first time he'd been assigned such a task, he'd been terrified—and he had been on a much smaller ship.

"Lieutenant Wallis, you will work with the purser and master-at-arms and master gunner to inventory our remaining ammunition." Ned sent up a quick prayer of thanks that William had the foresight to demand that both ships carry a full supply of cannonballs and powder when Admiral Glover tried to talk him into taking only a quarter of what a battle-ready warship needed.

"Aye, aye, sir."

"Lieutenant Duncan, you will work with the midshipmen who take over the watches for Hamilton and Martin. After I speak with them about their promotions, I will send them to assist you."

"Aye, aye, sir."

Ned turned to look at the warrant officers. "I would like reports from each of you on your areas before beat to quarters for inspection tomorrow evening."

Another chorus of "Aye, aye, sir." Every time Ned heard it, he could picture the eager sailors who had followed him in his first command with an "Aye, aye, sir," and gone to their early and unnecessary deaths.

"That is all."

The officers filed out of the dining cabin wordlessly. Ned waited until the door closed behind the last man before propping his elbows on the table and burying his face in his hands.

Someone cleared his throat. Ned jerked his head up. The wiry little man who had introduced himself as Parker's steward stood just inside the door. "Beggin' pardon, Cap'n. Wanted to know should I start supper for ye and what ye'll want to have, sir."

With the sour feeling in his stomach and the burning in his chest, Ned wasn't certain he would be able to eat, but he had to try. "Bring me whatever you would have cooked for Captain Parker—and his officers and the midshipmen of the watch." He was about to dismiss the steward, but then he remembered one of the privileges of his new rank. "Pass word for Midshipmen Hamilton and Martin to report to me."

"Aye, aye, sir." The steward disappeared.

Ned stood and crossed to the door leading to the day cabin. Willing his hand to stop trembling, he opened it. The lingering need to have permission to step into the captain's inner sanctum held him in the doorway.

Unlike William Ransome's plain, understated furnishings, Captain Parker's tastes had run to the ornate: large pieces covered in carved scrollwork, elaborate and bold upholstery, and an oilcloth upon the floor painted to look like black-and-white tile—as Admiral Lord Horatio Nelson reputedly had in his cabin aboard *Victory*.

Papers still lay atop the mahogany table in the middle of the room, as if Captain Parker were merely seeing to something out on deck and would be back in a moment to continue working on them. A book with a marker sticking out nearly halfway through the pages sat beside an ornate brass lamp on the stand beside the plush chair in the corner. And over the chest of drawers hung a portrait of a woman and two young girls.

Sorrow clutched Ned's heart. Parker's wife and daughters. William would send word to Mrs. Parker informing her of her husband's death when they made port in Madeira.

Rather than picturing Mrs. Parker, Ned imagined Charlotte Ransome weeping over receiving news that he had been killed in action. No. William had been right...before he had himself changed his mind. A naval officer had no business marrying.

At a knock on the dining cabin door, Ned gathered himself and turned away from the perusal of his new living quarters. "Enter."

Two young men stepped into the room. The one with light brown hair seemed self-assured and confident—but patches of red high on his cheeks made Ned suspicious that the midshipman might merely be good at hiding his emotion. Not so his mate. The taller, dark-haired boy wore his disquietude on his face.

"Midshipman Hamilton reporting as requested, sir." The boy with the lighter hair stared over Ned's right shoulder.

"Midshipman Martin reporting as requested, sir." Martin's deeper voice trembled.

"At your ease, gentlemen." Ned rested his hands on the top of the chair before him. Neither midshipman relaxed his stance. "Though we all would wish the circumstances to be different, I am pleased to congratulate you both on your promotion to acting lieutenant. Which of you is senior?"

"I am, sir." Hamilton's chin trembled, but with all his effort, the dimple that appeared in his cheek betrayed his joy in the announcement. Martin did not smile, but he visibly relaxed.

"Very good, then. Mr. Hamilton, you will be fourth; Mr. Martin, you will be fifth. I understand you both passed your lieutenancy examination?"

"Aye, sir," both boys chorused.

"Good. Then you know what is expected of you." Rather than go all the way around to the head of the table again, Ned pulled out the side chair he stood behind and sat. "Please, be seated."

The two acting lieutenants did as requested. "As the leaders of your respective watches, you have a better knowledge of the midshipmen under your command than the lieutenants might. Who would you recommend to take over your watches?" Though these things usually went by seniority, Ned himself had been the beneficiary of a captain who looked at his midshipmen's aptitude and readiness and not just his time of service as what made him suitable for leadership.

Martin looked to Hamilton. Ned tucked that away in his mind—to be certain Martin did not always look to others before making a decision or expressing his opinion when asked.

"Sir, though he does not have seniority, I would recommend Midshipman Lott as a watch leader. In fact, Captain Parker—God rest his soul—had just yesterday assigned Lott to the quarterdeck during his watch."

Lott—he'd wondered how the lad had fared aboard *Audacious*. He hid his smile at his own success in recognizing Lott's potential. "And the second?"

"Midshipman Jamison, sir. He's senior after Kent, and he would make a good watch leader." Hamilton seemed quite at his ease making recommendations for promotion. If his ability to see potential in others was as strong as his confidence, Ned would have a good crew working under him.

"Acting Lieutenant Hamilton, Acting Lieutenant Martin, you will join the rest of the lieutenants at three bells in the first dogwatch for supper with me tonight. And bring Midshipmen Kent, Jamison, and Lott with you."

"Aye, aye, sir." Hamilton and Martin stood, saluted, and left the cabin.

Good. Perhaps now, under closer observation, Ned could figure out why Midshipman Lott seemed so familiar to him.

Charlotte thought she might be ill. Supper with Ned Cochrane?

"You probably should not tell anyone else, but Martin and I recommended you to take over command of one of our watches."

"Why would you do something so utterly ridiculous? There are at least four others who have seniority over me." Truthfully, even young Isaac McLellan with his six months of service had seniority over her.

"But would you want to serve under any of them who are senior to you? Excepting Jamison, of course." Martin leaned in closer.

Charlotte ran through the names of the older boys aside from Hamilton, Martin, and Jamison. The other three over the age of sixteen were all Kent's friends and former *Lark* shipmates—and better at following Kent than they were at showing any leadership potential.

"No. I would not want to be assigned to their watches. But if I am put over a watch, all that will do is make them dislike me more than they already do—because I was shown favoritism by the captain who got me onto this ship in the first place."

"Captain Cochrane did that? I thought Lieutenant Howe recommended you." Hamilton paused in throwing his belongings into his sea chest to look up at Charlotte.

"Lieutenant Cochrane—I mean, Captain Cochrane recommended me to Howe first." And if Ned recognized her, if he somehow figured out what she'd done, not only would he most likely be furious with her, he would never want to see her again.

Not that she should care about that. Using Ned's seeming admiration of and liking for Charles Lott had been an expedient means to an end. It should not give her a hollow sensation in her chest to imagine his reaction when she finally revealed her identity when they arrived in Jamaica.

She helped Hamilton and Martin carry their belongings to the wardroom. At the opposite end of the room, silhouetted by the light from the stern windows, Lieutenant Gardiner stood in the doorway of one of the small cabins lining the room. The commotion of the new lieutenants' arrival drew his attention.

"Lott? Is that you? You look horrible. Did you have the doctor from *Alexandra* take a look at your face?" Gardiner came over and grabbed Charlotte's shoulder to turn the left side of her face toward the light.

"It looks worse than it feels, sir." She touched her throbbing, swollen cheek. Indeed, Hamilton's announcement that Ned wanted Charlotte to join the officers for dinner had momentarily taken her mind off the pain in her face.

"Still, you should have the doctor take a look. You could have some shards of wood imbedded in your skin, which could become infected and make you sick."

"I will do that. Thank you, sir." She glanced around the room.

Rather than the open-ended canvas stalls in the cockpit, the lieutenants had actual private cabins divided and enclosed with whitewashed wooden bulkheads complete with doors. They not only had the privacy afforded by those walls, but only four lieutenants had to share the larboard quarter-gallery privy—while the first lieutenant had the starboard quarter-gallery privy to himself—instead of having to share one head with more than a dozen midshipmen. Though illogical, as it meant she would come even more under Ned's scrutiny, she wished she'd been promoted to acting lieutenant.

Less than a fortnight ago, when she had toured *Alexandra*, she had looked upon the wardroom and the lieutenants' quarters as barely habitable. Now, after more than a week in the cockpit, they looked luxurious.

"Lott, what are you supposed to be doing now?"

Gardiner's question made her nervous. "Nothing, sir. I'm idle this watch."

"Good. I need help packing up Howe's and Crump's belongings and taking them below to the hold. The purser will store them until they can be sent back to England." Gardiner rubbed the bridge of his nose. "I do not know anything about Crump's family or to whom his belongings should be sent. Howe's will go to his wife." He shook his head.

"Howe was married?" Charlotte pictured the former first lieutenant. Serious and handsome, he had not struck her as the kind of man who would find courting enjoyable or easy.

"Aye. Married not a week before we weighed anchor. I stood up with him at the wedding. He'd known Jane since they were small children. Promised her if she waited for him, he would marry her as soon as the war ended. He considered resigning his commission, but Jane would not hear of it. She knew the navy was his life, and she would not let him give it up for her."

Emotion formed a lump in Charlotte's throat. How easily that could have been William or James or Philip…or Ned. Even though her own father had died at sea—of illness, not in battle—until this moment, she had never realized just how dangerous her brothers' chosen profession was or how close they may have come on numerous occasions to meeting the same fate as Parker, Howe, and Crump.

And if Charlotte herself had fallen from the shrouds during the storm, or if she had been hit by the cannonball instead of just the flying debris it created, no one would have known of her death. They would have buried her at sea and then gone through her belongings to discover nothing to link her to the Ransome family.

Howe had been tidy, so it did not take much time to pack away his belongings. Charlotte caught sight of herself in his shaving mirror mounted on the wall. Gardiner was right. With the whole side of her face swollen, scraped, and bruised, she looked hideous. Wonderful. Ned would never recognize her.

By the time Howe's and Crump's sea chests had been handed over to the purser and his mates for storage, Charlotte had to run back to the cockpit to change into her cleaner, spare waistcoat and brush her coat and hat free from the dust and lint they picked up during the day. She retied her neckcloth, taking note in the mirror borrowed from Jamison that the bruises around her neck were barely visible anymore. She shook her aching head. In the past two weeks, she'd been nearly strangled—twice; had bruised her hip and side falling into the side of the ship during the storm; had so many callouses and cuts and scrapes on her hands she no longer worried they would give her away, as they no longer looked feminine and smooth and white; and had been struck in the face with a piece of *Audacious*'s hull. And, with only ten days' genuine experience as a midshipman, she had been promoted to a watch commander.

"Lott, let's go!" Jamison urged her, apparently fearful they would be late for supper with their new commander. Hesitation, however, dragged at Charlotte's feet. She wanted to delay the meeting with Ned Cochrane as long as possible.

They passed through the wheelhouse just as the sailing master's mate struck the bell, joining the lieutenants at the door to the big cabin. Captain Parker's steward—now Ned's—opened the door and ushered them into the dining cabin, indicating where each was to sit. Charlotte breathed a relieved sigh when he told her she was to sit not just at the far end of the table but with her left profile toward Ned.

Ned entered from the big cabin, looking much more serious than she had ever seen him. He took his place at the head of the table. "Please, be seated."

Not wanting to give herself away by giving any indication she was accustomed to anything but naval life, Charlotte watched the men and mimicked their behavior—and discovered that they would have been quite acceptable at any formal dinner she had ever attended, unlike the more rustic manners she'd found in the cockpit at mealtimes.

After the steward and the sailors conscripted to act as footmen during the meal served the food, Ned had each officer give his experience and a brief history of his service. Charlotte found the revelations fascinating, especially from the lieutenants, as she had never had the opportunity to speak to any of them in a context in which personal information had been shared.

As the youngest and most junior officer at the table, Charlotte was, naturally, last to be called upon. She'd run through her fabricated history in her mind several times while the others spoke, so she was able to speak with confidence.

"Charles Lott, from Liverpool." That explained the northern lilt to her accent, and the story about having to travel three days in one direction to get home. "I was made a midshipman in June 1811. I saw only home service during the war, as I had the bad fortune to be assigned to a succession of ships that were laid up in ordinary shortly after I signed on." She once again silently thanked Geoffrey Seymour for that bit of history, as he had spent the first two years of his naval career in that manner.

"And what do you think of service in the Royal Navy now that you have been through battle, Mr. Lott?" Ned asked.

Even with Kent in the room, now was no time for false bravado. "It was much different than the accounts I read, sir. I thought I was prepared for it, but reading about it and actually being in the midst of it bear no comparison with each other."

"Very true. If only those who send us off to war would understand that concept, perhaps there would be no more war." Gardiner turned bright red after speaking. "If I may make so bold as to say so, sir."

"You may, Lieutenant. I think you will find there are few in the navy—and the army as well—who would disagree with you." Ned motioned for the steward to clear the plates from the table and pour more wine.

As soon as each glass had been refilled—excepting Charlotte's, as hers was still nearly full—Ned raised his glass. "Gentlemen, His Majesty the King."

Charlotte joined the others in raising their glasses and finishing the Loyal Toast with, "His Majesty, King George III." She sipped the potent wine.

Ned held up his glass again for the traditional Saturday toast. "To wives and sweethearts."

Everyone at the table looked at Charlotte. Panic closed her throat for a moment until she remembered that as the youngest present, it was her duty to give the unofficial second part of the toast. She raised her glass. "May they never meet."

As each of the men surrounding her chuckled, drank, and possibly thought of his own wife or sweetheart, Charlotte assiduously avoided looking at Ned Cochrane. To be in his presence once again, especially now seeing him in command of a ship, wreaked havoc with her ability to think solely of Henry Winchester.

She made her own silent toast as she and the other officers left Ned's cabin. *Henry Winchester and Ned Cochrane. May they never meet in my presence—as Henry is likely to suffer greatly by comparison and make me admit just how foolish I have been.*

Chapter Twenty-One

Charlotte focused on the pain in the side of her face and kept her eyes fixed on the horizon beyond the starboard side of the ship. Anything to keep from looking at the five bodies, sewn into their hammocks, laid out on the deck.

Captain Parker, Lieutenant Howe, Lieutenant Crump, a sailor from one of Martin's gun crews, and a marine sharpshooter who'd been shot and fallen from his perch on the mizzenmast top. And according to Hamilton, Dr. Hawthorne thought a few of the injured might not live through the night. Her throat tightened to the point she could hardly breathe. She flinched when the boatswain's whistle signaled for all hands to gather on the deck. She took her place between Jamison and McLellan.

Ned Cochrane stepped into the space between the bodies and the bulwark. He looked up at the mainmast, behind Charlotte, and called, "Raise the pennant to honor the dead."

She did not need to watch the action to know that a black pennant was being hoisted to fly from the highest point on the ship. Ned nodded at the two boatswain's mates who lifted the first body onto the top of a table from the sailors' mess and covered it with the Union Jack.

"Ship's company...off hats!" the bosun yelled.

Charlotte slipped hers off and held it in front of her the way Jamison did. The mates carried the board to the starboard entry port and balanced the end of it atop the bulwark railing.

Ned handed his hat to his steward and opened the small, thick book he carried. "We read in the thirtieth Psalm: 'Sing unto the LORD, O ye saints of his, and give thanks at the remembrance of his holiness. For his anger endureth but a moment; in his favour is life: weeping may endure for a night, but joy cometh in the morning… I cried to thee, O LORD; and unto the LORD I made supplication… Hear, O LORD, and have mercy upon me: LORD, be thou my helper. Thou hast turned for me my mourning into dancing: thou hast put off my sackcloth, and girded me with gladness; to the end that my glory may sing praise to thee, and not be silent. O LORD my God, I will give thanks unto thee for ever.'"

Ned looked up from the book and at the shrouded form ready to be laid to rest in the depths of the ocean. He pressed his lips together, closed his eyes briefly, and then continued. "In the sure and certain hope of the resurrection to eternal life through our Lord Jesus Christ, we commend to Almighty God our shipmates, and we commit their bodies to the depths. Ashes to ashes, dust to dust. The Lord bless and keep them. The Lord make His face to shine upon them and be gracious unto them. The Lord lift up His countenance upon them and give them peace. Amen."

"Amen," Charlotte murmured with the crew. Ned called the name of the marine, and the boatswain's mates upended the tabletop so the body slid feet first into the sea from under the flag. She could not watch. The same was repeated for the sailor, the lieutenants, and Captain Parker. With two cannonballs placed at each man's feet, the bodies would sink to the bottom quickly. But her imagination got away from her, and the picture of one of the shrouded figures floating beside the ship chilled her to the bone.

After Captain Parker was laid to rest, Ned turned to face the crew once more. "Let us pray. 'Our Father which art in heaven…'"

Charlotte joined in the recitation of the familiar and comforting words. "'Hallowed be thy name…'"

After the murmured "Amen," Ned left the deck. As soon as he had disappeared into his cabin, the bosun called, "On hats…dismissed!"

Though she was not entirely certain how, or if God would listen to her, Charlotte vowed to pray every night that they would not have to go through that ordeal again.

⁂

Ned paced the cabin. His first official duty in front of the entire crew had been to bury their captain. He hoped, he prayed that the problems Howe had shared with him before leaving Portsmouth had worked themselves out once *Audacious* put to sea. The last thing he needed in his first true command was a divided and antagonistic crew.

He squeezed the object in his hand until the corners bit into his fingers. He lifted the prayer book. A gift from his mother upon his being made lieutenant. Commodore Ransome read his daily, along with his Bible. And when William led the prayer service on Sunday mornings, Ned had always believed, even if just for a little while, that God was near and could not only hear his prayers but might even answer them.

He had read and said the expected words over the dead today, but tomorrow he would have to lead the crew in Sunday services.

Opening the book, he checked the liturgical calendar in the front. Never before had he seen that for each day of the year, the calendar listed Scriptures to be read morning and evening. He glanced around the cabin. Would Parker have kept a Bible? Or, like Ned's first captain, would he have been the type to read the collects and prayers from the book and leave it at that?

A row of books lined the top of the chest of drawers. Ned moved closer to read the titles. Mostly naval history. Parker's prayer book. Some biographies of men Ned had never heard of. But no Bible.

Perhaps one of the officers would have one he could borrow. Or, more likely, God was trying to tell him he was not worthy of reading the Holy Scriptures as someone with authority over others. After all, why would God forgive Ned for sending those sailors to their deaths when he could not forgive himself? No, he would read the collects and the prayers. Then, when they arrived in Jamaica and he returned to

Alexandra as William's first officer and someone more deserving took over command of *Audacious*, the new captain could worry about the eternal welfare of the men on this ship.

He returned to the table and opened the prayer book to the designated page for the fourteenth Sunday after Trinity. He liked the prayer, asking God to increase their faith, hope, and charity. The reading from one of Saint Paul's epistles was from the book of Galatians, and it spoke of sins of the flesh and fruit of the Spirit. He would have to spend more time reading that to understand it. The excerpt from the Gospels came from Luke.

Pulling the book closer, he read the story of ten lepers who begged Jesus to have mercy on them. Jesus sent them to the priests, and, as they walked away, they were healed. But only one returned to Jesus to thank Him. Ned turned the page, anxious to see how Jesus responded to this man's humble gratitude. He frowned when he read of Jesus asking the man where his nine companions were.

Ned supposed he had been in the Royal Navy too long to be surprised by the ingratitude of the majority of men.

But he had skipped the last line. *Arise, go thy way: thy faith hath made thee whole.*

He rocked back in his chair as if broadsided. It had not been the man's faith that had rid him of his leprosy. It had been Jesus. Jesus had every right to say, "I accept your gratitude for the wondrous work I have completed in you." How could a man's *faith* heal him, make him *whole*?

Again, he searched the cabin for a Bible, wanting to see if Jesus went on to explain what He meant by His cryptic statement, but no copy of the Scriptures was to be found.

His head hurt too much already to spend more time trying to figure out what the passage meant. Instead, he went into the sleeping cabin and pulled the box of important papers out of his sea chest and carried it to the table that had served as Parker's desk. He sorted through them until he found what he was looking for.

The paper was somewhat yellowed and the ink slightly faded, but he read through his promotion orders officially conferring on him the rank of lieutenant. From his pocket, he pulled the folded parchment William had handed him several hours ago. His field promotion to acting captain.

Spreading both out on the table, he found Parker's stock of paper, ink, and quills, and then he sat down to write up the orders conferring status of acting lieutenant on Hamilton and Martin.

Julia waved William aside. "I can do it myself."

Hands held up in surrender, he backed away a few steps.

Getting in and out of the hanging bed with its high canvas sides had been difficult to manage with two feet. But now that she could not put any weight onto her right foot, the simple act of getting out of bed in the morning seemed nearly insurmountable. And her husband's amusement at her attempts to do it on her own was not helping at all.

Yesterday, in the fear from hearing *Audacious* was under attack, she'd somehow managed to not only get out of the box bed, but grab her dress off the peg on the wall beside it and dress in a matter of minutes. However, she had discovered yesterday that trying to go about her normal daily activities with the use of only one foot proved to be difficult and frustrating.

Seven bells chimed.

"In half an hour I will call all hands to order for prayers. I would like for you to join me. Please let me know if you require my assistance." With a half bow, William left the sleeping cabin.

Julia blew a loose clump of hair out of her face. She could do this. She had climbed the shrouds to the foremast top at ten years old. Getting out of a hanging bed one-footed should be no problem. She pushed herself up onto her hands and knees and scooted over to the side, carefully balancing as the other side of the bed canted upward. She moved all of her weight onto her right knee and swung her left leg over the side.

She stretched...reached...success—her toes touched the floor. Shifting her weight to her left foot, she turned to put her right leg over the side.

But she misjudged the fact that with almost all of her weight on her foot of the floor, this side of the bed would come back up. Her right heel caught on the side, but her momentum carried her backward. Arms flailing, she finally managed to grab the side of the bed and break the worst of her fall, but not before wrenching her knee and injured foot, which stayed caught in the bedding as she landed on the deck.

Involuntary tears welled in her eyes from the pain and increased frustration.

"Why must you be so stubborn?" William reappeared and gently extricated her foot from the bed and then sat down on the floor beside her. "I offered to help you."

"But I need to be able to do it on my own." Julia dashed at the tears with the back of her hand.

"Why?"

"Because I do not want to..." She shook her head and looked away as the tears refused to stop.

"You do not want...?"

She closed her eyes and pressed her lips together. Success had come in every area of her life as long as she worked hard at it. This would be no different.

William hooked his finger under her chin and forced her to face him. "What do you not want?"

Blinking away the wretched tears, she found herself mere inches from the blue eyes she had dreamed of for nearly two decades. "I do not want to become dependent on you," she whispered. "I need to be able to take care of myself."

His nod seemed loaded with comprehension and understanding. "I see." He moved his hand from her chin to push her hair back and tuck it behind her ear. "I am sorrowed to know that I played a large role in teaching you to trust no one but yourself." He took and released a deep breath. "Do you know what I will speak of for the prayer service this morning?"

She shook her head.

"God's faithfulness. How He has promised He will never leave us nor forsake us. And how we are to reflect His faithfulness in our own lives by offering that kind of steadfastness to the ones we love. I know I betrayed your trust twelve years ago, but I promise I will never leave you nor forsake you, and I promise I will do whatever it takes to show you that you can depend on me."

An idyllic picture of William by her side at Tierra Dulce made her smile...but that image faded into one of her standing on a lonely dock waving as a boat rowed him out to his ship. "You will be at sea. And while I know you will always be faithful to me and I can trust in your steadfastness, I must still depend on myself and my strength and knowledge to see me through my daily life."

A hint of pain flickered through William's eyes, but he quickly slipped back into his mask of no emotion. "But I am here now, Julia. Let me help you while I can. Let me take the burden from you, if just for a short time, before you shoulder all of your duties and responsibilities."

She wanted to say no, to turn down his offer, but the ache in her foot and knee stopped her. "Agreed. I will try."

And she would try even harder to not allow this exercise in marital trust and dependence make her fall even more deeply in love with him than she already was. She could not become like her mother and waste away pining for him, losing more of herself the longer they were apart.

He helped her up and then insisted on assisting her to dress—requesting she wear one of the dresses that laced up the back rather than buttoned, since they were running short on time. After tying the laces, he unplaited her hair, running his fingers through it to remove the tangles.

"I do not have time to do anything with it."

"Leave it loose," he whispered in her ear. "You know I prefer it thus."

A pleasured tingle danced down her spine. "But it will be blowing in my face. Here"—she took the ribbon from him—"I will tie it back, like this." She gathered it all at the nape of her neck and tied it. "Now...my crutch."

He handed her the long stick with the short beam across the top that just fitted under her arm. She hopped along with it pretty well, thanks to the practice she'd had with it yesterday. She retrieved her straw bonnet from the hook on the side of the wardrobe. William picked up his prayer book and hat and then offered his arm to Julia. It took a few steps to accustom herself to balancing herself between the crutch and his arm, but she reveled in the relief his support provided.

She had just about determined how she would manage the steps up to the poop deck when William swept her up into his arms and carried her up them. He deposited her in a chair—she recognized it as one of the chairs from the dining cabin—and turned away from her to face the crew now gathering on deck as eight chimes rang out, followed by the bosun's whistle for all hands.

After her initial indignation, Julia found herself smiling. He knew her well and had avoided another disagreement over her stubbornly insisting she could climb the steps herself with no help by taking the decision out of her hands.

Dawling bustled over with a footstool. She shook her head but did allow him to take her crutch so it was out of the way. With her chair beside William, the lieutenants lined up behind them. She missed Ned's smiles, but it was good to see Gibson with the white patches removed from his collar and an epaulet on his shoulder indicating his promotion to acting lieutenant.

Hands clasped behind him, William leaned forward, a slight breeze ruffling his hair between hat and collar. "Good morning, crew of *Alexandra*."

The crew saluted and shouted their "good morning" back, and everyone removed his hat. As William quoted a verse from the book of Joel, Julia could not keep her eyes from him. Last Sunday, she had not gotten to witness him leading the crew in worship, as he had to use the time to read out the Articles of War, as prescribed by the Admiralty to be done once a month in place of prayers. He read the prayer book and his Bible every morning and, at her request, had taken to reading the passages and prayers aloud so she could have the benefit of them as well. But seeing him standing before more than seven hundred men and quoting Scripture and extolling God's love for them made Julia's heart swell with pride.

He moved on to read the Morning Prayers. And though the words had been written by someone else more than a century ago, William's heart shone through the words. When her father had given the Sunday service aboard *Indomitable*, it had been perfunctory—very much like the recitation of the Articles of War. For William, this was not merely a performance of his duty as captain of this ship; this was the only time when he allowed his true feelings to be seen by the men under his command…the feelings that stemmed from his love for God.

After the Collect and prayers and Scripture readings and William's soliloquy, Acting Lieutenant Gibson stepped forward and began singing a hymn. Julia closed her eyes. She had heard many tales of Gibson's talent, but to hear the rich, deep voice—so incongruous with the young man's appearance—she knew in that moment what the angel Gabriel must have sounded like when he appeared to Mary and then to the shepherds at the annunciation.

Perhaps, if William were to decide to leave the Royal Navy, he could enter the church and become a rector. In fact, the rector of the Tierra Dulce parish was quite old and could possibly be encouraged to retire if a replacement were readily at hand.

She focused on William again, and the fantasy faded like a wisp of steam. Like her father, William would never be happy away from the Royal Navy. She would do well to remember that, and to also guard her heart for the time when his duty would take him away from her. She must learn to enjoy the times when they were together.

She prayed there would be more reunions than partings.

Charlotte wrote the coordinates on the log board as Master Bolger called them out. After a few days and several duty shifts as the midshipman of the watch, the sense of panic every time she had to tell someone to do something—whether a sailor, one of the mids on her watch, or one of the warrant officers—had finally started dissipating.

And since Ned had been spending most of the time in his cabin—sometimes alone and sometimes with one or more of the lieutenants or warrant officers—her worry over his recognizing her had also diminished.

Isaac McLellan skidded to a stop and saluted Lieutenant Duncan. "Midshipman Clerke's regards, sir. We have closed within thirty yards of the ship ahead, sir."

"Very good." Duncan dismissed the eager young midshipman and then turned to Charlotte. "Lott, my respects to Captain Cochrane. Please inform him we are in position and I respectfully request to reef tops'ls."

Before she could respond, another voice said, "I will do it, sir."

Charlotte narrowed her eyes at Kent. Normally, she would have been grateful for anyone's offer to keep her from being face-to-face with Ned. But not Kent. She liked Ned too much to leave him to Kent's sycophantic ways.

"I ordered Lott to do it." Duncan, barely older than Hamilton and Martin, fixed Kent with a challenging gaze. "And as you are not on duty, Mr. Kent, you should not be in the wheelhouse."

Kent moved closer to the third lieutenant, as if trying to intimidate him into backing down. She'd seen him do it with Martin before Martin's promotion, but Duncan would have none of it. When Duncan stood firm, Kent changed his tactics and gave Duncan a tight-lipped smile.

Charlotte moved slowly toward the big-cabin door, not wanting to miss the end of the encounter.

"The captain passed word to see me," Kent said. "That's why I offered to take the information to him, since I am going in there anyway."

Charlotte turned and hurried the last few steps to the door, anxious to have done with her duty before she had to witness Kent's toadying. The marine guard knocked for her.

"Enter." Ned's voice rang clearly from within.

Taking a deep breath, she did as commanded and entered the dining cabin. The double doors to the day cabin stood open, framing Ned, sitting at an ornate round table with paperwork spread out in front of him.

He finished writing something, wiped his quill, and entered the dining cabin to stand across the big table from her.

Her knees quaked. She was alone with Ned Cochrane, something she had stopped herself from dreaming and thinking about many, many times. "Lieutenant Duncan's respects, sir. We have closed to within thirty yards of the ship ahead, sir, and Lieutenant Duncan requests permission to reef topsails."

Before Ned could respond, the marine knocked on the door again. The muscles in Charlotte's neck tightened so much, she feared they might snap.

"Enter," Ned called.

Kent bounded in, stood beside Charlotte, and swept his hat off his head in much the same way Charlotte had seen Julia's smarmy cousin, Sir Drake, do. "Midshipman Kent reporting as ordered, sir."

Charlotte tried to keep her dislike of Kent from showing in her face—Ned kept looking at her, and she did not want him marking her as a malcontent or troublemaker and deciding to keep a close eye on her.

"We shall have to postpone our meeting a few minutes, Mr. Kent." Ned turned and retrieved his bicorne from the other room. "We are going to need the crew on duty to man their stations to reef tops'ls." He came around the table and preceded them from his quarters.

Charlotte allowed Kent to exit ahead of her—after all, he did have seniority, and she did not want to do anything to further antagonize him. The fact he had made no mention of her promotion to watch commander, that nothing had happened to her since the crew had been informed of all of the promotions, made her fear he was planning something extreme at a time when she least expected it. Better not to turn her back on him.

She hurried forward as the whistle blew so she could supervise from a better vantage point the midshipmen of her watch and the crew climbing up to the mast tops to shorten the topmost sails.

Duncan joined her. He kept an eye on their surroundings, and especially the stern of the ship just off their larboard bow, while Charlotte kept her attention aloft.

By the time the order to lay off was given, her neck ached from looking up so long. She dismissed the crew and midshipmen back to their regular duty stations and walked back to the wheelhouse with Duncan, just in time to see Kent follow Ned back into the big cabin.

"Should have known he'd find a way..." Duncan muttered, shaking his head and then turning his back on the cabin.

"Find a way, sir?" Charlotte picked up her log book to record the time and completion of reefing the sails.

"To try to get in good with the new captain. Captain Yates would never have allowed a mid to behave the way Kent does."

No, Charlotte could well imagine that Collin would not have tolerated Kent's antics. Nor would William. But Ned? She glanced at the closed door one more time. Though she guessed him to still be in his twenties, his experience as William's first officer aboard *Alexandra* for the past few years gave her hope he would not fall for Kent's flattery. Because she had a feeling that whatever Kent was planning to do to retaliate against Charlotte for gaining a promotion, he was right now laying some of the groundwork by trying to win Ned over.

❧

"Mr. Kent, please be seated." Ned motioned the lad to take the chair on the opposite side of the table from him. Even after four days as captain of *Audacious*, Ned still felt more comfortable sitting along the side of the table rather than at the head.

The sharp-faced young man pulled out the chair and sat. "Congratulations on your promotion, Captain Cochrane. I am certain you will be a great asset to *Audacious* and her crew."

Ned tapped his fingers on top of his leg—under the table where Kent would not see it. "Thank you, Mr. Kent. However, in the future you will please remember that you are not to speak freely unless given permission. Understood?"

The boy's face turned nearly as pale as his white-blond hair. "Aye, sir."

Ned folded his hands in his lap and concentrated on trying to appear relaxed. "I have been reading through Captain Parker's logs and journal, and I came across several reports of incidents in which you were involved."

Kent's eyes narrowed, and his expression grew stony.

"Captain Parker seemed concerned that there was a division amongst the crew—between the men who served on *Audacious* under Captain Yates and those who came over with Captain Parker from his previous command. Would you say his observation is true, Mr. Kent?"

The boy's adam's apple bobbed a couple of times before he attempted an answer. "Aye, sir, I would say that is an accurate description of the crew. It has been difficult for those of us who came with Captain Parker—God rest his soul—to feel like we have been accepted by the *Audacious* crew. They have not been overly welcoming."

"I see. Would you say that has been the attitude of the *Audacious* crew toward everyone new aboard, or just toward those who served with Captain Parker on *Lark*?"

Again, Kent hesitated briefly before responding. "I would have to say that it has been only toward those of us from *Lark*, sir."

"Interesting." Ned steepled his fingers and tapped his forefingers against his chin, as he had seen William do on many occasions. "Mr. Kent, the reason I asked you, specifically, to come in to talk about this issue is because I need to know that all of the officers and midshipmen on *Audacious* are of the same mind—that everyone aboard wants to be part of an organized, well-functioning crew in which there are no rivalries and no animosities between any of the members. I trust that you are someone who wants that as well."

Kent looked as though he was about to be ill. "Aye, sir."

"So we'll have no more incidents of controversy between you and any of the other midshipmen or officers?" Ned struggled to keep his facial expression serious and not smile over the midshipman's inability to mask his frustration.

"Aye, sir."

"Very good. You may be dismissed, Mr. Kent." Outside the door, eight bells chimed. "Pass word for Mr. Lott to come in."

Kent hesitated at the mention of Lott's name. "Aye, aye, sir."

So that was how it went—bad blood between Kent and Lott. Parker's journal entry had mentioned a few run-ins between the boys, culminating in disciplinary action against both of them, which had been extended for Kent.

Lott entered moments later, and Ned motioned him to sit in the chair Kent had vacated. Ned's mind cast about for what it was that seemed so familiar about the boy, but he came up with nothing once again. Of course, the bruises obscuring the left side of Lott's face would have made it hard for the boy's own mother to recognize him now.

"Mr. Lott, I know you are aware that Mr. Kent was just in here with me. I would imagine you are also aware that you are mentioned in Captain Parker's journal, along with the punishment you recently received along with Mr. Kent."

Lott nodded. "Aye, sir."

He half expected the boy to continue, to try to explain the circumstances, but the lad stayed quiet. Impressive. "Would you care to explain what happened that led to the punishment?"

"It was a misunderstanding between the two of us in the cockpit, sir."

Ned raised his eyebrows. "A misunderstanding? From what I read in Captain Parker's journal, Kent accused you of trying to poison him."

The unbruised side of Lott's face flushed pink. "I respectfully maintain, sir, that it stemmed from a misunderstanding."

"Who do you think put the turpentine in your grog, then?" Ned leaned forward, fascinated by the boy's unwillingness to make an accusation against Kent.

"I do not know, sir."

In Ned's experience, when a rivalry went both ways, given an opportunity like this, either participant would be only too happy to cast aspersions on his rival. Lott had proven himself to have a high sense of honor. Ned's respect for the lad, and his determination to see him succeed, increased.

"Tell me, Mr. Lott, do you feel there is a division amongst the crew?"

"Aye, sir."

"And have you, as a newcomer, felt that the crew of the *Audacious*—those who were here before Captain Parker came aboard with men from his previous ship—have made you feel unwelcomed?"

"Not at all, sir. It is—" Lott clamped his lips together and looked down at his lap.

With the concerns Howe had expressed back in Portsmouth, combined with inferences Ned had made from what Parker had *not* written in his journal, Ned now had a relatively clear understanding of why this crew had been plagued with disciplinary problems. Parker had recruited men who tended toward arrogance and entitlement. And when he had shown favoritism for them over Collin's officers and crew, they had taken advantage.

"Mr. Lott, tell me, do you have brothers serving in the Royal Navy?" Ned had no idea where that question had come from, but he had to figure out how he knew this kid.

Even under the color from his contusions, it was almost alarming how pale Lott's face turned. "Aye, sir."

Ned leaned forward, intrigued by the unusual reaction. "Yes? Brothers in the Royal Navy?"

Lott's shoulders drooped in an almost resigned movement. "Aye, sir. Brothers in the Royal Navy. Two still at sea, one now at home."

Though he thought the information might help, he could not think of any other Lott he knew. Ah, well, he had several more weeks to try to figure it out. Back to the real reason for asking him to come in. "I trust you will work hard to ensure that the crew and officers of *Audacious* work well together and that there will be no more incidents."

Lott nodded. "Aye, sir, to the best of my ability."

"That is all I can ask. You may be dismissed."

"Thank you, sir." Lott slid both legs around and stood up beside his chair rather than simply pushing it back and stepping around it.

Something about it struck him as odd—it wasn't anything Ned had ever seen a sailor do. It was...well, it was the way a woman might do it if she did not have a man to pull the chair back for her. Perhaps Lott had picked up the mannerism from his mother.

Several hours later, when Ned went about the ship for evening inspection, he had a hard time keeping his gaze from drifting to Lott when he was on the upper gun deck. Not very tall, Lott's uniform only served to emphasize his slim, almost delicate, frame. And though he stood in the same position as the rest of the midshipmen and lieutenants—feet shoulder-width apart, hands clasped behind the back—to Ned, Lott did not look like one of them.

He dismissed the crew and returned to his cabin, unsettled. He found Howe's journal under a stack of Parker's paperwork he'd been working on for the past several days. He thumbed through it, finding two places where Lott's name was mentioned. The first was upon Lott's reporting for duty. Howe had been impressed with the boy's book learning, but once he saw Lott in action, he worried whether the lad would be strong enough to survive a transatlantic voyage.

Lott seemed to have proven the former first officer wrong on that account.

The second mention was a recounting of the poisoning "misunderstanding." Howe seemed to think Kent at fault, but he praised Lott for his forbearance in not retaliating and accusing Kent with no firm evidence.

Ned closed his friend's journal and set it aside. His steward entered and tried to assist him in readying for bed, but Ned preferred to undress himself. The steward bustled about straightening everything in the room but the paperwork on the table and taking the pieces of clothing Ned discarded as each item came off.

Finally, he dismissed the servant, doused the lamps, and climbed into his hammock. With the gun port closed, no light penetrated the small room. Ned closed his eyes and was instantly bombarded by images and voices of everything that had happened in the past five days. One by one, he dismissed each errant thought until only one remained.

Charles Lott. Everything about the boy struck Ned as odd, slightly off. Not right. He was too delicate, too small, his proportions not quite right for a fifteen-year-old. He was too effeminate.

Even that epithet did not put Ned's mind to rest. Effeminate tendencies were not unusual in the Royal Navy, but there was more to it with Lott. Rather than being a man with a few feminine mannerisms, it was as if Charles Lott were a woman with a few masculine mannerisms.

Ned's eyes flew open. Yes, that was it. That was what felt so wrong about Charles Lott. He looked and moved more like a woman than a man.

And directly on the heels of that realization—

Ned bolted upright, nearly flipping himself out of the hammock. Surely not. Charles Lott...Charlotte.

No. It could not be. Charlotte Ransome had no reason to disguise herself and put herself through the arduous life of a midshipman on a warship. Not when she could have traveled in comfort with Julia and William as a passenger on *Alexandra*.

But it fit. As soon as her name came to mind, he knew it was her. He had avoided her as much as he could while in Portsmouth, but he had admired her from afar often enough to know, almost beyond a doubt, that Charles Lott was Charlotte Ransome.

He now wished that instead of taking promotion to acting captain of *Audacious* he had thrown himself overboard.

They would make port in Madeira in a few more days. By then, he would confirm Charlotte's identity and turn her over to her brother. Yes, that was the best course of action. He could not be responsible for the welfare of Commodore William Ransome's only sister.

No matter how much he admired her for being able to fool a ship full of experienced sailors and officers, she would be in constant danger of discovery. And if the men on this ship discovered they had been taking orders from a woman, mutiny would be the least of Ned's problems.

The sooner he got her off this ship, the better.

Julia was bored. She tried to hide it, but the difference in her demeanor was obvious. William wished he could spend more time with her, but he had to be seen by the men as not neglecting his duties on account of his wife. Her injured foot kept her from taking walks on deck. The only thing he could do to try to give her some relief from the daily monotony was to invite his officers and midshipmen to dine with them. At table, with several people surrounding her, the sparkle rekindled in her green eyes, the wan expression left her face.

After supper he assisted her into the day cabin. "How are you at calculus?"

She looked at him askance. "Calculus?"

"Yes. You see, Dr. Hawthorne was instructing the midshipmen in calculus. And now that he's aboard *Audacious*, no one is keeping up with their lessons. I thought I remembered your saying you studied all of the same lessons as Michael, even after he went to sea."

Julia sank onto the sofa and swung her legs around to stretch them out on the seat. "I would probably need to review the textbook. But it will be difficult for me to join them out on deck and stand while instructing them."

"They will come to you—in the dining cabin. You can sit at the head of the table."

"Will they take issue with being instructed by a woman?"

"You are not 'a woman.' You are Mrs. Commodore, and as such they will pay you proper respect—or I will teach them proper respect."

He picked up the mathematics book from his desk and handed it to her. "Best review it tonight. Hawthorne marked his place. Your first lesson is at four bells in the forenoon watch tomorrow."

Julia opened the book and scanned a few pages. She gave him a questioning glance. "Will Dr. Hawthorne be rejoining us at Madeira?"

"I hope so. But only as long as the injured men he is treating are sufficiently recovered. If he does not feel comfortable leaving them to *Audacious*'s surgeon's mate, then he will stay."

She looked over another page and then closed the book. "How do you suppose Ned is getting on with the *Audacious* crew?"

William shrugged out of his coat and draped it across the back of his chair before sitting. "He told me before we left Portsmouth that the first lieutenant expressed concerns about some divisiveness amongst the crew. But I know Ned Cochrane, and I know of what he is capable. He will get them sorted."

"So if it is not worry over Ned that kept you awake most of the night, what was it?"

He took his turn casting a questioning glance at her. He had lain still, staring at the patch of moonlight coming through the open gun port almost all night. He had not tossed and turned. She, on the other hand, had seemed to sleep soundly.

"I was thinking of Charlotte and the trouble with Lord Rotheram. I know there is naught I can do, yet I spent the night thinking through everything I should have instructed Collin to do to ensure her safety."

A slight smile interrupted the concern on Julia's face. "But I know Collin Yates, and I know of what he is capable. He will get it sorted." She adjusted her dress to cover her feet better. "I know it is different—trusting Ned to sort out an unruly crew comprised of men you do not know, and trusting Collin to take care of your sister and solve the legal dilemma she found herself in. But will God not be as faithful and steadfast in both instances?"

Something he found endearing—and, at the same time, annoying—about Julia was her tendency to remember and challenge him with his own words. "Aye. But if you have difficulty putting your faith in me and coming to rely on me, when I am here with you, you can see how much more difficult it is to let go of doubt and rely completely on God."

Julia sighed. "Now you understand my plight."

He looked up from his folded hands, uncertain she had truly grasped what he said. Humor danced in her eyes. He shook his head, but not before his own grasp of the irony drew a smile from him.

Julia laughed in response, and the sound acted as a salve for his worry-abraded soul. She had not laughed enough since their marriage—at least, not when she was alone with him. He feared it was the necessity—and habit—of hiding his own emotions wearing off onto her.

"You deserve better."

The levity instantly left her. "Pardon?"

"You deserve better—a happier, more interesting life than what I can give you."

"You believe I am not happy? And that my life is not more interesting than the majority of women can boast already? William, if you tried to make it more interesting, I do not know I could survive it."

"But you are not happy here, aboard *Alexandra*."

"Only because a ship is no place for a woman, even if she is 'Mrs. Commodore.' And especially if she is tied by the leg from doing anything—quite literally."

William tried to take her at her word, and yet a remnant of insecurity remained. Not an hour ago, she had talked and laughed and told stories from her life in Jamaica to the rapt lieutenants and midshipmen. Here, in their private quarters, she rarely laughed; and, though they enjoyed conversation in the evenings, the subjects tended toward more serious topics such as theology, politics, the war. She tried to elicit anecdotes from him about his experiences, but he firmly believed the past should stay in the past. He did not want to become like Admiral Glover, whom people avoided at social gatherings rather than be regaled, again, with tales of his exploits. But perhaps an occasional story of his life would not be amiss.

He opened his mouth to begin to relate the history of *Alexandra*'s brief posting in the waters off Sicily—but was preempted by a loud knocking on the door. "Enter."

Dawling came in. "Mr. Kennedy's compliments, sir, and a message is coming in from *Audacious*."

William stood and donned his coat. "Thank you, Dawling. Please see to Mrs. Ransome's comfort." He inclined his head toward Julia but left the cabin without registering her expression. Disappointment, no doubt, that their private time had once again been cut short by his duty.

He made his way up to the stern of the poop. Kennedy stood with telescope to eye in the waning sunlight, reading out the message being raised in the bow of the ship following them. One of the younger midshipmen recorded it in the log book.

Finally, Kennedy lowered his glass. "Commodore Ransome, sir, *Audacious* reports two more have died. They will be buried at sea within the hour."

William checked the time. "Send word to the fleet: All ships are to raise black pennant until three bells of the second dogwatch to honor the dead."

"Aye, aye, sir."

Rather than return to the cabin, William wandered the ship, stopping to speak with the midshipmen and officers only to set their minds at ease over his unusual behavior. A decision lay before him. Either he could make an effort to open himself—his past, his emotions—to Julia and risk becoming more vulnerable by deepening his attachment to her, or he could continue on as he had started his marriage, providing Julia the protection of his name, the hope of a future family, and a modest level of affection.

Indeed, the same choice lay before both of them. The fear that he would choose the opposite of Julia's choice kept him anchored to the quarterdeck, staring out at the silver-streaked ocean long after he knew Julia would have retired for the night.

❧

Ned made sure he was on deck when the third watch reported at eight bells in the afternoon watch. Once again, Midshipman Lott had been the first to calculate and mark noon. The more he watched Lott, the more certain he became that Charles Lott was Charlotte Ransome. Although he could fathom no explanation for why she would choose to put herself in such a position, he grudgingly admitted she performed the duty of a midshipman admirably. Though not as strong as a lad of fifteen, she had mastered the fine art of command in a way that most lieutenants of one or two years' experience had yet to learn.

The majority of the crew liked and respected Midshipman Lott, including almost all of the young men with whom she was berthed. He cringed and closed his eyes a moment. If anyone in England learned she had spent more than a fortnight living in the same room as seventeen men, her reputation would be ruined—and it would reflect poorly on Commodore Ransome and his entire family.

That consequence of revealing Charlotte's identity—in conjunction with the crew's expected negative reaction—kept Ned from dragging her into his cabin and confronting her with the truth. And if he handed her over to William when they made port in Madeira tomorrow, it would leave *Audacious* dangerously understaffed in command positions. Now that he'd had almost a week to observe and meet all of the midshipmen, he could not think of another who would be capable of assuming her role as midshipman of the watch.

He paced the quarterdeck, hands clasped behind his back, head down. When faced with so dire a dilemma, William would have counseled him to pray for a solution. But though Ned formed the reverent words in his mind, such a prayer seemed to do no better than his continual mulling of the facts.

The late August sun beat down on him unmercifully. He left the quarterdeck and paused in the wheelhouse to review the log board before retiring to his cabin. He exercised his prerogative as captain and did not speak to anyone in the shaded area in front of his cabin—especially Midshipman Lott. It was not like him to run away or hide from a problem, but in this case, not sure what he should do and afraid he would give Charlotte away inadvertently, avoidance seemed the best policy.

Seemingly endless reams of paperwork gave him the excuse he needed to stay in his cabin the next several hours. Later, after supper, when he'd started to think about turning in, a knock came at the main door.

"Enter."

Midshipman Jamison entered and saluted. "Lieutenant Gardiner's compliments, sir. Signal from lead ship—they have sighted Madeira. We are to prepare to drop anchor before noon tomorrow."

"Thank you, Mr. Jamison." Having stopped at Madeira a few times to resupply over the years, Ned could picture the approach to the harbor clearly. Even following a dozen ships in, the task should be simple. However, as it had been a few years since the last time, he pulled out the most up-to-date charts to make sure there had been no shifting of sandbars or reefs since his last anchorage here.

He plotted the course and mentally went through the orders to the crew to make it happen. Maneuvering into position at the rear of the convoy in the predawn darkness would add a bit of hazard to the experience, but so far this crew had given him no reason to doubt their ability to pull together when necessitated.

After a few fitful hours of sleep, he dressed and joined the midshipman of the forenoon watch on deck.

"Good morning, Mr. Lott." Ned squinted against the sunlight at the lump of land beyond the bow of the ship.

"'Morning, Captain Cochrane." She did a good job of keeping her voice pitched lower than what he'd become accustomed to hearing in Portsmouth.

The first lieutenant joined them at the binnacle.

"Mr. Gardiner, signal all hands to prepare the ship for making anchor."

"Aye, aye, Captain." The young officer carried out the order, and soon the formerly calm, quiet ship was teeming with sailors hoisting sails and manning the capstan in preparation for lowering the anchor.

For the first time in a week, Ned caught sight of *Alexandra*'s bluff lines. Though both ships had come from the same yard, *Alexandra*, nearly twenty years older than *Audacious*, had been built during a time when craftsmanship was more important than haste when it came to the finishing touches.

Ned was about to start calling orders when he remembered his position. "Take us in, Lieutenant Gardiner."

The first lieutenant, rather than appear excited, looked as if he were about to lose his breakfast. "Aye, aye, sir." He stepped forward and began yelling the same commands Ned had planned last night, leaving Ned nothing to worry about—except for Charlotte Ransome, who, even now, hung twenty feet above the deck supported by the ropes and ratlines of the foremast shroud.

Once the anchor dropped and *Audacious* came to rest near *Alexandra*, Ned released the breath that had been caught in his chest. Gardiner had been slower with issuing some commands than Ned was comfortable with, but the memory of his own first few attempts at bringing a ship into harbor kept him from stepping forward and taking over.

Released from duty, the sailors crowded the sides of the ship as boats bearing everything imaginable flocked around the new arrivals.

"No one is to come aboard," Ned told the lieutenants, catching a glimpse of a boat full of women of ill repute headed their direction.

"Aye, aye, sir."

"Captain Cochrane, sir." Midshipman Lott came to a breathless stop a few paces from him. Ned took a deep breath and schooled his expression before turning to look at her—no, him. He had to keep thinking of Lott as a boy, not as Charlotte Ransome.

"What is it, Mr. Lott?" Ned clasped his hands behind his back.

"Signal from flagship, sir. All captains to report to *Alexandra*." Lott stared straight ahead at Ned's chest, appearing as though not wanting to make eye contact any more than Ned did.

"Very good. Lieutenant Gardiner, make ready the ship's boat." Ned returned to his cabin without a backward look at Lott. It would have been logical for him to select Lott to accompany him to *Alexandra*, but if he recognized Lott as Charlotte Ransome, surely her brother and Julia would recognize her as well. As he was unsure what he wanted to do about the situation, he did not want to risk their recognizing her before he made his decision.

Twenty minutes later, Ned climbed up the accommodation ladder in *Alexandra*'s side. Familiar faces lined the waist, greeting him like a long-lost brother. Seeing them all again made him wish to return to duty on *Alexandra* even more, yet he had to admit that after week as acting captain, he was enjoying command more than he ever thought he would.

William greeted him on the quarterdeck. Ned could tell the commodore wanted to question him about his first week on board *Audacious*; however, with the presence of several of the captains of the convoy ships, he was unable to do so. Instead, he introduced Ned to the other captains while they waited for the rest to arrive.

When all were present, William ushered them into the dining cabin. Ned caught a glimpse of Julia in the day cabin before Dawling closed the door between the two rooms. William motioned for Ned to sit at the foot of the table, while the convoy captains lined the sides.

William gave a report on the loss of *Buzzard* to the pirates followed by a strongly worded admonition on the importance of maintaining a tight formation for the remainder of the voyage. Ned tried to keep his focus on the commodore, but the image of Charles Lott kept interfering. Once they left Madeira he would not have the opportunity to speak to Julia or William for at least a fortnight, until they reached Barbados and stopped again to resupply. He realized the knowledge of Charlotte's presence aboard *Audacious* was a burden he could not carry by himself. He decided he would speak to Julia alone, if the opportunity presented itself.

William called the ships' masters into the room and spread the charts out on the table. The next hour was spent plotting their course from Madeira to Barbados. Ned's sailing master took copious notes in his log book, which Ned double-checked against his own. Once assured that everybody had the correct course and heading, William dismissed them with the expectation that they would have all supplies purchased and stowed aboard their ships by dawn day after tomorrow.

Ned stayed back after everyone else had left. "Commodore Ransome, sir, I hoped to take the opportunity to call on Mrs. Ransome while I'm here." He hoped William would not take offense to his request.

"Mrs. Ransome is anxious to see you, Ned. Please take your time, and I would be remiss if I did not tell you that you are expected for supper tonight." William donned his hat and left the dining cabin.

Ned waited until the door closed behind William before he knocked on the door to the day cabin. It opened, and Ned found himself face-to-face with the commodore's burly steward.

Ned cleared his throat nervously. "I hope to call upon Mrs. Ransome, if she is receiving."

Dawling stepped back and motioned Ned into the cabin. "Welcome back to *Alexandra,* Cap'n Cochrane." The steward turned and saluted Julia Ransome, who sat at her desk. "Acting Captain Ned Cochrane to see you, mum."

With a beaming smile, Julia extended her hand toward Ned without rising from her chair. "Captain Cochrane, how wonderful it is to see you again. I had hoped we would have a chance to speak before you left *Alexandra*. You will forgive me for not rising to greet you properly, but I injured my foot the night of the attack. And with Dr. Hawthorne aboard your ship, I have been unable to convince William that I should be allowed to walk on it now."

Ned crossed to her side and let her press his hand between hers. "Dr. Hawthorne returned to *Alexandra* with me, ma'am, so I hope he will clear you to return to your normal activities before the day is over."

She motioned him to the sofa beside her desk, and he perched on the edge of it. He answered her questions about his new command and officers and about the frustration that came from trying to split the crew into three watches instead of two.

After several minutes, conversation lagged. A few long moments of silence ensued, and then Ned looked up from his perusal of the rug spread under Julia's sofa.

"While I do so enjoy seeing you, Ned, I cannot help but think there is something you wanted to tell me—more than just of your first few days as a captain."

Ned could sit no longer. He leapt to his feet and paced the length of the cabin. When he returned to Julia's position on the larboard side of the room, he stopped and clasped his hands behind his back. "What I am about to divulge is of the utmost confidence. If I tell you, I must beg that you tell no one, especially Commodore Ransome."

Chapter Twenty-Four

Julia stared at Ned for a moment, indecision warring within her. She wanted to help him, but agreeing to keep something from William…

"Perhaps it is wrong of me to ask you to keep this from your husband," Ned said. "So I will ask you to tell him only when you think it is prudent."

"Thank you for understanding that it would be impossible for me to promise to keep something from Commodore Ransome. I will promise you that I shall use my best judgment in deciding when to tell him." Her concern for Ned rose as he started pacing the cabin again.

He took two turns about the room before returning to his seat on the sofa. He perched on the edge, propped his elbows on his knees, and clenched his hands together. "Now that I am here, I hardly know where to start." He stared at his thumbs for a few moments. "It's about Charlotte."

"Charlotte? Charlotte Ransome?" Julia turned her head away to hide her smile as an idea started to form as to the nature of Ned's discomfort. Although the two had seemed to avoid each other in Portsmouth, the way they had watched each other had not escaped her notice.

"Yes. She is aboard *Audacious*."

"She is…where?" Julia was not certain if she was supposed to laugh, but what else could she do at such an absurd statement? "Charlotte is most likely at this moment on her way home to her mother. Collin Yates promised he would see to that when he visited us the night before we weighed anchor."

"Nay, Mrs. Ransome. I guarantee you, Miss Ransome is not at Gateacre." Ned finally looked up at her. "Not only is she aboard *Audacious*, she is in disguise as a midshipman."

She opened her mouth to protest again, to assure Ned that he was incorrect, but the earnestness in his expression stayed her words. "Why would she do such a thing?"

"I had hoped you could tell me. Is there any reason why Miss Ransome would want to leave England in secret? Why she would want to travel to Jamaica without anyone—including her family—knowing?"

The fragment of the letter Julia had accidentally read flew into her mind with stabbing accusation. Or could it be that Charlotte had anticipated the reprisal from Lord Rotheram? "If it is she, I am certain she has her reasons. Have you…have you spoken to her? Has she given you any sense of her thinking?"

"She does not know I have recognized her—though I cannot understand how no one else has seen her for a woman." Ned ran his fingers through his thick, golden-brown hair. "Every time I am near her, I fear I will accidentally reveal her secret to everyone else."

Julia shook her head. "I am amazed she has survived two weeks in such harsh conditions without revealing the secret herself. You should have brought her with you rather than condemning her to continue living in such conditions."

The corner of Ned's mouth quirked up. "But she does not seem to mind. In fact," he hooked his hand behind his neck, "she is thriving. She was just promoted to midshipman of the watch. Truth be told, she rather seems to be enjoying herself."

Though horrified at the idea of a gentlewoman of Charlotte's social stature working as hard as the duty of a midshipman required, Julia could not help but smile in remembrance of her own insistence at the age of twelve that she should be allowed to join the Royal Navy along with Michael.

Her mirth faded quickly. "Oh, dear. You mean she has been living in the cockpit with the rest of the midshipmen?"

Ned's half smile faded as well. "Thus my reluctance to bring her identity to anyone's attention. Disregarding the reaction the crew of *Audacious* would have to the knowledge they have been taking orders from a woman, of greatest concern is the effect such a revelation would have on her reputation."

"And on William's," Julia breathed, pressing her hand to her chest.

"Aye." Ned nodded. "I cannot imagine it would go well with the Admiralty if they discovered Commodore Ransome's sister had done such a thing."

Though well over her seasickness, Julia began to feel nauseated. "Are you certain she is well and no harm has come to her? We shall be here almost two days. Surely we can find a way to smuggle her off your ship and bring her secretly onto *Alexandra*."

"And what would you tell the crew of *Alexandra*? How would you explain her presence here, if you're unable to explain her presence on *Audacious*?"

The urge to pace was so great, Julia's legs twitched. "But how can we justify leaving her on *Audacious* in such a precarious position? You yourself said she is in constant danger of discovery. What will you do if her identity is discovered in the middle of the crossing to Barbados?"

"Not only has she managed to stay hidden, she has become an integral part of the crew. Indeed, if she were to leave *Audacious*, I would have difficulty replacing her. As I had to promote two midshipmen to lieutenants, I now have a dearth of midshipmen qualified to lead watches. You may find it hard to believe, but Charlotte Ransome is one of the most capable midshipmen I have ever served with."

Julia could not decide between rubbing her aching head or her churning stomach, so she settled for wringing her hands instead. Aside from the perilous possibilities arising from Charlotte's presence on *Audacious*, Julia feared William's reaction when he learned of it. He would want to bring her onto *Alexandra*, to keep her safe, to try to undo the damage to her reputation—without any thought to his own.

"What are you going to tell Commodore Ransome?" Ned stood and straightened his waistcoat.

"I do not know. I need to meditate on this. Charlotte must have a compelling reason for choosing this means of transportation to Jamaica, and an equally compelling reason for not wanting her brother, or me, to know she is traveling with us." She pressed her thumb and middle finger to the inside corners of her eyes, trying to rid herself of the headache starting there. "I never mentioned it to her, but I asked Commodore Ransome if Charlotte could travel with me as my companion. But he reminded me of my own opinion that it would be better for her prospects if she stayed in England and took advantage of the opportunities provided her by Lady Dalrymple and the Fairfaxes."

"She must have determined her prospects lay elsewhere—whether in the Royal Navy or on the other side of the Atlantic I will leave to you to discover. But now I must come to the question and then be on my way. Do I tell Commodore Ransome, reveal Charlotte's presence, and turn her over to him, or do I continue on, feigning ignorance and allowing her to maintain her secret?"

Julia's mind wanted to tear itself apart. Half of her wanted to see Charlotte safely installed right here, right now, in *Alexandra*'s big cabin; the other half wanted to allow Charlotte the freedom the young woman had gone to such dire measures to secure for herself.

If she were in Charlotte's position, what would she want? She knew in an instant that she would want to continue on in her disguise, to be allowed to see her journey through. Julia rubbed her dry tongue against the roof of her mouth. "Keep her secret...for now." Her chest tightened with the painful knowledge she would once more be breaking her promise to William. "Do your best to keep her from being discovered by anyone else."

Relief, followed by a different expression of concern, filled Ned's eyes. "I will." He bowed. "Mrs. Ransome, thank you for being my confidante in this matter. It will be easier for me to handle this situation knowing I am not alone in my worry and concern."

"I do not know how long I will be able to hide this from the commodore. I will try to keep it from him as long as I can; however, I cannot lie to him, Ned. I will seek the right opportunity to tell him."

Ned looked slightly ill at the idea of William's finding out. "I understand." He bowed again. "I shall wish you good afternoon, Mrs. Ransome."

"Good afternoon to you, also."

He turned and reached for the doorknob.

"Oh, and Ned?"

He spun on his heel to face her again. "Yes, ma'am?"

"Keep a watchful eye on our girl. If you believe she is in danger—whether in physical danger or in danger of discovery—I trust you will know what to do."

He inclined his head in a nod. "Yes, ma'am. I shall protect her with my very life if need be."

She had no doubt he would. As soon as he was gone, she rose and, walking on the heel of her injured foot, did her best to resume Ned's pacing.

William must be told. Not only as Charlotte's brother, but as the commander of this small fleet of ships, if Charlotte's presence became known and William discovered both Ned and Julia had known of it and tried to keep it a secret, Ned's career would be ruined...as would Julia's marriage. This was no mere run-in with a drunken lord Julia was keeping from him this time.

She could not tell him while they were docked. She had no doubt that if he found out now, he would storm *Audacious*'s quarterdeck and drag his sister back to *Alexandra*—and would probably find a ship bound for England to send her home on.

The letter fragment from a man declaring his love for Charlotte, asking her to marry him, made the girl's motivation clear: She was running away from England to marry a man of whom she knew her mother and brothers would not approve. Julia knew nothing of the anonymous letter writer, but given that Charlotte had kept the letters hidden and that she now fled to Jamaica incognito, Julia had to assume the young man had found disfavor with Mrs. Ransome, and thus with William.

No, she could not tell him now. She would wait until they were once again at sea…until they were closer to their final destination. Until she was certain that William could not do anything drastic.

William tried not to think too much of the amount of time Ned had been in the cabin with Julia. He trusted both of them. He simply wished he could spend such uninterrupted time talking with her.

Ned emerged from the cabin so deep in thought that he walked past O'Rourke without acknowledging the new first lieutenant's greeting until O'Rourke reached out and touched Ned's arm. What could be so troubling that Ned could speak of it only to Julia?

William pressed his lips together and returned his gaze to the list of supplies the purser wanted him to approve for purchase. He signed the order and gave it back to the warrant officer.

Ned approached with a salute. William reciprocated.

"Unless you require my presence further, sir, I shall return to *Audacious* and see if my officers have completed their supply list." Ned's usually laughing eyes seemed dull and distant.

William kept his concern to himself. Julia would tell him if anything was amiss with Ned that would have an ill effect on his ship or crew. "You have permission to leave the ship, Captain Cochrane. However, you will report at three bells in the second dogwatch for supper."

"Aye, sir." Ned gave a half bow and departed through the starboard waist entry port. William tried to turn his attention to other matters, but Ned's unusual demeanor continued to claim part of his focus. He wanted to return to the cabin and ask Julia for an explanation of his former first officer's behavior, but duty forced him to stay on deck for the remainder of the afternoon.

"Boat coming up, Commodore."

"Where away?" William asked the question even though he knew where and whom it would be.

"Starboard side, sir. 'Tis Lieutenant—Captain Cochrane, sir."

Permission for Ned to board *Alexandra* was requested and given. William scrutinized him when he appeared on deck. Much of the traces of melancholy William thought he had seen before were no longer as evident, though Ned's smile took longer to develop and stayed a briefer time than usual.

He ushered Ned toward the cabin, and they were joined by *Alexandra*'s six lieutenants. Tomorrow night William would play host to the captains of all the ships. Tonight was for his officers.

Dawling was just pushing Julia's chair in when William and the officers entered the dining cabin. Ned and each of the lieutenants stopped and gave her a polite bow before taking their regular places at the table. As Gibson had been added to their number as the acting sixth lieutenant, he hung back and waited for everyone else to claim his seat before taking the open chair in the middle. As the honored guest, Ned sat at Julia's right hand, at the opposite end of the table from William.

No one could have called the meal exquisite—nothing like what Collin's French-trained steward had been able to prepare—but the meal Dawling and Cook had prepared for them was hearty and tasty.

The lieutenants, naturally, wanted to hear about Ned's first week in command of a ship of the line.

"It has gone well," Ned responded. "Though there have been some rough waters along the way." Here, Ned stole a sidelong glance at Julia, who gave him a tight-lipped smile.

The bite of beef in William's mouth lost all flavor. Ned *had* confided something to Julia. William wanted to demand a full telling of it, but he exerted his self-control to wait until his private time with Julia later tonight.

"What problems have you faced?" Lieutenant Eastwick asked.

Ned took another glance at Julia before answering. "I learned almost as soon as I took command of the vessel that it is not a unified crew. The majority of the officers served under Captain Yates. But Captain Parker—God rest his soul—brought several over with him. Midshipmen, warrant officers, and lieutenants. It seems a rivalry formed between the two groups, with Parker's officers feeling they had the captain's favor and therefore lording it over those who had served under Captain Yates. So I have spent much of my first week as an acting captain trying to figure out ways I can forge these two factions into one united crew."

William relaxed, understanding now what Ned's long interview with Julia earlier had been about. When Ned had shared his concerns about the *Audacious* crew to William, he had mentioned he had a few ideas on how to help his crew work together better. Realizing Julia's experience in managing vast numbers of workers who probably did not always get along, Ned must have decided to run his ideas past her to get her input on their viability.

He enjoyed the rest of the dinner party, having worked out the meaning behind the occasional glances between Ned and Julia. After dinner ended, William walked Ned to the waist entry port.

"I will see you tomorrow at three bells in the second dogwatch, Captain Cochrane." He hoped Ned would volunteer his ideas for unifying his crew, but perhaps he thought William did not have time to deal with such issues. "If you would like to come early and discuss any of the issues you are having with your crew, I would be more than happy to make the time."

"Thank you, Commodore Ransome. And please thank Mrs. Ransome for a lovely meal." Ned saluted before disappearing down the side of the ship.

William watched until the small boat had almost reached *Audacious*. A glance at the sky informed him it was almost time for evening call to quarters and inspection. He returned to the wheelhouse and waited a few minutes until eight bells signaled the beginning of the evening watch.

"Lieutenant O'Rourke, beat to quarters for inspection." William stood beside the binnacle, hands clasped behind his back, and observed as his crew efficiently made their way to battle stations. Though many might not understand his strict adherence to the custom of evening beat to quarters, William had been in the navy—and at war—far too long to relax his guard. He did not want to think ill of the dead, but he wondered if Captain Parker had been as scrupulous in training and inspecting his crew.

After making a complete inspection of the ship, William dismissed the men. As the majority of them would be on make-and-mend tomorrow, rather than immediately going below decks and hanging their hammocks, most lingered above to spend their hard-earned money on trinkets, fresh fruit and vegetables, and other goods offered them from the small boats that had swarmed about them ever since they docked.

As his presence was no longer needed on deck, William returned to the cabin. Julia sat at her desk writing furiously.

"What time will you deliver the packet of correspondence tomorrow?" she asked, the nib of her quill hovering over the page.

"Not until the afternoon. You have plenty of time to write a great long letter to your father." He wanted to press Julia for details on the ideas Ned had presented to her, but if Ned had wanted William to know, he would have told him. William himself might not tell a commanding officer that he had sought advice from a woman, no matter how intelligent and accomplished she was.

"Good. I was afraid you might be sending it first thing in the morning and that I might not have time to finish." She set her quill down. "I understand Dr. Hawthorne came aboard this afternoon. I hoped I might speak with him this evening."

William called for Dawling, who appeared moments later. "Pass word for Dr. Hawthorne."

"Aye, aye, sir." Dawling knuckled his forehead and left the cabin.

"Had you a good visit with Ned this afternoon?" He sat at his desk and opened his own stationery box to complete the correspondence he also needed to send tomorrow.

"Yes. He had a concern about his crew that he wished for my opinion on."

Once again, William was struck by Julia's ability to mask what she was feeling. She had promised she would not keep anything important from him again, so as she did not share more of her conversation with Ned, he had to trust that it was nothing more than she said.

Because one thing he knew about Julia, she was a woman of her word.

Chapter Twenty-Five

Charlotte was not certain what happened when Ned was aboard *Alexandra*, but in the days following the brief stopover in Madeira, she felt his eyes constantly upon her. He could not possibly know her secret or else, she was certain, he would have turned her over to William. However, with the constant vigil he now seemed to keep over her, she worried he might suspect something. So she made it her business to get away from him when she was not on duty by trying to avoid everyone altogether.

Occasionally she could find solitude in the cockpit, but those not on duty came in and out often enough to disrupt her peace.

The only quiet place she could find on the ship was the infirmary, and with most of the injured sailors now recovered enough to return to duty, Charlotte took her journal or her stationery box and a candle, found a quiet corner, and spent many a pleasant hour writing or sketching. The surgeon's mate now in charge of the infirmary ensured the others working with him did not bother her, and she never outstayed her welcome.

The letter she had sent to Mama from Madeira had been short, hastily scrawled in the last moments before the correspondence packet had been handed over to the captain of an English merchant ship headed for Portsmouth. She had not wanted to risk discovery by someone seeing her writing the long letter of explanation she wished she could send to her mother. But she hoped that even the short note assuring

Mama that she was safe and well and under William's protection would relieve the worry she knew she had caused.

"Mr. Lott, are you still here?" The surgeon's mate stepped out of the shadows and leaned over her position on the floor. "'Tis almost eight bells. You'll be late for duty if you aren't careful."

Charlotte closed her journal and wrapped its leather thong around it; then she jumped to her feet and bent down to retrieve her quill, ink bottle, and hat. "Thank you for telling me, Jack."

"You've always been nice to me, Mr. Lott, and I like to return good for good. Now, if you were that Mr. Kent, I might have let you sit here and be late."

Charlotte bit the inside of her cheek to keep from laughing. "You know it is not good to play favorites." Even though protesting the sentiment was the right thing to do, pleasure tingled in Charlotte's stomach at the idea that even ordinary seamen liked her more than Kent.

The surgeon's mate knuckled his forehead and gave her a sardonic grin, as if to say he knew she protested only out of politeness.

Charlotte returned the salute and rushed away to the cockpit to stow her writing supplies before reporting to the quarterdeck for duty.

The echo of the last of the eight chimes faded away just as Charlotte came to a stop in the wheelhouse. The sailing master looked at her in surprise. "Cutting it a mite short this time, Mr. Lott?"

"I lost track of time." Charlotte tried to catch her breath from the mad dash from the cockpit in the bow to the wheelhouse in the stern. She turned her attention to the log board, reviewing Midshipman Jamison's notations of their speed and bearing over the last four hours. She copied them into her log book and then wrote down the new information the sailing master gave her.

Nerves already taut, Charlotte's heart gave a little leap every time the marine standing guard at the door of the big cabin shifted position or made any kind of noise. By the time her watch ended at four o'clock, her back ached from the constant fear of Ned emerging from the cabin and exposing her identity.

Though she still hated the taste of it, she drank her entire ration of grog that evening at supper, feeling for the first time the relaxing effects of the rum. She wished for more, but then she understood why her mother had always warned her about the evils of strong drink. She needed to keep her wits about her at all times in order to remember who she was supposed to be so that those around her would never suspect who she really was.

Isaac cajoled Charlotte into returning above deck with him and most of the other idle midshipmen after supper. Since Ned had taken over command of *Audacious*, he had allowed the off-duty midshipmen and officers to idle on deck for an hour in the evenings. They soon discovered Lieutenant Duncan played the fiddle quite well and knew virtually every sea chantey the others asked him to play. In fact, it became a competition between the lieutenants and midshipmen to see who would be the first one to come up with a song Duncan did not know.

After singing along with two tunes she had recently learned, Charlotte slipped away from the boisterous group and moved toward the bow of the ship. In the forecastle a tall, lone figure stood beside the foremast, hands clasped behind his back. Charlotte stopped, her shoe making the tiniest scraping sound against the deck. The silhouetted figure turned, revealing it to be Lieutenant Martin.

"Please forgive me, sir. I had no wish to disturb you."

"Are you not enjoying the music this evening, Mr. Lott?" Martin relaxed his stance and smiled at her.

"I find I am not in the mood for such lively activity tonight." Charlotte hesitated, but at a signal from Martin she climbed up onto the forecastle deck to stand beside him, staring out over the dark waters beyond the bow of the ship. She mimicked his stance, hands clasped behind her back, feet shoulder-width apart, knees easy. Over the past month she had become so accustomed to the pitch and roll of the ship that she had almost forgotten what it felt like to stand on solid ground.

From the corner of her eye she caught the motion of Martin's nod. "I wondered if you might not be like me. While I occasionally enjoy the music and the laughter, I also have to find times when I can be alone and quiet. I have discovered over the years how hard this is to do on a large ship at war, but it is necessary for me. And I have learned to recognize and take advantage of the opportunities when they come. It can be hard though, trying to explain the need for solitude to others."

Charlotte had never given it any consideration, but upon further reflection she now realized that, like Martin, she had always sought out a quiet hour before or after a dinner party or ball at which she was sure to be surrounded by talking, laughter, music, and noise.

Although this would have been the perfect time to strike up a conversation with Martin and learn more about him, to break the silence between them would have been as unthinkable as laughing in church.

Though she could still hear it clearly, standing here, gazing out over the dark water seemed to mute the irksome noise the rest of the officers were making. And when it died away, her ears rang from the lack of sound. The sound of *Audacious* cutting through the waves filled the void. Charlotte closed her eyes, breathed deeply of the salt air, and relaxed more fully than even the grog had coaxed her to do earlier. The midshipman who was assigned the duty of the forecastle this watch reported himself to Lieutenant Martin and moved forward to resume watching for any signal from the ship ahead of them.

"I do believe that is your signal to return to the cockpit, Mr. Lott." Martin looked down at her with an almost apologetic smile.

"Thank you for allowing me to pass the hour with you, Lieutenant Martin." Charlotte touched the rim of her hat in salute.

Martin pinched the forepoint of his hat between thumb and forefinger. "Any time, Mr. Lott."

The confined space of the cockpit served to both amplify and muddle the noise the midshipmen had been making on deck. Once again, it seemed no one had been able to stump Lieutenant Duncan. Charlotte slipped into her berth and started to remove her coat, but in the dim light cast by the few candles out on the table, she realized something was amiss.

She stood very still and looked around to try to figure out what had caught her attention as being out of place. There. The lid to her sea chest was slightly ajar, with what looked like the cuff of her other jacket sticking out. She reached down to lift the lid, but took her hand away when it came in contact with something wet. She turned her palm toward the light coming from the main part of the cockpit. A dark smudge stained her fingertips. She sniffed it—ink.

She dropped to her knees and, touching only the corners of the lid, opened the chest. She could not see well, but it was easy enough to tell that her clothing was no longer neatly folded, as she had left it. Someone had been rifling through her belongings. Fear tightened like a fist in her chest. She ran a mental inventory of the trunk's contents: extra clothing, stockings, shoes, stationery—which she had been drawing on, not writing anything someone might use against her—her log book, and a few personal items, such as a plain comb, a sliver of unscented soap she had acquired on one of her many secret outings in Portsmouth, and…

She dug down under her clothing and stationery box. Finding the stack of thick cotton rags and fabric belt still neatly folded together, seemingly untouched, she rocked back on her heels with a sigh. Though whoever rummaged through her trunk might not know what they were for, their mere presence would raise questions.

She closed the trunk and stood, touching her hand to the small of her back. Not only did tucking her journal under her waistband help keep her pants up, it assured her nothing she wrote in it would fall under unfriendly eyes.

She stepped out of her cubicle and took one of the lighted candles from the table. Its glow illuminated the mess inside her trunk. Before she went on duty, she had set her ink bottle down on top of the folded clothes, thinking she would return it to the stationery box tonight, in which it was unlikely to be overturned. Only she knew the cork had a crack that allowed the bottle to leak when turned on its side.

Tomorrow she would discover the responsible party through careful observation. The culprit's hands would bear evidence against him.

She slept for a couple of hours before reporting for the middle watch at midnight. As expected, all remained quiet during the darkest time of night, when everyone except the watch on duty was asleep. At least, she hoped all of the other midshipmen were asleep and not rummaging in her trunk again. Perhaps when the intruder realized he'd upset the ink bottle, he'd stopped shortly after beginning his invasion of her privacy.

Upon returning to the midshipmen's berth, she discarded her jacket and waistcoat, climbed into her hammock, and fell almost immediately to sleep.

Less than four hours later, she grudgingly rolled out of bed at the "out or down" call and the shrill piping of the "hammocks up" whistle. She pulled her hammock down from its moorings and folded it in preparation to stow it, along with the rest of the crew's, in the netting that lined the sides of the ship. Yawning, she stepped into her shoes and bent to retrieve her waistcoat from the floor where it had slipped off of her sea chest.

A crash and several yelled oaths snapped her upright again.

"Watch what you're doing there!"

"What's the idea?"

"You've ruined my log book!"

Forgetting her vest and coat, Charlotte stepped out of her cubicle—and her heart sank. More than half the midshipmen stood back from the table splattered in varying degrees with ink stains. At least eight boys had ink on their hands.

Kent was on duty, so he could not have been personally responsible for the act that eliminated the clear identification of the boy who had violated Charlotte's privacy. It also meant he was unlikely to be the one who had entered her cubicle and gone through her belongings. He would not be able to explain ink stains on his hands when everyone knew he was not here for the "accident."

She returned to her area and finished dressing. Now it would be hard for her to go to Lieutenant Gardiner and tell him of the incident. With no way to positively mark the guilty party, with more than half of the midshipmen now bearing the mark of guilt, and with nothing missing as far as she could determine, complaining of it would only bring her undue attention.

The sea chest that locked had been just five guineas more. She should have ignored the clerk when he told her only lieutenants bought those.

Securing her journal into the waistband of her pants, she buttoned her waistcoat and jacket and joined the others—who had cleaned up the spilled ink—for breakfast.

❧

"Enter." Ned pushed his empty breakfast plate back and looked down to inspect the white expanse of his waistcoat for crumbs or spills. He saw none.

The purser entered the forecabin, knit cap in hand. He knuckled his forehead. "Cap'n Cochrane, sir."

"Yes? What is it, Mr. Harley?"

"I thought you should know, sir, that food is missing from the stores."

Ned started. "Food missing? How much? When was this noticed?"

"Cook brought it to my attention this morning, sir. It is not a vast quantity. A chunk cut from a wheel of cheese and a tin of biscuits, but it means someone has broken into the hold and stolen food meant for the crew, sir."

Ned was well aware of the implications of even the smallest amount of food missing. Stealing anything from the ship's stores was a hanging offense.

"Should we search the ship and have every sailor turn out his belongings to see who took it, sir?" An eager flicker of retribution gleamed in the warrant officer's eyes.

Ned considered saying no. The evidence was probably already gone—consumed by the thief, the tin and wrappers thrown overboard when no one was looking. However, a public search of everyone's belongings would either reveal the thief or discourage him from doing it again.

He stood and buttoned his coat. "Come with me, Mr. Harley." He exited the cabin and stepped out from under the shade of the wheelhouse into the bright morning light.

"Pass word for Bosun Parr and the captain of the marines," he commanded Midshipman Jamison.

"Aye, aye, sir." The teen scurried away.

Ned scanned the faces of the men currently on deck. Had one of them done it? Would that man, there, soon be standing before Ned to receive his punishment? And just what punishment would that be?

Lieutenant Gardiner joined him. Ned inclined his head in acknowledgment of his first officer's presence but did not say anything to him. Gardiner frowned, but he did not press Ned for an explanation.

The boatswain and the captain of the marines both joined him at the same time, followed by Jamison.

Ned tapped his hand against his leg, but stopped as soon as he realized he was doing it. He clenched his hands into fists instead. "Lieutenant Gardiner, Mr. Parr, Captain Macarthy, it has come to my attention we have a thief aboard. Purser Harley informed me that food is missing from the stores. We must discover the responsible party. Mr. Parr, you will pipe all hands for berth inspection. The three of you will conduct the search." He swallowed and looked at Gardiner. "The entire crew's dunnage is to be searched—including the officers, midshipmen, and marines."

Gardiner could not keep his shock from his expression. "Sir, you cannot believe that an officer would steal?"

"I hope not, Mr. Gardiner, but as I cannot be certain, I must not be prejudicial against the seamen. Search the officers' and midshipmen's berths first. If the foodstuffs are not found, they are to help inspect the remainder. Men are to be released to duty as soon as they clear inspection."

"Aye, aye, sir." Gardiner's voice still held incredulity, while the purser's and the marine captain's held nothing but excitement.

"If you find the thief, bring him to me." He looked at each of the three men and received their acquiescence. "Bosun Parr, pipe all hands."

"Aye, aye, sir." Parr stepped forward and repeated the order to his mates, who had followed him to the wheelhouse. Simultaneously, all four of them raised brass whistles to their lips and blew a short series of notes that carried throughout the ship.

Dutifully—but with questioning looks and murmuring amongst themselves—the sailors, midshipmen, and marines on deck went below, leaving only a skeleton crew manning the sails.

Though he could see the question in the sailing master's eyes as he passed the binnacle, Ned said nothing. He had just given an order that could forever alter his officers' opinion of him. By including them in the search, he put them on the same level—if even just for a moment—of the lowest landsman in the crew. He hoped they would understand his need to react in the strongest manner possible to even a hint of misconduct. If not...he was still their captain, and they would have to continue to obey him whether they resented his actions today or not.

He tried to settle down to his reports back in his cabin, but imagining the officers' and midshipmen's reactions to having their personal possessions searched kept him from being able to concentrate. He spent the rest of the morning pacing. Almost two hours after sending the three men to begin the inspection, a knock rattled the door.

"Enter!" Ned's arms vibrated with the desire to yank the door open.

Lieutenant Gardiner entered, followed by the boatswain and the marine captain.

"Repo—" The end of the word caught in Ned's throat when behind Captain Macarthy came a decidedly nervous-looking Midshipman Lott.

Ned had been correct—he should have jumped overboard before taking on this command.

Chapter Twenty-Six

The fear in Charlotte's—Charles Lott's expression nearly matched Ned's own. He began to pray as he had never prayed before for deliverance for himself and for Charlotte. How would he explain to William Ransome that he, Ned Cochrane, had sentenced the commodore's little sister to hanging for stealing less than a full meal for one man?

"Sir, Midshipman Lott told us something very interesting when we arrived to inspect his berth." Gardiner motioned Lott forward. "Tell the captain what you told us."

"Sir..." Lott cleared her—his—throat when it squeaked. "Sir," Lott said in a lower timbre, "when I returned to my berth last night after the entertainment on deck, I discovered someone had gotten into my sea chest and rummaged through it."

Ned grabbed onto the top rung of the chair before him, relief weakening his knees. "How do you know this?"

Lott explained about finding the lid ajar and splashed with ink, the clothing inside no longer folded, and the ink bottle tipped over.

"It should be easy to find the guilty one, then, by looking for someone with ink on his hands." Ned straightened.

"Not so easy, sir." Gardiner shook his head. "One of the mids knocked over a bottle of ink at the midshipmen's table this morning when several were updating their log books before breakfast. Eight of them now wear ink on their hands. None would admit to the act when questioned, sir."

Ned looked at the thin, pale midshipman dwarfed by the men surrounding him. "Was anything taken?"

"No, sir. I believe when the ink bottle began to leak, it frightened him and stopped him before he did whatever it was he'd set out to do." Lott worried the lowest button on his coat—in much the same way Charlotte Ransome had twisted the end of her sash around her fingers on her visit to *Alexandra* so many weeks ago.

Ned started to worry again—but this time for a different reason. He looked at the other officers. "The three of you continue your inspection. Mr. Lott, stay a moment."

Before the door closed behind them, Ned started pacing, turning whenever he reached the head or foot of the table. From the corner of his eye, whenever he passed the center of the room, he could see Lott standing in the same position, tense and nervous.

Twice he paused, opening his mouth to tell Charlotte he knew who she was. Both times as soon as he looked at her, fear and indecision got the better of him. He should not have been so hasty in dismissing his inspectors. He could have questioned them further, biding his time until he had decided what to do with Charles Lott.

Even when clinging to the ratlines of the foremast shroud, Charlotte had not experienced fear akin to what she now felt. The dread that Ned had indeed recognized her was greater even than the horror she experienced when the first lieutenant, the boatswain, and the marine captain had arrived in the cockpit and announced they would be inspecting everyone's belongings for food stolen from the hold. She had not looked through her sea chest thoroughly enough to ensure that the stolen food had not been stashed there.

"You are certain nothing was taken from your sea chest?" Ned finally stopped pacing, coming to stand directly across the table from her again.

"Aye, sir. When the first lieutenant removed everything, I was able to see that nothing was missing."

"And are you certain that someone else did this? That in your haste to report for duty, you did not yourself leave your sea chest in such a state?"

Charlotte understood his need to find the simplest explanation for the incident. If the person who stole the food was not the same person who had gone through Charlotte's trunk, it meant there was more than one wrongdoer for Ned to deal with. Of course, she could have given him a list of midshipmen she personally suspected of either or both crimes, but to do so would appear to be divisive at best and, at worst, vindictive.

"I am certain this was done by somebody else." Charlotte ran the backs of her thumbs along the outside seams of her pants. "I always keep my clothing neatly folded, and I know my ink bottle leaks when tipped, so I put it away very carefully each time."

Ned folded his lips together and began pacing again. After a few more turns, he paused again. "Do you have any idea who might have done this to you?"

She hesitated before answering. "No, sir."

His brows raised. "No?"

"No, sir." She tried to infuse confidence into her answer this time.

"You do not suspect anyone, or you are not willing to say?" He crossed his arms.

Charlotte lowered her gaze, not wanting to admire the breadth of his shoulders, the flattering cut of his coat, or the way the indigo wool emphasized the unusual gray hue of his eyes. "I do not know who did it, sir, therefore I will make no accusation without supporting proof." She risked a quick look at his face to gauge his reaction.

Ned looked as if he wished to yell—or swear—at her for not giving him what he wanted: a name, some way to rectify the situation, the truth behind the mystery. He grabbed the top of the chair again, his fingers twitching as they wrapped around the rung.

"Is there anything else you wish to tell me?" he asked, his eyes locking with hers.

He knew. She knew he knew. He knew she knew he knew. Her knees quaked and stomach churned—all while her heart leapt at the idea of telling him and having him not only swear to protect her, but confess his undying love for her. Since that was as unlikely to happen as Kent's confessing to everything he'd done to Charlotte since she'd come aboard…"No, sir."

"Very well, then. You are dismissed, Mr. Lott."

Charlotte spun and dashed from the cabin, paying no heed to the startled yells of the sailors she brushed past in her haste to find a quiet spot to collect herself. At the bottom of each companionway, around every turn—men. The officers still worked at inspecting the sailors' belongings. Those who had already been cleared stood around watching the spectacle, wanting to see the guilty one caught.

Down she continued, past the main gun deck, past the lower gun deck. Finally, she stepped off the bottom step and looked around. A fraction of sunlight trickled through the multiple layers of gratings in the decks above her. With the officers searching for someone who had stolen food, here—on the deck containing the hold and food storage areas—was probably not the best place to be.

She started back up the steps, her legs weak and wobbly. If Ned knew who she was, why hadn't he said anything?

"Mr. Lott!" She turned. At the other end of the crowded lower gun deck, Lieutenant Gardiner motioned her toward him. Stifling a groan, she wended through the sailors crowding the deck.

"Ah, good, Mr. Lott, if you are finished with the captain, we need help completing the inspection. Take two boys from your watch and go to the aft section of the deck and begin your search there." Lieutenant Gardiner's expression was made even grimmer by the light flickering up from the lantern in his hand.

"Aye, aye, sir." And while she searched the ship for stolen food, was someone even now in the cockpit once again searching through her belongings?

A few hours later, Charlotte was able to lay off searching to report for her watch. Then, after two hours of nothing more interesting than recording the ship's speed, bearing, and location on the log board, Lieutenant Gardiner, Boatswain Parr, and Captain Macarthy arrived and were admitted to Ned's cabin.

The sailing master looked at Charlotte with raised brows. "They didn't bring no one with them. Must not have found the thief."

Charlotte shrugged and tried not to picture Ned's handsome face set in concentration as he listened to his officers' report. A few minutes later, they left again.

As a woman, Charlotte wanted to go into the cabin and comfort Ned, offer him the opportunity to speak of his frustration with the obviously fruitless search for the offender. As a midshipman—after more than a month on *Audacious*, she no longer thought of herself as merely pretending to be one—she trusted him to make whatever decisions necessary to ensure the safety and order of everyone aboard.

And, as a midshipman, Charlotte turned her mind toward her duty and tried to shut down the part that wanted to dwell on Ned's handsome face, his fine figure, his distinguished mantle of authority.

Eight bells chimed and Charlotte exchanged a terse nod with Kent, who always came to the wheelhouse to report for duty before he took over as midshipman of the watch and rested his oars in the forecastle. She needed to write in her journal, needed to express her thoughts and feelings from everything that had happened today.

In the blaring sunlight and the equatorial heat, she longed for one of her lightweight muslin gowns, a wide-brimmed bonnet, a fan, and a parasol. The heat was even more stifling below deck as she started down the stairs toward the midshipmen's berth in the bow of the ship. Lady Dalrymple's garden, with its vine-covered bowers and ancient, towering oaks, was a lovely place to pass a hot afternoon. She could picture herself sitting there now, eating a lemon ice, flirting with Ned—no, with Henry Winchester. But it was Ned's face, Ned's impeccable uniform, that filled her mind.

Her eyes took a while to transition to the dimness below deck as she descended the companion stairs, but she was now so familiar with the ship she knew exactly how many steps there were between decks. She counted them to try to rid herself of the all-too-pleasing fiction of being called upon by Ned Cochrane. Five…six…seven…

Her ankle hit something hard, hovering above the eighth step, but her momentum carried her, pitching her forward into the darkness. She raised her arms to try to catch hold of something, anything to break her fall. Too late. She twisted and covered her head with her hands. Her shoulder and the back of her head took the worst of the blow when she hit the deck below. Bright lights flickered in her closed eyes, and she could not catch her breath.

"Who goes—?" Footsteps shuffled over to her. "Mr. Lott? That you?"

Charlotte jerked, trying to breathe, tears smarting her eyes. Finally, she gasped and glorious—though hot and foul-smelling—air filled her lungs. Along with it came the awareness of pain in her shoulder, her head, and her back.

"Yes," she croaked. "It is I."

"What're ye doing down there?"

"I…" What had happened? She inventoried the pains throbbing in her body. Her head had hit the deck. Same with her shoulder and back. So why did the front of her ankle throb? "I tripped on something and fell down the last four steps. There is an obstruction on the eighth step coming down."

The sailor—a man from one of her gun crews—stepped up to inspect it. "I don't see nothing, sir." He came back down and thrust his hand toward her. She gladly accepted his assistance up. "But we've all taken a fall now and again. That's life in the navy."

Charlotte grabbed onto the edge of one of the steps as a wave of dizziness crashed into her.

"Ye all right there, Mr. Lott?"

"I think…" She gulped a few steadying breaths and the motion of the ship seemed to settle back to its regular pitch-and-roll motion. "I believe I will be fine. Thank you."

The sailor knuckled his forehead and strolled away.

Charlotte made her way forward, to the cockpit. Sitting on the table and making full use of the open grating above, she pulled up her pant leg and examined her ankle. A red streak blazed across the skin right where it hurt. She touched it and flinched from the tenderness.

"What happened?" Jamison looked up from writing in his journal.

"I…" Charlotte glanced around. The berth was almost empty—only two other boys, both on Jamison's watch, both formerly of Collin's crew, were in here with them. She lowered her voice. "I believe someone tripped me apurpose when I was coming down the stairs just now." She told him what had happened.

Jamison's expression grew dark. "When you relieved me of watch, I returned here and found Kent and his mates huddled around the table whispering together. I was convinced they were up to no good, but they dispersed as soon as I entered. I had no cause to say anything to them."

A trickle of fear mingled with the thread of annoyance that cut through the throbbing pain in Charlotte's head. "And once again, there is no proof. Only suspicion."

"You must say something to Lieutenant Gardiner."

She let her pant leg down and climbed down from the table to take the chair next to her counterpart. "And what will I say? I *think* someone tripped me on purpose, but I saw no one and neither did the sailor who found me just after I fell. It was dark, and I am not the first person to fall when going down the stairs too quickly."

"But the mark on your leg," Jamison protested. "That is proof."

Shaking her head, Charlotte almost grinned at the vast change five weeks on this ship had wrought—she had thought nothing of Jamison's seeing her bare ankle just moments ago. "A mark like that could have happened at any time, anywhere on the ship. I took your advice and told Lieutenant Gardiner about my sea chest—and nothing has come of that." Except to upset Ned to the point she was certain he knew her true identity. "If I make another accusation and it reaches Captain Cochrane's ears, I will become known as a troublemaker."

"Then tell Ham or Martin. Even though they could not officially do anything for you, they need to be made aware of Kent's continual misconduct so they can watch for more blatant examples of it and do something about it."

Jamison had a point. And as she considered the two young acting lieutenants friends—and on her side when it came to Kent already—telling one of them would probably not land her back in front of Ned.

Six hours later, when she reported for duty, she was relieved to find Hamilton coming on as the lieutenant of the watch. She quickly reviewed the log board and double-checked it against the compass in the binnacle, made her calculations and notations in her log book, and conferred with the master's mate currently at the wheel.

Finally, she joined Hamilton on the quarterdeck. "Sir, might I have a moment?"

"Of course, Mr. Lott." Hamilton's dimples appeared when he looked down at her.

In a low voice she told him what happened, and the dimples disappeared. "I know it could not have been Kent. He had just relieved me as midshipman of the watch. But I have two of his mates on my watch, and Jamison has three." She went on to tell him what Jamison had seen in the cockpit, along with their suspicion that two of Kent's mates who were senior to Charlotte but had been passed over for promotion were the instigators of the mischief. "However, there is no evidence, not solid proof, that any of them did anything, so I cannot go to Lieutenant Gardiner and make an accusation."

Hamilton chewed his bottom lip, his eyes scanning the sails and rigging above them. After several long moments, he dragged his gaze away and pinned it on Charlotte once again. "I assume Jamison is the one who encouraged you to speak up about this?"

She nodded. "Aye, sir."

"How are your injuries?"

She reached up and touched the back of her head. "I have a knot here. And my shoulder is tender. But I am otherwise unharmed and, as you can see, fit for duty." She did not mention the pounding headache. Her experience with injuries over the recent past had taught her that the aches brought on by bumps and bruises eventually went away.

"Did you speak with one of the surgeon's mates about it?"

"No, sir. I saw no need."

He made an indistinguishable sound in the back of his throat and turned his attention toward the sails again.

She stood beside him, watching the activity of the sailors on the quarterdeck, wondering what he was thinking.

"Do you trust me, Mr. Lott?"

She looked up at the tall young man. "Sir?"

He turned toward her. "Do you trust me to deal with this situation in the manner in which I see fit?"

"Aye, sir." The answer came easily. If she did not trust him, she would not have told him despite Jamison's cajoling.

"Good. Carry on, Mr. Lott." Hamilton touched the forepoint of his hat, effectively dismissing her.

She saluted and returned to the wheelhouse. The half hour chimed, and Charlotte made a mark on the log board.

The door of the captain's cabin opened. Charlotte sucked in a breath and nearly choked when she tried to swallow at the same time. She sputtered and coughed, drawing the attention of everyone—including Ned.

"Are you ill, Mr. Lott? Do you need to be relieved?" Ned paused beside her, worry wrinkling what she could see of his brow under his hat.

She worked to relax her throat, taking a normal breath. "No, sir." The rasp in her voice tried to belie her denial and pulled the heat of embarrassment into her cheeks. "I am well."

"Carry on, then."

"Thank you, sir."

She cleared her throat and kept her eyes pinned to Ned's back. He stopped to speak to Hamilton—and Charlotte nearly choked again. From the length of their conversation and Ned's increased agitation, she did not need to hear what passed between them to know Hamilton was telling their captain of her fall down the stairs.

From now on, unless she could not stop the bleeding, she was not going to tell anyone on this ship about anything that happened to her.

Chapter Twenty-Seven

Guilt ate at Julia. Each time she sat down to a meal with her husband, every morning when he read from the prayer book and the Bible, every evening in the short time they had together before going to bed, whenever she looked at him, the news that Charlotte was aboard *Audacious* burned in her mind. Her inability to figure out how to tell him, how to confess to her husband she had kept this secret from him for ten days…eleven days…twelve days, settled like a weight on her chest.

At night she lay awake, staring at William's profile as he slept. On several occasions, she thought to whisper the truth in those dark hours to try to alleviate her conscience. But the longer she waited for the appropriate opportunity to tell him, the less one seemed likely to occur.

Finally, her lack of sleep gave her the excuse she needed to avoid her husband altogether: a severe headache, pronounced by Dr. Hawthorne to be a migraine. He recommended rest and cold compresses and avoidance of light and noise. Julia had never heard the term applied to the aches, from which she had suffered for most of her life, but she latched onto the doctor's suggested cure and retreated to the sleeping cabin, trusting William's solicitude to keep him from disturbing her until she declared herself well again.

Though it nearly ripped her heart from her chest, she did not mount a protest when he removed his old canvas hammock from his sea chest and hung it in the day cabin so as not to disrupt her sleep by his comings and goings. Dawling plied her with tea and soups and pastries, but the offense against her husband whittled away her appetite until none remained.

After two days, it was not her black mood that drove her from the sleeping cabin, but the overwhelming heat, which the closed gun port only exacerbated. She needed fresh air—and to bathe. She called for Dawling, announced herself well, and asked him to bring her water for washing.

While he went to comply, she stepped into the main cabin to retrieve clean clothing from the wardrobe. She stopped only two paces from the door.

From his desk, William stood and crossed to her, resting his hands on her shoulders. "Are you well?"

She nodded, unable to meet his earnest blue eyes. "Dawling is bringing me water so that I can bathe and wash my hair. I came to retrieve fresh clothing."

William pulled her into a gentle embrace. "I hoped you would be recovered today. We have arrived at Barbados and will be docking by midday. I will send word to Captain Cochrane to join us for supper."

Her stomach churned. Would Ned arrive with Charlotte in tow, expecting that Julia had told William? "It...will be good to see him again."

He held her at arm's length, his gaze searching. "My dear, are you certain you are well?"

"Weak and tired. I need fresh air." And to clear her conscience. She started forming the words in her mind, but then he smiled at her, and she could not bring herself to change that look, full of trust and caring, to something full of hurt, resentment, and anger.

"Come join me on the poop deck when you are ready." He squeezed her shoulders and then bowed away.

"William, wait. I...there is something I need to tell you."

He returned to her. "What is it?"

She was going to tell him. Until he reached out and brushed her limp hair back from her face, brushing his fingers across her cheek.

"What is this? Are you afraid to tell me?" His face betrayed neither concern nor amusement, but his eyes held hers with an intimacy that curled her toes.

Tears welled in her eyes. "I…I love you."

His expressionless mask melted away, replaced by a look so tender, it broke her heart. "There, now. That was not so hard, was it?" He cupped her jaw with his hands and kissed her forehead. "I love you, Mrs. Ransome."

"I do not deserve your love." His face blurred; she blinked away the moisture from her eyes.

"Yet you have it. You have possessed my heart for a very long time."

And she had squandered that gift. After he learned the truth, he would never look at her like this again. She committed this moment to her memory so that she could remember in the future she once held his full trust and love.

"Is there more you wanted to say?"

Why had Ned told her? Why had he burdened her with such a terrible secret?

"You are trembling. You should still be abed."

"No. I am—I need to recover my strength. I have lingered too long already." And played the coward too long. "I will bathe and dress and meet you on deck."

As soon as he departed, Julia wrapped her arms around her middle and bent over with a groan. *Oh, Lord, how will I explain Charlotte to him? How will he ever forgive me?*

Rustling sounds from the sleeping cabin alerted her to Dawling's presence. She retrieved her clothing from the wardrobe and carried it into the smaller chamber. Dawling was not in the room but reappeared a moment later carrying a tea tray.

"I know you didn't ask for it, mum, but I thought you could use a spot of food to start rebuilding your strength." He set the tray atop William's sea chest.

"Thank you, Dawling. I appreciate all your efforts on my behalf while I have been ill."

"My pleasure, mum." He knuckled his forehead and backed out the door that connected to the captain's galley beyond.

Julia undressed and dunked a clean cloth into the wash basin, the tepid water cooling her hot skin and filling the air with the scent of honeysuckle from the soap Susan had given her. After bathing, she leaned over the washstand and dunked her hair into the shallow water. She soaped her scalp and rinsed it, trying to rub away the heaviness of the guilt along with the grime.

Then she dressed, having pulled out her favorite yellow day dress, and secured her damp hair behind her neck with a ribbon. But she paused before she left the cabin. She could not tell William while they were on deck, with others around. She would have to find a way to tell him before Ned arrived for supper.

Or perhaps she could find a way to pull Ned aside and let him know she thought William might take the news better from Ned than from her.

"Message from lead ship. 'Captain, *Audacious*, to report to flagship four bells in the first dogwatch.'"

Ned glanced up from the charts spread out on his table and looked at the young midshipman carrying the message. "Is that all? No indication as to why?"

The boy shrugged. "No, sir."

"Very good. Dismissed." Ned thought he might be sick. If Julia had told William about Charlotte, Ned could very well be on his way to his doom in just a little while.

Bolger called his attention back to the charts as they calculated their own navigation into port at Barbados. The message had already been sent down the line as to the commodore's orders for docking, but no matter whom the orders came from, Ned had been taught to never rely on another ship's navigational directions without checking them for himself.

Satisfied that *Audacious* would not be torn apart by a sunken reef or grounded in shallow shoals, he relayed his orders for docking to his sailing master and lieutenants.

All hands were called to their stations. Ned, from his position at the fore of the poop deck, spotted Charlotte easily, his frozen lungs squeezing his heart as she scampered up the foremast shroud to observe the sailors on her station as they raised and secured the sails.

Ned's skin prickled and a chill like melted snow ran down his back. The heat, combined with his concern for his commodore's sister, did not agree with him.

Audacious came to rest easily at her assigned mooring. While Ned might have wished for a spot on the opposite side of the eleven remaining ships of the convoy, William wanted him close by, so they lay a score of yards off *Alexandra*'s larboard stern.

Once he dismissed the crew, he returned to his cabin. He sank into his desk chair, hoping to alleviate the aches in his back. His steward carried in a tray of pastries along with his tea, but Ned waved the whole thing away. The very sight of it made him queasy.

If Julia had not already told William about Charlotte, it would fall on Ned—should fall on him—to tell the tale. Although he still was not certain prayer worked, he prayed for the strength not only to speak the words, but to submit to whatever punishment William meted out afterward.

His head started pounding. But now was no time to allow the symptoms of his guilt to keep him from his duty. He recalled his steward.

"Pass word for Midshipman Lott."

"Aye, sir."

To keep from sitting at the table with his head buried in his arms, Ned paced. The action had become a habit—something he had never seen William Ransome do, but it was the only way Ned could find to keep himself calm before his men.

Though Lieutenant Hamilton had not mentioned Lott's name, his story of overhearing some boys discussing a practical joke they had played on another mid—standing below the stairs and holding something out over a step to make the person trip and fall—had not fooled Ned. The surgeon's mate reported all injuries to the captain and had informed Ned that Charles Lott had been to see him about a goose-egg-sized lump on the back of his head from falling down the steps. A few days later, Ned himself had noticed Charlotte limping, but when he asked about the injury, she shrugged and mentioned how easy it was to trip over an unknown object in the darkness of the cockpit.

Now that they were docked and only a few men were needed on watch—mostly to perform lookout and security duties—anyone wishing to do Charlotte harm would have ample time to plot and execute their plans. At Madeira, he had taken Jamison the first night and Kent the second night. He could not afford to raise any questions by not allowing Lott to go this time.

Though taking her to *Alexandra* would be dangerous, she knew the risk and would be cautious to hide her face from William or Julia. If Ned was invited for supper, Charlotte would dine in the midshipmen's berth. And with Charlotte aboard *Alexandra*, one of two things would happen. William would recognize her before anything could be said, and he would take matters into his own hands; or Ned would be put through the agony of confessing, William would send for *Charles Lott* to be brought to the big cabin, and he would take matters into his own hands.

He jumped when the knock came. "Enter."

Midshipman Lott came in. The bruises and swelling that had partially obscured her face when he'd first come aboard had faded away, leaving a long, red scar across her left cheek. She appeared wan, almost gaunt, but the continual oppression she suffered at Kent's and his mates' hands could explain that.

"Mr. Lott, you will form a detail to man the ship's boat that will take me to *Alexandra* by four bells in the first dogwatch."

"You want me to—" She swallowed convulsively, blue eyes wide. "Aye, sir."

If he thought he could get away with it, he would take one of the ship's boats and run away with her, saving both of them from facing her brother's anger and disappointment. His imagination showed him the idyllic picture of the two of them together—Charlotte in a white gown, as he'd been accustomed to seeing her—in a garden, behaving like normal people.

But they weren't normal people. "That is all, Mr. Lott."

For a moment it seemed that she would protest, but then she exited instead.

Ned sank into the closest chair. If he survived tonight, it would be a miracle. He folded his arms atop the table and rested his head on them. *"To sleep, perchance to dream..."* of a way to get out of the mess of his own making.

A knocking on the door awoke him. Groggy and bleary eyed, he raised his head. "Enter."

Charlotte came in. "The boat is ready, sir."

"So soon?"

She frowned. "We must leave almost immediately to get to *Alexandra* by four bells, sir."

Ned pulled out his watch. He'd slept for more than an hour. No wonder his head felt heavy. And when he stood...pain arced through his back, and a wave of dizziness struck him with such force that he had to grab the side of the table to keep from losing his balance. If this was what the tropical heat did to him, he was not going to enjoy being assigned to Jamaica station. If he did not lose his commission in the next few hours.

While he should have changed into his other, fresher uniform, he now had not the time or the energy. "Very well, then. Let us be off."

He straightened his waistcoat, took his hat from his steward, and led the way from the cabin to the waist entry port. He looked down at the boat waiting for him at the bottom of the accommodation ladder and had to grab the bulwark rail to keep from pitching headlong over the side. Though the ship lay quietly at her moorings, with the way his head was spinning, he felt as though he were on a ship in the midst of a hurricane.

But it would not do for the captain of the ship, acting or no, to have to be lowered down with the bosun's chair. Gathering his strength, Ned turned. "Mr. Gardiner, you have the ship."

"Aye, sir." Gardiner saluted.

Ned returned it, took a deep breath, and started down the side of the ship. Only his experience with using the narrow slots to climb up and down the sides of ships kept him from falling into the boat. The surgeon's mate offered him a steadying hand when he stepped in, which Ned accepted readily.

Charlotte was last to descend to the boat. Her foot slipped from the last slot, and she pitched backward. Ned, still standing, was in perfect position to catch her and keep her from falling over the side. His hands clamped around her waist—and he was shocked at just how thin she truly was under her layers of voluminous uniform. He waited until certain she regained her balance before releasing her.

They took their seats, and Charlotte took charge of commanding the sailors to row the boat around *Alexandra*'s stern to her starboard entry port.

After gaining permission to board, Ned climbed up first, fighting nausea the entire time. He would have to do it straight off. Until he confessed, his guilt would continue attacking him.

He ordered Charlotte to the midshipmen's berth, and she complied, following Midshipman Kennedy down the nearest companionway. The surgeon's mate asked permission to visit Dr. Hawthorne, which Ned gave with alacrity. The rest of the sailors would find their way among *Alexandra*'s crew.

Ned trudged toward the big cabin. William stood before the wheelhouse, waiting for him. As usual, the commodore's expression revealed nothing of his thoughts.

"Come. We have much to discuss." William motioned Ned to follow him to the big cabin.

When the door closed behind him, Ned flinched, imagining the shackles of the bilbo clamping down over his ankles.

"Report."

"Sir?"

William frowned. "Report on your ship's activities since your last report in Madeira."

Oh, yes. If it had not been to clap Ned in irons over Charlotte, the other reason William would have ordered him to *Alexandra* was to report upon his ship. He pulled out his journal from his coat pocket and gave William the important parts.

"...We searched the ship from bow to stern. No trace of the stolen food, and no one would confess to having done it."

"Searching the entire ship was a good idea, especially by including the officers. The sailors will respect you more for that."

"Thank you, sir." Would now be a good time to tell William, when he was happy with something Ned had done? "Sir, there is something—"

The door from the day cabin opened. Julia stood framed in the opening, hesitant and looking from William to Ned and back. "I am sorry for interrupting, but I wanted to greet Captain Cochrane and assure him that we miss him considerably."

Ned stood, but he kept his hands braced against the tabletop to keep his balance. Chills rushed over the surface of his skin. He was starting to think that these might not be the symptoms of guilt but of something much simpler. He was getting sick. A risk every sailor ran when coming to the tropics for the first time.

"Thank you, Mrs. Ransome. I miss serving on *Alexandra*."

"Have you—did you determine what to do about the problem you spoke to me about at Madeira?" Julia's green eyes were piercing.

She had not told William. "Nay, but it should be resolved shortly."

William looked back and forth between the two of them. "May I be privy to the secret?"

Julia clasped her hands in front of her, looking almost as ill as Ned felt.

"You cannot blame Mrs. Ransome, Commodore. I alone bear the responsibility."

William pressed his own palms against the tabletop and leaned forward. "Speak."

Wave after wave of chills broke over Ned, and he began to tremble. "Sir, when I first reported to *Audacious,* I noticed a problem with one of the—"

A knock on the door interrupted him.

William stepped around behind Ned and opened it. Kennedy and another midshipman stood there.

"What is it?" William demanded.

"Sir, it's Midshipman Lott. He fainted, sir. We took him to Dr. Hawthorne, and he said to come tell you it's a serious fever."

William's demeanor changed from annoyance to concern. "Is he recommending quarantine?"

"Not for the ship, sir, but—"

"Oh, dear." Ned reached for his chair, but his knees gave out on him and he fell to the floor, succumbing to a swirling blackness.

William tried to hold Julia back, but she pulled her arm free and knelt beside the fallen officer. He staunched his jealousy when she pressed her hands to Ned's cheeks and forehead.

"He burns with fever." She looked over her shoulder at William.

"Mr. Kennedy, pass word for Dr. Hawthorne and his mates." William put his hands around Julia's waist and lifted her away from Ned.

"Aye, aye, sir." Kennedy rushed away, the other midshipman on his heels.

As soon as William released Julia, she hoisted her skirt and hurried into the day cabin. He was happy to have her away from Ned. The headache had brought her so low the last two days, he feared she might catch whatever Ned had. "Dawling!"

The steward threw open the main door. "Aye, sir?"

"Fetch water and cloths."

"No need." Julia returned with the bowl of water from the washstand and several clean rags. She again knelt beside the prone figure, placed a wet rag across his forehead, and bathed his face with another.

Ned groaned and stirred.

"Shh. Do not try to move." Julia pressed down on his shoulders when he tried to sit up.

William moved around to Ned's other side and knelt as well. "The doctor is coming."

"*Audacious*...and Char—"

"Hush, now, save your strength." Julia dipped the cloth in the water, wrung it out, and continued bathing Ned's face.

Watching her tender ministrations, William remembered the time he had taken a shard of wood in his leg many years ago. When it became infected and he landed in the sick berth with a high fever, he had dreamed of Julia—as he had last seen her at seventeen years old—hovering over his hammock, whispering endearments to him.

Dr. Hawthorne arrived. "Has he been vomiting? Complaining of back pain? Headache?"

William stood and allowed the doctor to take his place beside Ned.

Julia sat back on her heels. "You believe it is yellow fever?"

The doctor nodded. "The young midshipman from *Audacious* presented with those symptoms, which are commonly associated with the disease." Hawthorne looked at Julia with concern. "You are from this part of the world, are you not, Mrs. Ransome?"

"Yes, I spent most of my life in Jamaica."

"Do you know if you have ever contracted yellow fever?"

"Yes. When I was a girl."

Hawthorne nodded. "You are unlikely to become sick with it again." The doctor stood and faced William. "May I request that Mrs. Ransome help with nursing the sick? I would like to limit exposure to keep it from spreading to the rest of the crew, if possible."

"No—"

"Yes, I will be happy to help in whatever way I can." Julia stood, drawing the doctor's attention to herself and cutting off William's protest.

"Ah...I shall leave the decision to the two of you." Hawthorne cleared his throat and then ordered Ned placed in the canvas litter his mates had carried in with them.

Julia disappeared into the day cabin while William helped lift Ned. He joined her after the doctor and his mates took his former first officer away. In just the few moments that had taken, Julia had changed out of her green evening gown into the yellow gown she called a work dress. At his entrance she turned, arms lifted as she tied a kerchief over her bundled hair.

"Julia, you will not risk yourself by attending the sick berth."

She finished tying up her hair and then turned to retrieve a large apron from the bottom drawer of the wardrobe. When she finished dressing, she moved to stand before him.

"If it were James or Philip, would you ban me from the sick room? Did not you, yourself, allay my fears back in Portsmouth by reassuring me that I would not sicken with yellow fever and die, as I have had it once before?" She rested her hands on the lapels of his coat. "William, I have had no duty, no effectual function since I have been aboard except teaching two calculus lessons to the midshipmen."

Her color heightened, her eyes sparkling with energy, William admitted defeat. Julia needed to feel useful, needed to contribute to the workings of life around her—something she had been denied since boarding his ship. "Very well. But you will take every caution, and you will obey the doctor. If he sends you away, you will leave."

She nodded, raised up on her toes, and kissed him. "Pray for them, William."

He pulled her close for a moment. "I will pray for you as well."

Julia nodded again and departed.

William stepped out onto the deck, and the officers and crew—who had lined the sides of the ship chattering and trading with the merchants that always swarmed around an arriving ship—now looked upon him with a mixture of curiosity and fear. As soon as he stepped out from under the shade of the poop deck awning, the questions started—all the sailors speaking at once, yelling to be heard over one another.

A raised hand was all it took to silence them. William looked around at the familiar faces of the men who had pledged their lives to serve him, this ship, the Royal Navy, and King George.

"Captain Cochrane and one of his crew members who came with him from *Audacious* are taken ill. Dr. Hawthorne believes it might be yellow fever. They are to be quarantined in the sick berth. There is no reason to fear a plague. It is expected that a few men will fall ill with fever upon arrival in the Caribbean, but pass word to your mates that if you begin to feel feverish, nauseated, or faint, you are to report to Dr. Hawthorne immediately. Is that understood?"

"Aye, sir," chorused from the men.

"Good. As you were." He waited until the men returned to duty or idling and then turned. As he hoped, his first officer awaited him in the wheelhouse.

"Mr. O'Rourke, prepare the ship's boat to take me to *Audacious*. Captain Cochrane is too ill to return and command her, so I must go confer with his first lieutenant and ensure he is competent to command the ship into Jamaica."

"Aye, sir." The Irishman worried his bottom lip with his teeth. "Sir, is it safe for you to board *Audacious*?"

William raised his brows. "Are you questioning my judgment, Mr. O'Rourke?"

"No, sir!" O'Rourke snapped to attention, his eyes showing his horror at the idea. "I will go prepare the ship's boat now, sir."

"Very good." William returned to the cabin and changed from his formal frock coat to the plain one he wore daily. He returned to deck just as the men finished lowering the jolly boat into the water. The sailors O'Rourke had designated to man the oars quickly filled the boat.

"Lieutenant O'Rourke, you have command until I return." He inclined his head toward his first officer and then climbed down the side of his ship.

His mind replayed the last hour, settling on the odd interaction between Ned and Julia before Ned's swoon had interrupted them.

The two shared a secret; of that, William had no doubt. He could be patient...to a point. But before they reached Jamaica, he would have the truth from them.

The doctor and his mates worked at getting Ned into a hammock.

Julia took the opportunity to lean over Midshipman Charles Lott. Charlotte's gaunt face startled her—as did the angry red scar across her cheek. Julia's decision not to tell William about his sister came into vivid relief. If Julia had told William and he had sent for her, Charlotte might not have suffered such pain and indignity.

"Mrs. Ransome, would you mind divesting the midshipman of his coat and waistcoat?" Dr. Hawthorne glanced at her over Ned's hammock. "One of my mates will join you shortly and take charge of removing the rest of the lad's clothing."

Julia shook her head. "There is something...Doctor, may I speak with you privately a moment?" She could not believe she was about to reveal Charlotte's identity to Hawthorne before William.

Frowning, Hawthorne turned Ned's care over to his mates and motioned Julia toward his small cabin, which served as both office and sleeping quarters. "Is there a problem, Mrs. Ransome?"

"A problem. Um, yes. Well, more of a complication. You see, Midshipman Lott...well, he is not actually a boy." Julia chewed the tip of her thumb, trying to figure out how to explain what she meant without revealing who lay in the sick berth behind her.

"I am unclear as to your meaning."

She sighed. Best to come right out and say it. "The midshipman is not a boy, but a young woman disguised as a boy."

The doctor's jaw slackened and his mouth hung open a moment. "Are you certain?"

She nodded. "Captain Cochrane confided this to me."

"Then I shall rely on you more than I originally thought. Have you served as a nurse in a sick chamber before, Mrs. Ransome?"

"I have been called upon many times to tend ill workers on my plantation when the doctor was busy elsewhere." Including tending her mother those final weeks of her life. She swallowed hard. If Charlotte died, and Julia could have saved her by revealing her secret to William, not only would she never expect or deserve William's forgiveness, she would never forgive herself.

"Good. We shall work together to get them hale and healthy again."

She followed him out of the cabin and busied herself with removing Charlotte's coat and vest while Hawthorne informed his mates that Julia would be responsible for the midshipman.

When Julia put her hand under Charlotte's side to roll her so she could remove the excess clothing, she could feel each of Charlotte's ribs. The young woman weighed practically nothing, enabling Julia to manipulate and move her easily—and increasing Julia's concern over Charlotte's eventual recovery. While Charlotte's figure had not been ample before, Julia had a hard time imagining she had been this thin when dining upon the rich foods served her at the Yateses' and Lady Dalrymple's homes.

Several years ago a half-starved slave sought refuge at Tierra Dulce. When Julia helped her undress to bathe, she had been horrified by the way her skin clung to her bones, showing the definition of each one. Although Julia, Jerusha, and the doctor had done everything they could, the young woman developed a fever and died a few days later. All they had been able to do was make her as comfortable as possible, and she died with a smile on her face, a song on her lips.

Fear formed a lump in Julia's throat. She would not allow Charlotte to die.

Another lump gave her concern—until she reached under the blouse and extracted a leather-bound book, a journal, from under the waistband of Charlotte's pants. Impressed by the girl's ingenuity at finding a hiding place for her most personal of possessions, she set it aside with the clothing and began bathing Charlotte.

Charlotte moaned and tossed her head.

Julia shushed her. "It is all right. You are safe."

"Mama?"

The word, spoken with a child's inflection, broke Julia's heart. "Nay, 'tis Julia. I am here to nurse you through your fever."

"Tell Mama…about me…if I die, they won't know. No one will know to tell Mama…William." Charlotte opened her eyes, and though she looked at Julia, there was no recognition in her eyes.

"I will tell them. Have no fear."

"And Ned. I need…to apologize."

Julia glanced across at the other hammock, where Dr. Hawthorne leaned over, ear pressed to Ned's chest. "You will tell him yourself when you are recovered."

Tears trickled from the corners of Charlotte's blue eyes. "I've been foolish. I should have stayed in Portsmouth. But I needed…wanted to go."

Julia shushed her again, even though Charlotte's voice barely rose above a whisper. She needed to keep the doctor and his mates from learning who she was—at least until she told William.

Charlotte continued to mumble, but the words slurred together until incoherent. Her eyes fluttered closed, and she slept.

Julia straightened, a hand to the small of her back, which ached from leaning over the hammock to bathe Charlotte as best she could without completely undressing her. With the doctor's assistance cutting through it at the back as Julia held Charlotte up on her side, they removed the muslin wrapped around Charlotte's chest. Even in her sleep, Charlotte shivered when Julia ran the cool, wet cloth over the red marks the binding left behind. The doctor brought a clean blouse and trousers, and sent his men to fetch various items or discard others while Julia changed Charlotte's clothes.

The light coming through the gun ports waned, and Hawthorne lit more candles and lanterns. "You should rest, Mrs. Ransome. Return to your cabin, take some tea, and eat something. 'Twill be a long night."

Julia pressed her fingertips to the sides of her neck. "Thank you, Doctor. I believe I will." She retrieved Charlotte's journal and made her way up to the open air of the quarterdeck and into the cabin. Dawling had replaced the bowl in the washstand and refilled it with fresh water. To try to get the sour smell of the air below decks from her nose, she washed her hands, arms, and face with the honeysuckle soap.

A noise from the day cabin startled her. Carrying the drying cloth with her, she stepped out into the room.

William looked at her in question. "How is Ned?"

"The doctor has not given his opinion yet." She returned to the sleeping cabin, dunked a cloth into the water, and returned to the sitting room, where she used it to wipe the sweat from her husband's face. He should at least be comfortable when she told him.

He caught her hand in his and kissed her palm. "Thank you."

She nodded, afraid to open her mouth before she had organized her thoughts.

William called for Dawling to bring tea and some of the supper he and the cook had prepared earlier. At the dining table, Julia sat at William's right hand, biding her time until he had eaten his fill.

"Two others aboard *Audacious* are ill. One cargo ship reported that they have one man with fever." William pushed his empty plate back.

Julia had eaten as much as she could, taking heed of the doctor's warning, though she had no appetite. "And is the first lieutenant of *Audacious* capable of commanding her to Jamaica?"

"I believe so. He is young but competent. And it will be for less than a fortnight. I am sending Lieutenant Campbell over to serve as his first lieutenant."

"But with the threat from pirates...?"

"I spoke with Mr. Gardiner at length. He commanded a small brig during an engagement and lost none of his crew. He is aware of the increased security measures his crew will need to take once we leave Barbados."

Julia could think of nothing else to ask him on the subject. She ran her tongue along the edges of her upper teeth, trying to determine how best to broach the subject of Charlotte.

William settled back in his chair. "I can see you have something you wish to say to me."

She nodded and looked down at the half-eaten beef and onions on her plate; she shoved it away and stood. "When Ned paid his respects to me at Madeira, he confided a secret so great, I have been unable to find a way to tell you."

William's expression did not change. "I assumed he had spoken to you of his crew, of the problems he was having with some of them."

Unable to continue to meet his unwavering, unreadable gaze, Julia walked slowly toward the other end of the table. At her chair at the foot, where she sat when others joined them for meals, she stopped and grabbed the finials adorning the back. "Ned wished to speak to me of one person particularly. One of his midshipmen."

"I see."

"Midshipman Lott, as a matter of fact."

"The one who is even now in my sick berth?" The question conveyed no surprise, no indication of any change in William's calmness.

"Yes. Midshipman *Charles Lott*." Would her emphasis of the name make him understand? She finally looked up the table at him.

The slight raising of his brows indicated nothing other than a desire for her to continue.

"Midshipman Charles Lott is not who he claimed to be."

"Is that so?"

She looked down at the chair before her. "Yes. You see, Midshipman Charles Lott is actually a young woman." She glanced up at him again.

"A...woman?"

"Yes, William." *Lord, give me strength.* "Yes. A young woman."

"I see." Still the same, calm intonation.

"But she is not just any young woman." She took a deep breath. "Midshipman Charles Lott is your sister. Charlotte."

Julia's father would have exploded from his chair, face mottled red with fury, and started yelling. William steepled his fingers and pressed his forefingers to his lips.

Words of apology, of begging his forgiveness, flew through Julia's mind, but she did not speak. Until William spoke, she needed to tread carefully so she did not anger him further.

"You need not explain why you have kept this from me until now." William spoke through tight lips. "That is something we will discuss at another time. Have you any idea why my sister would do such a thing?"

Her husband's gaze met hers with such a piercing intensity that she could hardly breathe. She nodded. "While I have heard no explanation from her, I have a suspicion."

"And that is…?"

"The day after our engagement, when I went to Charlotte's room to dress for dinner at Collin and Susan's home, I discovered a page from a letter that I believe belonged to Charlotte. It was not addressed nor signed, so I cannot be certain, but it seemed to be from a young man…who asked Charlotte to marry him."

William remained still, his eyes still boring into hers.

"I believe Charlotte disguised herself as a midshipman and signed on to *Audacious* to marry this young man." Silence stretched out after this statement. Julia chewed the inside corner of her bottom lip until it was raw.

"Is that all?"

"That is all I know."

"Then I thank you for entrusting me with the information."

"What…what will you do?"

"That is yet to be decided." William stood. "But I can assure you. My sister will not be marrying anyone at the end of this voyage."

Chapter Twenty-Nine

After sunset beat-to-quarters inspection, William finally made his way to the sick berth. Since Julia had made her confession more than an hour ago, the thought that Charlotte might be dying had kept his mind—and his heart—frozen. Performing the routine action of inspecting his crew at their battle stations enabled him to clear away everything but the cold, hard facts.

Charlotte had lied to her family and put herself, the crew of *Audacious*, and the entire convoy in danger.

Ned had known since before making port in Madeira and had not immediately told him; rather, he confided the information to Julia.

And Julia had feared telling him.

When she began her tale, his annoyance rose at her seeming nervousness and fear of him. Anger quickly conquered the annoyance. How often had they talked about trust? She had promised she would not keep anything from him. A secret fiancé? Charlotte stowing away—in plain sight—on a warship of the Royal Navy? Not important?

William stopped just outside the sick berth and calmed himself. Revisiting his anger benefitted no one. How many times had he seen Admiral Witherington explode with the passion of his ire? And if he recognized the admiral's tendency to react in anger, how could he blame Julia for being fearful that he would behave the same way? With a resolve to show his wife he was unlike her father in that respect, he opened the door in the removable bulkhead that cordoned off the infirmary and entered.

Both Ned and Charlotte were in the midst of emptying their stomach contents into buckets held by the doctor's mates, while Julia and Hawthorne held them upright.

He waited until they were cleaned up and once again resting in their hammocks. He moved to the opposite side of Charlotte's hammock from where Julia stood, wiping Charlotte's neck and arms with a damp cloth.

Pain constricted William's chest. Eleven years ago, he had stood beside Charlotte's bed and scolded her for climbing a rotted rope ladder and dislocating her shoulder. She had announced then, at six years old, her intention to join the Royal Navy.

Now, as then, the only sign of pain Charlotte betrayed were the tears that streamed from the corners of her eyes. "Mama...and William. You have to tell them. They won't know I'm here..."

Julia leaned over and whispered comforting words to his sister. When Charlotte closed her eyes and appeared to sleep, Julia straightened. She glanced over her shoulder to ensure the doctor and his mates were out of hearing range. "She fears she will die and no one will know her real name so they can let your family know of her death. I try to reassure her that you do know, that you have been told, but it plagues her mind."

"The fever?"

"Still high." She bent to dip her cloth in the bucket of water beside her feet, wrung it out, and began wiping Charlotte's face with it.

"I want her moved to our cabin. Tonight."

Julia looked startled. "But...what about Captain Cochrane?"

"Hawthorne and his mates can tend to him." He passed his hand through his hair and settled his hat back on his head. "Have the doctor and his mates prepare her for transport, and I will have Dawling hang my old hammock in the great cabin for her."

"Yes, William." That she acquiesced without asking for a reason he took as a sign of her remorse.

He returned to the cabin and, rather than summoning Dawling, set about hanging the hammock himself. He was none too quick in doing so; just as he secured the last knot, Julia entered. Hawthorne followed, carrying Charlotte in his arms. William helped him settle her into the hammock.

Though he hoped the doctor would not spread word about the midshipman who had turned out to be a girl, he could not bring himself to ask Hawthorne to keep the information secret.

"I had already released the mates to their supper and a time to rest before rotating the watches all night in the sick berth," Hawthorne said. "Mrs. Ransome understands my instructions for treatment, and I know she will send word for me if this...patient takes a turn for the worse."

"And what will you tell your mates when they return to only one invalid?" Julia asked.

"That the second is no longer with us. That is all they need to know." Hawthorne nodded. "Now if you will excuse me, I must return to Captain Cochrane. I do not wish to leave him alone longer than necessary."

"Thank you, Dr. Hawthorne." Julia walked him to the door of the dining cabin and closed it behind him.

William stood over his sister's inert form. He understood the implications of Charlotte's living as a boy on a ship for more than a month. And he would do what he could to minimize the ruination of her reputation in society—if anything could be done. But he also understood the damage her action could have on Cochrane's career as well as his own. For any woman to have been found masquerading as an officer, even a midshipman, and giving orders to men was bad. But for it to be a commodore's younger sister—William's career might never recover, no matter that he was son-in-law to Admiral Sir Edward Witherington. Even Sir Edward might not be able to keep William from being drummed out of the navy over this.

"William?" Julia stood in the middle of the cabin, her hair hanging in a limp braid down her back. She didn't look at him as she tied a fresh apron around her waist.

"Was she truly so unhappy in England that she thought her only recourse, at seventeen years old, was to run away to the far side of the world and marry someone of whom her family would not approve?" The words tumbled out before he could stop them.

"How do you know you would not approve of him?"

"A man who would carry on a secret correspondence with a young woman? Who would ask her to marry him without first gaining her family's permission? How can he be someone worthy of her affection?" He stopped, calmed himself, and modulated his tone. "In the past two years, my mother has written me only once in concern over Charlotte's forming a serious attachment to a young man. Mother did not approve of him. Not simply because he was poor with no prospects of future wealth—and thus after Charlotte's legacy—but because Mother believed him to be duplicitous, deceitful, and manipulative, toying with a young girl's eager affections."

"And your mother forbade her to keep company with him?"

"That was my advice. But months later, when I received her next letter, she told me the problem had resolved itself—the man had moved on. Gone…to the Caribbean as a steward on a sugar plantation." He cocked his head, and frowned, trying to remember if his mother had ever said exactly where in the Caribbean the man had vanished to.

"Did your mother mention this man's name?" Julia began to unplait her hair.

"Henry…something. Henry…" He tried to picture his mother's letter in his mind. Ah, yes, there it was. "Henry Winchester."

Julia froze, fingers still twined in her hair. "Henry Winchester—are you certain?"

"Yes. I have her letter in my lap desk if you wish to see it. Why? Have you heard of him?"

She glanced toward her desk, where the plantation's ledgers and the letters from Jeremiah lay in a drawer. "Henry Winchester is the name of the steward I hired at Tierra Dulce before I left for England.

He had just arrived in Jamaica and had a letter of introduction from another plantation owner with whom I am acquainted."

"Your steward—the one you believe is cheating you?" For once, William could not hide his incredulity.

"Yes, the very one. Could there be more than one man on this side of the ocean bearing that name?" She finished unbraiding her hair and reached into the top drawer of the wardrobe for her brush.

"I find it unlikely. Mother indicated in her letter the man had left England to seek his fortune. He apprenticed as a clerk for a wealthy merchant in Liverpool."

"Mr. Winchester said he received his training in Liverpool." Julia sank onto the bench seat under the stern windows, dropping the brush to her lap. "Could he have known of our families' connection? Do you think that is, perhaps, why he sought employment at Tierra Dulce?"

William shook his head and crossed the cabin to sit near her. "I doubt it. The connection is not known outside of naval circles. Or Portsmouth. It may simply be a coincidence. You were in need of a steward at the same time he was in search of a position."

She turned and studied his profile. "Forgive me."

He looked down and then at her. "Why, Julia? Why did you feel you could not tell me of the peril my sister had put herself in?"

Julia told him everything Ned had said to her in Madeira. "I knew I should tell you. I wanted to tell you. But..."

"But you were afraid I might behave out of character and act before considering all the ramifications and possible outcomes?"

"When my father learned Michael's ship had been attacked and the crew either killed or held for ransom, he took his ship, and the two under his command, and left port without orders, without permission to search for him. He almost lost his commission...he could have lost much more than that if he had been court-martialed for treason for stealing three ships from the Royal Navy. But he brought back information on several other pirates operating in the Caribbean and Gulf of Mexico whom the navy was then able to apprehend. I was afraid... worried that if you found out about Charlotte, you would row the jolly boat to *Audacious* yourself to retrieve her and bring her here, and that both crews would learn what happened."

William turned his face so his profile was once again to her. "Have you not yet learned that while I highly regard your father, I am not like him?"

"I have been his daughter for almost thirty years, and I feel I know very little about him. I have been your wife for six weeks. There is still much we both need to learn about each other."

He reached over and twined his fingers through hers. "Aye, there is that."

They sat, holding hands, for a long while—until Charlotte's groans reminded them of her presence.

Dawling knocked and gained permission to enter just as they settled Charlotte back down into the hammock. William sent the steward away with the bucket of sick.

"What will you tell him? What will you tell everyone?"

"Not much. Tomorrow we will go ashore, and you will buy clothing—dresses—for Charlotte. I am not mistaken, am I, that your dresses will not fit her?"

She smiled, picturing Charlotte trying to wear one of her dresses. "No. Aside from being too long, my dresses would be too large all over for her. She would look like a child sneaking into her mother's wardrobe."

"Make a tracing of her foot and we will get proper shoes for her as well. When she emerges from this cabin after she recovers, she will no longer be Midshipman Lott but Miss Charlotte Ransome. And if the crew want to speculate how she came to be on board, they are welcome to do so."

Charlotte awoke staring at an unfamiliar, whitewashed ceiling. Her head spun and her ears rang, but her stomach had finally settled, and her back no longer ached. She lay still, enjoying for the first time in—hours? days?—the lulling rock-and-pitch motion of a ship under full sail.

She tried to remember everything that had happened and why she was in an unfamiliar berth. Ned. Ned had ordered her to command the boat transporting him from *Audacious* to *Alexandra*. She had boarded *Alexandra*—had she not? Yes, she vaguely remembered hanging on to the slots in *Alexandra*'s side, trying to not fall off. Midshipman Kennedy had taken her down to the midshipmen's berth. They had just sat down to supper when…

Heat flared in her face. She had pitched forward into her plate of food. Good thing Kent had not been there to see it, or he would never let her forget the ignominy of it.

Light blazed to her right—more than a few candles or lanterns. Turning her head took more effort than it should have, but she accomplished it. A bank of windows lined the length of the room, the brightness blinding her momentarily to all other detail.

"You are awake." A figure moved between Charlotte and the light. A figure in a flowered, yellow dress.

Charlotte rolled her head back to center, wincing at the still-tender spot at the back. "Miss Witherington?"

Julia smiled down at her. "No. It is Mrs. Ransome now. But as we are sisters, you are supposed to call me Julia."

"How did I…?" Charlotte lifted the blanket and looked down at her body. Someone had changed her from her uniform into a white sleeping gown, with feminine ruffles at the wrists and high neck. Her eyes snapped back up to Julia. "If you…then William…oh, no!"

"Yes, William knows. You and Captain Cochrane came aboard five days ago. He is still quite ill. You had us worried for a few days, but your case turned out to be milder than Mr. Cochrane's."

"Is Ned—Captain Cochrane—is he going to recover?"

"Yes. His fever has yet to break, but the doctor is hopeful he will be well again by the time we reach Jamaica."

"William does not blame Captain Cochrane, does he? I have no desire for him to pay the price for my foolish actions." The idea Ned might lose his commission and be disrated back down to midshipman—or worse, be made an ordinary seaman—or be thrown out of the navy altogether weighed down on her as if the ship itself sat atop her chest.

"William will deal with Captain Cochrane as he sees fit."

"And me?" Charlotte hated the wispiness, the childishness, in her voice.

"I will not dissemble. He is still angry with you—especially now that the danger is past and he knows you will recover." Julia straightened the blanket. "Why did you do this, Charlotte? Was it because of Henry Winchester?"

Charlotte had closed her eyes in preparation to feign sleep but popped them open again at the mention of Henry's name. "Henry Winchester?"

"The steward at Tierra Dulce. The man your mother wrote to William about almost two years ago expressing her concern over his attentions to you. The man who has been writing you letters in secret and asked you to marry him. William and I concluded that your disguise, your willingness to suffer through working as a midshipman to journey to Jamaica was in an effort to marry Henry Winchester and not because of the legal troubles with Lord Rotheram."

"What legal troubles with Lord Rotheram?"

Charlotte listened in horror as Julia told her of Collin's visit to William the night before they left Portsmouth. "Mama must have been frantic when they could not find me. I sent her a brief letter from Madeira. I made it sound as if I was traveling with you and William so she would not worry." She reached up and dashed at the tears that escaped. "I never meant to hurt her or William or you. I only wanted to get to Henry."

"Do you truly love him so much?"

Astonished by Julia's surprised tone, Charlotte stopped drying her face with a corner of the blanket. "Yes...well...I thought I did when I left Portsmouth."

"What changed?" Julia pulled a handkerchief from under her sash and wiped away the remaining moisture from Charlotte's cheeks.

"I changed. Becoming a midshipman, learning what I could do, meeting N—other people." Charlotte closed her eyes against the comprehension that flooded Julia's expression.

"Ned Cochrane." She tweaked Charlotte's chin. "You could do worse than the acting captain of His Majesty's Ship *Audacious*."

"I was so young when I knew Henry—not quite sixteen. I know, it has been less than two years, but so much has happened since then. Julia, I do not even remember his face or the sound of his voice. And whenever I think about Ned..." She groaned and covered her face with her hands.

"You feel very much like another seventeen-year-old girl did when she fell in love with a handsome but poor lieutenant just home from the war."

Charlotte opened her eyes and studied her sister-in-law's face, trying to imagine Julia as anything other than the distinguished woman she knew. "You?"

Julia laughed. "I. When I was your age, my father retrieved my mother and me from Jamaica during the Peace of Amiens. It was the first time I had been to England since he took us to the plantation when I was ten. It was also the first time I had seen your brother since then. He seemed to be courting me; he seemed to admire me as much as I admired him. And at the ball to celebrate my father's knighthood, when your brother invited me for a stroll in the gardens, I accepted, expecting he would propose to me."

As Julia warmed to her story, Charlotte could see more of the young woman she used to be. "And did he?"

"I did not." William's voice startled both of them. "But it was a mistake God allowed me to rectify." He slipped his arm around Julia's waist and kissed her temple.

Charlotte's heart raced, but not at the unusual show of affection from her brother toward his wife. "William, I am sorry. I made a foolish choice."

"Aye, you did. And we shall discuss the consequences of your actions soon. But first you must recover your strength." William gave her a brief, almost terse nod, and, after a rustling of papers on his desk, departed as quietly as he'd appeared.

Charlotte tried to push herself into more of a sitting position, but even in the box-style hammock, sitting was nigh impossible. "Does... does the crew know who I am? Why I am here?"

Julia assisted her by propping her pillow behind her back. "The doctor knows you are the young woman who came from *Audacious* dressed as a midshipman. Only William's steward knows your true identity—he recognized you from having seen you so often in Collin's home—but he swore to William he would not reveal your presence to anyone. The rest of the crew know there has been a young woman in the great cabin since we departed from Barbados, but most believe you came aboard there because you are the daughter of someone important who needed transport to Jamaica. I believe, from the doctor's vague explanation to his mates as to Midshipman Charles Lott's disappearance from the sick berth, word that the boy did not survive the yellow fever has proliferated throughout the ship."

The idea of the death of Charles Lott struck Charlotte almost as hard as if he had been someone she knew for a long time—a childhood friend. "When can I visit the sick berth? I wish to explain and apologize to Captain Cochrane."

"As soon as Ned's fever has broken and you are strong enough to walk so far."

"How long until we dock in Jamaica?"

"Five days." Julia probably did not realize how wide her smile grew nor how her eyes sparkled at the knowledge they were less than a week from arriving at her home.

Very well, then. Charlotte had five days to regain her strength, convince Ned to forgive her, and resign herself to marrying Henry Winchester. After all, she had given him her word.

Ned awoke to the familiar rocking of the hammock. Six days he'd been aboard *Alexandra*. Yesterday, when his fever broke and he could think coherently, he informed William of his intent to resign his commision. He had yet to receive a response from the commodore.

He turned his face toward the light streaming in through the gun port. A woman in a pale gown was perched atop the cannon, reading. He had never seen Julia wear one of the white, fluffy mobcaps his mother and sister were so fond of, nor could he imagine her seated in such a casual manner on the enormous piece of artillery.

"Charlotte?" His voice came out rough and raspy.

The figure turned. "You are awake." She slid down from her perch, set the book on a nearby trunk, and came to stand beside the bed. "How do you feel?"

He frowned. "You are out of uniform."

Her smile brightened the room. "Aye, sir. I am."

"Then they know?"

"William and Julia know—and the doctor. And William's steward. Everyone else believes I am a passenger being taken by William as a favor to an old friend from Barbados to Jamaica."

"And Midshipman Lott?" Ned looked over at the empty hammock she had spent her first few hours aboard *Alexandra* in.

She hung her head to the side in an approximation of sorrow. "Poor Mr. Lott did not survive yellow fever. He was buried quietly at sea—well, he would have been if William had agreed to my suggestion."

"You are well? Fully recovered?"

"I tire easily, and my appetite has not returned. And you? How do you feel?"

"Like a ship capsized in a storm and smashed upon a rocky shore."

"How did you know?"

The question took him aback. "Know what?"

"About me? And why did you never say anything to me?" Charlotte reached up and started twining the ribbon that hung from the mobcap around her fingers.

Despite feeling he dragged *Alexandra*'s and *Audacious*'s anchors up with it, he raised his hand and captured hers. "This, for one. Charles Lott worried the buttons on his coat the same way Charlotte Ransome worries her ribbons."

She looked down at their joined hands, and he released her.

"I do apologize. I meant no offense."

"I was not—you did not offend me in the slightest."

"Your face."

"My face?"

He closed his eyes a moment, realizing how mad he sounded, speaking in discombobulated bits and pieces. He looked at her before speaking again. "Your face is too beautiful to be a boy's face. And your eyes. How could I forget having looked into them when we danced at your debut ball?"

Charlotte's cheeks changed from pale to bright red in an instant.

"How did you manage it, Miss Ransome? You had the book learning; I knew that from questioning you myself. But the physical labor. You could have had little opportunity to test yourself in such a manner." Drawing together the little strength he possessed, he pushed himself up with his elbows into a more upright position.

"With only Mama and me at home, I had great freedom. If she knew I spent my afternoons, when she thought I was visiting with friends or tucked away in a corner of the garden reading, learning how to tie a rope ladder, and then climbing a tree to hang it from to simulate climbing the shrouds, she would never have let me out of her sight."

"So you had been planning for a long time to do this?"

"No. I started doing it as a little girl because I wanted to be like my brothers. I continued doing it because I enjoyed the physical exertion." She helped him adjust the pillow behind his back and then crossed to the small table and poured him a cup of water.

He had not realized how thirsty he was until the liquid touched his lips. "Living in the cockpit, you managed to keep your true self hidden."

"Yes. With access to the privacy of the roundhouse privy and the need to change one's clothes only rarely, the boys suspected nothing."

The question he wanted to ask ever since discovering who Charles Lott was tumbled out. "What do you want that is so important you would not only submit yourself to the demanding life and duties of a midshipman, but that you would continue to do it after you made an enemy of Mr. Kent?"

She shrugged and reached up to toy with the ribbon again. "I had—have my reasons. Looking back, I was being childish and selfish. I fear I created more problems for everyone—you, William, my entire family. But even though I was foolhardy to choose the action I took, I promised something and I will follow through on that promise."

The ruffled cap slipped off her head, revealing the short, blunt hair he'd become accustomed to seeing on Mr. Lott.

"And you, Captain Cochrane? Why have you told my brother that you desire to resign your commission? The fault is completely mine. I have taken full responsibility."

For the first time, the voices came back—the echoes of their screams. "No. I should never have agreed to command *Audacious*. Both times I have been put in command of a vessel, I have made an ill-informed decision that proves my unfitness to be a ship's captain."

"The crew of *Audacious*—most of them—would disagree with you. Particularly those who served under Captain Yates before serving under Captain Parker. Hamilton, Martin, Jamison, and many others sang your praises and hoped you would be confirmed as captain and have *Audacious* as your posting."

Ned clamped his back teeth together. He had made a decision he felt benefitted the ship—letting Charlotte continue with her masquerade. But would Commodore Ransome see it that way?

"Captain Cochrane, please allow me to beg your forgiveness. Although I would never have wished either of us ill, it is only because our illness—some might call it an act of Providence—that we were able to leave *Audacious* with my identity and your reputation intact. I could have ruined the career of one of the best officers in the Royal Navy. For that I deeply apologize, and I hope that one day you might think better of me."

How could he think better of her than he did now? He loved her. Before he could articulate this, however, the doctor entered.

"Good afternoon, Miss Charlotte. Captain Cochrane, it is good to see you awake and able to make the effort to sit up. Do not overtax him, Miss Charlotte. He needs his rest to regain his strength. We dock in Kingston in four days." The doctor nodded at both of them and then disappeared into his office.

Ned reached for Charlotte's hand again. "Charlotte, I lo—"

"Oh, good. You're awake." William entered the sick berth with Julia just behind him. "Charlotte, Julia will walk you back to the cabin. I wish to speak with Mr. Cochrane."

Ned did not miss the implication of William's use of *mister*. It was better he have this talk with William, to determine if he had a future that could promise Charlotte anything but poverty, before he spoke to her of his feelings.

He struggled to push himself into even more of an upright position as William stood near the foot of the hammock and clasped his hands behind his back. Dr. Hawthorne stepped out of his office, took one look at William, and then went back into the small room, closing the door behind him.

William waited until the door closed behind Julia and Charlotte before speaking. "I have carefully considered your request regarding your resignation. Your reasons for wishing to be released from service were cogent and logically argued."

Hollowness consumed Ned, but he tried to keep his face as expressionless as William's. "Thank you, sir."

"Request denied."

"I will take my leave—I beg your pardon?"

"Your request to resign your position is denied."

"But...Miss Ransome..."

"You made an error in judgment. I would make myself a liar if I said I always made the correct decisions." William released a soft sigh. "There are two choices you can make from your mistake, Ned. You can let it take you aback, throw you off course, and sink you, or you can determine a new heading and let what you've learned from your mistake guide you."

William turned and reached to open the door. "The choice is yours. I expect to know your final decision before we make port at Jamaica." With a quick nod, he left the sick berth.

Ned released the tension in his upper body and melted down into the hammock. The choice was his. He could resign and walk away from the navy and, hopefully, never have to make life-and-death decisions again, or he could stay and face his seeming inability to make the correct choice in the face of danger or disaster.

If he thought of it in other terms, he could quit and have no income—and no prospects of income—to support a wife, or he could stay in the navy, learn how to be a better officer, and expand his prospects for future promotion and means and perhaps someday soon be considered a worthy suitor for...someone.

He stared up at the planks of the deck above and hoped William's faith that God did indeed listen to and answer prayers was justified. Because, as past and recent history proved, Ned could not trust himself to make the correct decision on his own.

"Where is she?"

Julia looked up from the list of questions she wanted to ask Henry Winchester as soon as she arrived home. "Pardon?"

"Charlotte. She is supposed to stay in the cabin with you." William clapped his hat down onto his desk.

Despite Julia's best efforts, the young woman had slipped away on three occasions since rising from her sickbed two days ago and being instructed to stay in the great cabin. Julia glanced around and sighed. "She was reading on the window seat only a short while ago. I apologize. I became immersed in my work."

"It is unfair for you to have to serve as her jailer." He crossed to look over her shoulder at the papers and ledgers spread out before her. "Have you informed her yet?"

"That I suspect the man she has secretly been carrying on a correspondence with and formed an illicit engagement with has stolen more than ten thousand pounds from me? No." Julia set down her quill, placed her hands on the small of her back, and stretched away the stiffness of hours spent pouring over the ledgers and Jeremiah's letters. "I still hold on to the hope that she will listen to her brother and give up the idea that she must marry Winchester because she sent him a letter—without the knowledge of her family—stating that she would."

William's lips quirked in a half smile. "I have long given up hope that the women in my life will listen to anything I have to say."

"Some may yet learn."

Her husband's forgiveness, and the ease with which he had accepted her apologies and excuses for why she had kept such a secret from him, made her feel at once better and worse—better that the burden of the conspiratorial knowledge no longer stood between them, and worse because she knew she did not deserve such grace, mercy, and love. Both drove her to determine she would never do anything that would risk his good opinion again.

"You did not hear her leave?"

Julia glanced around again, still finding a cabin devoid of Charlotte Ransome. "No, but I can easily guess where she went." She tucked the letters and lists into the ledger, closed it, and set it down in the top desk drawer. "I shall retrieve her."

"I will be on the poop deck sending instructions to the other ships.

Send Dawling for me when you return." He retrieved his hat and returned to duty.

Julia took a lantern and went down the companionway just outside of the great cabin. She preferred walking across the deck, in the delicious sunlight, before heading down into the dark, dank gun decks below, but with the heightened security measures William had set in place because of the increased risk of pirate attacks, he had requested she stay off the upper decks as much as possible.

As expected, she found Charlotte in the sick berth, seated across a small table from Ned, playing backgammon with him. He looked up and stood as soon as he saw Julia.

She waved him back down into his chair, though he did not take his seat again. "You are looking well this morning, Captain Cochrane." Though still gaunt from his illness, emphasized by the way his uniform hung on him, color filled his cheeks and his eyes sparked with life. "I do apologize, but I must interrupt your game. Charlotte, you are needed in the great cabin."

The set of the young woman's shoulders and the exasperation around her mouth reminded Julia far too much of herself at the same age, but she attended Julia without protest.

"Mrs. Ransome, before you go, might I have a private word with Miss Ransome?" Ned's gray eyes pled with her.

"Of course you may." Charlotte's countenance glowed in the dim light.

Julia clamped her teeth together and gave them a tight smile. That they loved each other was obvious. But she despaired of any hope for their future together.

"I shall await you outside, Charlotte." Julia looked between the two of them once again before exiting the sick berth.

Charlotte turned to put the game away, trying to control the fluttering in her belly. She should not have come down here, should not have spent so much time with Ned alone already. Coming to care for him even more deeply would only make it harder when she had to part with him in three days' time.

Her heart leapt when his hand closed over hers, stopping her from returning the game pieces to their holder.

"Miss Ransome…Charlotte…"

She turned and looked into his face, and her heart was utterly and completely lost. In this moment, there was no angry older brother, no fiancé waiting in Jamaica. There was only Charlotte and Ned. "Yes, Ned?"

"I will never be able to offer you wealth or a grand home or titles and land. But what I have, I wish to offer to you: I offer you my heart. It is fully yours, if you want it. Will you marry me?"

Happiness crashed against her with more force than a storm surge—only to rush out again as quickly and leave a void of despair.

Ned must have seen the change in her expression, as his own changed to reflect it. He released her hand. "I knew better than to hope you might return my affection. I beg your forgiveness if I have caused you any pain or inconvenience."

She grabbed his hand to keep him from turning away from her. "No, you do not understand. I want to marry you. I do." Her heart ached at the joy that flickered back to life in his beautiful eyes. "But I cannot."

"If it is a matter of money, I am willing to wait if you are. I plan to tell the commodore I no longer wish to resign my commission. I will work, long and hard, to accumulate enough money so that I can provide a comfortable life for you."

She smiled to stave off the tears that wished to flow. "It is not money that is the problem—there is the legacy my brothers have set aside for me. I know ten thousand pounds is not a vast fortune, but it is enough for a comfortable life—"

"If it is your brother, I will work just as long and hard to earn his approval and blessing, no matter how long it takes."

"Nay, it is not William or any of my family who stands in my way of accepting your proposal—"

"Then I do not understand—"

She touched her fingertips to his lips. If he continued to provide arguments in favor of the match, she might never say what needed saying. "Ned, I cannot marry you because I am already engaged. That is why I became a midshipman. To travel to Jamaica and get married."

"Engaged?" Ned staggered back and sank onto his chair. "Engaged? But why, then, were you traveling illicitly?"

Charlotte crossed her arms, her stomach aching. "Because my family did not know. I intended to tell them after Henry and I were married. I never expected..." She looked at him and hot tears burned down her cheeks. "I never expected I would fall in love with someone else along the way."

Ned raised his eyes to meet hers, and then he stood and took her hands in his. "If you do not love him, you cannot marry him. Your family has not approved the match. Therefore, you cannot be held legally bound to him."

Though it was the last thing she wanted to do, Charlotte pulled her hands free and stepped back from him. "But I am bound to him by a promise. And I would not be someone worthy of your love if I were to break my word to him. I have not seen him in almost two years." She swallowed and wiped her eyes on her sleeve. "I know now that I never truly loved him. But if he loves me and still wants me, I will stay true to my promise and marry him."

"Even if it means you will be trapped in a marriage with someone you do not love for the remainder of your life?" Ned seemed to fold in on himself as the strength of Charlotte's resolve registered in his mind.

"Aye. Because that is the honorable thing to do." Even though it would break her heart.

Julia awoke before the sun. She managed to rise without disturbing William, and she dressed quietly so as not to wake Charlotte. She took William's telescope from his desk and slipped out of the cabin. She made a conspiratorial gesture to Master Ingleby at the wheel and Lieutenant O'Rourke and made her way to the starboard side of the quarterdeck, skirting around the men who knelt on the deck scrubbing it with holystones.

Standing beside the railing to gain the best vantage, she raised the scope to her eye.

Jamaica.

Home.

Heart racing, she scanned side to side, drinking in the sight of the island only a few hours' distance from them. Before the sun set, her feet would once again be on her beloved home soil. She hoped the letter she posted before her marriage had arrived. For if Jerusha and Jeremiah knew she was coming and they heard English ships had been sighted, they might even now be on their way to Kingston to meet her.

Lowering the glass, the island disappeared into a shrouded mystery—the dim, predawn light giving no differentiation between the water and the dark green of the land.

"I have asked you to stay out of sight for your own protection." William's breath tickled the side of her neck. But when she looked over her shoulder, he wore a smile. "My glass."

She placed the heavy scope in the hand he held out before her. "How long will it be before we dock?"

William, still standing behind her, raised the telescope and examined the island. "We will dock by noon. I must go ashore at Port Royal and confer with the commander at Fort Charles—to pass on Admiral Witherington's orders, turn over command of the convoy ships, and discuss the transfer of command. Tomorrow, we will take the ship's boat to Kingston."

"Tomorrow?" She tried to swallow her disappointment, but it rose anyway.

He squeezed her shoulder. "Tomorrow. As long as everything goes well at Fort Charles this afternoon."

"If it does not, I will come ashore to smooth it myself." She turned and tilted her head back to look up into her husband's face. "Tomorrow. I have your word?"

"If you would like to send word ahead to Tierra Dulce, I will have a messenger sent from Fort Charles as soon as I arrive."

All was not lost! "Yes. I would like that. Thank you." She bounced up onto her toes and kissed his cheek. "Thank you, William."

She rushed back to the cabin, already composing the note in her head.

Charlotte let out a startled squeak, and her hammock swung wildly when Julia entered. "What is it? What's wrong?" She jumped out of the hammock as if the all-hands signal had been sounded.

"Nothing. I am sorry. I did not mean to wake you." She smiled at her sister-in-law. "We are within sight of Jamaica."

Charlotte's face reflected none of Julia's excitement. "Oh, I see." She turned to take down the hammock, which she folded, rolled, and stuffed into her sea chest.

Julia did not allow the girl's sour mood to affect her own. Humming, she sat at her desk and withdrew her stationery box, ink, and quill.

The quick note to Jerusha to inform her of their arrival became a three-page letter. After dressing, Charlotte sat on the window seat, staring out at the waters behind them—as she had done for the past three days since the last time Julia had retrieved her from the sick berth. She had not pressed the girl for details of her private conversation with Ned, but she had a fair idea of what had been asked by one party and how the other had answered.

After addressing and sealing the letter, she rose to take it to William on deck—but stopped. As they would not dock for several hours more, she did not need to hand it over yet. He had already seen her disappointment once this morning. She did not need to compound it by showing herself overeager to leave his ship and remind him they would soon part ways.

She sank into her chair again. Once he saw her safely home to Tierra Dulce, William would return to *Alexandra* and to the duty her father had set for him. She barely roused when Dawling knocked on the door to announce breakfast.

At table, she longed for an excuse to brush her hand against William's, to fill Dawling's role in serving him, to coddle and pamper him. She had spent far too much time on this voyage avoiding him and keeping secrets from him. Precious, precious time she would never regain. Wasted time she would regret as soon as they made their farewells at Tierra Dulce.

Tears welled in her eyes, but she blinked them away. She would not do that to him. She would not show him her tears, not like her mother. If her heart broke, she would never let him know, never send him away with the burden of her sorrow.

"As we are in range of the ships that guard the perimeter of the harbor, it is safe for you to return to the deck. I can have Dawling carry chairs to the poop for you both, if you would like." William set his fork down and picked up his coffee cup.

The thought of watching as they drew closer to her home overrode her melancholy over their future parting. "I would like that. Thank you, William." She glanced across the table at Charlotte. "Will you join me?"

William's sister tried to muster a smile. "Yes. I would like that as well." The forced smile twisted into a wry grin. "I could be of help in the shrouds, directing the men on the foremast..." She gave her brother a sidelong glance.

William raised his eyes to the ceiling, but the corner of his mouth twitched, betraying him. "Why am I plagued with stubborn, hard-headed women who will not learn their place?"

Julia exchanged a smile with Charlotte, glad to see genuine amusement in the young woman's face for the first time in days. If William would agree to her request and allow Charlotte to stay with her at Tierra Dulce for a year—after they convinced her she could not marry Winchester, of course—Julia believed she and Charlotte could be a balm for each other's broken hearts.

The anchor hit the water with a crash; the thick rope groaned as it lowered its burden into water the same color blue as Charlotte Ransome's eyes.

Ned turned away from the sight and tried to stop imagining that the anchor carried his heart with it to the harbor floor. William had granted his last request, and as soon as they made port, Ned would return to *Audacious* and resume command. William had also stated that he had written a letter to Admiral Witherington recommending Ned be confirmed to the rank of post captain with *Audacious* as his command.

The blessing in such a scheme was that *Audacious* would stay on Jamaica station, under William's overall command, while Charlotte would be returned to England. At least, he assumed that was what William intended to do with her. Surely he would not allow her to go through with her intended marriage. The cog in the wheel was William's insistence that Ned accompany them to Kingston—and then on to Tierra Dulce—tomorrow.

The idea that he might meet Charlotte's supposed intended, and that he might, through comparison of himself to this other man, convince Charlotte not to marry him, gave him a flicker of hope. But he quickly snuffed it.

She was lost to him. Either she married her intended, despite her family's objections, or she returned to England and married a wealthy merchant or perhaps even a baronet or son of a noble.

Though he had not quarters of his own on *Alexandra,* the other lieutenants had made him quite welcome in the wardroom once again. He headed aft, speaking to sailors and midshipmen he had known for many years, but this ship no longer felt like home. He missed *Audacious*. His brief return today to pack a bag to take to Tierra Dulce would not be long enough.

"Captain Cochrane." Julia Ransome stepped out from under the shade of the wheelhouse. "I hoped I would find you. Would you join us for supper this evening? It is to be my last supper aboard *Alexandra*, and I would so enjoy your company."

How could he decline when she put it in such terms—and when he had no logical excuse to say no? "It would be my honor, Mrs. Ransome."

"William told me you are to join us when we journey from Kingston to Tierra Dulce and stay for a few days. No—no protests. Commodore's orders. I cannot wait to show you the hospitality my home is famous for."

He did not want to disappoint her, but he would again try to convince William he would be better used staying with the ships while William made the journey to the plantation. "Thank you for the kind invitation, Mrs. Ransome."

She nodded. "I see the boat is ready to take you to *Audacious*, so I will keep you no longer. I simply wanted to secure you for supper tonight."

He inclined his head and turned to leave. Movement on the poop deck steps stopped him.

Charlotte paused on the bottom step. A straw bonnet with blue lining that, along with the sky and ocean, only served to sear the aspect of her eyes even deeper into his soul, hid her short hair. He had become so accustomed to seeing her this way, with the short hair emphasizing the height of her cheekbones, the delicate curve of her neck and shoulders, that he could not remember what she looked like with long hair.

He made a semblance of a bow. "Miss Charlotte."

She took the last step down to the deck and bent her knees in a slight curtsey. "Captain Cochrane. Congratulations. I understand the commodore is recommending you for promotion to post captain."

"Yes. Thank you." He touched the forepoint of his hat. "Good day."

Before Charlotte could respond, he turned on his heel and quickly marched to the waist entry port. At the last moment, as he descended down the side of the ship, he took one last look.

She was gone.

William gritted his teeth, reminding himself Admiral Lord Horatio Nelson once served as commander of Fort Henry in his younger years. But in Nelson's day, the command post for the Royal Navy's activities in this part of the Caribbean must have been much more organized and efficient.

He finally established his identity and the authenticity of Admiral Witherington's orders and had the cargo ships' bills of lading stamped as approved, legal goods to be unloaded and stored in the Royal Navy warehouse in Kingston for supply of the Caribbean fleet.

Although his duties would keep him at sea most of the time once he took command of the Jamaica squadron, he would see to it that many policies and procedures at the fort would change when he returned in a fortnight.

He pulled the sailors away from the fascinations the foreign port—though staffed by British officers and sailors—afforded. The sun had almost fully set by the time they reached *Alexandra*. He gave orders to beat to quarters for inspection as soon as his feet touched the deck, annoyed O'Rourke had not done so in his absence. Ned would have seen to it.

As the men scurried to their battle stations, William reminded O'Rourke of his responsibilities as first officer and then made his rounds.

He dismissed the men and informed O'Rourke that he would have command of the ship from tomorrow morning until William returned from Tierra Dulce.

Over supper he told an excited Julia and a subdued Charlotte and Ned about his experience at Fort Henry. When none seemed to take in what he said about the lack of organization and the near disdain with which the commander had treated him, he quitted the topic. It did not take any coaxing beyond a simple question to get Julia to talk about Tierra Dulce, which she did for the next hour.

As Ned seemed anxious to return to the wardroom, and Charlotte to the day cabin, William dismissed them both. Julia's idea that Charlotte was in love with his former first officer, and that inviting him to dinner—and to accompany them to Tierra Dulce—was a good way to get her to give up her notion of marrying Henry Winchester did not seem to be working.

After supper William sat at his table in the big cabin, hoping to finish a few reports before taking two weeks away from his ship. But Julia was like a jolly boat on a stormy sea, tossed from one wave to the next. First at her desk, then the sofa, then the window seat, then back to her desk.

"Would you like a glass of wine to calm your nerves, Mrs. Ransome?" He set his quill down and rubbed his forehead. Charlotte had given up and gone to sit at the dining table to write her letter of full explanation to Mother.

"No. I do not want—we are so close, William. I can smell the air—the Jamaica air. I want to be there, on my island, at my home."

He breathed in through his nose, but all he could smell were the odors of a ship that had been at sea for more than seven weeks. Which was not nearly as bad as a ship that had been at sea for six months. But, still, Julia's imagination seemed to be overexerting itself.

Her restlessness continued. More than an hour after they retired for the night, William pulled her into his arms and covered her mouth with his hand to cease her constant chatter. Even then, the tension in her body kept him from doing more than dozing occasionally.

When morning came, his eyes were dry and grainy, his head whirling almost at the same speed Julia flew around the cabin packing the last few items she had needed this morning. Dawling stood by, helpless, as Julia did everything herself. She would have skipped breakfast, but William insisted—needing coffee more than food.

He would not have been surprised if Julia ran out on deck and commanded the sailors to work faster at lowering the boat and loading her dunnage into it. As soon as the sailors rowed toward the Kingston docks with her crates, valises, and trunks, William ordered a second boat lowered and crewed. His and Ned's small valises and Charlotte's sea chest were lowered into it.

Julia did not make a fuss about being lowered down to the boat in the bosun's chair. Charlotte did. He quelled her protest with one look, and she grudgingly obeyed.

Beside him on the seat in the boat, Julia trembled. She squeezed his hand until his fingers went numb. She would have been the first one to jump out at the quay, but William held her back, allowing the sailors to secure the boat to the dock first. He climbed out and turned to assist Julia and then Charlotte.

"Miss Witherington! Miss Witherington!"

Julia shaded her eyes, let out a cry, lifted her skirt, and ran up the pier. At the head she threw her arms around the necks of two figures. The people around them stared—as did William. The black man and woman were both taller than Julia and, from this distance, looked older—perhaps as old as Mother and the admiral.

William added his and Charlotte's baggage to the pile of Julia's and then made his way to where his wife stood, chatting animatedly with the dark-skinned couple.

The woman noticed him first. She patted Julia's arm until Julia stopped talking. "I believe the captain has something he needs to say to you, Miss Julia."

"The captain—?" She turned, and when she saw William, she laughed. "Come, William." She hooked her arm through his. "I want you to meet two of the most important people in my life." She motioned with her free hand. "Jerusha and Jeremiah Goodland, may I present Commodore William Ransome, my husband."

"I hoped by the way you grabbed onto his arm that he was some relation to you, young miss." Jeremiah Goodland extended his large, calloused right hand. "Welcome to Jamaica, Commodore."

William clasped hands with the man briefly. Jerusha curtseyed, and William bowed to her. "I am pleased to be making your acquaintance. Mrs. Ransome speaks of you often."

Jerusha turned sparkling hazel eyes on Julia. "'Mrs. Ransome.' How nice that sounds." She hugged Julia again.

William turned at the sound of a clearing throat. Charlotte and Ned had joined them. Julia made the introductions.

"Welcome, all." Jerusha beamed at them. "Miss...I mean, Mrs. Ransome, we brought the buggies and wagons, just as you requested. Jeremiah figured you'd have brought back more than what you went away with."

"Who drove?" Julia asked.

Jerusha began listing names, and Julia's excitement grew. She clasped the older woman around the elbow. "Come, I must see them."

The two of them moved through the crowd to the wagons waiting on the road.

The brick buildings and cobblestone streets of Kingston beyond the harbor were just as William remembered from his first view of them twenty years ago.

"It is good to have her home. Thank you, Commodore, for bringing her back to us." Jeremiah watched her greet each of the drivers as if each were a brother she had not seen in years. While four of the five men were black, the fifth was not—but his appearance consternated William even more. The man looked like a pirate, the kind featured in storybooks about the famous pirates Blackbeard and Morgan from almost two hundred years ago.

At a gesture from Julia, they left the wagons and buggies and made their way down the quay, filing past William, Ned, and Charlotte with polite nods. They turned down the sailors' offers of help in loading the large trunks and crates, handling them readily and quickly. In short order the wagons were loaded.

William returned to the end of the dock where Lieutenant O'Rourke waited. "Take the boats back to the ship. You are in command until I return. The commander from Fort Charles will take command of the supply ships this morning. Shore leave by watches—two watches on *Alexandra* at all times. Revocation of shore leave for the remainder of the time in port if they are late returning." He had conveyed all this, and more, to O'Rourke yesterday. He stepped back and touched two fingers to the forepoint of his hat. "You have your orders, Lieutenant."

O'Rourke returned the salute. "Aye, aye, sir."

When William rejoined his wife, tears streamed unchecked down her cheeks. "What is wrong?"

She shook her head. "I cannot help myself. I am so happy to be home, to see my friends once more, that I feel I am about to burst."

How would he ever be able to compete for her love when simply stepping off his boat onto the Kingston dock made her happier than he had ever seen her, even on their wedding day?

Chapter Thirty-Two

Charlotte bit her tongue as the carriage bumped over the packed-dirt road that cut through what appeared to be a forest of tall grass.

"This is the sugarcane," Julia announced, looking as pleased about the unruly, unkempt green fronds as Lady Dalrymple was about her prized climbing roses. "And just around this bend..."

The road curved and the wall of sugarcane on the left gave way to a rolling field of dark green grass—real grass—and the house. Charlotte had not expected something as grand as Lady Dalrymple's home, but with the way Julia had spoken of Tierra Dulce, and the rumors of her wealth the Fairfaxes had shared, she had expected something more like the Fairfaxes' home in Portsmouth than what she saw.

The low, white clapboard house, with its deep porches and steep, gabled roof, sprawled across the emerald lawn like a cat sunning itself.

Julia's excitement rose as people appeared beside the carriage—more dark faces, though not all of them were of African origin—and she greeted each one by name. But she did not speak to them as if they were mere servants, people to do her bidding and then be thought of or heard from no more; she spoke to them as if they were her friends and neighbors, asking about their children or parents, their friends and relatives, and their own health and happiness.

The closer they drew to the house—slowed now by the people surrounding the carriage—Charlotte's fear grew. What if Henry were nothing like what she remembered? She could not conjure an image of him in her mind. Would she recognize him?

She refused to look back at Ned, who rode with Jeremiah and Jerusha in the second carriage by his own choice.

Julia tried introducing her and William to everyone, but there were just too many. She shrugged. "You will learn their names as need arises." The carriage had not quite rolled to a stop when Julia jumped to her feet to get out. "Come!" She grabbed William's hand and pulled him down with her. Charlotte thought they might forget about her, let her sit outside for a while and work up her courage to face Henry, but Julia turned and motioned for her to join them.

Charlotte followed them up the few steps to the porch. All up and down it, doors and windows stood open; white, gauzy drapes fluttered in the slight breeze.

She could learn to like this place.

The interior of the house was just as different from anything Charlotte had seen as the outside. Above her, there was no ceiling. Instead, the large room opened up all the way to the exposed timbers and slats of the roof—all whitewashed to give it a light, bright feeling. Furniture that approximated the fancy pieces at the large homes and estates she had seen in England, but which were different enough to show they had been made locally, filled the enormous sitting room.

"You will want to refresh yourselves after the journey." Julia turned to find Jeremiah and Jerusha in the cluster of people gathered near the front door. "Jeremiah, will you please show Captain Cochrane to his quarters—the blue room? Jerusha, Miss Ransome could use your assistance—and she will need a lady's maid, as well." Julia touched Charlotte's shoulder. "You will be in my old room."

Charlotte followed the woman she assumed to be the housekeeper down a long hallway. The house appeared to be much larger than her original estimation, given how far from the main room her bedroom, at the end of the hallway, was.

The room, with its pale yellow walls and coverlet, the dark blue upholstery on the chaise, the desk chair, and the bench at the end of the bed, reminded Charlotte forcefully of Julia. No floral wallpaper—and she had seen wallpaper in a few rooms they passed—just yellow paint. As in the other rooms, a mat that looked as though made of straw lay on the floor where a carpet should be.

"That's woven out of the dried grass from the cane." Jerusha motioned a younger man into the room. He set Charlotte's sea chest down in front of the wardrobe and left without saying a word.

"The close stool is there, behind the screen, as is the washstand. There's fresh water, soap, and towels if you wish to wash up some before tea." Though thin, the way Jerusha moved toward the door could only be called bustling. "I will send Huldah to you."

"Thank you, Mrs. Goodland."

The housekeeper laughed, a loud, strong sound. "No one calls me that, miss. You can call me Jerusha, just the same as does Miss Julia—Mrs. Ransome. La, it will take time to get used to the change."

After making use of the necessary and washing her face, Charlotte stepped out through the open door onto the porch at the rear of the house. A white rocking chair sat looking out over the lawn, which sloped down toward the sugar fields—and beyond, an expanse of water. She frowned. They had driven several hours from Kingston and, she thought, away from the sea. But there it lay, sparkling and bright blue.

"Miss Charlotte?" A rusty voice came from the bedroom.

Charlotte pushed the drapes aside and entered the room. "You must be Huldah." The woman could only be a few years older than Charlotte. Her skin was neither dark nor light but a rich tan. Her hair curled in tight ringlets only a shade darker than her skin. And her eyes—the pale golden orbs seemed to be taking in Charlotte's appearance as she assessed her.

"Jerusha sent me to help you with anything you need, miss."

"I would love to take a bath—but I know there is not time before tea. Perhaps later. For now, I could use your help in changing clothes." Charlotte pulled the small mobcap off her head, and Huldah gasped and crossed herself. Charlotte spun to see what the maid reacted to, but saw nothing. "What is it?"

"Have you been ill, Miss Charlotte? Is that why they cut off all your hair?"

Self-consciously, Charlotte reached up and touched the blunt end of her hair, which now hung just below her ears. "I have been ill recently, but that is not why my hair is short. It was a mistake that never should have happened."

"I'll say. You're too pretty to be walking around looking like a shorn sheep, miss." Huldah's manner was so open and unaffected, Charlotte could not take offense. She laughed and showed her which dress she wanted to wear.

"Oh, you have been ill." Huldah draped the discarded dress over the screen and turned Charlotte by her shoulder to look at her. "But that's all right. Mama Virgie's cooking will fill in those gaps betwixt your ribs."

Charlotte had no choice but to surrender herself to Huldah's ministrations. Once she stopped trying to help, the process went much faster.

"There now. As soon as we cover up your hair, you're ready for tea." Huldah dug through the stack of mobcaps Julia had purchased for Charlotte in Barbados until she found one she liked, and she adjusted it until she liked the way it angled just slightly over Charlotte's right ear. "Tomorrow, I'll bring the hot irons and we will see what we can do with this here in the front."

"Thank you, Huldah." As a midshipman, wearing a midshipman's uniform and living without a lady's maid had been easy. But in this lifestyle, with stays and petticoats and gowns that buttoned in the back, Charlotte realized just how much she needed someone like Huldah.

The maid curtseyed. "Tea will be in the great room, just down the other end of the hall."

Charlotte thanked her again before she left. Taking a deep breath, she prepared for the worst and hoped for the best.

The worst came before she even made it to the sitting room.

Instead of walking down the hall, Charlotte decided to walk around the outside of the house on the porch, to see what could be seen.

What she saw was her fiancé, Henry Winchester, in close conference with a seedy-looking man. As soon as Henry saw her coming, he wrapped up his conversation and sent the other man scuttling away.

Henry turned toward her and bowed. "You must be of the party Miss Witherington brought with her from Kingston."

Charlotte shook her head, unsure if she had heard him correctly. "Do you not recognize me?"

"I apologize, miss. Have we met before? Perhaps at the Abingdons' ball last month?"

She wasn't sure if she wanted to laugh or cry. The confusion gathering in the lines around his eyes indicated he was not joking. "Henry—it is I, Charlotte Ransome."

"You mean to tell me—"

Henry whirled at William's voice from the other side of the porch.

"—that you are engaged to a man who does not recognize you when he sees you?"

"Engaged—" Henry turned back to face her. "Charlotte? Darling, it is you." He drew her into an embrace. "Two years...two long years." He pushed her back and held her at arm's length. "But what are you doing here? I did not expect to see you for years yet—until I sent for you."

"I came to see you, Henry. To marry you."

The expression that filled his eyes was more akin to frustration than happiness. "We cannot marry yet, dear. Not until I have finished what I came here to do."

William separated the two of them. "And what is that, Mr. Winchester?"

"Work until I have saved enough money to deserve Miss Ransome's hand."

Of the same height, William, in his uniform, seemed to tower over Henry, in his plain brown suit. The breeze ruffled his blond hair—had it been so light last she'd seen him?—and deep lines formed around his eyes as he squinted against the afternoon sun. Handsome. As she recalled. But not nearly as handsome as Ned.

But she was not engaged to Ned. She was engaged to Henry.

Ned stepped away from the window, having heard more of the conversation already than he should have. The harsh tones of men's voices had first drawn him to the open window, though he could not make out what they said. He had been about to step out and make his presence known, rather than skulking and eavesdropping, when Charlotte spoke.

He lowered himself onto the edge of the bench at the end of the bed. She had sounded so hurt and betrayed when Winchester did not recognize her that Ned wanted to burst through the door and challenge the man right then. Something that would now be left to her brother to handle.

And if he provided William with a viable alternative to Charlotte's marrying Winchester...

He smiled. He hated to see Charlotte hurt by Mrs. Ransome's steward, but he planned to take full advantage of the man's mistakes.

At the sound of the large clock in the hall striking four o'clock, Ned shrugged into his uniform coat and made his way back to the enormous room at the front of the house. Charlotte sat in a delicate chair beside the settee on which Julia sat. William stood behind Charlotte as if on his own quarterdeck, looking at Henry Winchester as if the steward were standing before a court martial accused of mutiny.

"Captain Cochrane, please join us." Julia set down the heavy silver pot and held a cup and saucer toward him.

He took the delicate china and sat in the chair on the other side of the low table—from which he could see all parties.

"My dear Commodore..." Julia gazed up at her husband with a cocked head.

William took her meaning and moved around Charlotte to sit beside his wife.

"Jerusha and Jeremiah asked me to pass along their apologies that they could not join us. They each had duties that called them away." Julia exchanged another look—this one unreadable—with her husband.

Ned tried to hide his consternation by looking down into his cup. Though uncertain the exact nature of the positions held by the older couple, the idea that they would have expected the Goodlands to be joining them for tea shocked him. He expected life in Jamaica to be different than in England. But to include servants at tea?

Julia broke the awkward silence by asking Winchester to give her a report on his expectation for the harvest in a few months. He tried couching his answers in general terms, but Julia continued questioning him for specifics.

Ned watched Charlotte during the exchange. Though she tried to appear interested in the subject, her blue eyes soon hazed over with indifference followed by boredom. Ned bit into a scone and relaxed. He might not have much to do to show Charlotte—and convince William—she would never be happy with Winchester, that she would be happiest married to a naval officer.

Charlotte had read somewhere, perhaps in the prayer book, a verse or proverb about fools. *The wise man's eyes are in his head; but the fool walketh in darkness.* As Henry danced around Julia's questions, causing her to ask each one in different ways several times, Charlotte's darkness began to lift.

At fifteen years old, and besotted by the first attentions she had received, Henry's patronizing ways seemed humorous, his way of teasing and flirting with her. Now that she had experienced more of life—and had lived for more than a month without being treated like a piece of fragile porcelain with fluff in her head rather than a capable, knowledgeable mind—Henry's refusal to give Julia direct answers, to try to flirt his way out of imparting the information he held, and the way he looked to William when he did share a few specific details, Charlotte grew angry—with Henry and with herself.

No appellation fit her better than *fool*. She had been a fool to fall for Henry's charms two years ago. She had been a fool to correspond with him—and to form a picture of him in her imagination built upon the nonsense in his letters. She had been a fool to agree to marry him, especially without her family's knowledge and approval. And she had been a fool to endanger herself—and people she loved—by becoming Charles Lott.

She flicked her gaze at Ned, who sat to her left, facing Julia and William on the sofa. Though he tried to appear more interested in the tea and food, a slight smile played around his chiseled lips—and it grew each time Henry said something that frustrated Julia.

Charlotte had been the biggest fool not to recognize, from the first time she saw Ned, that she had met the man she would love for the rest of her life.

William finally put a stop to Julia's questioning of Henry with the suggestion the ladies might like to rest before supper. Charlotte hopped up from her chair, eager to escape the uncomfortable setting.

Henry caught her before she entered the hall. "Might I entreat you to take a walk with me this evening after supper? The porch offers a delightful view of the cove."

"Excuse me." Ned inclined his head and brushed past Charlotte and continued down the hallway. She strained her neck to keep from turning to watch him walk away—or call after him to wait for her.

For better or worse, and for now, she was engaged to the man standing before her. She had to see if she could make things work or get him to agree to an amicable termination of their engagement.

"Yes, Henry. I will take a walk with you after supper."

He lifted her hand and kissed the back of it. Somehow, the amorous expression on his face was not reflected in his eyes. A chill climbed up her arm and settled in her chest. She bent her knees in curtsey, pulled her hand away, and did all within her power to walk, not run, down the hall.

In her bright, cheerful bedroom, Charlotte leaned against the closed door a moment, trying to rid herself of the lingering effects of her encounter with Henry.

She had the perfect escape from the entanglement: William's disapproval.

But she had never been one for doing things the easy way. Though it might take a little longer, she would find a way to convince Henry they should not marry.

An hour later, having worn herself out pacing and trying to formulate a plan, Charlotte had only one option left to her. She pulled a pillow off the chaise and tossed it to the floor in front of it. Then, mimicking the position she had assumed every Sunday her entire life, she knelt on the pillow, propped her elbows on the seat of the chaise, and clasped her hands together in what she assumed was a properly penitent position. She closed her eyes and knit her brow, the way William did when he prayed.

How did the prayers in the prayer book start?

"Almighty God in Heaven, our Father." Yes, that was a good and proper beginning. Now what? "You are...mighty and...in heaven and...our Father." No, that was not quite right. "Hallowed be Thy name." Better.

There was something else about kingdoms and wills, but as Charlotte grew up knowing she'd never be part of the aristocracy, she had not paid much attention to that part of the prayers. "We—I...humbly beseech Thee to hear my prayer."

She blew her breath out in a huff. This wasn't working. "God, if You truly are there, as William and Julia seem to believe, I know You will hear my prayer without all the fancy words from the prayer book. I have been foolish. And I believe the Scriptures equate foolishness with wickedness. I do not want to be wicked. I want to be good, like William. He looks to You for guidance. I am not certain how to do that, but I know I can learn. And I promise I will. I will start learning right away. But I hope, I pray, in the meantime that You will help me figure out how to break my engagement with Henry. Because though my sin of foolishness is great, I believe it would be a far greater sin for me to marry Henry when I am in love with Ned Cochrane."

No plan immediately filled her mind. But William had said in his address to the crew last Sunday that God did not usually answer prayers the moment they were prayed, nor in a manner immediately recognizable as an answer, but that the truly penitent in heart could be assured that God would hear his—or her—prayer and answer it.

"Uh…that is all I want to say. So…Amen."

She stood, replaced the pillow on the chaise, and bit her bottom lip as a smile overcame her.

Be patient, Ned. God is on our side now.

Charlotte silently thanked Julia for stopping William's protest before he could speak it when Henry asked his permission to take Charlotte for a stroll.

"We shall stay to the porches," Henry explained.

Charlotte rose and took Henry's arm before William could get his protest out, made a slight curtsey to her brother and sister-in-law, and practically dragged Henry from the room.

Once alone with him, though, uncertainty settled over her. She hardly knew this man, and what she had seen of him today did not dissuade her from the decision to try to end their engagement.

"I cannot help but be pleased—and flattered—that you traveled so far to come to me, Charlotte."

Hearing her Christian name on his lips annoyed her—as much as it thrilled her whenever Ned said it. "I wanted...I needed to...find out if we still had a chance at a future together. And I could not do that from England when you were here. When my brother married Julia Witherington, I knew I had to take the chance and come here, even before I knew you worked for my sister, to see you again."

The lights glowing from inside the house made it difficult to see much beyond the edge of the porch, so dark was the night. But once they moved beyond the windows of the great room, and past the darkened bedrooms, her eyes adjusted. Beyond the dark mass of the sugarcane fields, the sea stretched out like silver glass. Yes, she could definitely become accustomed to living here.

At the corner just outside her bedroom, Henry stopped and, placing his hands on her shoulders, turned her to face him. "How could you doubt we are still destined to be together? Did you not read my letters? I meant every word I said, every promise I made. For the past year, all I have been able to think of is you and our future."

"*Two* years, Henry. It has been two years." She caught the inside of her cheek between her teeth. If he wished to try to convince her he remembered more than he did, she would play this game with him. "You say you meant every word, every promise you made. So when you wrote me to say that you wished me to have the freedom to call off the engagement if I had a change of heart, you meant it?"

"I…well…when I wrote that…" He released her shoulders and waved his hands between them as he struggled for words. "That was when… when I did not know…" He stopped gesticulating. "You have not had a change of heart, have you?"

Ah. So he did not remember much of the drivel he had written to her over the years. "Henry, I was barely fifteen years old when we first knew each other—a girl still at school. What I have learned in the past two years, about myself and about the world around me, has changed me, has changed everything about me. I am no longer that naive, impressionable schoolgirl. I have studied, I have learned, I have been through difficulties you cannot begin to imagine"—because she did not intend to tell him about her misadventures aboard *Audacious*—"and I have gained wisdom that has taught me to reconsider many things I used to hold as truths."

A slow smile spread across his face, but it was not a comforting expression. "There is one thing you are forgetting."

"What is that?"

"This." He grabbed her about the waist, hauled her up against him, and smashed his mouth down on hers.

Charlotte struggled, pushing against his chest, but he was stronger than she expected. Anger overrode her fear. She stopped struggling, and as soon as she did so he relaxed his hold. She stomped the heel of her shoe down on his toe and sent her fist into his gut.

Sputtering, he staggered back, arms around his stomach, hopping on one foot. "What did you do that for?"

She swiped the back of her hand across her mouth. "For taking liberties that are not yours to take."

"Is everything all right here?"

Charlotte's heart leapt when Ned appeared out of the shadows. Though she could not see his eyes clearly, from the hint of amusement in his voice she imagined them twinkling.

"Aye—yes, Captain Cochrane. Mr. Winchester and I were clearing up a little misunderstanding." She stepped forward, feeling no guilt for pretending Henry had given her the promise of release. "Mr. Winchester, I am going to take you up on your promise to release me from our engagement. I have had a change of heart." She glanced over her shoulder at Ned. "In fact, I love someone else and wish to marry him."

Henry stopped groaning and hopping. He dropped all pretense at flirtation and looked between Charlotte and Ned. "We shall see about that. You agreed to marry me, Miss Ransome. Which means your legacy is mine for the claiming."

She rubbed her lips together and then cocked her head. "You are more than welcome to take your case to my brother. It is he who controls my dowry, and it is he who never had knowledge of or gave permission for our ill-advised engagement. I am certain he will be happy to come to terms with you. But pray, do not plague me with your attentions any longer. I know you do not love me. I know you want only my money. Therefore, we have nothing further to say to each other."

Henry gave her one more malevolent look and then stalked off into the darkness.

"Now I understand." Ned leaned against the porch railing, arms crossed. The glow of light coming from the other end of the porch gave limited definition to the side of his face and showed his smile.

"Understand what?" Charlotte moved closer, needing to pull comfort and strength from his presence.

"How you made an enemy of Kent and lived to tell the tale." He shook his head and stood. "Have you *no* common sense? Do you not know better than to taunt a hungry shark?"

She settled her hands on her hips. "It is the shark who should not taunt *me*. Have I not proven I am capable of surviving anything that comes my way? Have I not shown that I can do what a man can do as well as a man can do it? Have I not demonstrated—"

His lips pressed against hers in a kiss so gentle and sweet, the hairs on the back of her neck tingled. She grabbed the lapels of his coat to keep from melting into a puddle on the floor. With one hand, he pressed the small of her back, with the other, he pulled off her mobcap and caressed the back of her head.

The kiss ended, and Charlotte settled into his embrace, not minding the scratchy wool of his coat under her cheek.

"Aye, you have proven all those things."

"I was a good midshipman, was I not?" Though she tried to sound confident, insecurity tinged her voice.

His laugh vibrated through his chest. "Yes. One of the best I have ever had the pleasure to serve with. But it makes me worry."

She pushed back far enough to look into his eyes. "Worry?"

"Aye. Will you be content to give up your prospects for further promotion in the navy to become merely the wife of an officer?"

Joy knotted her throat, and she swallowed hard against it. "Aye, sir. It would make me most content to be the wife of Captain Ned Cochrane."

The light breeze ruffled Julia's hair. The sound of the waves kissing the beach warmed her—as did the feel of William's hand clasped around hers. At first, he had not been convinced of the wisdom to take the long walk down to the cove. But once he had seen it...

"Are you certain we should have let her walk out with Winchester? I do not trust him." William stopped and looked back up at the house.

Julia sighed and turned with him. Her home was barely visible in the dark, moonless night—a small glow atop the rise that provided its majestic view of the cove lapping softly against the sand behind them.

"She lived as a midshipman for a month. Before that, she proved her resilience by fending off the unwanted advances of Lord Rotheram. Henry Winchester knows none of these things. Do you believe he will be able to do anything she cannot handle? And if he does try anything, Jeremiah is only a few feet away. As is Ned."

"Ned?"

"You think he is going to leave her alone with Winchester?" Julia harrumphed.

"Ned?" William finally turned his attention away from the house and to her again. "Ned Cochrane? And my sister? I suspected, but once I learned of her attachment to Winchester—"

"Ned Cochrane and your sister." She reached up and ran her thumb across the creases in his brow, trying to soothe them, but he would not be deterred.

"Ned Cochrane...and Charlotte." He stared out at the water a long moment and then shrugged. "I would wish him wealthier, but he is a good man. So you believe it to be serious?"

"She loves him. And I believe he loves her."

"They have known each other too short a time to know if they are in love." William's mouth settled into a tight line.

Julia squeezed his hand until he looked at her. "I knew the first—or perhaps the second—time I clapped eyes on you that I loved you. 'Twas you who made me wait twenty years."

The absurdity of her statement finally dragged him out of his worry, and he pulled her into his arms. "Aye, I can well imagine what your father's reaction would have been if I had gone to him as a midshipman and told him I was in love with his ten-year-old daughter. There would not have been a Lieutenant Ransome to disappoint you seven years later. Though, I suppose you could have proven your love for me by weeping for me at my burial."

She slid her arms around his waist. "Yes, I would have made such a show of my love for you, the likes of which not even Shakespeare could compose. But as the Bard would say, all's well that ends well."

He cupped her jaw in his hand and lifted her face for a kiss. "But, my dear, we are only at the beginning."

"I will not weep for you when you leave me."

"I would hope not."

"Nor when you return from sea."

"I expect nothing more than calm disdain at my comings and goings." He squeezed her tightly and then released the embrace. Taking her hand again, he started up the beach toward the road leading back to the house.

"I will not pine for you when you are away."

"Nay. You will have too much to occupy your mind between running the plantation and tending to our children."

Her skin tingled. "You will not be disappointed if children do not come immediately?"

"Children will come when God decides it is time, and not before." He released her hand and wrapped his arm around her waist, tucking her into his side. "Will you be disappointed if more promotions do not come and I am stuck at the rank of post captain, with the posting of commodore, for the rest of my life?"

She smiled, even though she knew he could not see it in the darkness. "Promotion will come when God decides it is time, and not before." Of course, to gain promotion, he needed to be at sea, making his name more widely known amongst the Admiralty. She wrapped her arms around his waist, almost throwing both of them off balance. "You will be cautious. You will come home to me more often than you go to sea."

He kissed the top of her head. "Aye, Mrs. Ransome. I will always come home to you, even though I must live with the knowledge that you will not weep upon my return."

His gentle humor staved off her melancholy…for now.

The breeze whistled through the thick grass blades at the tops of the cane stalks, the white, frilly seed fronds whispering together as Julia and William passed quietly under them.

"I can see now why you love this place so intensely," William whispered.

"I hope you will come to love it too. It is your home now—"

William shoved her against the wall of sugarcane.

"What—?"

"Quiet." He stilled, eyes fixed on the road before them. "I heard something."

Julia heard nothing but her pounding heart. "You are unfamiliar with Tierra Dulce. It is probably nothing."

"I will take no chances."

She slowed her breathing and strained her ears. There—a rustling that did not come from the cane. An animal? Or something more sinister?

When nothing happened after several moments, William stepped back onto the road. "Stay behind me."

She grabbed hold of the back of his coat with trembling hands and followed him the remaining few yards until the corridor opened onto the lawn.

"Who goes there?" A figure carrying a lantern bobbed down from the porch and moved swiftly toward them.

"Commodore William Ransome. Identify yourself."

"Captain Ned Cochrane." He stopped and leaned over, panting for breath. Another figure took the lantern from him.

Julia stepped out from behind William. "Jeremiah? What—" But before she could complete her question, Ned stood. The light fell on his face and revealed a stream of blood coming from a gash on his temple. She yanked her handkerchief from her sleeve and moved forward, pressing the cloth to the wound, and then she noticed the pistol in Ned's right hand. "What happened?"

He took the handkerchief from her and wiped the worst of the blood from his face with it. "Pirates." He spat the word. "They attacked me from behind. The blow disoriented me. By the time I could see straight, they were gone."

Ned locked eyes with William. "They took Charlotte."

About the Author

Kaye Dacus lives in Nashville, Tennessee, and holds a master of fine arts degree in writing popular fiction from Seton Hill University, is a former vice president of American Christian Fiction Writers, and currently serves as the president of Middle Tennessee Christian Writers. She loves action movies and British costume dramas, and when she's not writing she enjoys knitting scarves and lap blankets (she's a master of the straight-line knit and purl stitches!). To learn more about Kaye and her books, visit her online at kayedacus.com.

Ransome's Honor

Book 1 of The Ransome Trilogy

Once Youthful Sweethearts—Can Their Love Be Renewed?

When young Julia Witherington doesn't receive the proposal for marriage she expects from William Ransome, she determines to never forgive him. They go their separate ways—she returns to her family's Caribbean plantation, and he returns to the Royal Navy.

Now, twelve years later, Julia is about to receive a substantial inheritance, including her beloved plantation. When unscrupulous relatives try to gain the inheritance by forcing her into a marriage, she turns to the only eligible man to whom her father, Admiral Sir Edward Witherington, will not object—his most trusted captain and the man who broke her heart, William Ransome. Julia offers William her thirty-thousand-pound dowry to feign marriage for one year, but then something she could never have imagined happens: She starts to fall in love with him again.

Can two people overcome their hurt, reconcile their conflicting desires, and find a way to be happy together? Duty and honor, faith and love are intertwined in this intriguing tale from the Regency era.